P9-DUY-475

NEW
LEGENDS

OTHER BOOKS BY GREG BEAR

Hegira
Psychlone
Beyond Heaven's River
Strength of Stones
The Wind from a Burning Woman
Blood Music
Eon
The Forge of God
Eternity
Hardfought
Tangents
Heads
Queen of Angels
Anvil of Stars
Moving Mars
Songs of Earth and Power
Legacy

NEW LEGENDS

EDITED BY

GREG BEAR

WITH

MARTIN H. GREENBERG

A TOM DOHERTY ASSOCIATES BOOK
NEW YORK

This is a work of fiction. All the characters and events portrayed in this book are fictitious or are used fictitiously.

NEW LEGENDS

Copyright © 1995 by Greg Bear and Martin H. Greenberg

All rights reserved, including the right to reproduce this book, or portions thereof, in any form.

This book is printed on acid-free paper.

Design by Lynn Newmark

A Tor Book
Published by Tom Doherty Associates, Inc.
175 Fifth Avenue
New York, N.Y. 10010

Tor® is a registered trademark of Tom Doherty Associates, Inc.

Library of Congress Cataloging-in-Publication Data

New legends/Greg Bear, editor.
        p.   cm.
    "A Tom Doherty Associates book."
    ISBN 0-312-85930-9
    1. Science fiction, American.   I. Bear, Greg
PS648.S3N45   1995
813'.0876208—dc20   95-14719
                                                            CIP

First edition: August 1995

Printed in the United States of America

0 9 8 7 6 5 4 3 2 1

Copyright Acknowledgments

Introduction copyright © 1995 by Greg Bear
"Elegy" copyright © 1995 by Mary Rosenblum
"A Desperate Calculus" copyright © 1995 by Abbenford Associates
"Scenes from a Future Marriage" copyright © 1995 by James Stevens-Arce
"Coming of Age in Karhide" copyright © 1995 by Ursula K. Le Guin
"High Abyss" copyright © 1995 by Abbenford Associates
"Recording Angel" copyright © 1995 by Paul J. McAuley
"When Strangers Meet" copyright © 1995 by Sonia Orin Lyris
"The Day the Aliens Came" copyright © 1995 by Robert Sheckley
"Gnota" copyright © 1995 by Greg Abraham
"Rorvik's War" copyright © 1995 by Geoffrey A. Landis
"Radiance" copyright © 1995 by Carter Scholz
"Old Legends" copyright © 1995 by Abbenford Associates
"The Red Blaze Is the Morning" copyright © 1995 by Robert Silverberg
"One" copyright © 1995 by George Alec Effinger
"Scarecrow" copyright © 1995 by Poul Anderson
"Wang's Carpets" copyright © 1995 by Greg Egan
Afterword copyright © 1995 by Greg Bear

Contents

NEW
LEGENDS

Introduction

A few years ago, my wife, Astrid, and I hosted a lakeside party for the Clarion West Writer's Workshop. We've held these parties at our home every year since 1988, to give the students a break as they survive the mid-point of a grueling six-week schedule. On this occasion, it was a cool day, cloudy—not unusual for Seattle in the summer. The lake spread quiet and calm, with barely a ripple, to the trees and houses on the opposite shore. I sat on the end of our small dock with one of the students, talking. In jest, I said, "Well, if you really want to know the secret, I'll tell you what it takes to become a great writer . . ."

The student looked at me soberly and said, "What *does* it take?"

Having put myself on the spot, I was about to laugh when a fey little blonde girl of three and a half, the daughter of good friends, stepped between us, sat down with a wriggle and a vague, far-seeing look, and said, "I don't know the Lithuanian word for tree."

The student regarded her with astonishment, the conversation veered elsewhere, and the secret stayed secret.

In 1993, I taught at Clarion West for the sixth and last week. The students were dragged-out, skeptical, hardened by hearing from so many writers. A tough crowd to please. On the last day, conversation in the classroom ebbed. Everyone stared glumly around the circled tables, knowing the group would very soon break up and wander back to the real world. Finally, a student asked, "What does it take to be a great writer?"

Without hesitating, I said, "A great soul." Everybody thought about that, then nodded their heads.

The secret was out. And it's true.

Science fiction has always been powerful and important in our society. It is the only form of literature that clearly and consistently criticizes the Western paradigm: scientific investigation and technological endeavor. By criticism, I mean examination, dialog, and, well, *criticism:* catching problems before they overwhelm, or preparing us for inevitable changes. The criticism may extend to the paradigm itself. Science fiction has never been completely pro-science or progressive.

Over the years, however, and with cruel injustice, science fiction has been chastized by some as a non-literature, a restrictive genre without *soul.* The same charge, ironically, was once leveled against jazz.

I know the lie well; it hasn't stopped me from pouring my creative life into science fiction. To ignore science fiction is to abandon a pretty lofty pulpit from which to scream and shout and dance out semaphores of warning. We need these shouts and dances more than ever.

Martin Greenberg, the most prolific and capable anthologist of all time, and one of the pre-eminent experts on the short story, called one afternoon and asked if I would be interested in doing an anthology of science fiction stories. Something sparked in my head. *Yes.* But not just any anthology.

Something that would point the way. A collection of new stories that would pool the finest talents in our field, and show that the science fiction neighborhood can still grow mental athletes stronger and more agile than ever before. Something big and exciting . . .

Science fiction with a great soul.

What I needed to discover was whether there were still enough writers out there, particularly new and young writers, who could dance the frantic dances and shout the desperate warnings, engage in the dialog of science fiction, play with ideas as if they were real and important.

I said, "Marty, let's think big. An all-original anthology, a thick book. Every single story has to be dramatically strong, well-written, with believable characters, and it must be *science fiction.* No catering to the in-between stories, however good they might be. No fantasy, because we need a critical focus. And whatever we do, we won't call it *hard science fiction.* Because that phrase has been so abused and misused. Each story must engage *strong emotions."* I added, "And you know, Marty, for me, Sense of Wonder is a very strong emotion."

Marty was enthusiastic. His instincts told him the time was ripe. And lo, our editor, John Jarrold, and publisher, Random Century U.K., agreed. Weeks later, in an airport lounge waiting for a flight, I made a list of possible titles for the anthology. *New Legends* popped to the top of the list.

Legends define the character of a civilization. Legends are a kind of myth—and they are also individuals whose excellence makes them household names.

In the same airport, I prepared the invitation that would go out to over a hundred writers, and refined one crucial criterion: what science fiction means to me. Each science fiction story has to demonstrate how the reader can get from where he or she is, to where the story is, *without magic.* A science fiction story has to take place in the universe as perceived by science, or as science might come to perceive it. I wanted to leave the reader with the sublime impression that *these stories might actually happen, if not to you and me, then to our children, our grandchildren. Our descendants.*

Response to our announcement was light at first. The stories came in dribs and drabs across the months; I wondered if we could fill the anthology in time. With only four stories bought, I extended the deadline.

I learned what it meant to be an editor. I loved to buy stories, hated to reject them. Some stories I enjoyed so much I put them aside for a while, to let my enthusiasms cool; but my first impressions did not fail me.

I rejected some very fine stories, simply because they were not science fiction, or not the kind of science fiction I was looking for. A few writers—surprisingly few—expressed displeasure with me.

The publishers grew impatient. Fingers tapped on corporate desks across the broad Atlantic.

More stories arrived, finally; not a flood, but a substantial flow. Four, five, six a week. And from them, with delight, I plucked the gems I needed.

With some concern, I realized a substantial number of Gregs were involved. And only three women. Did this somehow reflect our field—a predisposition of Gregs to write SF, and reluctance among women, after all these decades of striving for equality? I consoled myself that the excess of Gregs and the deficit of women was, after all, merely chance . . . I bought the best of what was sent to me. (And I spent a lot of time encouraging women to send me stories. I wish more had obliged.)

In January of 1994, I closed the anthology after nine months of editing. I stacked the stories in a tall pile and grinned. My colleagues had confirmed my faith. *New Legends* is diverse, elegant: an anthology with a great soul.

These stories challenge me to think and feel in new and compelling ways. I have not arranged them in order of quality, as is often done in anthologies, with favored stories placed first and last; I would hate to have to make that judgment, with so many fine stories. Instead, I have placed them according to theme. Some are more familiar and immediate; others take a long or satirical view. They all remind me that our neighborhood is alive with gossip and dialog; we *talk* with each other all the time, through our stories or in person.

We are rich with ideas that belong to nobody in particular. Grab an idea, run with it, and the only rule is that you must do a better job than any writer before you.

But the neighborhood is not limited to dreamers. *New Legends* is part of the vital dialog between fellow dreamers, and between dreamers and doers:

blue-collar working stiffs, white-collar bank managers, politicians, physicists, biologists, sociologists, psychologists, engineers, doctors, computer experts, software moguls, and impoverished students who may become any of the above . . . Anybody who cares about the future, and who needs to think as well as dream.

The SF neighborhood reaches across the length and breadth of the universe, from the beginning of time to the end.

As do these stories.

—Greg Bear

I

CHOICES

Elegy

Mary Rosenblum

MARY ROSENBLUM HAS PUBLISHED THREE WELL-RECEIVED SCIENCE FICTION NOVELS, *DRYLANDS, CHIMERA,* AND *THE STONE GARDEN,* AND A GOOD NUMBER OF SHORT STORIES. HER SENSE OF STYLE AND ATTENTION TO SCIENTIFIC AS WELL AS EMOTIONAL DETAIL MAKE HER WORK EXCEPTIONAL.

"ELEGY" IS A CLASSICALLY STRUCTURED STORY ABOUT DILEMMAS AND EXCHANGES. WHAT DO WE OWE NATURE, IN RETURN FOR ITS BOUNTY—AND HOW CAN WE EVER REPAY?

AMANDA CARNACK TIPPED backward off the anchored zodiac, pressing her mask against her face with one hand. The surface exploded around her in silver bubbles and her SCUBA tanks bumped her back as the water closed over her head. Chilly, not cold. Sea-sound wrapped her; the rasp of her breathing, gurgle of exhaled air. Beyond that the sea's voice; a sense of sound just beyond hearing, almost a *texture.* Amanda rolled onto her belly and scooped great sweeps of water with her fins, some of her tension draining away as she angled down into blue-green twilight.

The surgery would go fine, she told herself. The squid neurons would differentiate as expected. And she would have done it.

Would the media name her, or would they refer to her as "Roberta Guilliam's daughter"?

What did it matter? Angry suddenly, Amanda kicked hard, her thigh muscles driving her like an orca through the water. Roberta had taught her how to dive, how to spear fish, how to design a good experimental procedure. And then, she had turned her back. Forever.

Kelp stems undulated gently in the filtered light and the sea caressed her with its song, a hum of life, not so much heard as *felt.* Life. Such a precious thing. Amanda spread her fingers, savoring the rush of water against her palm. It was more than life, what she was trying to save. Life was heart muscle and the mindless tumble of cells through vessel walls. The ER docs were good at keeping that going.

Her mother's words? *Life is more than tissue and blood. I leave that to the ER docs.* Roberta had said it . . . where? The memory faded as abruptly as it had burst on her, leaving doubt in its wake. *Had* Roberta really said that? Amanda drifted, struggling to recall. Surely, she could *remember.* Silver flashed in the murky distance and she focused on it, relieved at the diversion. Squid. She drifted motionless as the school sped toward her. The small cephalopods veered here and there in a flash of whip-flick motion; Gonatus *fabricii.* They could always use a few more for the laboratory tanks. Slowly, afraid she'd startle them, she disentangled the net from her belt. Small cousins of the giant squids, their split-second dance in the water was a gift of their specially evolved nervous system. Large primitive neurons let signals zip through their bodies at incredible speeds. She could transform those neurons with her biochemical magic, turn them into silver threads that could stitch up a torn human brain.

Or restore a lost yesterday?

Could anyone do that?

Maybe. *Come to me,* Amanda crooned in her throat. *Come to me. I love you.* As if they had heard her, the school halted instantly and completely. They rotated to face her in eerie ballet unison, their suckered arms gathered tightly, sticking straight out, as if they were pointing at her. Their great, dark eyes seemed to stare at her and bands of tan, rusty red, and black rippled across the school. For an instant, Amanda thought that the patterns coalesced into a recognizable shape . . .

She flicked the net, not nearly squid-fast but fast enough. The school jetted away into the gray-green distance, trailing dark clouds of ink. In the meshes of her net, her captives drifted, nearly colorless now, arms curled into writhing knots. They didn't struggle. They never struggled. Amanda kicked her way to the surface with her unexpected prize, wondering why that bothered her.

"I had a weird dream last night." Closeted in her non-sterile cubicle, Amanda watched Doctor Ahmed nod on the main screen. "I think I was . . . a fish." She had been tiny, struggling in terror as filmy strands of chaos tangled her. There had been no comprehensible shape to those strangling threads, but they had cut into her, crushed her together with a thousand other struggling bodies, and she had felt herself . . . all of them . . . begin to die. One by one, like lights going out, tiny sparks of fear and pain had vanished. And slowly, the sea had gone blue and clear. Sterile. Lifeless. "It scared me." Amanda's throat closed briefly on that remembered *desolation.*

"Fish are Freudian." Scrubbed and gowned, nearly large as life on the big screen, Ahmed held out her hands to the circulating nurse, fingers spread for her gloves. She did the gross surgery, giving entrance to Amanda's delicate virtual fingers. "I dream about gardens. And spiders. Spiders signify mothers, I believe."

"I always dream about the sea." A *net,* that's what the awful, tangling fibers had been. A drift-net? Something huge, anyway. "I think I was a squid," Amanda said. "They follow me around when I'm diving. Like they want me to catch them." Her laugh stuck in her throat and Amanda had a sudden memory of the squid school hovering motionless in the water, staring at her, pointing with their hundreds of arms. Waiting to be netted?

"You sound rather nervous."

Amanda couldn't tell if Ahmed was smiling behind her mask or not. Well, hell. She *was* nervous. Seized by adrenaline, she ran over her mental checklist one more time; neurons prepped and ready, backups loaded. Gerald would have double-checked all this. Her assistant never forgot. *Calm,* she scolded herself. She hadn't been so nervous since her first time in an OR. "Blood pressure?" she snapped.

"Ninety over seventy and steady." The anesthesiologist glared up at one of the video cameras. "It's on your screen."

Right, right, he was right. What was his name? She blanked, groped for it, struggling with a twinge of panic. Roberts? Robertson? So she couldn't remember—blame it on her jitters, OK? On screen, the sheeted body looked unreal beneath the bright floods. Ahmed and the rest of the surgical team clustered around the head of the table as they opened the skull. Arthur Montagne. Thirty-two, black, and painfully uncomfortable around doctors—or around her, at any rate. An actor, moderately successful, acting in plays that she'd never heard of. Not that she ever saw much live theater.

One ordinary afternoon, walking home from the store with a bag of groceries, he had gotten in the way of a drive-by shooting. Just another one of those ugly incidents you tuned out on the morning news. A bullet had caught Arthur Montagne in the head. Projectile-caused intracranial hematoma. They'd cleaned up the trauma, but a leaking artery in a bad site had left him with partial paralysis of the face.

Amanda looked at the green-sheeted mound portrayed in various views on various screens. She tried to visualize the dark skin, the slack muscles, and curl of pubic hair beneath the drapes, couldn't do it. That dream sea had been so *blue.* It was a sterile color. Like a desert, Amanda thought, and that sense of *desolation* clutched her, closing her throat like a squeezing hand. Briefly the cubicle vanished, dissolving to blue water, and a sound like wailing in the distance . . . Stop it. With difficulty, Amanda blinked the vision away. What the hell was going *on* here? She shook herself, focused on the screen in front of her, fright twisting in her belly.

Nothing worse than the jitters—Ahmed was right about that. Sure, had to be. Amanda reached for her goggles. She was about to walk around inside this man's brain, trespassing on memories of a lover's kiss, his fifth birthday, his ability to wiggle his little toe or comb his hair. And it worked in virtual but this was flesh, and of course she was jumpy, of course it wasn't anything else. She hung her virtual goggles around her neck, telling herself she was reassured. On screen, Ahmed bent over the green-sheeted mound that was a man. Neurons were dying in his brain, more each day as blood seeped from that leaking artery. Sealing the artery would be easy, but he wouldn't smile again. Human neurons don't regenerate. She began to pull on the soft fabric of the virtual gloves.

Only she could give him back his smile. As her mother had given her back her own . . .

"Skull is open." Ahmed dropped the bloodied piece of bone into a pan of saline, didn't look up at the cameras. "Ready."

She sounded so damn calm. Amanda took a deep breath. "Engage unit one. How's the soup, Gerald?"

"Waiting for you." Gerald's voice came over her ear-plugs, sounding as unruffled as Ahmed.

Amanda scowled as the microsurgical unit whined slowly down from its ceiling track. In a separate cubicle, Gerald was guiding it into place. With a nearly inaudible sigh it settled delicately over Arthur's head, hiding the last square centimeters of skin and flesh left exposed by the drapes.

"Microsurgical unit is in place." Ahmed enunciated for the video log. "Patient is stable. It's all yours, Amanda."

OK. "System access." Don't let me lose it again. Amanda mouthed the silent prayer as she pulled on her goggles. Nervous or not, this wasn't the time. Eyes closed against the disorienting shift, she entered virtual.

When she opened them, she stood in a wilderness of colored spider web; red, silver, yellow, and soft turquoise. The microcameras fed her system pictures of the patient's individual cells, tinting them with representative colors. Pulsing silver meant healthy neurons, red meant damage. Dusky crimson webbed the silver, down and to the left. Amanda faced it, stretching out her right hand to bring it into focus. *Aha, yes.* "It's right there, just like in the model." She pulled the knot of crimson damage closer. The human brain wasn't backyard-familiar yet. They could have been off by a virtual mile, in spite of the stereo-taxic mapping they'd done. Bracketing the pulsing tangle, she stretched her hands apart, enlarging the view. A few dead cells, and Arthur Montagne was no longer an actor. The brain was such a *fragile* thing. Bad timing on a shopping trip, a few microliters of leaking blood. A fall . . . You could lose so damn much. A handful of withered neurons, and a Nobel prize-winning biochemist was what? A senile old woman. No. Even before those neurons shriveled, Roberta Guilliam had stopped being a prize-winning biochemist. Or a mother.

The neuron-tangle blurred for an instant, and Amanda fought for calm. Don't think about Roberta. Not here. Not *now*. Don't let yourself lose it. She sucked in a quick breath and snapped her fingers. One fingertip glowed white, and she stroked the thick, scaly wall of the damaged artery. Careful . . . Slowly, the ragged tear sealed closed. Beneath the sterile microsurgical hood in the OR, a laser scalpel followed the dance of her fingers with its infinitesimally more delicate dance. So . . . Leak sealed, she cleaned up the seepage, then began to cut around the damaged neurons. One at a time, she pulled them free. (Beneath the hood filaments of rigid silicon, spun in orbital weightlessness, teased the excised neurons from the tangle.) "Ready for the soup."

"Ready."

Gerald sounded *cheerful,* damn him. "Switch to system B." She didn't shut her eyes in time, swallowed a twitch of nausea as the neuron-web shimmered, fragmented into a mosaic of gleaming silver. Amanda squeezed the focus down until she could see the individual neurons swimming in their nutrient bath. Squid neurons were wonderfully primitive. You could jump them through a lot of hoops once you'd figured out the chemical commands. Do a little DNA cut-and-paste with retroviruses, and you could make yourself a nice batch of primitive, antigenically human neurons, all ready to differentiate at need in Arthur Montagne's brain. Minimal rejection risk, maximum restoration of function.

That was the model, anyway.

It worked, in virtual.

Amanda swallowed, her mouth suddenly dry. "Transfer. Switch to system A, overlay B." This was the tough part. The scene blurred and she was looking at the tangled brain-web again, only this time, the bright neuron-school floated in the lower right-hand corner of her field of vision. For an unsettling instant, they looked like tiny squid, like the school in her cove. Any second now, they might jet away, trailing ink . . . Amanda blinked and banished the intrusive vision. *Concentrate,* for God's sake. The neurons were outlined in purple, which meant that they weren't in position yet. Come *on,* Gerald. She clenched her teeth, frightened all over again by her own distraction. Was this the jitters or . . . something more?

"Ready."

The purple outline vanished as Gerald spoke. "Proportional," she snapped, and waited as the squid neurons swelled larger. What would it be like to have a squid's reaction time? A sudden vision of the school turning as one to stare at her overlaid the neuronal webwork. Amanda shook her head, dizzy with a glimpse of that blue desolation, hands wanting to tremble in the gloves. Come on, come *on*. This was no different than the model. And not a lot different from the procedure that had earned Roberta Guilliam her Nobel Prize. Only she had been using fetal cells, back before the Supreme Court decision that ended all fetal cell research.

Amanda reached, framed a single neuron gently with both hands. It moved easily, sliding into the small space she'd freed for it, overlapping the silvery web of healthy neurons. Gently, she teased another into place, holding her breath. If this worked, the new neurons would settle happily into their new home, accepting signals as if they'd been there from birth, filling in the gap of damage.

If it worked.

Nothing was certain in this damn world. Not life, not fame, not the mind. What the hell was the anesthesiologist's name? One by one, she eased the neurons into place, reweaving the shining web that was the virtual metaphor for the firm clasp of a hand, a smile, a line spoken on stage. A hundred. A thousand . . . stitching up this man's torn future. Amanda reached, pointed, reached again. Once, her own future had been so torn. Roberta Guilliam had repaired it . . . to any purpose? What *was* that anesthesiologist's name? Where had those overwhelming visions come from? Amanda blinked, sweat stinging her eyes, hands trembling for real, now. Finished? Yes. "System, endit." The words came out in a rush of breath.

"Blood pressure steady, ninety over sixty-nine."

The soft hum of the retracting remote came to her over the screen. "Closing," Ahmed said.

Oh, God, she was going to start shaking . . . "Exit." Amanda pulled off her goggles.

"Bingo, Doc." Gerald grinned from a screen. "Very slick."

"Yeah. Thanks." She rubbed at the marks the goggles had left and began to strip off her gloves. "It'll be slick when our patient can smile into the mirror and like it." She didn't look at the main screen where Ahmed and her team were finishing up. "I'm going back to the lab."

"Yeah, sure." Gerald sounded puzzled.

There was no point in watching. Amanda left the OR and headed for the elevator. Ahmed wasn't going to lose this patient. They'd finish, send him into Recovery, and eventually back to his room. Tomorrow morning, she'd go see him, and even then it would be too soon. The elevator doors whisked open and she got in, ignoring the young phlebotomist with her tray of needles, syringes, and collection tubes. Roberta had worked with trauma damage, too. Her methods, pre-micro-remotes and VR, had been crude. But they had *worked*. Thank God. Amanda fingered the tiny ridge of scar tissue that curved across her scalp, invisible beneath her hair.

She slid her fingers down across her cheekbone, feeling the small rough-nesses of her thirty-eight-year-old skin, aware of the pressure of her finger-tip, compressing epidermis and muscle against unyielding cheekbone, the lift of skin and muscle as she smiled. A million molecules of acetylcholine drifted across the tiny gap between a few hundred thousand neurons to let her feel this.

Some hundreds of thousands more let her remember her name, where she'd parked her car, yesterday. Until those neurons died. She had felt so *strange,* immersed in that blue desolation. Not herself . . . The door whis-pered open and Amanda took her hand away from her face, aware that the phlebotomist was giving her a strange look. She marched past the woman, stomped down the hall to their lab. The familiar hum of equipment and the indefinable scent of chemicals and fish enfolded her, comforting her. On the big wall screen, Ahmed straightened suddenly, took an instrument from her tray, then bent over the table again. The hulking tangle of the remote apparatus loomed above her like a malign robot from a grade-B sci-fi video.

"Lab, lights." Amanda snapped her fingers.

The overhead strips brightened slowly, dimming Ahmed and her green-gowned team. In the big tanks along the far wall, dozens of squid hovered in orderly ranks. Amanda walked across to peer through the glass. They faced the same direction in every tank, arms writhing slowly in the gently circulating sea water, bodies shimmering with rippling bands of soft buff and orange. The neuron donors had come from this tank. Amanda reached over the top, let her fingers trail in the cool water. As one, every squid in every tank turned toward her.

Weird. Mottled patterns of orange, brown, and yellow succeeded each other in a soft pulse of color along the squids' bodies. For a dizzy instant, the notion seized Amanda that each squid was an individual piece of a giant jigsaw puzzle. If she put them into a single tank they would combine to form a picture. A picture of what? Amanda shivered and took her hand quickly out of the water. The loose sleeve of her shirt was wet to the middle of her forearm, its zig-zag stripes of gold and green darkened by the water. On the wall screen, Ahmed was backing away from the table, leaving the final details of closure to her team.

The surgery was over. In a few minutes, the entire staff would burst in here wanting to celebrate. Stifling a sudden twinge of panic, Amanda grabbed her coat and carryall off the hook. She couldn't face it, not when Arthur Montagne wasn't even in Recovery yet. The surgery itself didn't meant shit. She fled down the hall to the public restroom to change in one of the stalls and slip out of the hospital through the service elevator. As she turned the corner, she heard the hiss of the elevator doors and the first high-pitched voices.

What *was* that anesthesiologist's name?

Her mother's apartment in the Complex smelled faintly of pine. Not tree-pine, but the pine scent used in bathroom cleaners and air fresheners. Pine and piss, just a trace, but there. Her stomach stirred uneasily. "Hello, Roberta." Amanda closed the door behind her. "How are you?"

"Where's my juice?" Nearly lost in the deep armchair, Roberta Guilliam leaned forward. "I asked you hours ago." Her voice was high-pitched, childish. "I'm going to tell Brent if you don't give me my juice."

Memory seized Amanda—Roberta in their little zodiac, shaking water from her hair as she stripped out of her scuba gear, head tilted back, laughing at the blue sky. Throat tight, Amanda turned away. She looked like her mother—everyone had told her so, all her life. It was a frightening mirror, that fragile, confused face. "It's me. Amanda," she said. "Did you want some juice?"

"I've told you and I've told you. If you don't close the incubator door, we'll lose the whole damn run." These words came out in Doctor Roberta Guilliam's harsh, confidant voice, and for an instant, her face firmed. Then her lip trembled and that fleeting echo of strength and purpose vanished. "Brent's dead, isn't he?" She lapsed once more into an uncertain quaver. "Amanda? When did you get here?"

Brent had been Roberta's lab assistant and briefly, very briefly, her husband. "Yes, Roberta. Dad's dead." For a long, long time now. "I brought you some daffodils." Amanda went over to the kitchen counter that took up part of one wall, rummaging in an overhead cupboard for a vase. The vases were all plastic, like the dishes, unbreakable and safe for the senile elderly who could afford to live here. Roberta Guilliam had hated plastic-ware. "Aren't they nice?" She ran water, plopped the thick bunch of flowers into the vase and set it on the table, hating herself for her chirping fake voice, for being here at all, for feeling like she *had* to be here. "We implanted our first squid neurons into a patient, today. I don't know if it works yet or not."

"That's nice, dear." Roberta's eyes had gone glazed and dreamy. "They're very pretty."

Why had she told her? Amanda tweaked a daffodil into place. Once, she had shared a lot of her life with her busy, brilliant, obsessive mother—school work, troubles, everything. Back before the fetal-cell ban. Back before Roberta had shut her out—had *blamed* her. "I've got to go." The bright words fell like bits of broken glass onto the thick carpet. "I'll stop by tomorrow."

"Good." Roberta looked at her, frowning a little. "Thank you for the candy. Oh, it wasn't candy, was it?" She looked away. "I'm sorry. I . . . forget things."

Was that how it started? With small forgetfulnesses, like the name of an anesthesiologist? Or had it begun with unexpected lapses into day-dreams, like her vision of empty blue sea in the OR? "Good-bye." Amanda drew a shallow breath, tasting cheap pine scent, her stomach queasy. "I'll see you tomorrow."

"Daffodils." Roberta looked out her window into the garden that was actually a hologram. "You brought me daffodils. There aren't any daffodils outside." She turned suddenly, her eyes meeting Amanda's. "I like daffodils."

Her eyes were the color of water in a peat bog, clear and shallow, so shallow that you could see the bottom. Again that vision came to her— Roberta laughing, sea-wet, so *alive*. Pain clutched Amanda. What had *happened* to everything—all the memories, the imagination, the quick connections between fact and fact? What had happened to the temper, the impatience, and the unyielding, egocentric, obsessive intensity? Was it still there? Locked away somewhere behind a wall of shriveled neurons? Or was it gone forever?

How many neurons were shriveling in her own brain?

"Good-bye, Mother." Amanda's voice shook. "I'll stop by tomorrow." She opened the door and fled.

The carpeted hall smelled like pine and piss, too, but it was as clean as the neat room. Roberta Guilliam's space had never been neat. It had always been cluttered with stacks of journals, half-written articles, dirty clothes, and the remains of take-out dinners. The aides here did the housekeeping. Maybe they dressed her, too. Amanda hadn't asked, but every month, they did a little more for Roberta Guilliam.

Alzheimer's. You could always get funding for Alzheimer's research. The average age increased every year and people wanted their minds to live as long as their bodies. Some of her own money came from the American Alzheimer's Foundation. You could break up the plaques that formed in the brain with focused sound waves. That helped, but the atrophied neurons were gone forever. Amanda reached the lobby that had been decorated like an upscale hotel, and stopped short beside the receptionist's desk. Daniel waited for her on the sofa, his long arms spread along the back. The receptionist was staring surreptitiously because he was gorgeous—dark-haired and lanky. Way too gorgeous to be community college bio instructor. Amanda smiled in spite of her mood.

"What are *you* doing here?" She opened her arms to him in a rush of pleased surprise. "Did they fire you?"

"This is Wednesday, remember? I only have one lecture class, this quarter. I went by the lab. Gerald said you took off right after the surgery." He tucked his arm through hers as he ushered her out the door. "Are you OK, 'Manda? Gerald said it went fine."

He looked worried.

"Oh, it did. Just like the model." Amanda looked away from his intent gaze. "It's too damn early to celebrate." She waited for the lobby doors to open, stepped through. "Why did you come *here* to look for me?" she asked over her shoulder.

Daniel shrugged. "I thought you'd be here." He took her hand as they walked out to the parking lot together. "You want her to be proud of you."

"Do I?" Sudden anger squeezed Amanda. "Don't play mind-reader with me, Daniel. You don't have a clue." She yanked her hand free, fumbled for her keys. Her anger trickled away as suddenly as it had come, leaving her stranded like a beached dolphin. "Oh . . . I don't know. I'm sorry. I stopped wanting her to be proud of me about the time she told me what she thought of my choice in research." She yanked the door open. "And it's too late now, anyway."

"I guess. 'Manda?" Daniel touched her arm gently. "Want me to drive?"

"I'm fine." She threw herself behind the wheel. "I'm going out to the house tonight."

"I wish I could come." He sighed. "But I've got to finish grading those last lab reports. Can you drop me at the light-rail?"

"Sure." She squashed an unexpected pang of disappointment, covered it with the mechanics of starting the little car. Daniel offered comfort, didn't ask for much in return. Sometimes his undemanding *acceptance* of her made her impatient. Sometimes . . . she needed it. *"You're* the biologist," she said abruptly. "What do you know about squid?"

"Squid?" Daniel rolled an eye at her. "I'm just a teacher. You're the expert on squid."

"All I know is how their neurons work." She eyed a wandering triple trailer rig as she eased the car onto the freeway. "I can keep them alive in the tanks. I can turn their neurons into pretty fair approximations of human cells. They're not an endangered species." Although that could happen. Those dreams of empty, sterile blue water kept haunting her. "I don't really know much about their behavior. Every squid does the same thing at the same time."

"Vibration." He nodded sagely. "Like schooling fish. The vibrations from the movements of the other squid in the school tell an individual what's going on, and it reacts in the same way."

"That's not how they do it." Vibration didn't transmit across the airspace between tanks. "And what about the colors?"

"It *is* how they do it. You appointed me expert, remember?" He raised one eyebrow. "Color is camouflage, but I think I read somewhere that it might also serve as some kind of primitive communication." He touched her cheek with one fingertip. "What's eating you, 'Manda?"

"I don't know." The proximity alert beeped and she hit the brake, swearing under her breath as she eased back from the car ahead of her. "Roberta started with squid. She roughed out the procedure I'm using today—a crude approximation of it anyway—with squid neurons before she moved on to fetal tissue. You know, we're at about the same phase of development Roberta had reached when the Supreme Court decision went down. Experimental application in live patients." She gave a short laugh. "I think it scares me. I think that's why I'm having all these dreams and visions. I'm superstitious."

"What dreams and visions?" He shot her a quick, hard look.

"Nothing in particular." The intensity of his gaze bothered Amanda. "I'm just not sleeping well." Which was true, so what was bothering her? That all her dreams seemed to connect with the sea, or diving with Roberta? Some Freudian message here after all?

"You know, I've always wondered . . ." Blessedly, Daniel changed the subject. "How come your mother didn't just move her research to Europe? France was still funding fetal cell work."

"Don't ask me." Amanda took the exit ramp too fast, tires whining in protest. "She could have. She didn't. She just quit." Anger seized her again; anger at herself for saying so much to Daniel, anger at him, for his silence. "Oh hell. You know, this *is* just reaction to the surgery." She pulled into the big parking-lot around the maglev platform and braked to a stop in the drop-off lane. "So I'm sorry I dumped it in your lap and I'll see you."

"Yeah." He opened his door, his expression troubled. "Why don't you stay in town tonight? Those reports won't take too long to finish."

"No." Troubled, she looked away. She needed solitude. Or was it the sea she needed? Refuge. "No thanks." Amanda managed a smile for him. "I'll see you."

She watched him thread his way gracefully through the pedestrian traffic, graceful for all his lanky build. Quiet comfort, Daniel, so comfortable within his skin. Where did that comfort, that *self* come from? Did it reside within that complex tapestry of neurons, a fragile presence vulnerable to a bullet or a tearing blood vessel?

Or withering neurons, or a fall? She touched her scalp, finding that old scar, remembering earth and sky wheeling past, remembering the shock of impact that hadn't been pain, but an instant of . . . surprise.

Such a fragile thing, the mind. Amanda rolled down her window, meaning to call him back, say that she'd go home with him after all. He had already vanished into the station. With a jerky shrug, she rolled up the window and put the car into gear.

Rathbone. It came to her as she pulled away from the curb. The anesthesiologist's name was Rathbone.

It was a long drive out to the beach house, but worth it. Roberta had signed it over to Amanda on Amanda's thirtieth birthday—not long before she'd entered the Complex. Amanda hung onto it, even though the taxes and necessary repairs strained her budget at times. The road curved up and over the hills, wound down into one of the little creek canyons that led down to the shore. She had left the suburban sprawl behind, was passing through the orderly landscape of drip-irrigated, machine-tended crops. Most week nights she stayed at her tiny apartment near the med school. Or with Daniel. Why not tonight? she asked herself, braking for a curve. Because she needed the solitude.

Or was it the sea that she needed?

The road had dropped to the bank of the sluggish creek, burst out suddenly onto rolling coastal grassland. The house was on the leeward side of a headland, along a barren stretch of road between two tiny towns. A few locals passed her in battered pickups or on salt-eaten bicycles. Not too many tourists, this time of year. She pulled onto the rocky, grass-grown drive beneath the ancient creosoted piers that supported the downhill side of the house. The damp, salt-scented breeze stroked her face as she climbed out of her car, whipping her short hair back from her face, fluttering the hem of her long shirt. Surf roared and broke, murky green and white, not sterile blue, its rhythm a voice calling her, or maybe the voice was there beyond the crash of water on sand.

She ran up the rickety steps that she needed to replace, and unlocked the front door. The musty, familiar, comforting smell of the house closed her throat with a hard knot of unexpected tears. She almost called to Roberta, half expected to see her curled up on the sofa with a bag of corn chips and a journal, or her laptop. Amanda yanked off her shirt, kicked off her shoes and stripped out of tights and underpants. The red and white flowered suit on the back of the bathroom door ridged her skin with gooseflesh as she pulled it on, clammy with leftover salt because she'd forgotten to rinse it, last visit.

With a shiver, she went out the back door and ran down the path to the beach, jumping from rock to rock, hopping over the tideline of dead seaweed, broken shells, and plastic trash. Dead fish lay nose to tail in weirdly neat lines, raw spots marring their silver sides. Pollution? Some kind of disease? She leaped over them, hoping the tide would take them before they started to stink.

The sea came to meet her in a foamy rush, catching at her legs as she ran, tripping her so that she stumbled, arms flailing for balance as she floundered deeper into the surf. She threw herself into a sweeping crawl, fighting her way up the curl of the oncoming breaker, sliding down the back side as it crashed into foamy ruin behind her. The tide was just turning and the wind-driven swells lifted her high enough to see the main road when she treaded water.

Was he right? Daniel. Did she want Roberta to be proud of her, to acknowledge that she, Amanda, had succeeded where Roberta had had to fail?

Roberta could have done it. With squid. She could have *tried*, anyway. The tears threatened again and Amanda kicked harder, pushing herself to the limit. She had brought news of her funding like a gift, so long ago. A big grant—partly bestowed because she was Roberta Guilliam's daughter, and that had hurt, but she had *wanted* that money. And she had been *proud* of it—a grant that would let her at least try to continue what Roberta had had to give up.

And she had told her mother, her words faltering as Roberta's eyes grew colder and colder, as her face hardened from living flesh to something like stone. *So you think you're going to get there with squid?* Roberta had said, and her bitterness had burned like acid. *You think you're that good? I doubt it.*

Stunned, as stunned as if Roberta had slapped her, Amanda could only whisper, *Yes.*

Amanda hadn't said one word about her research after that, had waited for Roberta to ask, to apologize, damn it. Roberta hadn't asked. Or apologized. And then . . . it was too late.

"I'm doing it, Roberta." Amanda treaded water, gasping for breath, her sudden spurt of energy exhausted. "You were wrong and it's going to work. Yes, I'm good enough." Maybe. Silver flashed in the water, and she shook her hair out of her eyes.

Squid. They appeared in an eyeblink, thousands of them, surrounding her in a slick of nervous, glittering silver. Slowly, they turned toward her in eerie unison like the squid in the tank. Amanda shivered, fought down a twinge of uneasiness, because she'd never seen squid do that out here. "You're the key," she said as they slid up and over a swell. It was so *easy* to steal a lover or a child, leave a stranger looking from their eyes. So easy for the mind to simply wither and die. "We'll fix it," she whispered. "You and I. We'll give a million people their lives again." Suddenly she was sorry she'd come here, needed to tiptoe into Arthur Montagne's hospital room *right now*, touch that slack cheek and feel for an answering twitch of muscle.

All around her, the squid closed ranks until she wore a huge flared skirt of squid-flesh. Uneasy, a little frightened, Amanda sculled backward, felt the writhing touch of tentacles against her back, the tiny bite of sucker cups as they fastened briefly to her skin. She shivered and treaded water, scared and wanting to laugh too, because this was so *crazy*. Color swept across the massed squid; a storm of bright red, fading to white in random blotches. No . . . not random.

Amanda touched the fabric of her suit; bright tropical red, splashed with white flowers. Same pattern, only the squid had enlarged it a little. Dizzy, she reached out a hand, swept it through her matching squid-skirt. Small bodies parted and closed in behind her hand, blurring the pattern for only a moment.

The flowers darkened and blurred, dissolving into green and ocher. Stripes? The stripe-pattern took on an odd shape—sort of rectangular, a patch of plain ochre or tan at one end. Where had she seen . . . ? Without warning, the colors disappeared, and the school jetted downward, vanishing almost instantly. Offshore, porpoises leaped out of the water in a white shower of spray. Hunting flower-patterned squid? The fear possessed her suddenly, and she swam for shore, flinging herself into a hard, sloppy stroke, kicking hard. Her skin crawled with the memory of small squid-arms stroking her flesh and she swam faster, panting, eyes on the distant safety of the rocky beach

She was in the shower when she heard the front door bang. "Who's there?" She turned off the water, grabbed for a towel.

"It's me." Daniel's voice. "Steamy!" He stuck his head in the door, waving at the dense clouds. "What is this, a temporary sauna?"

"I was cold. I thought you were grading papers." Amanda wrapped her robe around herself, her pleasure at seeing him diluted with unexpected ambivalence. "I got caught in the current and wound up coming in on the south side of the headland."

"I'll finish them tomorrow. 'Manda, I worry about your swimming by yourself." Daniel caught her shoulders as she tried to edge past him. "You could drown out here and who would know?"

"The squid would know." The words tumbled out on their own and Amanda stilled a twinge of fear. "As long as you're here, maybe we should celebrate after all." She tucked a quick arm through his, tugged him into the main room before he could say anything about squid. "I've got a merlot we could open."

"I'll go for that." He sounded a little uncertain, but he smiled. "I brought champagne, but I'll put it in the refrigerator for when your patient wakes up and is cured."

"Not cured. He wasn't sick." Amanda broke away from him. "Call it . . . restored." A restoration of a career? Could you restore vanished yesterdays? Were they still there, somewhere beyond a curtain of damage? "Our mind, our memories—it's who we are." She went to get the wine from the rack on the back porch. "When you damage it, you damage *us*. Our soul, maybe." She twisted out the cork with a single pull. "Our *self* anyway."

"I'm not arguing." Daniel came up behind her as she poured blood-colored wine into the glasses. "But you'll have to discuss 'soul' with the preachers."

"What *is* our soul, if it isn't what we know, what we've learned and experienced? Who we *are*." Amanda picked up a glass. Roberta had bought these the summer after Amanda's senior year in high school. The Complex wouldn't allow glassware in the apartment. Too dangerous. "Damn," Amanda said softly. "Just . . . damn it."

Daniel took the glasses from her and set them on the table, pulled her onto the sofa beside him. "What's the trouble?" He put his arm around her, worried, holding her close. "The operation? Is that all?"

"Isn't that enough?" She kept seeing her mother's shallow eyes. "I've spent my whole life working up to this moment." *Do you think you're that good? I don't.* Roberta Guilliam's bitter words echoed in her head.

Amanda reached for her glass, swallowed wine she barely tasted. "How smart are squid? Can they . . . duplicate specific patterns? With their color-changes, I mean."

"They duplicate background colors for camouflage. I told you, in the car. That wine's too good to gulp." He took the glass gently from her hand. "You're not Roberta." He wouldn't let her turn away from him. "You're not going to lose your funding. You're not going to quit. Your squid cells are going to work and you know it."

"Are you so sure I'm not her?" Her lips twitched.

"You don't have Alzheimer's." His eyes held hers, warm and steady.

And she wanted to believe him, but down in those dark, compassionate depths, way down there . . . something flickered. Doubt? A hint of *lie?* Amanda sighed. "If you stick a pattern into a tank with a school of squid, will they mimic it?"

"*I* don't know. Ask a marine biologist."

"I was just . . . I want to know." Maybe that's all it was—squid camou-flaging themselves against her suit to escape the porpoises. Uh-huh, oh *sure.* She got up, hiding her expression by refilling both their glasses. Why not just tell him?

Hey, Daniel, this school of squid admired my swimsuit today . . . He'd think she was losing it, like Roberta had. That doubt in his eyes would surface. It would eat her.

"I didn't think about dinner." She retreated into the kitchen and activ-ity. "I've got crackers." She opened the refrigerator. "And some cheese."

Amanda frowned as he followed her into the kitchen. "Why don't you cut up those apples. The ones in the bowl on the counter."

If he sensed her mood, he didn't say anything as he cut up apples and arranged them on a plate. They ate their cheese and fruit by the glow of an antique oil lamp, watching purple twilight thicken into night. At the edge of vision, brief light flickered on the dark water. Squid? Once, out night-diving with Roberta, a school of squid had erupted from the depths, streaking past the boat, glowing a ghostly bioluminescent green in the darkness. The beauty of that moment—the slap of water against the boat, the darkness, the quick brightness of the squid—still made her shiver. "We can't grow squid neurons in the lab," she said softly. "Oh, we can, but they won't work."

"There are plenty of squid." Daniel pulled her against him, pillowing her head on his shoulder. "They're slippery, tough as leather if you don't cook them right, and they have tentacles. They change color, and they're full of wonderful neurons. We have now covered the entire subject of squid." He laughed softly and stroked her cheek with one fingertip. "You know, as romantic conversation goes, yours sucks. No more squid, please. Not tonight." He kissed her.

Her body responded, banishing visions of Arthur Montagne beneath his green drapes, her mother's empty eyes, and the red-and-white squid-skirt. Amanda broke free at last, twining her fingers with his, pulling him to his feet. Daniel carried the lamp into the bedroom and they made love by its warm light. It was refuge, almost as much a sanctuary as the sea, and she welcomed it, drowned herself in it.

Finally, Daniel fell asleep. Head pillowed on his shoulder, she listened to his heartbeat and the soft rasp of his breathing, wondering if she'd dream about the sea again, dream of diving with Roberta maybe, in that sterile blue desert. Thick grief clogged her throat suddenly, knotting in her chest. Grief for what? For whom? It had an . . . alien feel. As if it belonged to someone else. More strangeness. The chemical echo of withering neurons? Blinking, she focused on the familiar shapes of dresser, mirror, and bookshelves. Her shirt still lay in a crumpled heap near the door where she'd shed it this afternoon. She was as messy as Roberta. Was that who the grief had been for?

It had felt . . . larger than that. Distorted by those dying cells? Dear God.

The lamp touched the stripes with shadow and yellow light, deepening the green and turning the tan stripes into gold.

Green and gold zig-zag stripes, with a blob of tan at one end. Like the distorted, too-large image of an arm sweeping down into a tank of squid?

An image that had been made of squid bodies, this afternoon?

Amanda stiffened, not sleepy anymore. She had dipped her arm into that laboratory tank. The one that was a hundred miles from here, separated by roads and fields, concrete and oblivious people. Oh, come *on*. She stared into the darkness, populating the shadows with a thousand ghostly squid. They all pointed at her, their arms straight and accusing. When Daniel stirred in his sleep, she held very still, afraid that he would wake.

Afraid of what she might tell him if he did. There wasn't anything that would work if she couldn't use the squid.

Which didn't really matter at all, because this was *her,* her brain, her dying neurons talking. Reality was Alzheimer's. Insanity.

Amanda buried her face in the pillow and waited for dawn.

Arthur Montagne looked up as she walked in. He had the room to himself, so the curtains around his bed had been drawn completely back, letting in the flood of morning sunshine. "Hi." He kept his face half-turned on the pillow as he always did. Hiding the slack, drooping flesh.

"How are you feeling?" She paused at the foot of his bed, touched his chart up onto the console screen. Chemistry good, everything looking normal. No sign of rejection or reaction, although it was too soon to write it off as a danger. "Any problems?"

"No," he mumbled through soft lips. A silver thread of drool glimmered at the corner of his mouth. "I . . . it feels different. My face. I . . . think so. Maybe . . . I just want it to."

Tortured eyes, slow slurred words from those clumsy lips. She wondered what her face was showing him. She didn't deal with patients enough to have the neutral look down pat. No, she dealt with squid who managed to communicate across miles of dry land. Amanda closed her eyes briefly, swallowed a laugh that would probably sound hysterical. Just *listen* to yourself, lady. You *know* what's really going on . . . "It's very early to expect much progress." She put lots of cheer into her smile. "The implanted cells are stimulated to differentiate by their environment." Courtesy of Roberta Guilliam's research, begun before she'd lost her funding, before her brain began to die, before she'd turned her back on her daughter. "There's no concrete schedule for when they'll begin to conduct messages. Let's see." She took him gently by the chin.

He flinched, tensed, then relaxed and let her turn his head toward her. His skin felt warm, dry, and slightly rough. She tapped his cheek lightly, felt a tiny twitch of response in the flaccid tissue. His eyes looked past her shoulder, fixed on some inner vision or a spot on the wall. She tugged his lip gently, nodded. "Response," she said softly. "Did you feel it?" Not as much as she'd hoped for, but response, damn it. A fucking *response!* "Congratulations, Arthur."

"Good. I'm . . . sick of . . . drooling." His lips quivered—not a smile, not yet, but *movement.*

"No mirror yet, OK?" She met his eyes, smiled, hoping with his hope, squeezing his hand tightly. "Give it a couple of days and you'll be impressed."

"I'll . . . pray," he mumbled softly. "I've . . . remembered how."

"You do that." She squeezed his hand again, seeing that silver school of cells inside his head, imagining the electrical impulses reaching the end of each healthy neuron, translating into released acetylcholine that drifted molecule by molecule across the vast gap between it and the next, new neuron. "It'll work." She put his hand down gently on the bed, fuck professional distance, fuck caution. "Believe it."

His lips twitched again.

"I'll see you tomorrow," she said and turned to leave, praying she wasn't wrong—don't think about that now, too late to take back those premature hopeful words.

"Doc . . . tor Car . . . nack?" His voice stopped her at the door. "What does . . . it mean? To you. Doing this?"

Amanda paused, a little at a loss because no one, not even Daniel had ever asked her this question—not so bluntly anyway. A dozen easy answers came to mind, and she discarded them, one by one. Frowning, she looked back at him, and for an instant, she saw her own face on that pillow. "I'm not quite sure." She blinked the vision away and smiled for him. "I'll see you tomorrow," she said and left quickly, before he could say anything more.

Gerald was in the lab, staring into one of the squid tanks. He raised his eyebrows as she came to stand beside him. "He's got more mobility than before," she answered his unspoken question. "More muscle tension in his face. The pathways are reestablishing—at least to some degree."

"*I* didn't doubt it." He grinned at her.

"You know, when I was a kid, our neighbor had bees." Amanda tapped the glass, watched all the squid ripple in reaction. "He sold beachplum honey to the tourists and he let me put on a veil and watch him when he worked with the hives. He never wore anything, said the stings didn't hurt him anymore." She watched the closest squid curl and uncurl its tentacles, exposing the small, white disks of the suckers. "He told me it was a mistake to talk about *bees.* He said the organism was actually the hive, that the bees were just cells. They didn't have any life or will of their own."

As if someone had given a signal, every squid in the lab turned to face her. Amanda looked quickly at Gerald, but he didn't seem startled. "Why do they do that?"

"I don't know." He shrugged. "They just do. Maybe they're bored."

The individual squids rippled with shades of brown ranging from dark mahogany to pale buff. The water in the tank was so clear. Gerald must have just cleaned it. Not blue, but just as empty, devoid of any life other than the captive squid. Will we do this to the sea one day? she thought, and felt that strange, alien *grief* again. In the tank, the squid darkened to magenta. "I wonder," she said softly. "If they were all together out in the ocean, what would we see?"

"A lot of squid disappearing over the horizon?" Gerald shrugged. "I'm going to go mix up that new medium. If we could get those damn neurons to grow, and work as implants, we could dump our little donors back into the ocean. No more tanks to clean." He moved off in the direction of the store-room. "It smells like a fishbowl in here."

Donors. Nice polite term.

Was she really thinking of a squid-mind, made up of a million tentacled neurons? Or was she hiding from that ugly reality of her dying brain? Amanda smiled crookedly and stuck her fingers into the cold water. "Speak to me, O squid," she murmured. "What do you use for acetylcholine? What carries the signal?"

In the tank, the squids' colors brightened feverishly, and Amanda felt a sudden clutch of fear.

"What are you trying to tell me?" she whispered.

Every squid turned its tail to her and went unanimously pale.

Which was nothing more than enigmatic squid behavior. Squid were long on speed and reaction time and very short on intelligence.

A single neuron wasn't so smart either.

"I'm leaving." Amanda turned her back on the tank, bending to unlock the drawer where she kept her purse. "I'm going home. Don't call me unless it's an emergency."

"OK," Gerald yelled from the sterile hood. "You want me to finish setting up the new cell cultures today?"

"Yes." And they probably wouldn't work any better than their other attempts. She slammed the drawer. "I'll see you tomorrow."

She didn't catch his answer, was already out the door. Down the hall, the elevator was just closing its doors. She ran to catch it, shoved her hand into the narrow gap. The rubber bumpers gripped her briefly and hard, then the doors hissed open and let her on.

She had intended to stop by and see her mother, but instead, she drove straight out to the beach house, speeding shamelessly in the midday lull between flex-time traffic rushes. A few days ago she had stuck her hand in a glass fish tank in her lab, had seen an oversized replay of that gesture reproduced by a school of squid out in the ocean.

She missed her exit and swore because it was three more miles until she could get off and turn around. Why pick on *her?* Why not? she asked herself bitterly. She probably spent more time with Gonatus *fabricii* than anyone short of an obsessed graduate student. Maybe obsessed graduate students never went swimming with their squid. If she lived in town, if she only saw them through the glass of the tanks, what would she see? Colors. A random expression of squid angst . . . what Gerald had seen. The people who would know about neon squid were probably the factory trawler crews; the ones who caught anything and everything and ground it into surimi. And maybe the squid knew better than to try and talk to *them. Talk* to them. Oh *God,* from color change to communication now? She swallowed a sour half laugh as she took the exit, crossed over the freeway and headed back toward her missed exit.

What if the squid were trying to say something specific to *her?*

Like: *Hey lady, stop grinding us up?* Better talk to the big drift-net operations, Squiddie. I'm just small time. Amanda wanted to laugh again, but this time it wouldn't come out.

The phone was ringing when she got home, and she heard Daniel's voice on the machine as she unlocked the door. She locked the door behind her and erased the message without playing it.

If she listened to it, she might call him. She might tell him about the squid and the patterns, because she needed to tell *someone.* He might think she was going senile, plaques clogging her brain, a premature version of her mother.

What scared her was that he might *not.*

Amanda closed her eyes briefly, seeing her mother's glazed shallow face against the black screen of her eyelids. What is the soul? Or can we only define it by its absence? The red and white flowered suit hung from the bathroom doorknob. She kept noticing it as she took off her coat, as if it were stalking her. She didn't put it on, instead donned a faded blue one that she kept for unexpected and suitless guests. She let herself out the back door, slammed it so hard that the glass rattled.

The squid mimicked patterns. So what? The green and gold zig-zags had been coincidence, or imagination, or camouflage. Not communication. What is communication? What is a soul? Arthur Montagne would walk on stage again, would move men and women perhaps to tears, or laughter, or nothing more than a heightened awareness of themselves in the scheme of life. Maybe he was a shitty actor. And did that matter? Amanda jumped from rock to rock, smelling something dead as she crossed the tideline. It was a harbor seal, bloated like a balloon, eyes already snatched out by crows or gulls. The empty, bloodied sockets seemed to follow her as she picked her way down to the foamy edge of the sea.

A wave tumbled toward her in a rush of foam, washing the sand from beneath her feet until she lost her balance and had to step sideways. Cold. She shivered as the water surged around her calves, stepping high to clear the white welter as she waded toward the surf line. Not much wind today, and at tide's ebb, the waves were small and tame. She leaped into an oncoming wave, breasting the foamy crest, sliding down the glassy seaward slope. They wouldn't be out here, she told herself, and couldn't even come up with a reason for the urgency that squeezed her. Why *should* they be waiting for her? They were cephalopods, operating on instincts and the goads of hunger and survival.

She felt a tiny tickle of relief at their absence.

Then, in the space of a single breath, they surrounded her. Amanda's rhythm slowed until she treaded water, hemmed in by silvery squid-flesh. The water was murky, blue-green today, rich in algae and glittering jellyfish drifting on the tide. But suddenly, it all felt *dead.* Jellies, fish, plankton. She swam in a festering soup of decay. "No!" The word burst from her, and she gagged, choking on a thick stench.

Then . . . it was over. She swam in cold green sea water again, smelling salt and sea and nothing else. Was this how it had started for Roberta? Brain cells withering, short-circuiting in bursts of brilliant vision? Or . . . was this something else? Afraid now, she breast-stroked toward a nearby rock. Barnacles crusted its flank, dry and gray between tides, fringed by hanks of slick green weed.

The squid swam with her. They bumped against her chest, slid writhing tentacles across her shoulders and breasts, tapping at her arms and thighs like a thousand importuning fingers. Alzheimer's or . . . what? A squid-whisper in her ear? Amanda shivered and nearly went under. She kicked convulsively, shivered again at the slick cold feel of squid-flesh against her left foot. She reached, clutched a mussel-covered knob of rock. The swell tugged at her, but she pulled herself closer, knees scraping on invisible barnacles, scrambling to get her feet under her. Squid tangled in her hair let go, plopping into the water as she staggered to her feet.

The next swell lapped around her feet and receded, trailing lacy foam. Anemones bloomed in the pooled water at her feet, groping for a meal. Panting, heart pounding, Amanda pushed wet hair out of her eyes. The squid crowded the sea in front of her, a silvery pool of endless motion, glinting with light in the bright sun.

"What do you want?" Amanda's voice trembled. "What are you trying to say to me? Are you trying to say *anything?* Or, dear God, am I just going *nuts?*"

The silvery squid darkened suddenly, as if someone had turned off a light. Slowly, colors emerged, brightening here, remaining dark there.

Knuckles pressed to her mouth, Amanda watched, her brain sorting the colors, trying to identify the pattern. Brown there, lighter *there,* a glint of pure white . . . In an instant of comprehension the swirls and blotches of color came together for her.

Three meters across, Arthur Montagne's face stared up at her from the slow sea swell.

Amanda took her hand away from her mouth, tasting blood on her lips. *How could they know?* Movement caught her eye and she looked shoreward. Someone was walking down the path from the house. Daniel? He'd called to say he was coming over? She looked down at the image of Arthur. It seemed to smile at her. In another dozen strides, Daniel would be able to see beyond the headland rocks. And maybe, from where he stood, he'd see what the squid school was showing her.

Roberta had gotten to this point. She'd made it *work,* and then the courts had taken it away from her. So she had quit. And then, she had started to die . . .

"Get *out!*" Amanda leaped from the rock, arms spread, legs scissored like a kid leaping into a swimming pool. With a gasp, she splashed into the swell, eyes squeezing shut as she went under. *Get out of here!* She screamed silently; an inner shrill note of anger, desperation, fear, and guilt. *Out!* Floundering, she struggled to the surface flailing her arms like a drowning swimmer. "Now!" she shrieked out loud, gasping for breath. "Get out of here *now,* do you hear me? Get *out! Get out!*"

The surface seethed with dusky red, like old blood. For the space of three heartbeats, the blood-colored squid surrounded her as if she had cut her throat and was bleeding to death. Then, in an eyeblink, they dove and vanished. Sobbing for breath, Amanda treaded water, staring down into the murky gray-green depths. Gone. Every one of them. "I don't care what you're trying to say," she whispered. "I won't listen. I can't, so don't come back. Not ever."

On the beach, Daniel was running for the surf. Amanda waved a leaden arm, wondering what he'd seen. Maybe nothing. She swam for shore, kicking sluggishly, weighed down by a stone of pain in her chest.

"Amanda!" Daniel splashed through the surf, his face taut with worry. "Are you OK?" He caught her as she staggered to her feet, arms going around her. "I thought you were drowning. I thought a shark was after you. You're bleeding."

"I just . . . jumped off the rock. For fun." She clenched her chattering teeth. Blood welled up from shell cuts on her thigh, dark as the squid, diluting to orange in the water that ran down her legs. "I must have scraped myself on some barnacles. I'm . . . getting you all wet."

"Yeah, you are." He kept his arm around her, eyes still worried. " 'Manda, what's wrong? And don't tell me *nothing*."

"Don't be angry at me, Daniel. I'm too cold." She laughed, hiccoughed, and shut up before it could turn into a sob. "Is it important? What I'm doing? Does it matter?"

"Matter?" He took her by the shoulders and turned her around to face him. "How can you even ask that? Is that what's bothering you?" He gave her a gentle shake, his eyes dark with compassion. "There's a message on your machine. Gerald just called. He says your patient is smiling and likes what he sees. Does that make sense?"

She leaned her forehead against Daniel's chest, tears stinging her eyes, burning worse than sea water. "It makes sense. It worked."

"How can you even *ask* if it matters?" He pressed his face against her wet hair. "Look what you can *do*. How can you *doubt?*"

How can I doubt? Amanda sighed and straightened, that stone still heavy in her chest. And what if I told you that there is a being out there, a creature like a hive of bees is a creature—a mind made up of squid, as the human brain is made up of neurons? And it has been . . . talking to me, Daniel. Or trying to. Mourning for the sea that we're killing. And instead of listening, I'm killing it—bits of it anyway, and I won't tell anyone about it, because I *need* it. I need to kill it.

"Arthur—my patient—asked me why I do this." Amanda drew a shuddering breath. "When I was ten, I . . . fell off the headland cliffs. I wasn't supposed to be climbing up there, but I was. And I slipped." She pressed her lips together, remembering that cartwheeling chaos of sky and sand, the fearful wakening to white chaos and darkness, alternating in flashes that lasted for seconds or eternities. No movement, no speech, she had been trapped in silence and terror. "Brain damage," she whispered. "Roberta did the repair. Herself. Her procedure—it was still in the early experimental stages." Crude, compared to her own methods, but it had worked. Or her brain had recovered on its own. Over the course of a year, therapy had given her back all that she had thought she'd lost. "That's why I do it." She bowed her head, remembering that *terror*—that she would be forever trapped in silence. "That's why."

"I didn't know." Daniel put his arms around me. "You're shivering," he said tenderly. "You need a long, hot shower, and then I think it's time to open that champagne."

"Yeah, sure." She leaned against him, needing his warmth, the warmth of his self, his *soul,* whatever it was made of. "Let's go have our shower and our champagne. I should celebrate."

*　*　*

Her mother's apartment still smelled like pine. The piss smell seemed stronger today. Amanda stood just inside the door, watching her mother sleep in the recliner in the tiny living room. The chair was turned toward the garden window, which showed a spring-green lawn bordered with a riot of daffodils. Puffy clouds floated above a distant wood. Amanda wondered if her mother had asked for this scene, or if some kind aide had programmed it after the daffodils had wilted. She had brought more; a thick bunch of yellow-green, half-open buds, flown in from some greenhouse or exotic flower farm somewhere, because daffodil season was over.

Amanda tiptoed across the clean, uncluttered carpet to the kitchen to get one of the plastic, safely unbreakable vases from the cupboard above the sink. The splash of water sounded loud in the sleepy quiet, and Amanda glanced quickly at Roberta. Still asleep. She set the vase on the small table beside the recliner, arranging the stems into a bright explosion that mimicked the springtime garden.

In the chair, Roberta Guilliam snored gently. Her head was turned sideways on her slack, skinny neck, scalp gleaming pinkly between wisps of white hair, face flaccid, without will to give it shape. A tiny thread of drool gleamed at the corner of her pale lips. Arthur didn't drool anymore. Amanda looked away, out at the unreal garden. When had Roberta Guilliam begun to notice the first small erosions of self? Had she already *known*, back in those bitter days after the court decision? Was that why she had quit? Because she knew what was happening? Because she was already aware of her small losses?

Had that been the source of her bitterness? That Amanda was going to do what she had so much wanted to do?

You think you're that good? I doubt it. It still hurt, would always hurt. "Why didn't you tell *me?*" Amanda said softly. "How could you *blame* me? I didn't take your research away from you. The Alzheimer's did that."

Roberta Guilliam stirred, whimpering softly in her sleep. Gently, Amanda touched her frail shoulder, stroked a wisp of hair back from her face. "It worked," she said softly. "We'll get funding. A lot more people will start using our technique. Someday, we'll be able to fix almost any damage. It's going to happen."

Too late to help Roberta Guilliam, perhaps. And what about herself, Roberta Guilliam's genetic daughter? Amanda tweaked a daffodil into place. "When I fell . . . did you use squid cells or were they fetal neurons?" It had been early on in Roberta's research; she might have used squid. Amanda had asked Gerry to search for the journal article in the lab database. "I never thought you were a quitter," she said softly. "I wish you had told me."

Too late now to change it. Too late for a lot of things. Amanda paused in the door, looked back. "Good-bye, Mother. I'll come by tomorrow." The piss smell wasn't as bad in the hall. Amanda walked quickly, eyes dazzled by the evening light streaming through the big lobby windows. The team had an article coming out in *Lancet,* others pending. The media had picked up the story, had blown it all out of proportion, of course. And they had referred to her as Roberta Guilliam's daughter. Which I *am,* Amanda thought. It occurred to her that she had called Roberta, *Mother.* She hadn't called her that since childhood. Amanda fumbled her key out of her pocket and started to unlock her car.

"Doctor Carnack?"

Arthur Montagne's voice? Here? Amanda looked up quickly. Yes, it was him, discharged a week ago. She could just see the white bandage that covered the surgery site beneath the baseball cap he wore. "Arthur." She nodded, at a loss for words. "Hello."

"I . . . I'm sorry to intrude." He didn't quite meet her eyes. "I wanted to talk to you again before they discharged me, but you never came by. So after I got out, I . . . asked a hacker friend of mine to dig up your address. I'm sorry." He blushed. "This man at your house told me you might be here."

Daniel. He was spending the weekend. Amanda nodded stiffly.

"I just wanted to tell you what it means." Arthur's eyes met hers at last, full of light and shadow. He lifted his head, smiled slowly. "When I'm on stage, I can *reach* people. I can *touch* them. I can . . . make a difference. I told myself that I'd dealt with it—that I wasn't going to be acting, but I'd do something else. I told myself that I'd handled it. But I hadn't. Not really." He held out his hand slowly. "It matters, the acting. I just want to say . . . thank you."

His eyes were so full of light. Amanda took his hand, squeezed it hard and briefly. "You're welcome," she said softly.

"That's all." The shyness came down over him like a curtain. "I won't bother you again." He smiled. "How about if I send you tickets to the next play I'm in? Would that be OK?"

"I'll come if I can." Amanda watched him walk away and get into a battered car driven by a woman. It had *mattered* to Arthur Montagne. Perhaps . . . she had given him back his soul after all. Part of it, at least? She let her breath out in a slow sigh, got into her car, and started home.

Daniel felt it, a shadow between them—a wall of silence that was there, even when they made love. He had felt it, but he hadn't said anything, was waiting for her to speak first. Maybe he thought she was getting bored with him. Amanda drove carefully, pushing empty air ahead of her as she took the exit for the beach. Maybe that wall would fade with time. She hoped so. Maybe they'd finally succeed in growing the neurons *in vitro,* and she could take him swimming in the cove. And maybe the cultured cells would never work. They'd never been part of that squid-mind. Maybe that made a difference. She thought of the squid, hovering in their clean water, waiting to die.

What is communication? What are its boundaries and what is intelligence?

What is a soul?

Midnight questions. Amanda clutched the wheel, forcing herself to pay attention to the winding road. This was not midnight.

The sun was setting as she parked in front of the beach house, staining the sea with bloody light. Daniel was gone, shopping perhaps, or walking on the beach. The light on the answering machine was flashing. Amanda hit playback and went into the kitchen for a drink of water.

Amanda? Gerry's voice sounded loud in the silence. *I found that article you asked for. Roberta Guilliam used squid neurons on the patient. Pretty crude procedure if you ask me—she sort of splashed the stuff around—but it worked in that case, anyway. Is that what you wanted? I'll be around until four finishing that incubation, so call me if you need anything else. Bye.*

The message ended with a beep. Glass in hand, Amanda stared at the machine. She touched her scalp, shivered as she found that tiny ridge of scar tissue. She wondered if this was how Arthur felt. She put her glass of water down and went out into the sunset glare. Long shadows stretched across the road, lapping at the rising hills beyond. Leaving her shoes on the steps, Amanda took the path down to the beach.

The sea was quiet, waves breaking gently as the tide ebbed. She waded out to an offshore rock and climbed onto it, to where she could see beyond the surf, out to where the squid swam. Wet pants clinging to her legs, she stood ankle deep in the foamy rush and retreat of the sea, one hand shading her eyes as she searched the bloody water. The water was empty, patched only with lacy foam. Not even a resting gull marred the smooth swells. Would environmental and animal rights groups rise up as one to protect talking squid? *Scientists Torture Sentient Squid.* She could see the headlines, now.

"I can't hear what you're telling me." She cupped her hands around her mouth, as if they—it—might be listening. "It's my decision, no one else's. My choice. My sin." Amanda closed her eyes seeing Arthur Montagne's face in the sun-baked parking-lot, seeing her mother's shallow empty eyes like a mirror reflecting her own future. Remembering terror and silence in a white hospital room. "I can't tell anyone. And I can't quit." She drew a deep breath, lungs crowded by the stone in her chest. "I'm sorry," she said. Suddenly the water filled with squid. They shone silver in the dying light, sliding shoreward in a gleaming rush, glittering in the breaking surf. "Don't!" she cried. They'd end up on the beach, washed ashore to flop and die on the rocks.

Still they came, swirling around the rock, bumping against her ankles as the waves lifted them. Stiffly, slowly, Amanda stepped down into the water, knee deep, thigh deep. The undertow tugged at her, trying to steal her balance. They gathered around her, a shifting, squirming canvas of constant motion as they struggled against the rush of the waves. The colors swirled and formed, took shape . . . This time, the picture was blurred, softened by the wave motion. But she recognized it. Amanda's hands flew to her mouth as she stared at her mother's face. Roberta Guilliam. "Is that it?" she whispered. "Are you reading my mind?" Seeing through her eyes, or the eyes of her memory? "You're sending me those dreams, aren't you? *Talking* to me." Slowly, gently, Roberta Guilliam smiled. With pride.

What is the soul, if not memory, past, who we are . . . Perhaps it was there, to be recaptured with a net woven of silver neurons. At whatever price . . . The stone in Amanda's chest softened, dissolving into tears. The first drop fell into the water, salt into salt, from sea back to sea again. "We did it," she said softly. "*We,* Mother. You and I. I won't quit and . . . I love you." Amanda stretched out her hands, spread her fingers wrist deep in the cold water. Squid bumped her palm, flicked tentacles around her fingers with the ghostly feel of hands clasping hers.

Then, they were gone, diving back through the surf, on out into the sea.

Slowly, Amanda waded back to the shore. A single squid lay on the sand, pale in death. She picked the creature up, stroking the sleek mantle, winding a limp tentacle around a finger. Her tears dripped onto it, and with an overhand toss, she threw it far out beyond the surf, to where the current would carry it out of the cove, out to where the sea could reclaim it. "Go talk to someone else," she said bitterly. "Someone who can hear you."

The sea remained dark and empty.

Slowly, Amanda trudged up the path to the dark house. Today, Arthur Montagne. Tomorrow, someone else—a hundred, a thousand, a million someone elses. More lives recaptured, netted with silver threads.

Like herself . . .

Did Arthur Montagne dream about the sea? On the front porch, Amanda hesitated. Did he dream about blue desolation, wake to a vast clench of alien grief in his chest? Beneath the evening star, a single gull skimmed low to scoop something from the water.

"You won't just talk to me," Amanda whispered. "You'll tell *him,* too?" She remembered the neurons in her virtual model, like a school of tiny squid. A new excitement tingled in her blood—tinged with just a touch of fear, too. Who *are* you? What is it that you want from us?

Maybe, it could tell them after all.

"Is that the bargain?" She cupped her hands around her mouth, although she probably didn't need to shout or even speak out loud, not with squid neurons in her brain. "Is that the deal you want? You'll give us your cells, and in return, we'll listen to you? We'll be afraid of that empty ocean, too?"

Out on that dark water, light flashed and faded, a splash of pale bioluminescence like the wave of a hand.

"I'll give you more people who can listen," she said softly. She touched the tiny ridge of scar tissue on her scalp. "I'll give you a lot of them."

Shaking sand from her shoes, filled with excitement, and fear, and anticipation, she returned to her mother's house.

In a day or two, when she had absorbed all this and truly believed, she would call Arthur Montagne and ask him if he dreamed about the sea.

For Lilly.

A Desperate Calculus

Sterling Blake

S TERLING BLAKE IS A NEW NAME WITH THE VIGOROUS VOICE OF A SEASONED WRITER. HIS FIRST NOVEL, *CHILLER*, DE-SCRIBED THE NEAR-FUTURE CONSEQUENCES—LEGAL, ETHICAL, AND PSYCHOLOG-ICAL—OF THE CRYONICS MOVEMENT. LIKE *CHILLER*, THIS TALE DEALS WITH DEEP COLD, PRESERVATION, AND LIFE AND DEATH—WITH A STARTLINGLY FRESH CON-CEPT AT ITS CORE.

AMY INCHED SHUT the frail wooden door of her hotel room and switched on the light. Cockroaches—or at least she hoped they were mere cock-roaches—scuttled for dark corners. They were so big she could hear them bumping into the tin plating along one wall.

She shucked off her dusty field jacket, threw it at the lone pine chair and sprawled on the bed. Under the dangling, naked light bulb she slit open her husband's letter eagerly, using a dirty fingernail. Frying fat flavors seeped through the planking but she forgot the smells and noises of the African village. Her eyes raced along the lurching penmanship.

> God, I do really need you. What's more, I know it's my 'juice' speak-ing—only been two weeks, but just at what point do I have to be rea-sonable? Hey, two scientists who work next to disasterville can afford a little loopy irrationality, right? Thinking about your alabaster breasts a lot. Our eagerly awaited rendezvous will be deep in the sultry jungle, in my tent. I recall your beautiful eyes that evening at Boccifani's and am counting the days . . .
> This "superflu" thing is knocking our crew people down pretty fierce now. With our schedule already packed solid, now comes two-week Earth Summit V in São Paulo. Speeches, press, more talk, more dumb delay. Hoist a few with buddies, sure, but pointless, I think. Maybe I can scare up some more funding. Takes plenty juice!—just to

keep this operation going! Wish me luck and I'll not even glance at the Latin beauties, promise. Really.

She rolled over onto her side to ease the ache in her back, keeping the letter in the yellow glow that seemed to be dimming. The crackly pages were wrinkled as if they had gotten wet in transit.

A distant generator coughed, stuttered, stopped. The light went out. She lay in the sultry dark, thinking about him and decoding all that the letter said and implied. In the distance a dog yapped and she smelled the sour lick of charcoal on the air. It did not cover the vile sickly-sweet odor of bodies left out in the street. Already they were swelling. Autumn was fairly warm in this brush-country slice of Tanzania and the village lay quiet with the still of the fallen. In a few minutes the generator huffed sluggishly back into its coughing rhythm and the bulb glowed. Watery light seeped into the room. Cockroaches scuttled again.

She finished the letter, which went on in rather impressively salacious detail about portions of her anatomy and did the job she knew Todd had intended. If any Tanzanian snoops got into her mail, they probably would not have the courage to admit it. And it did make her moist, yes.

The day's heavy heat now ebbed. A whispering breeze dispersed the wet, infesting warmth.

Todd got the new site coordinates from their uplink, through their microwave dish. He squatted beside the compact, black matte-finish module and its metallic ear, cupped to hear a satellite far out in chilly vacuum. That such a remote, desiccated, and silvery craft in the empty sky could be locked in electromagnetic embrace with this place of leafy heaviness, transfixed by sweet rot and the stink of distant fires, was to Todd a mute miracle.

Manuel yelled at him in Spanish from below. "Miz Cabrina says to come! Right away!"

"I'm nearly through."

"Right away! She says it is the cops!"

The kid had seen too much American TV. Cop spun like a bright coin in the syrup of thickly accented Spanish. Cops. Authorities. The weight of what he had to do. A fretwork of irksome memories. He stared off into infinity, missing Amy.

He was high up on the slope of thick forest. Toward him flew a rainbird. It came in languid slow motion, flapping in the mild breeze off the far Atlantic, a murmuring wind that lifted the warm weight from the stinging day. The bird's translucent shape flickered against big-bellied clouds and Todd thought of the bird as a gliding bag of genes, biological memories ancient and wrinkled and yet still coming forth. Distant time, floating toward him now across the layered air.

He waved to Manuel. "Tell her to stall them."

He finished getting the data and messages, letting the cool and precise part of him do the job. Every time some rural bigshot showed up his stomach lurched and he forced down jumpy confusions. He struggled to insulate the calm, unsettled center of himself so that he could work. He had thought this whole thing would get easier, but it never did.

The solar panels atop their van caught more power if he parked it in the day's full glare, but then he couldn't get into it without letting the interior cool off. He had driven up here to get a clear view of the rest of the team. He left the van and headed toward where the salvaging team was working.

Coming back down through kilometers of jungle took him through terrain that reflected his inner turmoil. Rotting logs shone with a vile, vivid emerald. Swirls of iridescent lichen engulfed thick-barked trees. He left the cross-country van on the clay road and continued, boots sinking into the thick mat.

Nothing held sway here for long. Hand-sized spiders scuttled like black motes across the intricate green radiance. Exotic vitality, myriad threats. A conservation biologist, he had learned to spot the jungle's traps and viper seductions. He sidestepped a blood vine's barbs, wisely gave a column of lime ants their way. Rustlings escorted him through dappled shadows which held a million minute violences. Carrion moths fluttered by on charcoal wings in search of the fallen. Tall grass blades cut the shifting sunlight. Birds cooed and warbled and stabbed insects from the air. Casually brutal beauty.

He vectored in on the salvaging site. As he worked downslope the insecticidal fog bombs popped off in the high canopy. Species pattered down through the branches, thumped on logs, a dying rain. The gray haze descended, touched the jungle floor, settled into nooks. Then a vagrant breeze blew it away. His team moved across the hundred-meter perimeter, sweeping uphill.

Smash and grab, Todd thought, watching the workers in floppy jeans and blue work shirts get down on hands and knees. They inched forward, digging out soil samples, picking up fallen insects, fronds, stems, small mammals. Everything, anything. Some snipped samples from the larger plants. Others shinnied up the slick-barked trees and rummaged for the resident ants and spiders and myriad creatures who had not fallen out when the fog hit them. A special team took leaves and branches—too much trouble to haul away whole trees. And even if they'd wanted to, the politicos would scream; timbering rights here had already been auctioned off.

Todd angled along behind the sweeping line of workers, all from Argentina. He caught a few grubs and leaves that had escaped and dropped them into a woman's bag. She smiled and nodded respectfully. Most of them were embarrassingly thankful to have a job. The key idea in the Bio-Salvage Program was to use local labor. That created a native constituency wherever they went. It also kept costs manageable. The urban North was funding this last-ditch effort. Only the depressed wages of the rural South made it affordable.

And here came the freezers. A thinner line of men carrying Styrofoam dry ice boxes, like heavy-duty picnic coolers. Into these went each filled sack. Stapled to the neck of each bag was a yellow bar-code strip giving location, date, terrain description. He had run them off in the van this morning. Three more batches were waiting in his pack for the day's work further up the valley.

His pack straps cut into his roll of shoulder muscle, reminding him of how much more remained to do. To save. He could see in the valley below the press of population on the lush land. A crude work camp sprawled like a tan fungus. Among the jungle's riot of emerald invention a dirt road wound like a dirty snake.

He left the team and headed toward the trouble, angling by faded stucco buildings. Puddles from a rain shower mirrored an iron cross over the entrance gate of a Catholic mission. The Pope's presence. Be fruitful, ye innocent, and multiply. Spread like locusts across God's green works.

Ramshackle sheds lay toward the work camp, soiling the air with greasy wood smoke. In the jungle beyond, chain saws snarled in their labors. Beside the clay ruts of the road lay crushed aluminum beer cans and a lurid tabloid about movie stars.

He reached the knot of men as Cabrina started shouting.

"Yes we do! Signed by your own lieutenant governor *especial!*"

She waved papers at three uniformed types, who wore swarthy scowls and revolvers in hip holsters.

"No, no." An officer jerked a finger at the crowd. "These, they say it interferes with their toil."

Here at the edge of the work camp they had already attracted at least fifty. Worn men slouched against a stained yellow wall, scrawny and raw-boned and faces slack with fatigue. They were sour twists of men, *maraneros* from the jungle, a machete their single tool, their worn skins sporting once-jaunty tattoos of wide-winged eagles and rampant bulls and grinning skulls.

"The hell it does." Cabrina crossed her arms over her red jumper and her lips whitened.

"The chemicals, they make coughing and—"

"We went through all that with the foreman. And I have documents—"

"These say nothing about—"

Todd tuned out the details and watched lines deepen in the officer's face. Trouble coming, and fast. He was supposed to let Cabrina, as a native, run the interference. Trouble was, these were macho backcountry types. He nodded respectfully to the head officer and said, "Our schedule bothering them?"

The officer looked relieved to deal with a man. "They do not like the fumes or having to stay away from the area."

"Let's see if we can do something about that. Suppose they work upwind?"

So then it got into a back-and-forth negotiation. He hated cutting in on Cabrina but the officer had been near the breaking point. Todd gradually eased Cabrina back in and the officer saw how things were going to go. He accepted that with some facesaving talk and pretty soon it was settled.

Todd walked Cabrina a bit back toward the jungle. "Don't let them rile you. Just stick to the documents."

"But they are so stupid!" Flashing anger, a wrenched mouth.

"Tell me something new."

Their ice van growled into view. It already had the sample sacks from the fogging above. Time to move a kilometer on and repeat the process. All so they could get into this valley and take their samples before these butchers with their bovine complacency could chop it down for cropland or grazing or just to make charcoal. But Todd did not let any of this into his face. Instead he told Cabrina to show the van where to go. Then he went over and spoke to several of the men in his halting Spanish. Smoothing the way. He made sure to stand close to them and speak in the private and respectful way that worked around here.

Amy followed the rest of her team into the ward. It was the same as yesterday and the day before. All beds filled, patients on the floors, haggard faces, nurses looking as bad as the patients. The infection rate here was at least eighty percent of the population. These were just the cases which had made it to the hospital and then had the clout to get in.

Freddie went through the list prepared by the hospital director. They were there to survey and take blood samples but the director seemed to think his visitors bore some cure. Or at least advice.

"Fever, frequent coughing, swellings in the groin," Freddie read, his long black hair getting in the way. He was French and found everything about this place a source of irritation. Amy did not blame him but it was not smart to show it. "Seven percent of cases display septic shock, indicating that the blood stream is directly infected."

"I hope these results will be of help to your researches," the director said. He was a short man with a look that alternated between pleading and outright panic. Amy did her best to not look at him. His eyes were always asking, asking.

Freddie waved his clipboard. "All is consistent with spread directly among humans by inhalation of infected respiratory droplets?"

The director nodded rapidly. "But we cannot isolate the chain. It seems—"

"Yes, yes, it is so everywhere. The incubation period of the infection is at least two weeks, though it can be up to a month. By that time the original source is impossible to stipulate." Freddie rattled this off because he had said the same thing a dozen times already in Tanzania.

Amy said mildly, "I note that you have not attempted to isolate the septic cases."

The director jerked as if reprimanded and went into an explanation, which did not matter to anyone but would make him feel better, she was sure. She asked for and received limbic fluids, mucus, and blood samples from the deceased patients. The director wanted to talk to someone of higher authority and their international team filled that need. Not that it did any good. They had no vaccine, no real advice except to keep the patients cool and not to use sedation which would suppress their lung function. They told him this and then told his staff and then told him again because he just kept looking at them with those eyes. Then they went away.

In the next town Amy got to a telephone and could hook up her modem. She got an uplink with only a half hour wait. They drove back into the capital city over dusty roads while she read the printouts.

Summary View.

This present plague is certainly a derived form of influenza. It is well known that the "flu" virus undergoes "antigenic" drifts—point mutations in the virus's outer protein coat which can enhance the ability of the virus to attack the human immune system. New pandemic viruses emerge at unpredictable intervals on the order of decades, though the rate of shifts may be increasing. The present pathogenic outbreak, with its unusual two- to three-week incubation period, allows rapid spreading before populations can begin to take precautions—isolation, face masks, etc. Fatality rate is 3% in cases which do not recover within five days. Origin: The apparent derivation of this plague from southern Asia has been obscured by its rapid transmission to both Africa and South America. However, this Asian origin, recently unmasked by detailed hospital studies and demographics, verifies the suspicions of the

United Nations Emergency Committee. Asia is the primary source of "flu" outbreaks because of the high incidence there of "integrated farming," which mingles fowl, pigs and fish close together. In Southeast Asia this has been an economic blessing, but a reverse-spin disaster for the North. Viruses from different species mix, recombining and undergoing gene reassortment at a rapid rate. Humans need time to synthesize specific antibodies as a defense. Genetic aspects: Preliminary results suggest that this is a recombinant virus. Influenza has seven segments of RNA, and several seem to have been modified. Some correlations suggest close connection to the swine flu derived from pigs. This is a shift, not a simple drift. Some recombination has occurred from another reservoir population—but which? Apparently, some rural environment in southern China.

She looked up as they jounced past scrubby farmland. No natural forest or grassland remained; humans had turned all arable land to crops. Insatiable appetite, eating nature itself.

Nobody visible. The superflu knocked everybody flat for at least three days, marvelously infective, and few felt like getting back to the fields right away. That would take another slice out of the food supply here. Behind the tide of illness would come some malnutrition. The U.N. would have to be ready for that, too.

Not my job, though, she thought, and mused longingly of Todd.

São Paulo. Earth Summit V, returning to South America for the first time since Summit I in the good old days of 1992. He was to give a talk about the program and then, by God, he'd be long gone.

On the drive in he had seen kindergarten-age children dig through cow dung, looking for corn kernels the cows hadn't digested. The usual colorful chaos laced with gray despair. Gangs of urchin thieves who didn't know their own last names. Gutters as sewers. Families living in cardboard boxes. Babies found discarded in trash heaps.

He had imagined that his grubby jeans and T-shirt made him look unremarkable, but desperation hones perceptions. The beggars were on him every chance. By now he had learned the trick which fended off the swarms of little urchins wanting Chiclets, the shadowy men with suitcases of silver jewelry, the women at traffic lights hawking bunches of roses. Natives didn't get their windshields washed unless they wanted it, nor did they say "no" a hundred times to accomplish the result. They just held up one finger and waggled it sideways, slowly. The pests magically dispersed. He had no idea what it meant, but it was so easy even a gringo could do it.

His "interest zone" at Earth Summit V was in a hodge-podge of sweltering tents erected in an outdoor park. The grass had been beaten into gray, flat blades. Already there was a dispute between the North delegates, who wanted a uniform pledge of seventy-five percent reduction in use of pesticides. Activists from the poor South worried about hunger more than purity, so the proposal died. This didn't stop anyone from dutifully signing the Earth Pledge which covered one whole wall in thick gray cardboard. After all, it wasn't legally binding.

Todd talked with a lot of the usual Northern crowd from the Nature Conservancy and World Wildlife Fund, who were major sponsors of Bio-Salvage. They were twittering about a Southern demand that everybody sign a "recognition of the historical, biological and cultural debt" the North owed the South. They roped him into it, because the background argument (in Spanish, so of course most of the condescending Northerners couldn't read it) named BioSalvage as "arrogantly entering our countries and pushing fashionable environmentalism over the needs of the people."

Todd heard this in a soft drink bar, swatting away flies. Before he could respond, a spindly man in a sack shirt elbowed his way into the Northern group. "I know who you are, Mr. Russell. We do not let your 'debt swap' thievery go by."

BioSalvage had some funding from agreements which traded money owed to foreign banks for salvaging rights and local labor. He smiled at the stranger. "All negotiated, friend."

"The debt was contracted illegally!" The man slapped the yellow plastic table, spilling Coke.

"By your governments."

"By the criminals!—who then stole great sums."

Todd spread his hands, still smiling though it was getting harder. "Hey, I'm no banker."

"You are part of a plot to keep us down," the man shot back.

"By saving some species?"

"You are killing them!"

"Yeah, maybe a few days before your countrymen get around to it."

Two other men and a woman joined the irate man. Todd was with several Northerners and a woman from Costa Rica who worked for the Environmental Defense Fund. He tried to keep his tone civil and easy but people started breaking in and pretty soon the Southerners were into Harangue Mode and it went to hell. The Northerners rolled their eyes and the Southerners accused them in quick, staccato jabs of being arrogant, impatient, irritated when somebody couldn't speak English, ready to walk out at the first sign of a long speech when there was so much to say after all.

Todd eased away from the table. The Northerners used words like "proactive" and "empowerment" and kept saying that before they were willing to discuss giving more grants they wanted accountability. They worried about corruption and got thin-lipped when told that they should give without being oppressors of the spirit by trying to manage the money. *"Imperialista!"* a Brazilian woman hissed, and Todd left.

He took a long walk down littered streets rank with garbage.

Megacities. Humanity growing by a hundred million fresh souls per year, with disease and disorder in ample attendance. Twenty-nine megacities now with more than ten million population. Twenty-five in the "developing" world—only nobody was developing anymore. Tokyo topped the list, as always, at thirty-six million. São Paulo was coming up fast on the outside with thirty-four million. Lagos, Nigeria, which nobody ever thought about, festered with seventeen million despite the multitudes lost to AIDS.

He kicked a can and shrugged off beggars. A man with sores drooling down his face approached but Todd did not dare give him a bill. Uncomfortably he wagged his finger. Indifference was far safer.

Megacities spawned the return of microbes that had toppled empires down through history. Cholera, the old foe. New antibiotic-resistant strains. Cysticercosis, a tapeworm that invades the brain, caught from eating vegetables grown in the city's effluent. Half the world's urban population had at least one skin rash per year.

And big cities demand standardized, easily transported foods. Farmers respond with monocrops, which are more vulnerable to pests and disease and drought. Cities preyed on the cropland and forests which sustain them. Plywood apartment walls in Nagasaki chewed up Borneo's woodlands.

When he reached his hotel room—bare concrete, tin sink in the room, john down the hall—he found a light blinking on the satellite comm. He located the São Paulo nexus and got a fastprint letter on his private number. It was from Amy and he read it eagerly, the gray walls around him forgotten.

I'm pretty sure friend Freddie is now catching holy hell for not being on top of this superflu faster. There's a pattern, he says. Check out the media feeding frenzy, if you have the time. Use my access codes onto SciNet, too. I'm more worried about Zambia, our next destination. Taking no recognition of U.N. warnings, both sides violating the ceasefire. We'll have armed escorts. Not much use against a virus! All our programs are going slowly, with locals dropping like flies.

The sweetness of her seemed to swarm up into his nostrils then, blotting out the disinfectant smell from the cracked linoleum. He could see her electric black hair tumbling like rolling smoke about her shoulders, spilling onto her full breasts in yellow candle light. After a tough day he would lift her onto him, setting her astride his muscular arch. The hair wreathed them both, making a humid space that was theirs only, musk-rich and silent. She could bounce and stroke and coax from him the tensions of time, and later they would have dark rum laced with lemon. Her eyes could widen with comic rapt amazement, go slit-thin with anger, become suddenly womanly as they reflected the serenity of the languid candle flame.

Remember to dodge the electronic media blood hounds. Sniffers and lickers, I call 'em. Freddie handles them for us, but I'm paranoid—seeing insults spelled out in my alphabet soup. Remember that I love you. Remember to see Kuipers if you get sick! See you in two weeks—so very long!

His gray computer screen held a WorldNet news item, letters shimmering. Todd's program had fished it out of the torrent of news, and it confirmed the worst of his fears. He used her code-keys to gain entry and global search/scan found all the hot buzz:

SUPERFLU EPIDEMIC WIDENS. SECRETARY-GENERAL CALLS FOR AIR TRAVEL BAN. DISEASE CONTROL CENTER TRACING VECTOR CARRIERS.

(AP) A world-sweeping contagion has now leaped from Asia to Africa and on to South America. Simultaneous outbreaks in Cairo, Johannesburg, Mexico City and Buenos Aires confirmed fears that the infection is spreading most rapidly through air travelers. Whole cities have been struck silent and prostrated as a majority of inhabitants succumb within a few days.

Secretary-General Imukurumba called for a total ban on international passenger air travel until the virus is better understood. Airlines have logged a sharp rise in ticket sales in affected regions, apparently from those fleeing.

The Center for Disease Control is reportedly attempting to correlate outbreaks with specific travelers, in an effort to pinpoint the source. Officials declined to confirm this extraordinary move, however.

He suspected that somebody at the CDC was behind this leak, but it might mean something more. More ominously, what point was there in tracing individuals? CDC was moving fast. This thing was a wildfire. And Amy was right in the middle of it.

He sat a long time at a fly-specked Formica table, staring at the remains of his lunch, a chipped blue plate holding rice and beans and a gnawed crescent of green tortilla. Todd felt the old swirl of emotions, unleashed as though they had lain in waiting all this time. Incoherent, disconnected images propelled him down musty corridors of self. Words formed on his lips but evaporated before spoken.

She hated autopsies. Freddie had told her to check this one, and the smell was enough to make her pass out. Slow fans churned at one end of the tiny morgue. Only the examining table was well lit. Its gutters ran with viscous, reeking fluids.

The slim black woman on the table was expertly "unzipped"—carved down from neck to pelvis, organs neatly extracted and lying across her chest and legs. Glistening tubes and lumpy vitals, so clean and smooth they seemed to be manufactured.

"A most interesting characteristic of these cases," the coroner went on in a serene voice that floated in the chilly room. He picked up an elongated gray sac. "The fallopians. Swollen, discolored. The ova sac is distended, you will be seeing here. And red."

Amy said, "Her records show very high temperatures. Could this be—"

"Being the cause of death, this temperature, yes. The contagion invaded the lower abdomen, however, causing further discomfort."

"So this is another variation on the, uh, superflu?"

"I think yes." The coroner elegantly opened the abdomen further and showed off kidneys and liver. "Here too, some swelling. But not as bad as in the reproductive organs."

Amy wanted desperately to get out of this place. Its cloying smells layered the air. Two local doctors stood beside her, watching her face more than the body. They were well-dressed men in their fifties and obviously had never seen a woman in a position of significance in their profession. She asked, "What percentage of your terminal cases display this?"

"About three quarters," the coroner said.

"In men and women alike?" Amy asked.

"Yes, though for the women these effects are more prominent."

"Well, thank you for your help." She nodded to them and left. The two doctors followed her. When she reached the street her driver was standing beside the car with two soldiers. Three more soldiers got out of a big jeep and one of the doctors said, "You are please to come."

There wasn't much to do about it. Nobody was interested in listening to her assertion that she was protected by the Zambia-U.N. terms. They escorted her to a low, squat building on the outskirts of town. As they marched her inside she remarked that the place looked like a bunker. The officer with her replied mildly that it was.

General Movotubo wore crisp fatigues and introduced himself formally. He invited her to sit in a well-decorated office without windows. Coffee?

Good. Biscuit? Very good. "And so you will be telling now what? That this disease is the product of my enemies."

"I am here as a United Nations—"

"Yes yes, but the truth, it must come out. The Landuokoma, they have brought this disease here, is this not so?"

"We don't know how it got here." She tried to understand the expressions which flitted across the heavy-set man's face, which was shiny with nervous sweat.

"Then you cannot say that the Landuokoma did not bring it, this is right?"

Amy stood up. General Movotubo was shorter than her and she recognized now his expression: a look of caged fear. "Listen, staying holed up in here isn't going to protect you against superflu. Not if your personnel go in and out, anyway."

"Then I will go to the countryside! The people will understand. They will see that the Landuokoma caused me to do so."

She started for the door. "Believe me, neither I nor the U.N. cares what you say to your newspapers. Just let me go."

There was a crowd outside the bunker. They did not retreat when she emerged and she had to push and shove her way to her car. The driver sat inside, petrified. But nobody tried to stop them. The faces beyond the window glass were filled with stark dread, not anger.

She linked onto WorldNet back at the hotel. The serene liquid crystal screen blotted out the awareness of the bleak streets beyond the grand marble columns of the foyer.

PULLDOWN SIDEBAR: News Analysis MIXED REACTION TO PLAGUE OUTBREAK

Environmental Hard Liners Say "Inevitable"(AP) . . . "What I'm saying," Earth First! spokesman Josh Leonard said, "is that we're wasting our resources trying to hold back the tide. It's pointless. Here in the North we have great medical expertise. Plenty of research has gone into fathoming the human immune system, to fixing our cardiovascular plumbing, and the like. But to expend it trying to fix every disease that pops up in the South is anti-Darwinian, and futile. Nature corrects its own mistakes."

. . . Many in the industrialized North privately admit being increasingly appalled with the South's runaway numbers. Their views are extreme. They point to how Megacities sprawl, teeming with seedy, impoverished masses. Torrents of illegal immigration pour over borders. Responding to deprivation, Southern politico/religious movements froth and foment, few of them appetizing as seen from a Northern distance. "The more the North thinks of humanity as a ma- lignancy," said psychophilosopher Norman Wills, "the more we will unconsciously long for disasters."

Amy was not really surprised. The Nets seethed with similar talk. Todd had been predicting this for years. That made her think of him, and she shut down her laptop.

He stopped at the BioSalvage Southern Repository to pick up the next set of instructions, maps, political spin. It was a huge complex—big, gray, concrete bunker-style for the actual freezing compartments, tin sheds for the sample processing. All the buzz and clatter of the rest of Caracas faded as he walked down alleys between the Repository buildings. Ranks of big liquid nitrogen dewars. Piping, automatic labeling machines, harried workers chattering in highly accented Spanish he could barely make out.

In the foyer a whole wall was devoted to the history of it. At the top was the abstract of Scott's first paper, proposing what he called the Library of Life. The Northern Repository was in fact called that, but here they were more stiff and official.

A broad program of freezing species in threatened ecospheres could pre-serve biodiversity for eventual use by future generations. Sampling without studying can lower costs dramatically. Local labor can do most of the gath-ering. Plausible costs of collecting and cryogenically suspending the tropi-cal rain forest species, at a sampling fraction of 10-6, are about two billion dollars for a full century. Much more information than species DNA will be saved, allowing future biotechnology to derive high information content and perhaps even resurrect then-extinct species. A parallel program of limited in situ *preservation is essential to allow later expression of frozen genomes in members of the same genus. This broad proposal should be debated throughout the entire scientific community.*

Todd had to wait for his appointment. He fidgeted in the foyer. A woman coming out of the executive area wobbled a bit, then collapsed, her clipboard clattering on marble. Nobody went to help. The secretaries and guards drew back, turned, were gone. Todd helped the woman struggle into a chair. She was already running a fever and could hardly speak. He knew there wasn't anything to do beyond getting her a glass of water. When he came back with one, a medical team was there. They simply loaded her onto a stretcher and took her out to an unmarked van. Probably they were just going to take her home. The hospitals were already jammed, he had heard.

He took his mind off matters by reading the rest of the Honor Wall, as it was labeled. Papers advocating the BioSalvage idea. A Nobel for Scott. Begrudging support from most conservation biologists.

Our situation resembles a browser in the ancient library at Alexandria, who suddenly notes that the trove he had begun inspecting has caught fire. Already a wing has burned, and the mobs outside seem certain to block any fire-fighting crews. What to do? There is no time to patrol the aisles, discerningly plucking forth a treatise of Aristotle, or deciding whether to leave behind Alexander the Great's laundry list. Instead, a better strategy is to run through the remaining library, tossing texts into a basket at random, sampling each section to give broad coverage. Perhaps it would be wise to take smaller texts, in order to carry more, and then flee into an unknown future.

"Dr. Russell? I am Leon Segueno."

The man in a severe black suit was not his usual monitor. "Where's Confuelos?"

"Ill, I believe. I'll give you the latest instructions."

Back into the executive area, another new wrinkle. Segueno went through the fresh maps with dispatch. Map coordinates, rendezvous points with the choppers, local authorities who would need soothing. A fresh package of local currency to grease palms, where necessary. Standard stuff.

"I take it you will be monitoring all three of your groups continuously?"

An odd question. Segueno didn't seem familiar with procedures. Probably a political hack.

"I get around as much as I can. Working the back roads, it isn't easy."

"You get to many towns."

"Gotta buy a few beers for the local brass hats."

"Have you difficulty with the superflu?"

"Some of the crew dropped out. We hired more."

"And you?"

"I keep away from anybody who's sniffling or coughing."

"But some say it is spread by ordinary breath."

He frowned. "Hadn't heard that."

"A United Nations team reported so."

"Might explain how it spreads so fast."

"*Sí, sí.* Your wife, I gather she is working for the U.N.?"

"On this same problem, right. I hadn't heard that angle, though."

"You must be very proud of her."

"Uh, yes." Where was this going?

"To be separated, it is not good. Will you see her soon?"

No reason to hide anything, even from an officious bureaucrat. "This week. She's joining me in the field."

Segueno chuckled. "Not the kind of reunion I would have picked. Well, good luck to you."

He tried to read the man's expression and got nothing but a polished blandness behind the eyes. Maybe the guy was angling for some kind of payoff? Nothing would surprise him anymore, even in the Repository.

He stopped off in the main bay. High sheet-metal ceiling, gantries, steel ramps. Stacks of blue plastic coolers, filled with the labeled sacks that teams like his own sent in. Sorting lines prepared them further. Each cooler was logged and integrated into a geographical inventory, so that future researchers could study correlations with other regions. Then the coolers went into big aluminum canisters. The gantries lowered these into permanent place. Tubes hooked up, monitors added, and then the liquid nitrogen pumped in with a hiss. A filmy fog, and another slice of vanishing life was on its way to the next age.

Todd wondered just when biology would advance to the point where these samples could be unfolded, their genes read. And then? Nobody could dictate to the future. They might resurrect extinct species, make leopards again pace the jungle paths. Or maybe they would revive beetles— God must have loved them, He made so many kinds, as Haldane himself had remarked. Maybe there was something wonderful in those shiny carapaces, and the future would need it.

Todd shrugged. It was reassuring to come here and feel a part of it all.

Going out through the foyer, he stopped and read the rest of the gilt lettering on polished black marble.

We must be prudent. Leading figures in biodiversity argue that a large scale species dieback seems inevitable, leading to a blighted world which will eventually learn the price of such folly. The political impact of such a disaster will be immense. Politics comes and goes, but extinction is forever. We may be judged harshly by our grandchildren, our era labeled the Great Dying or the Age of Appetite. A future generation could well reach out for means to recover their lost biological heritage. If scientific progress has followed the paths many envision today, they will have the means to perform seeming miracles. They will have developed ethical and social mechanisms we cannot guess, but we can prepare now the broad outlines of a recovery strategy, simply by banking biological information. These are the crucial years for us to act, as the Library of Life burns furiously around us, throughout the world.

He left. When he got into his rental Ford in the parking lot, he saw Segueno looking down at him through a high window.

He had not expected to get a telephone call. On a one-day stop in Goias, Brazil, to pick up more coolers and a fresh crew, there was little time to hang around the hotel. But somehow she traced him and got through on the sole telephone in the manager's office. He recognized Amy's voice immediately despite the bad connection.

"Todd? I was worried."

"Nothing's gone wrong with your plans, has it?"

"No no, I'll be there in two days. But I just heard from Freddie that a lot of people who were delegates at the Earth Summit have come down with superflu. Are you all right?"

"Sure, fine. How's it there?"

"I've got a million tales to tell. The civil war's still going on and we're pulling out. I wrote you a letter, I'll send it satellite squirt to your modem address."

"Great. God, I've missed you."

Her warm chuckle came through the purr of static. "I'll expect you to prove it."

"I'll be all set up in a fresh camp, just out from Maraba. A driver will pick you up."

"Terrif. Isn't it terrible, about the Earth Summit?"

"Nobody's immune."

"I guess not. We're seeing ninety percent affliction in some villages here."

"What about this ban on passenger travel? Will that—"

"It isn't sticking. Anyway, we have U.N. passes. Don't worry, lover, I'll get there if I have to walk."

He got her letter over modem within a few minutes.

We're pinning down the epidemiology. Higher fevers in women, but about 97% recover. Freddie's getting the lab results from the samples we sent in. He's convinced there'll be a vaccine, pronto.

But it's hard to concentrate, babe. This place is getting worse by the hour. We got a briefing on safety in Zambia, all very official, but most of the useful stuff we picked up from drivers, cops, locals on street corners. You have to watch details, like your license plates. I got some neutral plates from some distant country. People sell them in garages. Don't dare use the old dodge of putting a PRESS label on your car. Journalists draw fire here, and a TV label is worse. Locals see TV as more powerful than the lowly word-artists of newspapers. TV's the big propaganda club and everybody's got some reason to be mad at it.

We got a four-wheel job that'll go off-road. Had to be careful not to get one that looked like a military jeep. They draw fire. We settled on a white Bighorn, figuring that snipers might think we were U.N. peacekeeping forces. On the other hand, there's undoubtedly some faction that hates the U.N., too. Plenty of people here blame us—Westerners—for the superflu. We get hostile stares, a few thrown rocks. Freddie took a tomato in the chest today. Rotten, of course. Otherwise, somebody'd have eaten it.

We go out in convoys, seeking superflu vectors. Single cars are lots more vulnerable. And if we break down, like yesterday, you've got help.

I picked up some tips in case we come under fire. (Now don't be a nervous husband! You know I like field work . . .) Bad idea to ride in the back seat of a two-door—hard to get out fast. Sit in the front seat and keep the door slightly open so you can dive out. Windows open, too, so you can hear what's coming down.

Even in town we're careful with the lights. Minimal flashlight use. Shrouds over camera lights as much as you can. A camera crew interviewing us from CNN draped dark cloth over their heads so nobody could see the dim blue glow of the viewfinder leaking from around their eyes.

Not what you wanted your wife to be doing, right? But it's exciting! Sorry if this is unfeminine. You'll soon have a chance to check out whether all this macho stuff has changed my, uh, talents. Just a week! I'll try to be all frilly-frilly. Lover, store up that juice of yours.

He stared at the glimmering phosphors of his laptop. Superflu at the Earth Summit. Vaccine upcoming. Vectors colliding, and always outside the teeming city with its hoarse voices, squalling babies and swelling mothers, the rot of mad growth. Could a species which produced so many mouths be anything more than a blight? Their endless masses cast doubt upon the importance of any individual, diminished the mind's inner sense.

He read the letter again as if he were under water, bubbles springing from his lips and floating up into a filmy world he hoped someday to see. He and Amy struggled, knee-deep in the mud of lunatic mobs. How long, before they were dragged down? But at least for a few moments longer they had the shadowy recesses of each other.

He waited impatiently for her beside his tent. He had come back early from the crew sites and a visit to the local brass hats. It had gone pretty well but he could not repress his desire for her, his impatience. He calmed himself by sitting in his canvas-backed chair, boots propped up on a stump left by the land clearing. He had some background files from Amy and he idly paged through them on his laptop. A review paper in *Nature* tried to put the superflu in historical perspective.

There were in fact three bubonic plagues, each so named because the disease began with buboes—swollen lymph glands in the groin, armpit, neck. Its pneumonic form spread quickly, on breaths swarming with micro-organisms, every cough throwing micro-organisms to the wind. A bacterial disease, the bacillus *Pasteurella pestis* was carried by fleas on *Rattus rattus*.

In assessing the potentials of Superflu, consider the first bubonic pandemic. Termed the Plague of Justinian (540–590), who was the Caesar of the era, it began the decline of the Roman Empire, strengthened Christianity with its claims of an afterlife, and discredited Roman medicine, whose nostrums proved useless—thus strangling a baby science. By the second day of an ever-rising fever, the victims saw phantoms which called, beckoning toward the grave. The plague ended only when it killed so many, up to half the population of some cities, that it ran out of carriers. It killed a hundred million, a third of the region's population, and four times the Black Death toll of 1346–1361.

Our Superflu closely resembles the Spanish Influenza, which actually originated in Kansas. It was history's worst outbreak, as rated by deaths per day—thirty million in a single fall season of 1918. The virus mutated quickly. Accidental Russian lab release of a frozen sample in 1977 caused a minor outbreak . . .

He lay on his cot, waiting for the sound of his jeep, bearing Amy. Through the heavy air came the oddly weak slap of a distant shot. Then three more, quick.

He stumbled outside the tent. Bird rustlings, something scampering in the bush. He was pretty sure the shots had come from up the hill, where the dirt road meandered down. It was impossible to see anything in the twilight trees.

He had envisioned this many times before but that did not help with the biting visceral alarm, the blur of wild thoughts. He thought he had no illusions about what might happen. He walked quickly inside and slapped his laptop shut. Two moths battered at the lone lantern in his tent, throwing a shrapnel of shadows on the walls, magnified anxiety.

Automatically he picked up the micro-disks which carried his decoding routines and vital records. He kept none of it on hard disk so he did not need to erase the laptop. His backpack always carried a day's food and water and he swung it onto his back as he left the tent and trotted into the jungle.

Evening falls heavily beneath the canopy. He went through a mat of vines, slapping aside the stinging flies which rose angrily.

Boots thumping behind him? No, up on the dirt road. A man's shout. He bent over and worked his way down a steep slope. He wished he had remembered to bring his helmet. He crouched further to keep below the ferns but some caught him in the face. In the fading shafts of green radiance he went quietly, stooped forward. Cathedral pillars of old trees were furred with orange moss. The day's heat still thickened the air. He figured that if she got away from them she would go downhill. From the road that led quickly into a narrowing canyon. He angled to the left and ran along an open patch of rock and into the lip of the canyon about halfway down. Impossible to see anything in there but green masses.

There was enough light for them to search for her. She would keep moving and hope they didn't track her by the sound. Noise travels uphill better in a canyon. He plunged into lacerating fronds and worked his way toward where he knew a stream trickled down.

Somebody maybe twenty meters ahead and down slope. Todd angled up to get a look. His breath caught when he saw her, just a glimpse of her hair in a fading gleam of dusk. Branches snapped under his boots as he went after her. She heard as he had hoped and slipped behind a tree. He whispered, "Amy! Todd!" and there she was suddenly, gripping her pop-out pistol.

"Oh God!" she said and kissed him suddenly.

"Are you hurt?" he whispered.

"No." Her gaze ricocheted around the masses of green upslope from them. "I shot the driver of my jeep. In the shoulder, to make him stop. I had to, that Segueno—"

"Him. I wondered what the hell he was—Wait, what'd you shoot at after that?"

"The jeep behind us."

"They stopped?"

"Just around the curve, but they were running toward me."

"Where was Segueno?"

"In my jeep."

"He didn't shoot at you?"

"No, I don't think—"

"He probably didn't want to."

"Who is he? He said he was with World Emergency Services—"

"He's probably got a dozen IDs. Come on."

They forked off from the stream. It was clearer there and the obvious way to go so he figured to stay away from it and move laterally away from the camp. The best they could do would be to reach the highway about five kilometers away and hitch a ride before anybody covered that or stopped traffic. She had no more idea than he did how many people they had but the followup jeep implied they could get more pretty quickly. It probably had good comm gear in it. In the dark they would take several hours to reach the highway. Plenty of time to cover the escapes but they had to try it.

The thin light was almost gone now. Amy was gasping—probably from the shock more than anything else, he thought. She did look as though she had not been sleeping well. The leaden night was coming on fast when they stopped.

"What does he—"

She fished a crumpled page from her pocket. "I grabbed it to get his attention while I got this pistol out." She laughed suddenly, coughed. "He looked scared. I was really proud of myself. I didn't think I could ever use that little thing but when—"

Todd nodded, looking at the fax of his letter, words underlined:

God, I do really need you. What's more, I know it's my "juice" speak-ing—only been two weeks, but just at what point do I have to be rea-sonable? Hey, two scientists who work next to disasterville can afford a little loopy irrationality, right? Thinking about your alabaster breasts a lot. Our eagerly awaited rendezvous will be deep in the sultry jungle, in my tent. I recall your beautiful eyes that evening at Boccifani's and am counting the days . . .

"He thought he was being real smooth." She laughed again, higher this time. Brittle. "Maybe he thought I'd break down or something if he just showed me he was onto us." Todd saw that she was excited still but that would fade fast.

"How many men you think he could get right away?"

She frowned. "I don't know. Who is he, why—"

He knew that she would start to worry soon and it would be better to have her thinking about something else. "He's probably some UN security or something, sniffed us out. He may not know much."

"Special Operations, he told me." She was sobering, eyes bleak.

"He said he was BioSalvage when I saw him in Caracas."

"He's been after us for over a week, then."

He gritted his teeth, eyeing the inky jungle. Twilight bird calls came down from the canopy, soft and questioning. Nothing more. Where were they? "I guess we were too obvious."

"Rearranging Fibonacci into Boccifani? I thought it was pretty clever."

Todd had felt that way, too, he realized ruefully. A simple code: give an anagram of a mathematical series—Fibonacci's was easy to remember in the field, each new term just the sum of the two preceding integers—and then arranging the real message in those words of the letter. A real code-breaker probably thought of schemes like that automatically. Served him right for being an arrogant smartass. He said, "I tried to make the messages pretty vague."

Her smile was thin, tired. "I'll say. 'God I do need more juice at next rendezvous.' I had to scramble to be sure virus-3 was waiting at the Earth Summit."

"Sorry. I thought the short incubation strain might be more useful there."

She had stopped panting and now slid her arms around him. "I got that. 'This "superflu" thing knocking people with two-week delay. Juice!' I used that prime sequence—you got my letters?"

"Sure." That wasn't important now. Her heart was tripping, high and rapid against his chest.

"I . . . had some virus-4 with me."

"And now they have it. No matter."

Hesitantly she said, "We've . . . gotten farther than we thought we would, right?"

"It's a done deal. They can't stop it now."

"We're through then?" Eyes large.

"They haven't got us yet."

"Do you suppose they know about the others?"

"I hadn't thought of that." They probably tracked the contagion, correlated with travelers, popped up a list of suspects. He and several others had legitimate missions, traveled widely, and could receive frozen samples of the virus without arousing suspicion. Amy was a good nexus for messages, coded and tucked into her reports. All pretty simple, once somebody guessed that to spread varieties of the virus so fast demanded a systematic, international team. "They've probably got Esther and Clyde, then."

"Damn!" She hugged him fiercely.

Last glimmers of day gave a diffuse glow among the damp tangle of vines and fronds. A rustling alerted him. He caught a quick flitting shadow in time to turn.

A large man carrying a stubby rifle rushed at him. He pushed Amy away and the man came on, bringing the rifle down like a club. Todd ducked and drove a fist into the man's neck. They collided. Momentum slammed him into thick ferns. Rolling, elbows jabbing.

Together they slammed into a tree. Todd yanked on the man's hair, got a grip. He smacked the head against a prow of limestone that jutted up from the leafy forest floor. The man groaned and went limp.

Todd got up and looked for Amy and someone knocked him over from behind. The wind went out of him and when he rolled over there were two men, one holding Amy. The other was Mr. Segueno.

"It is pointless to continue," Segueno called.

"I thought some locals were raiding us." Might as well give it one more try.

No smile. "Of course you did."

The man Todd had knocked out was going to stay that way, apparently. Segueno and the other carried automatic pistols, both pointed politely at his feet. "What the hell is—"

"I assume you are not armed?"

"Look, Segueno—"

They took his pack and found the .38 buried beneath the packaged meals. Amy looked dazed, eyes large. They led them back along the slope. It was hard work and they were drenched in sweat when they reached his tent. There were half a dozen men wearing the subdued tan U.N. uniforms. One brought in a chair for Segueno.

Todd sat in his canvas chair and Amy on the bunk. She stretched out and stared numbly at the moths who still flailed against the unattainable lamp.

"What's this crap?" Todd asked, but he could not put any force into his voice. He wanted to make this easy on Amy. That was all he cared about now.

Segueno unfolded a tattered letter. "She did not destroy this—a mistake."

His letter to Amy. "It's personal. You have no right—"

"You are far beyond issues of rights, as I think you know."

"It was Freddie, wasn't it?" Amy said suddenly, voice sharp. "He was too friendly."

In the fluttering yellow light Segueno's smile gleamed. "I would never have caught such an adroit ruse. The name of a restaurant, a mathematical series. But then, I am not a code-breaker. And your second paragraph begins the sequence again—very economical."

Todd said nothing. One guard—he already thought of the uniformed types that way—blocked the tent exit, impassive, holding his 9 mm automatic at the ready. Over the men outside talking tensely he heard soft bird calls. He had always liked the birds best of all things in the jungle. Tonight their songs were long and plaintive.

Segueno next produced copies of Amy's letters. "I must say we have not unpuzzled these. She is not using the same series."

Amy stared at the moths now.

"So much about cars, movement—perhaps she was communicating

plans? But her use of 'juice' again suggests that she is bringing you some."
Segueno pursed his lips, plainly enjoying this.

"You've stooped to intercepting private messages on satellite phone?"

"We have sweeping authority."

"And who's this 'we' anyway?"

"United Nations Special Operations. We picked up the trail of your group a month ago, as the superflu began to spread. Now, what is this 'juice'?"

Todd shook his head silently, trying to hear the birds high in the dark canopy. Segueno slapped him expertly. Todd took it and didn't even look up.

"I am an epidemiologist," Segueno said smoothly. "Or rather, I was. And you are an asymptomatic carrier."

"Come on! How come my crew doesn't get it?" Might as well make him work for everything. Give Amy time to absorb the shock. She was still lying loosely, watching the moths seethe at the lamp.

"Sometimes they do. But you do not directly work with the local laborers, except by choice. Merely breathing in the vapor you emit can infect. And I suspect your immediate associates are inoculated—as, obviously, are you."

Todd hoped that Cabrina had gotten away. He wished he had worked out some alarm signal with her. He was an amateur at this.

"I want the whole story," Segueno said.

"I won't tell you the molecular description, if that's what you mean," Amy said flatly.

Segueno chuckled. "The University of California's Center for Molecular Genetics cracked that problem a week ago. That was when we knew someone had designed this plague."

Todd and Amy glanced at each other. Segueno smiled with relish. "You must have inoculated yourselves and all the rest in your conspiracy. Yet with some molecular twist, for you are all asymptomatic carriers."

"True." Amy's eyes were wary. "And I breathed in your face on my way in here."

Segueno laughed sourly. "I was inoculated three days ago. We already have a vaccine. Did you seriously think the best minds in medicine would take long to uncover this madness, and cure it?"

Todd said calmly, "Surprised it took this long."

"We have also tracked your contagion, spotted the carriers. You left a characteristic pattern. Quite intelligent, using those who had a legitimate mission and traveled widely. I gather you personally infected hundreds at Earth Summit V, Doctor Russell."

Todd shrugged. "I get around."

"To kill your colleagues."

"Call it a calculus of desperation," Todd said sharply. "Scientists are very mobile people. They spread a virus real well."

"A calculus? How can you be so—" Segueno caught himself, then went on, voice trembling slightly. "As an epidemiologist, I find puzzling two aspects. These strains vary in infectivity. Still, all seem like poor viral design, if one wants to plan a pandemic. First, they kill only a few percent of the cases. Even those are mostly the elderly, from the fever." He frowned scornfully. "Poor workmanship."

"Yeah, I guess we're just too dumb," Todd said.

"You and your gang—we estimate you number some hundred or more, correct?—are crazy, not stupid. So why, then, the concentration of the disorders in the abdominal organs? Influenza is most effective in the lungs."

Amy said crisply, "The virus had proteins which function as an ion channel. We modified those with amantadine to block the transport of fusion glycoproteins to the cell surface—but only in the lungs." She sounded as though she were reciting from something she had long ago planned to say. It was as stilted as the opening remarks in a seminar. "The modification enhances its effect in another specific site."

Segueno nodded. "We know the site—quite easy to trace, really. Abdominal."

"Game's over," Todd said soberly. The CDC must know by now. He felt a weight lifted from him. Their job was done. No need to conceal anything.

"This 'juice', it is the virus, yes?"

Amy hesitated. Her skin was stretched over her high cheekbones and glassy beneath the yellow light. Todd went over and sat beside her on the cot and patted her hand reassuringly. "Nothing he can do anyway, hon."

Amy nodded cautiously. "Yes, the virus—but a different strain."

Todd said wryly, "To put a li'l spin on the game."

Segueno's face pinched. "You swine."

"Feel like slapping me again?" Todd sat with coiled energy. He wished Segueno would come at him. He was pumped up from the fight earlier. His blood was singing the age-old adrenaline song. The guard was too far away. He watched Todd carefully.

Segueno visibly got control of himself. "Worse than that, I would like. But I am a man with principles."

"So am I."

"You? You are a pair of murderers."

Amy said stiffly, "We are soldiers."

"You are no troops. You are—crazed."

Her face hardened with the courage he so loved in her—the dedication they shared, that defined them. She said as if by rote, "We're fighting for something and we'll pay the price, too."

Segueno eyed Amy with distaste. "What I cannot quite fathom is why you bothered. The virus runs up temperature, but it does not damage the cubical cells or other constituents."

"The ovarian follicles," Amy said. "The virus stimulates production of luteninizing hormone."

Segueno frowned. "But that lasts only a few days."

"That's all it takes. That triggers interaction with the follicle-stimulating hormone." Amy spoke evenly, as though she had prepared herself for this moment, down through the years of work.

"So you force an ovarian follicle to rupture. Quite ordinary. That merely hastens the menstrual cycle."

"Not an ovarian follicle. All of them."

"All . . . ?" His brow wrinkled, puzzled—and then shock froze his face. "You trigger all the follicles? So that all the woman's eggs are released at once?"

Amy nodded. "Your people must know that by now, too."

Segueno nodded automatically, whispering. "I received a bulletin on the way here. Something about an unusual property . . ."

His voice trickled away. The moths threw frantic shadows over tight faces that gleamed with sweat.

"Then . . . they will recover. But be infertile."

Todd breathed out, tensions he did not know that he carried now released. "There. It's done."

"So you did not intend to kill many."

Amy said with cool deliberation, "That is an unavoidable side effect. The fever kills weak people, mostly elderly. We couldn't find any way to edit it out."

"My God . . . There will be no children."

Todd shook his head. "About fifteen percent of the time it doesn't work through all the ovarian follicles. The next generation will drop in population almost an order of magnitude."

Segueno's mouth compressed, lips white. "You are the greatest criminals of all time."

"Probably," Todd said. He felt suddenly tired now that the job was done. And he didn't much care what anybody thought.

"You will be executed."

"Probably," Amy said.

"How . . . how could you . . . ?"

"Our love got us through it," Todd said fiercely. "We could not have children ourselves—a tilted uterus. We simply extended the method."

Amy said in her flat, abstract tone, "We tried attaching an acrosome to sperm, but males can always make new ones. Females are the key. They've got a few hundred ova. Get those, you've solved the problem. Saved the world."

"To rescue the environment," Todd knew he had to say this right. "To stop the madness of more and more people."

Segueno looked at them with revulsion. "You know we will stop it. Distribute the vaccine."

Amy smiled, a slow sliding of lips beneath flinty eyes. "Sure. And you're wondering why we're so calm."

"That is obvious. You are insane. From the highest cultures, the most advanced—such savagery."

"Where else? We respect the environment. We don't breed like animals."

"You, you are . . ." Again Segueno's voice trickled away.

Todd saw the narrowed eyes, the straining jaw muscles, the sheen of sweat in this tight-lipped U.N. bureaucrat and wondered just how a man of such limited horizons could think his disapproval would matter to them. To people who had decided to give themselves to save the world. What a tiny, ordinary mind.

Amy hugged her husband. "At least now we'll be together."

Segueno said bitterly, "We shall try you under local statutes. Make an example. And the rest of your gang, too—we shall track them all down."

The two on the cot sat undisturbed, hugging each other tightly. Todd kissed Amy. They had lived through these moments in imagination many times.

Loudly Segueno said, "You shall live just long enough to see the vaccine stop your plan."

Amy kissed Todd, long and lingering, and then looked up. "Oh, really? And you believe the North will pay for it? When they can just drag their feet, and let it spread unchecked in the tropics?"

Todd smiled grimly. "After they've inoculated themselves, they'll be putting their energy into a 'womb race'—finding fertile women, a 'national natural resource'. Far too busy. And the superflu will do its job."

Segueno's face congested, reddened. Todd watched shock and fear and then rage flit across the man's face. The logic, the inevitable cool logic of it, had finally hit him.

Somehow this last twist had snagged somewhere in Segueno, pushed him over the line. Todd saw something compressed and dark in the face, too late. *My mouth,* he thought. *I've killed us both.*

Segueno snatched the pistol from the guard and Todd saw that they would not get to witness the last, pleasant irony, the dance of nations, acted out after all.

It was the last thing he thought, and yet it was only a mild regret.

II

GROWING UP

Scenes from a
Future Marriage

James Stevens-Arce

J AMES STEVENS-ARCE HAS BEEN WRITING AND SELLING SHORT FICTION FOR OVER TWO DECADES. IN THIS HAUNTING AND PAINFUL STORY OF HOW, FOR SOME, THE FUTURE DOES NOT AND CANNOT WORK, HE REVEALS TWO PERSONAL HELLS MADE ALL THE WORSE BY NEW POSSIBILITIES, NEW TECHNOLOGIES.

NOW

"SO, ALL RIGHT, so we lost," Bub says, floundering at first, but then pouncing on the perfect phrase that will put everything into proper perspective: "But I mean, you know, what the hell, huh?"

Well, nobody has ever accused him of having a way with words. Nervously, he awaits Kate's response.

Kate's silence cuts him like a scalpel. Kate hates him.

"I mean, it's not like we really lost anything," he says. "We just . . . we just didn't win anything."

Traffic on the beltway circling Minneapolis is even more fouled up than usual. It oo-oo-zes . . . it cra-a-w-wls . . . it cr-ee-ee-ps. Talk about your car claustrophobia. The heater of their junky old Hyundai Passé is still on the fritz, and Bub's fingers on the steering wheel are numb from the cold.

"It was only a game," he says, inching the Hyundai forward. "A dumb game."

He should know about games. He's a jock—well, an ex-jock, with a lean, athletic body whose streamlined muscles used to take Kate's breath away—and considers himself an authority on winning and losing. Sometimes you eat the bear, and sometimes the bear eats you. That's what Coach Keegan used to say. Today, they had been bear chow.

He takes a deep breath. "I know another way we can get money. Big money."

Kate ignores him. What desperate scheme will he come up with this time?

"We can make a baby. Get an abortion. Sell the fetus."

He speaks the words stiffly, almost angrily. They succeed in getting Kate's attention.

"That's illegal," she says.

"Of course it's illegal." Bub sounds offended. Does she think he's that ignorant? "That's why there's good money in it. I know a guy who knows a guy. He can set it up."

Kate huddles against the car door, as far from him as possible. Doesn't speak. Doesn't look at him. She breathes furiously through her nostrils and blinks rapidly. In spurts.

ONE YEAR AGO

Unblinking, she watched the blood spurt from her wrists. The cuts ran deep. Scalpels are so much sharper than razors. Surprisingly, it didn't hurt nearly as much as she had expected. A lot less than the miscarriage—no, she didn't want to think about that. No worse than a scraped knee, really, and Lord knows she had endured more than her share of those as a little girl mountain biking with her dad.

Tomorrow will be better than today. Her father had believed that. The great American leap of faith in a century gone sour. What crap. The future had fallen way short of its hype. Which was part of why she lay curled up in this cheap baby blue spa, where her blood could run down the drain and not stain anything. Daddy's neat little angel would be an easy clean-up job. Flip on the shower, fan the spray, sluice away the dark red juice of life. Probably wouldn't even make the DV news.

And why should it? Who gave a whiff if Kate Slade killed herself? Her dad was dead, a flash-frozen corpse in a breached exosuit somewhere at the bottom of a crevasse in the lunar Carpathians; her mother might as well be dead, unable to cope with the loss and locked away as a certified loony in a state-run sanatorium; and her husband . . . well, Bub had no idea who Kate Slade was nor what she might be capable of.

The only way Kate had ever wanted to be on DV was as a game show winner. Her great childhood dream. On a game show, you could win anything—that's what Kate loved about them. Scandinavian dinette sets, Japanese recreational vehicles, Brazilian cosmetic surgery, Himalayan ski weekends, good old American money. It was like a brush with heaven—God's Finger reaching down to spell out your name on the celestial wheel of fortune.

Her favorite game show was *The Bi-i-ig Boodle.* Sure, they decked you out in a ridiculous outfit and made you do humiliating things, but then, at the exciting finale, you got a shot at the millions of dollars inside module number one, two, or three. Guess right, and it was all yours—the thrill of winning, the Bi-i-ig Boodle and a shiny new lease on life!

Lord knows, she could have used a lift like that. The path of her existence had been mined with so many mishaps that, unlike her father, she had finally concluded that life stinks.

NOW

Bub sniffs. What is that stink? Is that exhaust seeping into the cockpit of their gas-guzzling dinosaur? They really need a nicer vehicle. Newer. Sunpowered. A Jeep Solarian or HumVee PhotoGlide, maybe.

But what are they going to buy it with? They have no money. His signing bonus with São Paulo is long gone, as is the huge chunk of change Kate got from her father's insurance, and they're mortgaged to the max. What had ever possessed him to think that a Cuban fast food franchise would ever go over in Dead Lake, Minnesota? She had certainly never had faith in it. Rightly so, as it turned out. Bay O'Pigs had bled them of practically every penny they had.

"I mean, try to look at it in a positive way, honey," Bub says. "We lost on a game show, but we can still be winners in the game of life."

Why do the things he says come out sounding like such bull? He sniffs again. Oh, Lord, it *is* carbon monoxide. He opens his window a crack, even though it's freezing outside. The icy air stings his cheek but helps clear his brain.

"C'mon, honey, say something, please. I feel stupid talking to myself here."

FOUR YEARS AGO

"You stupid, stupid boy," she said, sounding weary and infinitely sad. Winter moonlight etched the fragile bones of her face in silver. "For you," she whispered. "I saved myself for you."

"Don' wan' a virgin," Bub mumbled thickly again.

He was only seventeen, a virgin himself. Bub Bocigalupi, fleshly innocent. What did he know about sex? What *could* he know with no father to teach him the sexual ropes, to tell him what was what between men and women, man to man? The Bible said multiply and fill the earth, but his Sunday School teachers had hammered home that he should keep himself pure in body and mind. His hormones were raging, but he was a scared, confused boy who needed someone more experienced to tell him what to do.

Kate was older, nineteen tonight, a woman, and seemed to know about everything that mattered. But she was as innocent of the flesh as he. One thing was sure—this first-time sex thing was not going the way he had fantasized, and thinking she might not have understood him the first two times, he said again: "Don' wan' a virgin."

She rolled off him. Dressed. Left. A burst of hot gospel beat and teenage party chatter washed over him as the entrance to the bedroom module slid open and shut. He lay staring out the window at the full moon, which hung low in the winter sky like a child's yellow balloon.

Kate's father was up there, part of the construction crew assembling Galileo, the first lunar ville. Kate talked a lot about her father and mother. Big Kurt Slade and sweet, frail Meg. Kate came from a closeknit family. Not like Bub's. Aside from the fact that he bore an uncanny resemblance to his vanished old man that made his mother Thalia edgy and not much fun to be around, Bub knew nothing about his father and he *didn't care*. You couldn't let yourself care too much about anything, because then you could get hurt. Things broke, people left, nothing lasted. So, for your own protection, you had to keep yourself cool, aloof, distant, uncommitted.

He stared at the ceiling, blinking as little as possible. When he closed his eyes, the bed spun and the earth sucked at him. Though he was naked, the room still felt hot and stuffy.

If only he could wish away the present. Because the future was rosy. First, college on a veeball scholarship as a high-leaping, hard-spiking outside hitter in the rude, hopped-up version of the sport that had seized the imagination of twenty-first century DV hounds. Good times were coming! He would have his pick of sleek girls and hot wheels. And then there would be a zillion-dollar contract with one of the teams in the International League. Life was going to be great, if he could just get past feeling so sick. And so confused.

A gentler swell of crowd noise told him Kate had come back and the party was fading. His stomach had quieted, but he was still reluctant to turn his head suddenly.

The rustle of Kate's clothing settling on the rug. The heat of Kate's hand between his legs. Kate's mouth.

Before he could think to protest, her knees gripped his hips and he found himself smoothly inside her. Slick and swift. He was surprised at the sudden ease of entry, when just a short while earlier there had been that . . . obstacle. But his beer-dulled brain made no connections. Kate arched in ecstasy, and settled back on her heels. Bub's glazed eyes fixed on her.

She floated above him like an angel. Though she was as tall as Bub, she seemed to weigh no more than a puff of warm air. Bub imagined Kate's father peering down from his perch in the sky, the Man in the Moon watching over his angelic little girl as, mouth slightly open, tongue clinging to her upper lip, she surged against this confused but eager young stud . . . again . . . and again . . . and again. . . .

When finally she came, she laced her long fingers together as though in prayer, knuckles hard against her forehead. *Sssssss*—she sucked air in through her teeth, and tensed. A long whispered scream. Then her locked fists crashed down against the bridge of Bub's nose, splintering bone.

She fell forward, sobbing. Her damp body against his rubbery flesh. "You bastard," she shuddered against his ear. And also: "I love you."

NOW

"I love you," he ventures. As though asking her permission. He bullies the Hyundai into the clogged exit lane. Tentatively: "You hear me, Angel?"

He knows it tees her off when he uses her father's pet name for her, but it just slipped out. Maybe he does it because he'd like her to love him with the same unquestioning passion she lavished on her father. Maybe he wishes he could love her with the same selfless intensity her father bestowed upon her.

Bub glances at Kate's ghostly reflection in the dark windshield. He doesn't want to look at her directly. Maybe he's a little bit afraid to. So he gets mad instead, and feels a prickle of righteous anger creep across his shoulder blades.

"I wore that blessed maternity smock, didn't I?" he says resentfully. "Didn't I dress up like a breeder with a nine-month belly and wear that stupid sign: HEY, BROTHER RAY, I'LL TRADE YOU MY FIRSTBORN!?"

He had felt a twinge of guilt at that in light of Kate's miscarriage before they had even celebrated their first wedding anniversary. But that had been a long time ago, four years now, and, besides, the other contestants carried similar signs, it was all in the spirit of game show fun. Still, he had felt like a ditz in that stupid maternity dress with the padded stomach they had made him wear.

He sounds angry but pleading when he says, "I mean, I made a blessed idiot out of myself!"

"You're not an idiot, sweetheart," she soothed, her fingers like powdered snow drifting across the back of his neck.

"I broke it, didn't I?"

"Well . . . yes, but. . . ."

"But what?" he said. Challenging her.

"But it doesn't matter. It wasn't worth much."

"No," he said bitterly. "It was only a cheap little snowglobe that your father gave you just before he left to help build Galileo and never came back. You've told me the story only about a zillion times because it doesn't matter, right?"

He was right. Of course it mattered. This was just one more invisible scar he would leave on her soul. One more invisible scar on top of how many others?

But she had still cared about him then. He wasn't as demonstrative or affectionate as her father had been and she was starting to sense a certain disconcerting aloofness in him—a kind of icy core that no matter how she tried, she could not melt—but she still wanted to make the marriage work, especially since she sometimes suspected that he wouldn't have married her at all if she hadn't gotten pregnant. Which was maybe why she found herself defending him instead of trying to cut out his heart with one of the razor-sharp glass shards that lay scattered across the mock oak floor of their bedroom module.

She had treasured that cheap knick-knack, loved to watch the spun-glass angel at the heart of the globe vanish inside the sphere's artificial snowstorms. She had felt secure and, in some sense, comforted knowing it would re-emerge in all its serene beauty each time the swirling storm abated. More important, it was something her father had given her, and all she had left to remember him by.

"It doesn't matter, honey," she said. "Truly." She thought she meant it. They had been married barely a year then, she hadn't gotten over the miscarriage or her father's death yet, and she believed she still loved him. Even so, she was starting to suspect that if life was a game show, she had drawn a poor partner.

"It's just that I'm always doing things like that. Dumb-stupid-idiot things!"

He was always so wonderfully . . . *remorseful* afterwards, such a sweetly penitent little boy that Kate couldn't help forgiving him. Not then, and not even the time two years later when he came limping home after wrecking his knee in that dumb—and so unnecessary—playground pick-up game of veeball.

How could he have been so stupid? He knew that the signing bonus was already down the drain, sluiced away along with her dad's insurance money by the dead Bay O'Pigs franchise, and that he wouldn't start drawing his player's salary until the season began in two more months. Arnie—his agent—had warned him that something like this would void his contract and leave him out in the cold. And still he went and did it. So careless. Just like a little boy.

That was Bub: charming, handsome, sexy—but a little boy. It drove her crazy, but she forgave him. Even though the botched arthrosurgery to repair his right knee had left their dreams as dead as her Man-in-the-Moon daddy, she still forgave him—for the ruined knee, and the shattered snowglobe, and so many other broken promises and shattered dreams in between. He needed forgiving, and though they had so little of everything else and even fewer prospects after he blew out his knee, it seemed to her that forgiveness cost nothing and so was perhaps the only thing she could still afford to be generous with.

Except with herself. She had yet to forgive herself for the miscarriage. No. She had to get straight with herself. For the abortion.

She hadn't wanted it, but she had been only nineteen and could see no other choice when the DNA tests showed it couldn't be Bub's daughter. How could she tell him? What would he do if he found out he had married her because she was pregnant by Denny Castellano, Bub's teammate whom she had taken into the other bedroom module when Bub kept insisting he didn't want a virgin?

Oh, God, how could Bub have forced her to do that? She loved him and she had wanted *him* to be the first, not stupid, stuck-on-himself Denny, whom she'd used only because he was available. The notion that kept slinking into her mind whenever she remembered that ugly night sounded crude, but she couldn't help thinking there was more than a grain of truth in it—Bub didn't want the guilt for breaking her virginity, but he felt no guilt at all for having broken her heart.

As he had broken what had been her last link to her father . . . .

"Honey," she had said, voice trembling from trying to hold back the tears for the broken angel, for poor broken Kurt and Meg Slade and their shattered little girl Kate, "everybody has his . . . you just . . . you just break things. It's not important. I mean, it's . . . it's the kind of thing people love you for. Really. I love that in you, you know? You wouldn't be you if you didn't break things occasionally."

Though the words stuck in her throat, she forced them out: "It's no big thing, okay? Let's just forget it."

"Can't you just forget it?" he says, crushing the accelerator. The engine floods and starts to stall, then catches. The car lurches, bouncing them against their restraining webs.

It's not easy being married to Kate. She makes a federal case out of the weirdest things. "Losing on a DV game show isn't exactly up there with racking up your knee and being practically crippled for life, you know," he mutters.

They have finally escaped the glutinous traffic of the beltway. Because few vehicles frequent this ancient two-lane blacktop, he can nurse the Hyundai up to a chassis-rattling forty-five klicks per hour. Any faster and he won't be able to dodge the really major potholes and bumps. Only a few more hours to their hard-to-heat little cabin out there in the boonies on the north shore of frozen Dead Lake. The wind slicing through the crack in the car window feels icy against the tight skin of his face. The night air smells of impending snow.

"For all practical purposes, it's like it never happened. You understand what I'm saying?"

It's always like that for him. He wants her to look at things as having happened or not in terms of "practical purposes," not reality. Right after he'd blown out his knee only a year ago, she had—in reality—opened her wrists and tried to bleed to death. But since the suicide prevention team at St. Theresa's had successfully resurrected her, "for all practical purposes" it hadn't happened. So he didn't feel compelled to question the reasons behind it.

But it had happened. She had tried to kill herself. And he had been one of the reasons, if not the main one.

Now, if she could get him to address the subject at all, he would quickly say, "Hey, all I know is you dodged Doctor Death and, far as I'm concerned, that's all that matters. Case closed." No matter how much she remonstrated or cajoled after that, it was like talking to a dead man.

The truth was, she hadn't dodged "Doctor Death." Just the opposite, in fact. To bring her back to life, the team at St. Teresa's had had to pry her loose kicking and screaming from the good "Doctor's" cold embrace. This was God's way of punishing her, she realized now—making her come back to live with her guilt in the straitjacket of her marriage to Bub.

"I'm sorry," Bub says. "I've said I'm sorry. Sure, we could've picked module number *three* like you wanted, but *one's* always been my lucky number."

He considers the import of that thought. Six million dollars waiting for them inside the module Kate had begged him to pick, but he had been too high on the self-importance that had been a constant in his once-charmed life as a star athlete and had insisted on going with the number he'd always worn.

Bub tries to salve his wounds with a dose of Coach Keegan's ursine philosophy—*Sometimes the bear eats you*—but finds cold comfort in it.

"It was just luck," he mutters. "Bad luck."

Kate turns her face toward him slowly. It is devoid of emotion, like the scary blank face with which his mother used to regard him sometimes when he was younger. He called it her Dead Man's Face and still finds it upsetting and frightening.

"But then it would have been my bad luck," Kate says in a terrible whisper. "My bad luck. Not yours."

ONE YEAR AGO

It had been her bad luck to try to kill herself the same day Bub limped home early from what was supposed to have been his night out with the guys, only he picked a fight with Denny Castellano and the others told him to fuck off. As she lay curled up in that cramped, cheap spa, dark blood seeping from her veins, her last thoughts had been of her father and her mother and the dead baby—and the money she had secretly taken for it. Nothing of Bub. Not at the end. Wasn't that weird? Wasn't that heartbreakingly strange?

But Bub had found her. And called 911. And less than five minutes after she had embraced the welcome darkness, a two-man suicide prevention team was pulling her deathly pale, but still-warm, body from the baby blue tub. Despite her flat EKG and brainscan, they hooked her up to their van's cryopac and turned her into a corpsicle.

Domelights whirling, siren shrieking, they rushed her flash-frozen body to the newly inaugurated St. Teresa of Avila Resurrection Center. A team of doctors thawed her out and sealed up the sliced flesh of her wrists so neatly the scars were almost invisible. Then they pumped her full of new blood, jump-started her heart and nervous system, and brought her back to life, surprised as hell, but good as new and ready to be billed for medical services. The whole process took barely six hours and ate up every last cent of what little money they had left. And then some.

NOW

"It's the money, isn't it?" Bub says, goosing the Hyundai because they're approaching a relatively decent strip of highway. "Every time we've had a chance at some real money, I've screwed up, and that's screwed *us* up."

"It's not just the money," Kate says. In mock kindergarten teacher style, she sing-songs, *"Mon-ey can't buy hap-pi-ness."* You can almost see a gently admonishing finger marking the cadence. Her voice goes flat. "Everybody knows that."

"Yeah? Well, it can make a pretty good down payment, anyway."

Kate says nothing.

"Look, I know you don't want children," Bub says. "Not after the miscarriage. But if you were to get pregnant again, we could get out of the hole. Get a fresh start, you know?"

Kate looks at him. "No," she says, overenunciating each word. "No. I don't want to do that."

Bub glances over at her, then back at the road, anger and frustration darkening his pale eyes. "I'm not talking about having the baby, you know."

Kate turns away. "I know."

"It's good money." His voice is cajoling now, trying to tempt her, trying to make the idea irresistible. "Big money. More than my signing bonus, as much as you got from your dad's insurance."

Kate closes her eyes. That money hadn't come from her father. What meager insurance her dad had been able to afford had all gone to her mom. That big lump-sum payment had been the blood money for Denny's baby, though she's never told Bub that.

"It wouldn't be just for the money," he says. "The pharmaceuticals use the fetal cells to cure terrible diseases. We'd be helping sick people, people with Alzheimer's—like your mother—and Parkinson's and multiple sclerosis and sickle cell anemia and Lou Gehrig's disease and who knows what else." The list rolls off his tongue so glibly that she knows he must have been rehearsing it in his mind for a long time. "It wouldn't be a selfish thing. We'd be doing a lot of good."

Tears begin to roll down Kate's cheeks. Bub doesn't notice. His eyes are fixed on the road, his attention focused on the plan. His voice takes on that pleading tone that tells her this is really important to him.

"Will you just think about it?" he says. "Please? Will you at least just please *think* about it?"

ONE YEAR AGO

It was weird, when you stopped to think about it, how she finally got to be on DV. Because Kate Slade was St. Teresa's first self-inflicted death and St. Teresa's was the first of a chain of suicide prevention centers scheduled to go up all across the country, in less than one revolution of the planet her digitized image had been flashed across DV screens the nation over and—just like that—she was famous.

But Kate took no joy in her instant celebrity. The way she saw it, the doctors had snatched away the surcease she had sought in eternity, and cruelly wrenched her back into this wretched excuse for a life.

NOW

Kate grabs the steering wheel and wrenches it to the left, swinging the Hyundai into the oncoming lane. Bub slams on the brakes, jerks the steering wheel hard right. Big mistake.

They skid. Broadside. Toward the onrushing trucktrain, the fiery red letters on its sides screaming: FLAMMABLE.

Just like that, in the midst of life, we are in death. . . .

The trucktrain's brakes shriek as its one hundred two oversized tires erupt into clouds of thick black smoke. The trucktrain slews onto the two-lane's shoulder and its linked rigs start to accordion. The Hyundai screeches to a shuddering halt scant centimeters from the multitanker, the windows of Kate and Bub's rusting hulk barely a meter below the trucktrain's shiny new cockpit. Before the other driver can get a good look at them, Bub floors the Hyundai and they peel out, balding tires screaming.

"Why did you do that?" Bub says in a shaky voice. It is one thing for her to try to take herself out. But trying to take him with her. . . .

His flesh feels icy and his heart pounds fit to burst from his chest.

SIX MONTHS AGO

Before her brief bubble of fame burst, Kate applied for them to be contestants on *The Bi-i-ig Boodle.* Her remaining vestige of notoriety tipped the scales in their favor. When she received notification of their acceptance, she was enormously excited and, while she didn't like to admit that appearing on a DV game show might constitute the high point of her life, she could not have said offhand what other event might have beat it out. Though maybe if she had gone ahead and had Denny Castellano's little girl. . . .

Almost from the moment the recently developed glass moon test had confirmed her pregnancy and the embryo's gender, she had thought of the child as Meg, after her mother. But Kate had been only nineteen, she was afraid that Bub would find out it wasn't his baby and . . . oh, God, what kind of person was she, to have done what she had done? She had taken money, *she had taken money.* . . .

She hated to think about it. But she had felt there was no other way, she had to have the abortion. And if the baby was to be dead anyway, but its brain cells and other organ tissues could still be used to cure Alzheimer's and MS and other terrible diseases—well, wasn't that a good thing? And if archaic laws made a good thing like that illegal so the drug companies were compelled to force large amounts of under-the-table money on people like her in order to do good, where was the harm? Nothing could bring the unborn child back to life, but as fleeting as that life might have been, at least some good might come from tragedy and someone whose mind, like her mother's, was slipping into oblivion might be saved from years of living death.

Countless dark nights of the soul devoted to mulling such thoughts had failed to convince Kate, or to grant her any relief from the crushing guilt. She deserved Bub and this wretched life, her lost dreams and the torture of remembering who she had been before those dreams were lost. Before she made her decision, before she took the money, Kate had imagined that when Meg learned to speak, her little lost girl would call her Mavourneen—the same pet name Kate had had for her mother. Back then, Kate had liked to imagine a lot of things that were now only aching memories, lost dreams and fading yearnings.

With maybe one exception. The old yearning for a quick fix to life's pains in the form of free cash and fabulous prizes burned as brightly as ever—just *one* wave of the Digital Age's magic wand, a single touch of the moving Finger, was that too much to ask? But aside from that, in every other aspect of her life Kate had reached the point where she felt . . . nothing.

Beyond, of course, a wish to be dead.

NOW

Kate says nothing. She still wears her Dead Man's Face.

"Why did you do that?" Bub demands.

The trucktrain is already a dozen klicks behind, but Bub's heart is still in his mouth and he still can't catch his breath.

The snow that had threatened earlier is coming down hard now—thick and cold and impenetrable. Kate leans her head back against the Hyundai's frayed headrest. Closes her eyes. Sighs.

She pictures her father, for the millionth time tries to imagine how he must have felt at that terrible moment when the burning cold of near-vacuum burst into his exosuit and froze his flesh and bone. She visualizes her mother, remembers that last visit when frail Meg Slade sat staring up through the sanatorium skylight at a lost yellow balloon of a moon floating high in the cold winter sky, softly keening her sorrow. Kate considers herself and Bub, recalls the countless times she has huddled against him under their thin blankets seeking his warmth, only to feel a bitter cold he carries around inside him cut her like a scalpel. She remembers the dead child and the day she lost her in that cheery pink clean room attended by a fatherly physician and a kindly nurse amid sterile metal trays and almost invisible nanosurgical gear. And she imagines she can now feel the quickening of another new life in her belly, its presence detected purely by chance through a routine test only yesterday and still unknown to Bub.

Kate had planned on telling him this evening, intending the glad news that she is carrying his son to put the capper to what was supposed to have been the glorious day they finally brought home their happily-ever-after. Now, she doesn't know if she wants him to know.

Outside, the world is shrouded in snow, snow, snow. It falls in flurries; in curtains; in great, white, swirling sheets. A long sigh escapes Kate's dry lips: *Sssssss . . .* like a balloon deflating. The cold has slithered into her veins and sapped all her strength. She feels dead tired.

ONE MONTH AGO

"What was it like, being dead?"

She was surprised at the question. Not that he had asked it, but that he had been capable of asking it. She could tell by the way he spoke that he had been waiting a long time to ask. His timing might have been better, though. They had just finished making love.

"It was wonderful," she said without hesitation.

He got that hurt little boy look she had found so appealing in the early stages of their relationship, but which now made her want to puke.

"You mean you'd rather be dead than be with me?" he finally said.

He just didn't have a clue, did he? she thought, but said nothing.

When he realized she meant her silence to be her answer, he looked unhappy, but couldn't keep himself from asking again: "So what was it like?"

How could she explain it to him? Or to anyone? Like people said after an anecdote that was supposed to be hilarious bombed: You had to be there.

Well, she had been there. And ached to be there again. Death had a lot going for it. When she had opened her eyes to discover she was alive again, still trapped in her fleshly hell, Kate had thought she would go crazy, like her mother.

To her sad misfortune, she did not.

NOW

"That was crazy," Bub says, wide-eyed, still reliving the fearful sight of the onrushing trucktrain, voice still trembling from having barely dodged "Doctor Death."

Kate's silence cuts him like a scalpel.

"Blessed Savior," Bub murmurs in a stunned voice.

Tiredly, Kate closes her eyes, amazed at how clearly she sees everything now, despite the blinding snowstorm swirling all around them. She wonders if this is how an angel at the heart of a snowglobe might see things.

"It's not like we really lost anything, is it, Bub?" she says wearily. "It's not like we gambled away something we actually had."

They ride in silence amid the entombing snow. "No," he says after a moment, afraid to speak more. For the millionth time, he pictures her wrists, the scalpel, the almost invisible scars.

She opens her eyes and looks out the window, but the swirling snow hides the sky and the moon and the countryside, and turns everything gray and meaningless, even the subtle stirrings of life she imagines she can already feel within her. A vast lassitude envelops her, as though someone has beaten all the strength out of her. Maybe Bub's right. Maybe the money would make a difference. Maybe things will be better if she goes along. In any event, she feels exhausted, too tired to go on fighting the irresistible forces that shape her existence.

"It was just a stupid game, wasn't it?" she says, weary and infinitely sad. "All just a stupid, stupid game."

Bub smiles, relieved. He thinks she is talking about the DV show. "Sure," he says lightly, "what the hell."

He thinks they are finally on the same wavelength and decides to seize the moment. He takes a deep breath and shudders, like he's about to plunge naked into Dead Lake's icy waters.

"So, okay; so how about it; so you'll do it then?" he whispers, all his hopes twisted into one enormous knot in his throat.

Kate looks at him with her Dead Man's Face, realizes nothing has changed. For the zillionth time, she thinks of her wrists, the scalpel, the invisible scars.

"Sure," she says tonelessly. "What the hell."

Coming of Age
in Karhide

Sov Thade Tage em Ereb, of Rer, in Karhide, on Gethen (Ursula K. Le Guin)

U RSULA K. LE GUIN IS ONE OF AMER-
ICA'S FINEST WRITERS. SHE HAS EXCELLED IN MANY AREAS OF FICTION, BUT
MAKES SCIENCE FICTION AND FANTASY HER SPECIAL HOME. IN THIS STORY, SHE
RETURNS TO THE PLANET OF GETHEN (FIRST VISITED IN HER NOVEL, *THE LEFT
HAND OF DARKNESS*) TO SHOW US THAT COMING OF AGE IS NEVER EASY, BUT IN A
PROPER WORLD, AT A PROPER TIME, AND WITH THE PROPERLY PREPARED INDIVID-
UAL, IT CAN BE JOYOUS AND EVEN DELIGHTFUL.

I SUGGEST READING "COMING OF AGE IN KARHIDE" WITH A BELOVED PART-
NER NEARBY . . .

I LIVE IN the oldest city in the world. Long before there were kings in Karhide, Rer was a city, the marketplace and meeting ground for all the North-
east, the Plains, and Kerm Land. The Fastness of Rer was a center of
learning, a refuge, a judgment seat fifteen thousand years ago. Karhide became a nation here, under the Geger kings, who ruled for a thousand years.
In the thousandth year Sedern Geger, the Unking, cast the crown into the
River Arre from the palace towers, proclaiming an end to dominion. The
time they call the Flowering of Rer, the Summer Century, began then. It
ended when the Hearth of Harge took power and moved their capital across
the mountains to Erhenrang. The Old Palace has been empty for centuries.
But it stands. Nothing in Rer falls down. The Arre floods through the
street-tunnels every year in the Thaw, winter blizzards may bring thirty
feet of snow, but the city stands. Nobody knows how old the houses are,
because they have been rebuilt forever. Each one sits in its gardens without
respect to the position of any of the others, as vast and random and ancient

as hills. The roofed streets and canals angle about among them. Rer is all corners. We say that the Harges left because they were afraid of what might be around the corner.

Time is different here. I learned in school how the Orgota, the Ekumen, and most other people count years. They call the year of some portentous event Year One and number forward from it. Here it's always Year One. On Getheny Thern, New Year's Day, the Year One becomes one-ago, one-to-come becomes One, and so on. It's like Rer, everything always changing but the city never changing.

When I was fourteen (in the Year One, or fifty-ago) I came of age. I have been thinking about that a good deal recently.

It was a different world. Most of us had never seen an Alien, as we called them then. We might have heard the Mobile talk on the radio, and at school we saw pictures of Aliens—the ones with hair around their mouths were the most pleasingly savage and repulsive. Most of the pictures were disappointing. They looked too much like us. You couldn't even tell that they were always in kemmer. The female Aliens were supposed to have enormous breasts, but my Mothersib Dory had bigger breasts than the ones in the pictures.

When the Defenders of the Faith kicked them out of Orgoreyn, when King Emran got into the Border War and lost Erhenrang, even when their Mobiles were outlawed and forced into hiding at Estre in Kerm, the Ekumen did nothing much but wait. They had waited for two hundred years, as patient as Handdara. They did one thing: they took our young king off-world to foil a plot, and then brought the same king back sixty years later to end her wombchild's disastrous reign. Argaven XVII is the only king who ever ruled four years before her heir and forty years after.

The year I was born (the Year One, or sixty-four-ago) was the year Argaven's second reign began. By the time I was noticing anything beyond my own toes, the war was over, the West Fall was part of Karhide again, the capital was back in Erhenrang, and most of the damage done to Rer during the Overthrow of Emran had been repaired. The old houses had been rebuilt again. The Old Palace had been patched again. Argaven XVII was miraculously back on the throne again. Everything was the way it used to be, ought to be, back to normal, just like the old days—everybody said so.

Indeed those were quiet years, an interval of recovery before Argaven, the first Gethenian who ever left our planet, brought us at last fully into the Ekumen; before we, not they, became the Aliens; before we came of age. When I was a child we lived the way people had lived in Rer forever. It is that way, that timeless world, that world around the corner, I have been thinking about, and trying to describe for people who never knew it. Yet as

I write I see how also nothing changes, that it is truly the Year One always, for each child that comes of age, each lover who falls in love.

There were a couple of thousand people in the Ereb Hearths, and a hundred and forty of them lived in my Hearth, Ereb Tage. My name is Sov Thade Tage em Ereb, after the old way of naming we still use in Rer. The first thing I remember is a huge dark place full of shouting and shadows, and I am falling upward through a golden light into the darkness. In thrilling terror, I scream. I am caught in my fall, held, held close; I weep; a voice so close to me that it seems to speak through my body says softly, "Sov, Sov, Sov." And then I am given something wonderful to eat, something so sweet, so delicate that never again will I eat anything quite so good. . . .

I imagine that some of my wild elder hearthsibs had been throwing me about, and that my mother comforted me with a bit of festival cake. Later on when I was a wild elder sib we used to play catch with babies for balls; they always screamed, with terror or with delight, or both. It's the nearest to flying anyone of my generation knew. We had dozens of different words for the way snow falls, floats, descends, glides, blows, for the way clouds move, the way ice floats, the way boats sail; but not that word. Not yet. And so I don't remember "flying." I remember falling upward through the golden light.

Family houses in Rer are built around a big central hall. Each story has an inner balcony clear round that space, and we call the whole story, rooms and all, a balcony. My family occupied the whole second balcony of Ereb Tage. There were a lot of us. My grandmother had borne four children, and all of them had children, so I had a bunch of cousins as well as a younger and an older wombsib. "The Thades always kemmer as women and always get pregnant," I heard neighbors say, variously envious, disapproving, admiring. "And they never keep kemmer," somebody would add. The former was an exaggeration, but the latter was true. Not one of us kids had a father. I didn't know for years who my getter was, and never gave it a thought. Clannish, the Thades preferred not to bring outsiders, even other members of our own Hearth, into the family. If young people fell in love and started talking about keeping kemmer or making vows, Grandmother and the mothers were ruthless. "Vowing kemmer, what do you think you are, some kind of noble? some kind of fancy person? The kemmerhouse was good enough for me and it's good enough for you," the mothers said to their lovelorn children, and sent them away, clear off to the old Ereb Domain in the country, to hoe braties till they got over being in love.

So as a child I was a member of a flock, a school, a swarm, in and out of our warren of rooms, tearing up and down the staircases, working together and learning together and looking after the babies—in our own fashion—and terrorizing quieter hearthmates by our numbers and our noise. As far as I know we did no real harm. Our escapades were well within the rules and limits of the sedate, ancient Hearth, which we felt not as constraints but as protection, the walls that kept us safe. The only time we got punished was when my cousin Sether decided it would be exciting if we tied a long rope we'd found to the second-floor balcony railing, tied a big knot in the rope, held onto the knot, and jumped. "I'll go first," Sether said. Another misguided attempt at flight. The railing and Sether's broken leg were mended, and the rest of us had to clean the privies, all the privies of the Hearth, for a month. I think the rest of the Hearth had decided it was time the young Thades observed some discipline.

Although I really don't know what I was like as a child, I think that if I'd had any choice I might have been less noisy than my playmates, though just as unruly. I used to love to listen to the radio, and while the rest of them were racketing around the balconies or the centerhall in winter, or out in the streets and gardens in summer, I would crouch for hours in my mother's room behind the bed, playing her old serem-wood radio very softly so that my sibs wouldn't know I was there. I listened to anything, Lays and plays and hearthtales, the Palace news, the analyses of grain harvests and the detailed weather reports; I listened every day all one winter to an ancient saga from the Pering Storm-Border about snowghouls, perfidious traitors, and bloody ax-murders, which haunted me at night so that I couldn't sleep and would crawl into bed with my mother for comfort. Often my younger sib was already there in the warm, soft, breathing dark. We would sleep all entangled and curled up together like a nest of pesthry.

My mother, Guyr Thade Tage em Ereb, was impatient, warm-hearted, and impartial, not exerting much control over us three wombchildren, but keeping watch. The Thades were all tradespeople working in Ereb shops and masteries, with little or no cash to spend; but when I was ten, Guyr bought me a radio, a new one, and said where my sibs could hear, "You don't have to share it." I treasured it for years and finally shared it with my own wombchild.

So the years went along and I went along in the warmth and density and certainty of a family and a Hearth embedded in tradition, threads on the quick ever-repeating shuttle weaving the timeless web of custom and act and work and relationship, and at this distance I can hardly tell one year from the other or myself from the other children: until I turned fourteen.

The reason most people in my Hearth would remember that year is for the big party known as Dory's Somer-Forever Celebration. My Mothersib Dory had stopped going into kemmer that winter. Some people didn't do anything when they stopped going into kemmer; others went to the Fastness for a ritual; some stayed on at the Fastness for months after, or even moved there. Dory, who wasn't spiritually inclined, said, "If I can't have kids and can't have sex anymore and have to get old and die, at least I can have a party."

I have already had some trouble trying to tell this story in a language that has no somer pronouns, only gendered pronouns. In their last years of kemmer, as the hormone balance changes, many people tend to go into kemmer as men; Dory's kemmers had been male for over a year, so I'll call Dory "he," although of course the point was that he would never be either he or she again.

In any event, his party was tremendous. He invited everyone in our Hearth and the two neighboring Ereb Hearths, and it went on for three days. It had been a long winter and the spring was late and cold; people were ready for something new, something hot to happen. We cooked for a week, and a whole storeroom was packed full of beer kegs. A lot of people who were in the middle of going out of kemmer, or had already and hadn't done anything about it, came and joined in the ritual. That's what I remember vividly: in the firelit three-story centerhall of our Hearth, a circle of thirty or forty people, all middle-aged or old, singing and dancing, stamping the drumbeats. There was a fierce energy in them, their gray hair was loose and wild, they stamped as if their feet would go through the floor, their voices were deep and strong, they were laughing. The younger people watching them seemed pallid and shadowy. I looked at the dancers and wondered, why are they happy? Aren't they old? Why do they act like they'd got free? What's it like, then, kemmer?

No, I hadn't thought much about kemmer before. What would be the use? Until we come of age we have no gender and no sexuality, our hormones don't give us any trouble at all. And in a city Hearth we never see adults in kemmer. They kiss and go. Where's Maba? In the kemmerhouse, love, now eat your porridge. When's Maba coming back? Soon, love. And in a couple of days Maba comes back, looking sleepy and shiny and refreshed and exhausted. Is it like having a bath, Maba? Yes, a bit, love, and what have you been up to while I was away?

Of course we played kemmer, when we were seven or eight. This here's the kemmerhouse and I get to be the woman. No, I do. No, I do, I thought of it! And we rubbed our bodies together and rolled around laughing, and then maybe we stuffed a ball under our shirt and were pregnant, and then we gave birth, and then we played catch with the ball. Children will play whatever adults do; but the kemmer game wasn't much of a game. It often ended in a tickling match. And most children aren't even very ticklish, till they come of age.

After Dory's party, I was on duty in the Hearth crèche all through

Tuwa, the last month of spring; come summer I began my first apprentice-ship, in a furniture workshop in the Third Ward. I loved getting up early and running across the city on the wayroofs and up on the curbs of the open ways; after the late Thaw some of the ways were still full of water, deep enough for kayaks and poleboats. The air would be still and cold and clear; the sun would come up behind the old towers of the Unpalace, red as blood, and all the waters and the windows of the city would flash scarlet and gold. In the workshop there was the piercing sweet smell of fresh-cut wood and the company of grown people, hard-working, patient, and demanding, tak-ing me seriously. I wasn't a child anymore, I said to myself. I was an adult, a working person.

But why did I want to cry all the time? Why did I want to sleep all the time? Why did I get angry at Sether? Why did Sether keep bumping into me and saying "Oh sorry" in that stupid husky voice? Why was I so clumsy with the big electric lathe that I ruined six chair-legs one after the other? "Get that kid off the lathe," shouted old Marth, and I slunk away in a fury of humiliation. I would never be a carpenter, I would never be adult, who gave a shit for chair-legs anyway?

"I want to work in the gardens," I told my mother and grandmother.

"Finish your training and you can work in the gardens next summer," Grand said, and Mother nodded. This sensible counsel appeared to me as a heartless injustice, a failure of love, a condemnation to despair. I sulked. I raged.

"What's wrong with the furniture shop?" my elders asked after several days of sulk and rage.

"Why does stupid Sether have to be there!" I shouted. Dory, who was Sether's mother, raised an eyebrow and smiled.

"Are you all right?" my mother asked me as I slouched into the balcony after work, and I snarled, "I'm fine," and rushed to the privies and vomited.

I was sick. My back ached all the time. My head ached and got dizzy and heavy. Something I could not locate anywhere, some part of my soul, hurt with a keen, desolate, ceaseless pain. I was afraid of myself: of my tears, my rage, my sickness, my clumsy body. It did not feel like my body, like me. It felt like something else, an ill-fitting garment, a smelly, heavy over-coat that belonged to some old person, some dead person. It wasn't mine, it wasn't me. Tiny needles of agony shot through my nipples, hot as fire. When I winced and held my arms across my chest, I knew that everybody could see what was happening. Anybody could smell me. I smelled sour, strong, like blood, like raw pelts of animals. My clitopenis was swollen hugely and stuck out from between my labia, and then shrank nearly to nothing, so that it hurt to piss. My labia itched and reddened as with loathsome insect-bites. Deep in my belly something moved, some monstrous growth. I was utterly ashamed. I was dying.

"Sov," my mother said, sitting down beside me on my bed, with a curious, tender, complicitous smile, "shall we choose your kemmerday?"

"I'm not in kemmer," I said passionately.

"No," Guyr said. "But next month I think you will be."

"I *won't!*"

My mother stroked my hair and face and arm. *We shape each other to be human,* old people used to say as they stroked babies or children or one another with those long, slow, soft caresses.

After a while my mother said, "Sether's coming in, too. But a month or so later than you, I think. Dory said let's have a double kemmerday, but I think you should have your own day in your own time."

I burst into tears and cried, "I don't want one, I don't want to, I just want, I just want to go away. . . ."

"Sov," my mother said, "if you want to, you can go to the kemmerhouse at Gerodda Ereb, where you won't know anybody. But I think it would be better here, where people do know you. They'd like it. They'll be so glad for you. Oh, your Grand's so proud of you! 'Have you seen that grandchild of mine, Sov, have you seen what a beauty, what a *mahad!*' Everybody's bored to tears hearing about you. . . ."

Mahad is a dialect word, a Rer word; it means a strong, handsome, generous, upright person, a reliable person. My mother's stern mother, who commanded and thanked, but never praised, said I was a mahad? A terrifying idea, that dried my tears.

"All right," I said desperately, "Here. But not next month! It isn't. I'm not."

"Let me see," my mother said. Fiercely embarrassed yet relieved to obey, I stood up and undid my trousers.

My mother took a very brief and delicate look, hugged me, and said, "Next month, yes, I'm sure. You'll feel much better in a day or two. And next month it'll be different. It really will."

Sure enough, the next day the headache and the hot itching were gone, and though I was still tired and sleepy a lot of the time, I wasn't quite so stupid and clumsy at work. After a few more days I felt pretty much myself, light and easy in my limbs. Only if I thought about it there was still that queer feeling that wasn't quite in any part of my body, and that was sometimes very painful and sometimes only strange, almost something I wanted to feel again.

My cousin Sether and I had been apprenticed together at the furniture shop. We didn't go to work together because Sether was still slightly lame from that rope trick a couple of years earlier, and got a lift to work in a poleboat so long as there was water in the streets. When they closed the Arre Watergate and the ways went dry, Sether had to walk. So we walked together. The first couple of days we didn't talk much. I still felt angry at Sether. Because I couldn't run through the dawn anymore but had to walk at a lame-leg pace. And because Sether was always around. Always there. Taller than me, and quicker at the lathe, and with that long, heavy, shining hair. Why did anybody want to wear their hair so long, anyhow? I felt as if Sether's hair was in front of my own eyes.

We were walking home, tired, on a hot evening of Ockre, the first month of summer. I could see that Sether was limping and trying to hide or ignore it, trying to swing right along at my quick pace, very straight-backed, scowling. A great wave of pity and admiration overwhelmed me, and that thing, that growth, that new being, whatever it was in my bowels and in the ground of my soul moved and turned again, turned towards Sether, aching, yearning.

"Are you coming into kemmer?" I said in a hoarse, husky voice I had never heard come out of my mouth.

"In a couple of months," Sether said in a mumble, not looking at me, still very stiff and frowning.

"I guess I have to have this, do this, you know, this stuff, pretty soon."

"I wish I could," Sether said. "Get it over with."

We did not look at each other. Very gradually, unnoticeably, I was slowing my pace till we were going along side by side at an easy walk.

"Sometimes do you feel like your tits are on fire?" I asked without knowing that I was going to say anything.

Sether nodded.

After a while, Sether said, "Listen, does your pisser get. . . ."

I nodded.

"It must be what the Aliens look like," Sether said with revulsion. "This, this thing sticking out, it gets so *big* . . . it gets in the way."

We exchanged and compared symptoms for a mile or so. It was a relief to talk about it, to find company in misery, but it was also frightening to hear our misery confirmed by the other. Sether burst out, "I'll tell you what I hate, what I really *hate* about it—it's dehumanizing. To get jerked around like that by your own body, to lose control, I can't stand the idea. Of being just a sex machine. And everybody just turns into something to have sex with. You know that people in kemmer go crazy and *die* if there isn't any-body else in kemmer? That they'll even attack people in somer? Their own mothers?"

"They can't," I said, shocked.

"Yes they can. Tharry told me. This truck driver up in the High Kargav went into kemmer as a male while their caravan was stuck in the snow, and he was big and strong, and he went crazy and he, he did it to his cab-mate, and his cab-mate was in somer and got hurt, really hurt, trying to fight him off. And then the driver came out of kemmer and committed suicide."

This horrible story brought the sickness back up from the pit of my stomach, and I could say nothing.

Sether went on, "People in kemmer aren't even human anymore! And we have to do that—to be that way!"

Now that awful, desolate fear was out in the open. But it was not a relief to speak it. It was even larger and more terrible, spoken.

"It's stupid," Sether said. "It's a primitive device for continuing the species. There's no need for civilized people to undergo it. People who want to get pregnant could do it with injections. It would be genetically sound. You could choose your child's getter. There wouldn't be all this inbreeding, people fucking with their sibs, like animals. Why do we have to be animals?"

Sether's rage stirred me. I shared it. I also felt shocked and excited by the word "fucking," which I had never heard spoken. I looked again at my cousin, the thin, ruddy face, the heavy, long, shining hair. My age, Sether looked older. A half year in pain from a shattered leg had darkened and matured the adventurous, mischievous child, teaching anger, pride, endurance. "Sether," I said, "listen, it doesn't matter, you're human, even if you have to do that stuff, that fucking. You're a mahad."

"Getheny Kus," Grand said: the first day of the month of Kus, midsummer day.

"I won't be ready," I said.

"You'll be ready."

"I want to go into kemmer with Sether."

"Sether's got a month or two yet to go. Soon enough. It looks like you might be on the same moontime, though. Dark-of-the-mooners, eh? That's what I used to be. So, just stay on the same wavelength, you and Sether. . . ." Grand had never grinned at me this way, an inclusive grin, as if I were an equal.

My mother's mother was sixty years old, short, brawny, broad-hipped, with keen clear eyes, a stonemason by trade, an unquestioned autocrat in the Hearth. I, equal to this formidable person? It was my first intimation that I might be becoming more, rather than less, human.

"I'd like it," said Grand, "if you spent this halfmonth at the Fastness. But it's up to you."

"At the Fastness?" I said, taken by surprise. We Thades were all Handdara, but very inert Handdara, keeping only the great festivals, muttering the grace all in one garbled word, practicing none of the disciplines. None of my older hearthsibs had been sent off to the Fastness before their kemmerday. Was there something wrong with me?

"You've got a good brain," said Grand. "You and Sether. I'd like to see some of you lot casting some shadows, some day. We Thades sit here in our Hearth and breed like pesthry. Is that enough? It'd be a good thing if some of you got your heads out of the bedding."

"What do they do in the Fastness?" I asked, and Grand answered frankly, "I don't know. Go find out. They teach you. They can teach you how to control kemmer."

"All right," I said promptly. I would tell Sether that the Indwellers could control kemmer. Maybe I could learn how to do it and come home and teach it to Sether.

Grand looked at me with approval. I had taken up the challenge.

Of course I didn't learn how to control kemmer, in a halfmonth in the Fastness. The first couple of days there, I thought I wouldn't even be able to control my homesickness. From our warm, dark warren of rooms full of people talking, sleeping, eating, cooking, washing, playing remma, playing music, kids running around, noise, family, I went across the city to a huge, clean, cold, quiet house of strangers. They were courteous, they treated me with respect. I was terrified. Why should a person of forty, who knew magic disciplines of superhuman strength and fortitude, who could walk barefoot through blizzards, who could Foretell, whose eyes were the wisest and calmest I had ever seen, why should an Adept of the Handdara respect me?

"Because you are so ignorant," Ranharrer the Adept said, smiling, with great tenderness.

Having me only for a halfmonth, they didn't try to influence the nature of my ignorance very much. I practiced the Untrance several hours a day, and came to like it: that was quite enough for them, and they praised me. "At fourteen, most people go crazy moving slowly," my teacher said.

During my last six or seven days in the Fastness certain symptoms began to show up again, the headache, the swellings and shooting pains, the irritability. One morning the sheet of my cot in my bare, peaceful little room was bloodstained. I looked at the smear with horror and loathing. I thought I had scratched my itching labia to bleeding in my sleep, but I knew also what the blood was. I began to cry. I had to wash the sheet somehow. I had fouled, defiled this place where everything was clean, austere, and beautiful.

An old Indweller, finding me scrubbing desperately at the sheet in the washrooms, said nothing, but brought me some soap that bleached away the stain. I went back to my room, which I had come to love with the passion of one who had never before known any actual privacy, and crouched on the sheetless bed, miserable, checking every few minutes to be sure I was not bleeding again. I missed my Untrance practice time. The immense house was very quiet. Its peace sank into me. Again I felt that strangeness in my soul, but it was not pain now; it was a desolation like the air at evening, like the peaks of the Kargav seen far in the west in the clarity of winter. It was an immense enlargement.

Ranharrer the Adept knocked and entered at my word, looked at me for a minute, and asked gently, "What is it?"

"Everything is strange," I said.

The Adept smiled radiantly and said, "Yes."

I know now how Ranharrer cherished and honored my ignorance, in the Handdara sense. Then I knew only that somehow or other I had said the right thing and so pleased a person I wanted very much to please.

"We're doing some singing," Ranharrer said, "you might like to hear it."

They were in fact singing the Midsummer Chant, which goes on for the four days before Getheny Kus, night and day. Singers and drummers drop in and out at will, most of them singing on certain syllables in an endless group improvisation guided only by the drums and by melodic cues in the Chantbook, and falling into harmony with the soloist if one is present. At first I heard only a pleasantly thick-textured, droning sound over a quiet and subtle beat. I listened till I got bored and decided I could do it too. So I opened my mouth and sang "Aah" and heard all the other voices singing "Aah" above and with and below mine until I lost mine and heard only all the voices, and then only the music itself, and then suddenly the startling silvery rush of a single voice running across the weaving, against the current, and sinking into it and vanishing, and rising out of it again. . . . Ranharrer touched my arm. It was time for dinner, I had been singing since Third Hour. I went back to the chantry after dinner, and after supper. I spent the next three days there. I would have spent the nights there if they had let me. I wasn't sleepy at all anymore. I had sudden, endless energy, and couldn't sleep. In my little room I sang to myself, or read the strange Handdara poetry which was the only book they had given me, and practiced the Untrance, trying to ignore the heat and cold, the fire and ice in my body, till dawn came and I could go sing again.

And then it was Ottormenbod, midsummer's eve, and I must go home to my Hearth and the kemmerhouse.

To my surprise, my mother and grandmother and all the elders came to the Fastness to fetch me, wearing ceremonial hiebs and looking solemn. Ranharrer handed me over to them, saying to me only, "Come back to us."

My family paraded me through the streets in the hot summer morning; all the vines were in flower, perfuming the air, all the gardens were blooming, bearing, fruiting. "This is an excellent time," Grand said judiciously, "to come into kemmer."

The Hearth looked very dark to me after the Fastness, and somehow shrunken. I looked around for Sether, but it was a workday, Sether was at the shop. That gave me a sense of holiday, which was not unpleasant. And then up in the hearthroom of our balcony, Grand and the Hearth elders formally presented me with a whole set of new clothes, new everything, from the boots up, topped by a magnificently embroidered hieb. There was a spoken ritual that went with the clothes, not Handdara, I think, but a tradition of our Hearth; the words were all old and strange, the language of a thousand years ago. Grand rattled them out like somebody spitting rocks, and put the hieb on my shoulders. Everybody said, "Haya!"

All the elders, and a lot of younger kids, hung around helping me put on the new clothes as if I was a king or a baby, and some of the elders wanted to give me advice—"last advice," they called it, since you gain shif-grethor when you go into kemmer, and once you have shifgrethor advice is insulting. "Now you just keep away from that old Ebbeche," one of them told me shrilly. My mother took offense, snapping, "Keep your shadow to yourself, Tadsh!" And to me, "Don't listen to the old fish. Flapmouth Tadsh! But now listen, Sov."

I listened. Guyr had drawn me a little away from the others, and spoke gravely, with some embarrassment. "Remember, it will matter who you're with first."

I nodded. "I understand," I said.

"No, you don't," my mother snapped, forgetting to be embarrassed. "Just keep it in mind!"

"What, ah," I said. My mother waited. "If I, if I go into, as a, as fe-male," I said. "Don't I, shouldn't I—?"

"Ah," Guyr said. "Don't worry. It'll be a year or more before you can conceive. Or get. Don't worry, this time. The other people will see to it, just in case. They all know it's your first kemmer. But do keep it in mind, who you're with first! Around, oh, around Karrid, and Ebbeche, and some of them."

"Come on!" Dory shouted, and we all got into a procession again to go downstairs and across the centerhall, where everybody cheered "Haya Sov! Haya Sov!" and the cooks beat on their saucepans. I wanted to die. But they all seemed so cheerful, so happy about me, wishing me well; I wanted also to live.

We went out the west door and across the sunny gardens and came to the kemmerhouse. Tage Ereb shares a kemmerhouse with two other Ereb Hearths; it's a beautiful building, all carved with deep-figure friezes in the Old Dynasty style, terribly worn by the weather of a couple of thousand years. On the red stone steps my family all kissed me, murmuring, "Praise then Darkness," or "In the act of creation praise," and my mother gave me a hard push on my shoulders, what they call the sledge-push, for good luck, as I turned away from them and went in the door.

The doorkeeper was waiting for me; a queer-looking, rather stooped person, with coarse, pale skin.

Now I realized who this "Ebbeche" they'd been talking about was. I'd never met him, but I'd heard about him. He was the Doorkeeper of our kemmerhouse, a halfdead—that is, a person in permanent kemmer, like the Aliens.

There are always a few people born that way here. Some of them can be cured; those who can't or choose not to be usually live in a Fastness and learn the disciplines, or they become Doorkeepers. It's convenient for them, and for normal people too. After all, who else would want to *live* in a kemmerhouse? But there are drawbacks. If you come to the kemmerhouse in thorharmen, ready to gender, and the first person you meet is fully male, his pheromones are likely to gender you female right then, whether that's what you had in mind this month or not. Responsible Doorkeepers, of course, keep well away from anybody who doesn't invite them to come close. But permanent kemmer may not lead to responsibility of character; nor does being called *halfdead* and *pervert* all your life, I imagine. Obviously my family didn't trust Ebbeche to keep his hands and his pheromones off me. But they were unjust. He honored a first kemmer as much as anyone else. He greeted me by name and showed me where to take off my new boots. Then he began to speak the ancient ritual welcome, backing down the hall before me; the first time I ever heard the words I would hear so many times again for so many years.

> *You cross earth now.*
> *You cross water now.*
> *You cross the Ice now . . . .*

And the exulting ending, as we came into the centerhall:

> *Together we have crossed the Ice.*
> *Together we come into the Hearthplace,*
> *Into life, bringing life!*
> *In the act of creation, praise!*

The solemnity of the words moved me and distracted me somewhat from my intense self-consciousness. As I had in the Fastness, I felt the familiar reassurance of being part of something immensely older and larger than myself, even if it was strange and new to me. I must entrust myself to it and be what it made me. At the same time I was intensely alert. All my senses were extraordinarily keen, as they had been all morning. I was aware of everything, the beautiful blue color of the walls, the lightness and vigor of my steps as I walked, the texture of the wood under my bare feet, the sound and meaning of the ritual words, the Doorkeeper himself. He fascinated me. Ebbeche was certainly not handsome, and yet I noticed how musical his rather deep voice was; and pale skin was more attractive than I had ever thought it. I felt that he had been maligned, that his life must be a strange one. I wanted to talk to him. But as he finished the welcome, standing aside for me at the doorway of the centerhall, a tall person strode forward eagerly to meet me.

I was glad to see a familiar face: it was the head cook of my Hearth, Karrid Arrage. Like many cooks a rather fierce and temperamental person, Karrid had often taken notice of me, singling me out in a joking, challenging way, tossing me some delicacy—"Here, youngun! get some meat on your bones!" As I saw Karrid now I went through the most extraordinary multiplicity of awarenesses: that Karrid was naked and that this nakedness was not like the nakedness of people in the Hearth, but a significant nakedness—that he was not the Karrid I had seen before but transfigured into great beauty—that he was *he*—that my mother had warned me about him—that I wanted to touch him—that I was afraid of him.

He picked me right up in his arms and pressed me against him. I felt his clitopenis like a fist between my legs. "Easy, now," the Doorkeeper said to him, and some other people came forward from the room, which I could see only as large, dimly glowing, full of shadows and mist.

"Don't worry, don't worry," Karrid said to me and them, with his hard laugh. "I won't hurt my own get, will I? I just want to be the one that gives her kemmer. As a woman, like a proper Thade. I want to give you that joy, little Sov." He was undressing me as he spoke, slipping off my hieb and shirt with big, hot, hasty hands. The Doorkeeper and the others kept close watch, but did not interfere. I felt totally defenseless, helpless, humiliated. I struggled to get free, broke loose, and tried to pick up and put on my shirt. I was shaking and felt terribly weak, I could hardly stand up. Karrid helped me clumsily; his big arm supported me. I leaned against him, feeling his hot, vibrant skin against mine, a wonderful feeling, like sunlight, like firelight. I leaned more heavily against him, raising my arms so that our sides slid together. "Hey, now," he said. "Oh, you beauty, oh, you Sov, here, take her away, this won't do!" And he backed right away from me, laughing and yet really alarmed, his clitopenis standing up amazingly. I stood there half-dressed, on my rubbery legs, bewildered. My eyes were full of mist, I could see nothing clearly.

"Come on," somebody said, and took my hand, a soft, cool touch totally different from the fire of Karrid's skin. It was a person from one of the other Hearths, I didn't know her name. She seemed to me to shine like gold in the dim, misty place. "Oh, you're going so fast," she said, laughing and admiring and consoling. "Come on, come into the pool, take it easy for a while. Karrid shouldn't have come on to you like that! But you're lucky, first kemmer as a woman, there's nothing like it. I kemmered as a man three times before I got to kemmer as a woman, it made me so mad, every time I got into thorharmen all my damn friends would all be women already. Don't worry about me—I'd say Karrid's influence was decisive," and she laughed again. "Oh, you are so pretty!" and she bent her head and licked my nipples before I knew what she was doing.

It was wonderful, it cooled that stinging fire in them that nothing else could cool. She helped me finish undressing, and we stepped together into the warm water of the big, shallow pool that filled the whole center of this room. That was why it was so misty, why the echoes were so strange. The water lapped on my thighs, on my sex, on my belly. I turned to my friend and leaned forward to kiss her. It was a perfectly natural thing to do, it was what she wanted and I wanted, and I wanted her to lick and suck my nipples again, and she did. For a long time we lay in the shallow water playing, and I could have played forever. But then somebody else joined us, taking hold of my friend from behind, and she arched her body in the water like a golden fish leaping, threw her head back, and began to play with him.

I got out of the water and dried myself, feeling sad and shy and forsaken, and yet extremely interested in what had happened to my body. It felt wonderfully alive and electric, so that the roughness of the towel made me shiver with pleasure. Somebody had come closer to me, somebody that had been watching me play with my friend in the water. He sat down by me now.

It was a hearthmate a few years older than I, Arrad Tehemmy. I had worked in the gardens with Arrad all last summer, and liked him. He looked like Sether, I now thought, with heavy black hair and a long, thin face, but in him was that shining, that glory they all had here—all the kemmerers, the *women*, the *men*—such vivid beauty as I had never seen in any human beings. "Sov," he said, "I'd like—Your first—Will you—" His hands were already on me, and mine on him. "Come," he said, and I went with him. He took me into a beautiful little room, in which there was nothing but a fire burning in a fireplace, and a wide bed. There Arrad took me into his arms and I took Arrad into my arms, and then between my legs, and fell upward, upward through the golden light.

Arrad and I were together all that first night, and besides fucking a great deal, we ate a great deal. It had not occurred to me that there would be food at a kemmerhouse, I had thought you weren't allowed to do anything but fuck. There was a lot of food, very good, too, set out so that you could eat whenever you wanted. Drink was more limited; the person in charge, an old woman-halfdead, kept her canny eye on you, and wouldn't give you any more beer if you showed signs of getting wild or stupid. I didn't need any more beer. I didn't need any more fucking. I was complete. I was in love forever for all time all my life to eternity with Arrad. But Arrad (who was a day farther into kemmer than I) fell asleep and wouldn't wake up, and an extraordinary person named Hama sat down by me and began talking and also running his hand up and down my back in the most delicious way, so that before long we got further entangled, and began fucking, and it was entirely different with Hama than it had been with Arrad, so that I realized that I must be in love with Hama, until Gehardar joined us. After that I think I began to understand that I loved them all and they all loved me and that that was the secret of the kemmerhouse.

It's been nearly fifty years, and I have to admit I do not recall everyone from my first kemmer; only Karrid and Arrad, Hama and Gehardar, old Tubanny, the most exquisitely skillful lover as a male that I ever knew—I met him often in later kemmers—and Berre, my golden fish, with whom I ended up in drowsy, peaceful, blissful lovemaking in front of the great hearth till we both fell asleep. And when we woke we were not women. We were not men. We were not in kemmer. We were very tired young adults.

"You're still beautiful," I said to Berre.

"So are you," Berre said. "Where do you work?"

"Furniture shop, Third Ward."

I tried licking Berre's nipple, but it didn't work; Berre flinched a little, and I said "Sorry," and we both laughed.

"I'm in the radio trade," Berre said. "Did you ever think of trying that?"

"Making radios?"

"No. Broadcasting. I do the Fourth Hour news and weather."

"That's you?" I said, awed.

"Come over to the tower some time, I'll show you around," said Berre.

Which is how I found my lifelong trade and a lifelong friend. As I tried to tell Sether when I came back to the Hearth, kemmer isn't exactly what we thought it was; it's much more complicated.

Sether's first kemmer was on Getheny Gor, the first day of the first month of autumn, at the dark of the moon. One of the family brought Sether into kemmer as a woman, and then Sether brought me in. That was the first time I kemmered as a man. And we stayed on the same wavelength, as Grand put it. We never conceived together, being cousins and having some modern scruples, but we made love in every combination, every dark of the moon, for years. And Sether brought my child, Tamor, into first kemmer—as a woman, like a proper Thade.

Later on Sether went into the Handdara, and became an Indweller in the old Fastness, and now is an Adept. I go over there often to join in one of the Chants or practice the Untrance or just to visit, and every few days Sether comes back to the Hearth. And we talk. The old days or the new times, somer or kemmer, love is love.

III

THEM AND US

High Abyss

Gregory Benford

GREGORY BENFORD, PHYSICIST, SCIENCE FICTION WRITER, AND TWIN TO FELLOW PHYSICIST JAMES BENFORD, IS ARGUABLY ONE OF THE FINEST SCIENCE FICTION WRITERS WITH THE INITIALS GB. SOME CLAIM (AND I AM AMONG THEM) THAT HE'S ONE OF THE FINEST WRITERS WITH ANY INITIALS. HIS NOVEL *TIMESCAPE* IS A CLASSIC AND A NEBULA AWARD-WINNER, AND HIS MOST RECENT NOVELS, *ACROSS THE SEA OF SUNS* AND *FURIOUS GULF*, HAVE CONFIRMED HIS STATURE.

BENFORD BRINGS A THOROUGH SCIENTIFIC PERSPECTIVE TO HIS STORY OF A PLACE THAT NEVER WAS, A TIME THAT NEVER WILL BE . . . FOR US. AND AGAIN, NOT A SINGLE HUMAN CHARACTER, YET PLENTY OF CONFLICT AND EMOTIONS, PERHAPS DEFINING CERTAIN UNIVERSALS OF ALL CONSCIOUS BEINGS.

THERE WAS NO taste quite so sweet as a battle won, Lambda reflected.

The troops below milled and bellowed, their blocky bodies shot through with coronas of celebration: burnt-gold gouts, hot spearing blues. They had killed legions of the Doxes, a frightful slaughter.

Now they held the ridge line with solid ranks, a living wall against the dying past. The Doxes were already being gathered into the sad veil of history, Lambda thought, as it watched them retreat across the scarred plain below, their columns shattered.

But the Mother World worked on, indifferent to the puny rages surging over it. Radiance spread into Lambda's splayed disk feet. It relaxed for an easeful moment, spreading its pads to sop up fresh energies from the Mother. Lambda had expended much of its electrical stores and needed replenishment. Skittering surges tingled up its bony legs.

>Victory!< came cries from below. >Truth!<

Lambda basked in the moment, but as always the natural grandeur of the World drew its attention. Lambda was a scientist, after all, in its core.

At the feet of the slag-mountains, glaciers cut forth. Glinting they glided, great ships whose prows carved the grainy orange plain. Their gouges brought forth spurts of Aqua Vita, red rivulets which attacked the crystal ramparts. Melting was ecstasy. Eating was all.

Lambda felt a strange emotion as it watched this: the slow, stately progress of the World, while armies crawled across its promontories and plains like a spreading stain. A disease of understanding.

>O Prophet!< Lambda turned on four legs and watched its subcommander approach. A full guard marched behind, a prisoner staggering in their blunt care.

>Well rendered,< Lambda said. >No Dox will throw itself forward against our lines again.<

>All homage to you!< the co-commander shouted.

>You say too much.< Lambda answered the formal salute with the proper piety.

>Your strategy worked gloriously!<

>No, *your* strategy.<

>Prophet, *you* pointed out that seizing these heights would force the Doxes to attack Crossly.<

>It was an obvious point.<

>You orchestrated our columns with masterly grace.<

Lambda tired of this formal trading of compliments. Some of the manners of the military were more taxing than the combats. >Once this volcanic spire erupted, and we saw how to complete our experiment here, the rest followed naturally.<

>They struggled so against the Crossway inertial winds! You should have seen them try to give battle with torch and spark alike, while swimming like helpless motes!<

Spiritlessly it clacked two legs in ritual agreement. Lambda had indeed witnessed the Dox legions throw themselves counter to the warpage of the World, which blew against them like an embittered gale. The butchery had sickened Lambda, even as the fevered skirmishing, blood-blue and lacerating, turned in their favor. A theorem demonstrated, yet without pleasure.

RightMotion lay along the natural axis of the World, of course, and Right stretched on to infinity—as expeditions had proved with harrowing, epic marches in both directions along the axis. To move Crosswise bore the price of sluggish labor, and in all history few had invested such toil. Scientists and adventurers had only of late proved the true nature of the Mother. Only by prolonged Crosswise struggle could one circumnavigate the World round the Crosslength.

These two basic facts, of RightMotion and Crosswise, had given Lambda the great clue. And, of course, had led to taunts, jeers, followed by persecutions in even the hushed hallways of the Collegium. Then long periods of study and experiment, of intense concentration on matters that un-hinged most minds, and outraged others. After that, expulsion from the Collegium, scuffles, and even beatings at public speeches. Followed by long, aching times when Lambda could live and work only in secret, gathering adherents. To further the ideas that now grew apace within, Lambda had to adopt the mantle of the Prophet. Muster followers, form armies, learn the sly arts.

All for the vision. Their Kind had long lived in a benighted miasma, hugging to the warmth and sparking wealth of the Mother, thinking nought of the mind's stretch, the intellect's reach—

>We have prey, as well!< The co-commander broke into Lambda's sub-mind musings.

>Take it—< Lambda waved two arms in ritual dismissal, but then saw who tottered between the columns of guards. >Epsilon!<

The co-commander beamed, trotting the prize forward with a vicious gouge. >We caught Epsilon in the Dox high-officers' camp. Afraid to run, I judge.<

>Insults ill become a victor.< Epsilon's voice held the old sardonic edge, but floated thin in the teeming air.

>Indeed.< Lambda cantered forward to confront the old foe. >And we do you insult by sparing you, perhaps?<

>The truth falls from your mouths at last. To endure your company is indeed torture.<

The co-commander plucked up a spike and jabbed it at Epsilon, pricking its carapace. >Vermin! Your words will find their price.<

Lambda slapped the spike aside. >No vengeance! You mistake our battle with words, co-commander. It is no invitation to the physical, to the rude rub of edge and point. Old Epsilon favors the stab of speech.<

>Mark: I would favor the spike if it made my point better,< Epsilon allowed soberly.

>And today it has not. Your legions flee.<

>You best us in the realm of the concrete only in this moment. The future shall turn your heresies inward, piercing you as our points did not.<

Lambda allowed itself a bark of amusement. >You Doxes never ingest the truth, do you? You lost because you are *wrong*.<

>Right is uncorrelated with ferocity,< Epsilon said serenely. >You Skeptics won because you are mad. Fever favors valor.<

The honor guard belched with contempt at this remark, their gases bursting crimson in the bright airs. More of this and they would impale Epsilon as soon as Lambda averted its head.

Best to calm them; Lambda had seen enough mindless savagery. >We, driven by a crazed faith?< Lambda held up all four arms to still the guards, who had already formed in two-squares, ready to pierce Epsilon from all sides. >But we shall *show* that we are right.<

>Blindness never sees!< Epsilon made this last sour declaration and abruptly stumbled. Crashed to the ground. Gasped.

>Back!< Some guards had rushed in, fearing a trick. Lambda crouched and cradled Epsilon's head. Rivulets of exertion-waste ran from the neck, a foul odor. Epsilon's air-slits were leached white, overcome by heat and exhaustion.

The sight of this old foe, so reduced, provoked both a swelling pride and a softening pity. Lambda trilled, >Your task is finished. Give up the struggle when it has lost its point. Remember?<

For indeed this was a remark Epsilon itself had made in a lecture long ago, when Lambda was only coming to feel the strength of its own ideas, yet understood the wisdom of the old. Perhaps Lambda still did. But age and the weight of time did not constitute an argument. Only reason, aided by knowledge of the world, did that. Rude though its rub might be . . .

It led Epsilon uphill, to the ramparts of the ragged ridge which Lambda's troops had held so well. Not a single Dox had reached the sharp lip of pale rock. Their broken bodies littered the slopes.

There Lambda gave food and a lie-down-pause to Epsilon. The air felt easeful among the slanted stones, creamy condensing pools of layered quiet. Epsilon spread its pads and drank of the Mother. The World fed them all, its timeless energies seeping forth in spilling plentitude. What the Kind did not use, or the festooning wildlifes, rose up through ripe radiations to the Vault above.

Epsilon shuddered with ecstasy as its batteries fed. >You have not forgotten kindness.<

>I learned more from you than false Physik.<

>You think this heresy is mere Physik?< The famous flinty edge flashed in sharp eyes. >You would destroy the unity of the World!<

>If there is more to the All than the World, should we not know of it?<

>The All *is* the World!<

>An hypothesis.<

Epsilon lurched up from the shimmering sun-rock, ripping its pads free. >A truth! The Unity brought forth Its Creation—<

>Whatever that means, precisely—<

>—in the only geometry which nature commends! You will unhinge all the order our Kind have so struggled to build, with these blighting ideas. We live exactly and cleanly by the principles of Rightway and Crossway, the moral imperatives—<

>Spare me the invocation to prayer. I have business.<

Lambda pushed Epsilon back, not unkindly, so that the frayed one could absorb more of the energies which crackled across the sunrock. The radiance lanced up shimmering, to paint the dusky clouds of the eternal Vault. Epsilon rattled legs in protest, but finally eased down with a grateful sadness.

Battles seldom leave neat ends. Victory had come as swiftly as a Rightwise march, heady and buoyant. The aftermath was like carrying a heavy burden uphill and Crosswise.

Lambda spent much time sorting out details: wounded, pursuit of the enemy, prisoner policy. Everywhere troops cheered. Many slaughtered Doxes in tribute as Lambda passed. Rich blue blood sizzled on sunstone. Bodies crumpled, legs jerked a last few times. Lambda had to pretend to enjoy this.

Still, the fervor and quickening smell of victory had their effect. Lambda felt the power of its convictions in this latest turn of destiny. Now, with Epsilon under guard and Doxes scattered, the hunger for the final test of its vision came fresh. The experiment beckoned.

The Vault waxed dusky by the time Lambda returned to the ridge. Coming up the hard slant, tugging against the Crosswise thickening of air that had held the Kind in mental bondage for all history, Lambda felt a tremor. At first it seemed a mere surge in the viscosity of space. Then matters worsened. Lambda slipped, fell.

The ground shook. Lambda clambered up—a Prophet should not be seen asprawl by troops—and stood on shaky legs. It cocked knees, assuming the proper posture with long practice.

Tremors. Rock parted, lumpy vapors rose. Sheets of gray mass purled into gossamer veils. Sunrock smoked into momentary frothy loops. Mass burst into spray and billowed. It thinned, fine-grained and scalding, enclosing Lambda in a halo of itself. The spray somehow caught and momentarily reflected its angular body in the haze, as if the Prophet were both there and also flickering into the surroundings and joining them, mingled with slanting rays and then gone into refractive miasmas.

The mountains suffered most from a straightening, Lambda knew. As the geometry of Rightway altered, losing curvature as the All expanded, the crust of the World shifted. The splits belched forth the hot Aqua Vita, whose searing rivulets brought pain and death to the unwary. Yet in disaster lurked knowledge. These quakings were the great clue which had led Lambda to the Prophecy.

Peaks shattered, canyons slumped. The inevitable evolution of the universe went on, indifferent to the bitter battles and anguished deaths of its tiny inhabitants. Lambda pondered this, cast into momentary meditation. Such straightenings were to Doxes merely the weather, meaningless. To

Lambda, shaken by one in a terrified moment at the Collegium, the wrack-
ings firmed up artful abstractions, giving geometry a muscular reality. A
solid truth built on shakings.

It passed. Lambda and its escort labored on. To toil against Crosswise
inertias brought stinging fatigue to Lambda's joints, but a Prophet must
maintain a stoic indifference. The commonkind could avoid the compacted
stresses that space imposed on a Crosswise mover, with artful dodges, slips
down gravity-assisted slopes.

Under-officers hurried to help. Dignity prevented Lambda from accepting the merest such aid. It wheezed and paled as it surmounted the final
ridge.

The special guard left to protect Epsilon fell back as Lambda approached. Four-arm weapons shot aloft in salute. More cheers, which by
now only wearied Lambda. Mathematicians did not favor the ceaseless
grind of leadership.

Epsilon lay still wan and listless but visibly better. Lambda was pleased
and left Epsilon to soak more radiance from the World.

An under-officer approached diffidently as Lambda surveyed the plain
below, where fitful fires and the usual torture of the vanquished went on
apace. Lambda sent orders to stop it and turned to receive a new message,
one he relished.

>The Aqua Vita stirs, O Prophet,< the under-officer said.

>The great bag is ready?<

>Double-layered, as you ordered.<

>Prepare to launch.<

>Yes, Prophet. The pilot, Eta, believes the experiment may work this
time.<

>So Eta believed last time.<

The under-officer paused. Lambda's staff, stolid and reliable, never
knew quite how to take these moods and ironies. Quite understandable;
none were, at heart, mathematicians.

This under-officer chose the typical dodge, ignoring Lambda's implications. >Eta wishes to go alone, since there is danger and—<

>No. I shall accompany Eta. And a passenger, as well.<

The under-officers stirred with alarm. >But Prophet! Your person must
not be—<

>Quiet!< Lambda ordered. >Devote yourselves to your celebrations of
victory. I shall go forward to the caldera.<

An officer noted for diplomatic skills rattled forward in haste and ventured, >But—you must not! You are far too important even for such a sacred mission. The danger—<

>Silence. I wish to see the vindication of our views—and be the first.<

Lambda marched away from them with a heady sense of completion. To beat the Doxes in a grand struggle, and at the same moment carry forward their great experiment—that would crown a life spent in the service of truth. Yes, do it. And the final stroke would be to force the vanquished foe to witness the defeat of the old ideas, with its own eyes. Yes, yes.

Soldiers hoisted Epsilon erect—tired, wounded, staring at Lambda in disbelief. >You . . . will do this thing? Take me?<

>Come. I am an empiricist. I will show you how futile your ideas are.<

A single gesture, and guards quick-walked Epsilon behind Lambda as they made their way through the joyous camp. Troops cheered their Prophet lustily at every lane and hummock. Cooking discharges flickered with feasts abrimming. Soldiers brandished their tri-handed launchers at Epsilon, threw oaths. One rushed toward Epsilon with a multi-mace, the hatred steaming in lunatic eyes, and had to be beaten down by the guards.

They emerged at the rim of the great caldera. Epsilon gasped at the roiling tongues of white heat that fought below. >I—I have never seen it so—<

>Precisely. We occupied this chain because we knew the Aqua Vita should burst forth here.<

>I had guessed such. But such ferocity!<

>Our cause awaited this opportunity. The Aqua Vita here is the greatest source of energy we can muster. The only hope of proving our tenets.<

>Your athwart notions, you mean.<

>You mistake nature for truth.< Epsilon would never yield to abstract argument, as Lambda had learned long ago. The World stretched objects Rightwise, compressed them Crosswise. Things free to move naturally oriented themselves Rightly.

All of philosophy had seen in this a natural provenance. Moral order descended from this stretching, this disfavor of the Crosswise. Yet it was no Great Lesson, Lambda had realized. It was geometry. An audacious, abstract argument—but how to prove it? Only by immersing oneself in the World—and leaving it.

The fuming caldera yawned like a great mouth, gaping in rage at a smoldering sky. Fumes belched from the pustules of fury below. The energies here came from deep in the guts of the World. About the rim Mother's powers danced in ribbons, blistering as bubbles burst. Mesons sputtered, staining the air with their dying messages.

The Aqua Vita was the raw form which drove the sunstones, feeding the Mother's Kind and the entire brimming, verdant World. Now a deep bass murmur of slag and smoldering angers grew, speaking in acoustic voices up through their feet. They labored up, struggling Crosswise toward the bobbing balloon perched on the lip of the great fuming abyss.

The experiment clung to the lowest rim of the caldera, on a smooth ceramic lip recently formed of cooled Aqua Vita. Lambda could see on the fuming horizon the upper ranges of jagged rock, the crater stretching Rightwise along the ridges. Their carefully stitched and insulated gas bag bobbled in the howling winds here, looking ready at last to catch the updrafts and be gone into a sky mottled and mad with vexed, swarthy currents.

Eta ran to meet them. >The Vita is running more than I have ever seen!<

>Excellent.< Lambda prodded Epsilon forward.

Eta staggered back at the sight of Epsilon, gasped, but out of respect said nothing. Heavy, hollow notes sounded through the clotted air.

The ground crew was startled as well, pausing a bare moment, then back to their preparations. Winches creaked and the boxy gondola lifted from the ground as the bag strained upward.

Eta called above the muttering of the Aqua Vita, >I am not sure whether I can control the craft in such turbulence. Perhaps, O Prophet, if I go aloft first alone—<

>No! I will see it. Now.<

The weights and winches holding down the huge, patched gas bag were barely enough. Cables groaned to hold it down as the caldera's heat made the balloon swell visibly, like a vast swollen organ digesting a feast.

Lambda peered up at the vast curve of it, proud of their achievement. Long labor and cunning craft had shaped this, insulation and buffers intricately woven to allow lift without bursting seams or searing the skin. Theirs would be an epochal voyage, whether they broke through the Vault or not. But they would—they *must*. To cap this victory with a greater one, in a single—

Lambda did not see the bolt which struck its carapace. Sharp, bright pain bit—and Lambda was down, rolling helplessly. By the time it skidded to a stop the attack was halfway up the stony lip.

Doxes. A tight band, scuttling swiftly. A bolt sang above Lambda and narrowly missed Eta.

>A raid!< Eta cried. >If we run—<

>We'll not run!< Lambda shouted. >That Epsilon—where's the culprit?<

Epsilon had silently circled around the gondola. Lambda raced upslope as Eta fired two quick bolts at the Doxes. The ground crew, which had frozen, began letting go their holds on the balloon's cable winches. The gondola creaked and drifted higher.

Epsilon was old, slow. Lambda grabbed Epsilon and slammed it against the gondola's rough weave. >You have a telltale implanted in you, true?<

Epsilon answered mildly, >Of course.<

>So a suicide team—<

>Could halt this mad attempt. Perhaps even stop the all-knowing Prophet.<

Lambda cursed itself for not thinking through just why Epsilon would allow itself to be captured. A small commando team, hidden up here in the sulphurous folds, ready to pounce when the experiment drew near completion. Primed by instructions from Epsilon, who had feigned fatigue. Victory had blinded the victor.

Epsilon said quickly, >Give way now and I shall spare you. Desist—<

>Quiet!< Lambda fired a sidearm sling against the Doxes, more to gain time than inflict injury. In truth, it had never mastered the violent skills.

A lance cut through one of the gondola's cables. The strands popped free and the gondola lurched. The Doxes were closing fast. Only a few slings from the ground crew slowed their struggle up the stony slope. Heavily outnumbered, Eta and Lambda and the panicked ground crew could not stand against them.

Lambda bent, wrapped arms around its enemy, and grunted, >In!<

Lambda thrust Epsilon up into the gondola, then followed. >Eta—come!<

Eta scrambled after. A wailing Dox slinger cut another cable. The gondola thumped with impacts of slugs against the sides.

Eta readied the pitifully few instruments inside, calling out orders to the ground crew. >Release!<

Cables snapped free. The balloon rushed up the sky, acceleration crushing all three of them to the floor of the gondola. Slingers smacked against the underside, jolts coming up through Lambda's feet. Raw, red winds lashed around them.

The Doxes below dwindled. Their rage at the rising balloon turned to a frenzy. They turned upon the ground crew, and Lambda had to look away.

Then silence. Sudden calm as they shot skyward on prickly winds.

>You betrayed my mercy!< Lambda shouted.

Epsilon was oddly calm. >I made my last move. Alas, it failed.<

Lambda could think of nothing further to say. Epsilon stood stolidly across the narrow gondola, peering out.

Eta said, >We're in a fast thermal. I think I can compensate with weights for the cut cables. Then if—<

>Do so.<

Time to concentrate. Lambda had learned to put out of mind the most harrowing of incidents, to concentrate on the present. It looked down.

Never had it seen such searing violence as the livid rivers below. Orange bubbles burst into rising red mist. Quarks sputtered from the buried hadron fury. Plumes forked up at them, like tongues of deranged mouths. The rushing, dry wind struck fear in even a prepared mind.

Eta was busy with the massive bags arrayed along the gondola's webbing. >Maybe I can steer us inward, try to catch one of the updrafts and—<

>Go!< Lambda ordered. Eta would dither with details, lose the moment.

The Aqua Vita might wane, as it so often did. Indeed, its steamy energies had slowly lessened through the History of the Kind—another clue which had led Lambda to its new vision: of a World which was evolving, straightening its Rightwise geometry, which in turn suggested still larger spaces beyond the Vault. Spaces in which the World was but a part . . .

Lambda peered upward into the tunnel which the Aqua Vita's heat had already cut in the Vault. The perpetual shroud which hung above the World was leaden, torpid—except where the spire of hot gases pierced. Mottled, dusky haze lurked there. Already Lambda could view further up the cave of smoky wrack, as far as any of the Kind had ever seen.

>You are mad to do this!< Epsilon shouted over the searing roar of the caldera. >We will perish in the heat. And to no good end!<

Lambda thrust Epsilon against the mooring lines. >Look upward and you will bear witness. Then you can *never* deny. Watch!<

They shot upward into the murky tunnel, a vertical cavern between glowering clouds. The Vault was a necessary consequence of the Mother's eternal heat and crackling, life-giving voltages—a layer of fine dust and gas kept aloft by the perpetual energy flux from below.

It was also a blanket, smothering any knowledge of what lay beyond. Epsilon and the Doxes held that nothing existed beyond the Vault, that it was the Creator's natural boundary to a perfect cylindrical Mother World. It hung like a shroud boundary to the Crosswise dimensions, a proper cap to the Kind's knowledge.

But to show the Creator's powers, along the Rightwise axis there was no boundary. Distance there was infinite, allowed, clearly ordained by the Creator. The Kind could journey Rightwise forever, expanding into fresh territories, following their needs or ambitions. Only malcontents such as Lambda thought of moving in the most contrary of all senses, worse still than Crosswise motion—to rise through the Vault. To pierce heaven.

Lambda spat and watched droplets descend into the fraying winds. To Lambda, whose calculations showed that matter itself was a soufflé of empty space and furious probabilities, such ancient faiths were no better than the musings of children.

>See the World?< Lambda chided Epsilon. >None of the Kind have ever risen so. It grants new perspective, agreed?<

The whole caldera spread below them. The bountiful land shimmered with the eternal radiance which streamed forth, energies electrical and photonic, the food of the Kind. Beauty fumed everywhere. Rumpled ridges were no more than dwindling foot marks. Whole armies came into view, their ranks like thin fretted lines.

Epsilon said bitterly, >You will be eternally damned for this, this act of—<

>The only eternal is change. The straightening of the Rightwise axis, the ebbing of the Aqua Vita—all point to that.<

>These are but passing events. The Creator can arrange our World as it likes.<

>Properly pious, but not a theory.<

>Theory? I speak of the only natural geometry—the cylinder. We apprehend its beauties directly. It exists eternally because it is the most perfect of form, expressing the Creator's—<

>So I heard when I was but waist-high.< Lambda brusquely waved Epsilon aside, the better to see the expanding perspectives beyond their cramped gondola. Harsh heat swirled about them, fizzing among the cables.

In its best pontifical voice Epsilon shot back, >Surely you cannot challenge the ideal geometry we sense in our every step, the paths of Crosswise or Rightway?<

>Of course I can. Look up!<

Epsilon craned its necks at the gas bag, which now glowed a sullen red from the scalding winds. Above, beyond the bag, was nothing but a gray churn. The gondola's walls protected them from the worst of the heating, but Lambda felt the sweltering pressure on its carapace. How long could they endure this? And where would they be driven by these fevered currents? Theory stood mute.

Epsilon said, >I do not take your point.<

>The bag. The sphere! Surely it is more perfect a form.<

>Perfect? It is the perfection of the rudimentary, the naive.<

>Yet it is the way of the true, larger world.<

>Nonsense! Crosswise, Rightwise—these two paths instruct us that a meaningful world must be cylindrical.<

>I have let mathematics be my guide, Epsilon, rather than the other way around. I have constructed equations which show that the universe can favor the spherical.<

>Ha! Do you think that you alone can command the reaches of mathematical philosophy? I *taught* you this lore, remember?<

>And well you did—though you balked at the next step. I have gener-

alized your equations, found solutions which apply to a far grander vision.<

Epsilon's disdain rippled in its twinned eyes. >So grand, you need climb the fearsome Vault to see it?<

>To prove it, yes. But the vision dances in the mind's eye, if you would but gaze there.<

>The Vault is sacred. The Creator's boundary—<

>The Vault is the weather. Not fundamental. Even—<

The balloon veered sidewise. A blistering wind slammed into them and sent Lambda reeling. The old Epsilon gasped and clung to the webbing which held their gondola beneath the vast belly. Then Epsilon collapsed.

A part of Lambda ached to tell its mentor of the visions encased in dry, formal equations. And so at last Lambda blurted out its feelings, its dreams, in a torrent made no less wild by the whipping winds around them. Lambda knelt beside Epsilon and spoke rapidly, almost as an apology.

Lambda spoke of a universe dominated by a seemingly trivial force, mere gravity. Of that universe expanding, cooling like a simple gas, and yet failing as it grew.

>Like ice freezing on a pond!< Lambda cried, when Epsilon seemed unmoved. The ice was never smooth, for small denser crinkles and overlaps grew with the swelling space-time. All error and misalignment was squeezed into a small perimeter. Compacted folds in space-time, tangles of topology which smoothed themselves out as they expanded.

>The straightening, don't you see?< Lambda shouted.

>Our geometry is becoming more nearly perfect as time progresses,< Epsilon answered stiffly. >The Rightwise increases its already slight curvature. If the quakings bring forth mountains and quakes, so be it. That is the Creator's will, not of your equations.<

So Lambda spoke of cables which expanded with the wholeness of All, getting longer and grander as they grew with the larger realm, warped space-time which stretched across the wholeness, binding it together.

>This is why we have our geometry! The cylinder is a rope which binds together the wholeness, a band across the spherical symmetry that *underlies* our World.<

Lambda finished, panting. Yowling winds seemed to call derision to its ears as a scowl spread among Epsilon's eyes. At last Epsilon spoke.

>You would have us be dwellers on a *string?*<

When Lambda heard the once-loved, once-feared voice latent with such sour disdain, it knew Epsilon was beyond reach. Lambda's vision was of grandiosity, to be part of something spherical, perfect, and immensely larger than the bounds of the seething dusky Vault.

And yet Epsilon saw in this a scuttling Kind, confined to a thread in a tapestry which made the Kind meaningless.

Lambda had feared such failure. What it had not anticipated was the blow that Epsilon landed on its carapace.

>You'll not bring this to be!< Epsilon hammered hard at Lambda. An antenna snapped off.

Stunned, Lambda backed into the rigging. Eta rushed to help. Epsilon broke off and wrestled into the web that held the gondola.

>You'll see. I'll end this!< Epsilon clambered up on the outside of the webbing, oblivious to the torrid winds which rushed past, churning its feelers.

Eta said, >Let Epsilon go. It'll fall off in good time, anyway.<

>No. We can't count on that.< Lambda saw the plan. If Epsilon reached the balloon, a single cut could end their expedition. End their lives.

Up Lambda went. It grasped the netting with all legs and fought against the swaying of the gondola. They were rising up the heat-carved shaft, tormented clouds whirling by, closer now. Still nothing visible far above but a dark churn.

>Don't do this!< Lambda had no hope of dissuading Epsilon, but if it could distract the enemy, slow it—

The jerking legs above did pause for a moment as Epsilon replied, >I will not see you split heaven itself!—to bring down false knowledge.<

>You'll die for nothing!<

>No, you'll die for nothing. I'll die for my convictions.<

>You taught me to study, learn from the world—<

>I'll end my days happy, knowing that I have fought for the Creator.<

>Maybe the Creator doesn't need your help.<

Lambda had nearly reached Epsilon. Heat rippled the air around them, drove stinging knives under Lambda's carapace. It sucked in thinning air. The Vault was grainy, its meager vapors rasping. Lambda climbed faster still.

But Epsilon was within a final lunge of the balloon's glowing underbelly. Epsilon clung to the webbing and unfurled its projector limb. It was old and stained, but sported a sharp point. Quite enough to slit the balloon.

Lambda could see the point glinting as Epsilon labored up again. It gleamed, promising death in a single thrust. Lambda threw itself upward, racing to catch Epsilon's legs, snatch them from the webbing. No mercy now. It would cast this enemy into the mist, watch it tumble to a raw death below.

Only then did Lambda realize that the dusty swirl of the Vault was thinning.

Around them the clouds grew pale. Tattered patches of dark poked through. Then the whole shroud peeled away and Lambda saw that they had lifted above a broad, ivory plain.

A plain, then a plane, a smooth mathematical surface. Not of substance, but of steam and shadow. The top of the Vault.

Clotted clouds, stretching away. Along Rightwise the Vault tapered endlessly, narrowing into a stripe that arced up and afar. Its curve was barely perceptible before it faded into the blackness.

And Crosswise, the Vault curved steeply, ending in inky nothing. Shadowy reaches, unimaginably huge—

Lambda's mind lurched with the implication. An abyss of nothing, an utter meaningless blankness all around.

Was this the outcome of its equations? The World was a crack in nothingness? No—such a void could not be. A border between yawning emptinesses would have no purpose, no beauty, no grandeur, no design.

Epsilon screamed. The cry's anguish lashed at Lambda, but Lambda was concentrating, peering out into the inky nothing, straining. Then it was rewarded. It saw.

The hard darkness had surprised Lambda. What it witnessed next brought a stab of terror. Some . . . *things* . . . hung there in shadowy recesses.

Epsilon's second, more despairing cry came down, bitter and sharp, jolting Lambda—mingled fear and rage and then finally hopeless torment. A wail of absolute finality, as the aged scientist felt the comforting cloth of belief ripped away.

Epsilon moaned. It turned in the webbing to look at the enormity around them, its mournful cry turning to a shriek. Lambda saw then why Epsilon had so strongly opposed the Prophecy. Out of a terrible fear, the dread of just such an abyss. Too much to contemplate, even in airy abstractions of mathematics.

And then Epsilon cast itself off, free. Its legs spread wide as it plunged. For a moment it almost seemed to be liberated at last, flying into the comforting deck of clouds that had swept in under the still rising balloon. Then gone in a flicker.

The blank, hard blackness which had terrified Epsilon—that Lambda could have stood. Indeed, it had pondered such reaches many times. What it could not fathom were the points of brilliance that abided there.

It took all of Lambda's strength to cling to the webbing. To cling to its convictions, and not follow Epsilon into a long descending gyre.

Somehow, it had never thought that the World would be a mere small thing in a universe filled with *other* presences. A sky sprinkled with glowing balls of actinic energies, brittle points of utterly alien light.

The nearest and brightest were round disks.

Sphericity ruled all, everywhere, swimming in brilliance.

Overhead, the stars were coming in.

And these globes would command this vast space, Lambda saw—this universe they would rule, reducing Lambda's World to a mere boundary, to a sliver of nothing as the space-time expanded.

Lambda's wail was different from that of Epsilon.

Even as Lambda cried out in shock and strange ecstasy, yet there was triumph. A final note of self-knowledge, mingled pain and pride—for it had sought and found this grandeur, this enormity, and was thus and forever a part of it.

The Mother World was a mere note in the margin, a flaw.

It was a string. Cosmic, but merely a string.

Recording Angel

Paul J. McAuley

P<small>AUL</small> J. M<small>C</small>A<small>ULEY HAS MADE A SUB-</small>
<small>STANTIAL REPUTATION AS A WRITER OF CONVINCING, COLORFUL, AND DIVERSE</small>
<small>SCIENCE FICTION. H</small>IS <small>NOVELS INCLUDE</small> R<small>ED</small> D<small>UST,</small> E<small>TERNAL</small> L<small>IGHT,</small> <small>AND</small> P<small>AS-</small>
<small>QUALE'S</small> A<small>NGEL.</small> H<small>E IS CURRENTLY WORKING ON</small> F<small>AIRYLAND,</small> <small>A NEAR-FUTURE SF</small>
<small>NOVEL.</small>

<small>"R</small><small>ECORDING</small> A<small>NGEL" VENTURES INTO</small> E. M. F<small>ORSTER TERRITORY, WITH AN</small>
<small>EPOCHAL DETOUR THROUGH</small> C<small>ORDWAINER</small> S<small>MITH, PRODUCING AN EFFECT AT</small>
<small>ONCE RICH AND STRANGE . . . AND HIGHLY MEMORABLE.</small>

M<small>R</small> N<small>ARYAN, THE</small> Archivist of Sensch, still keeps to his habits as much as possible, despite all that has happened since Angel arrived in the city. He has clung to these personal rituals for a very long time now, and it is not easy to let them go. And so, on the day that Angel's ship is due to arrive and attempt to reclaim her, the day that will end in revolution, or so Angel has promised her followers, as ever, at dusk, as the Nearside edge of Confluence tips above the disc of its star and the Eye of the Preservers rises above the Farside Mountains, Mr Naryan walks across the long plaza at the edge of the city towards the Great River.

Rippling patterns swirl out from his feet, silver and gold racing away through the living marble. Above his head, clouds of little machines spin through the twilight: information's dense weave. At the margin of the plaza, broad steps shelve into the river's brown slop. Naked children scamper through the shallows, turning to watch as Mr Naryan, old and fat and leaning on his stick at every other stride, limps past and descends the submerged stair until only his hairless head is above water. He draws a breath and ducks completely under. His nostrils pinch shut. Membranes slide across his eyes. As always, the bass roar of the river's fall over the edge of the world stirs his heart. He surfaces, spouting water, and the children hoot. He ducks under again and comes up quickly, and the children scamper back from his spray, breathless with delight. Mr Naryan laughs with them and walks back up the steps, his loose, belted shirt shedding water and quickly drying in the parched dusk air.

Further on, a funeral party is launching little clay lamps into the river's swift currents. The men, waist-deep, turn as Mr Naryan limps past, knuckling their broad foreheads. Their wet skins gleam with the fire of the sunset that is now gathering in on itself across leagues of water. Mr Naryan genuflects in acknowledgment, feeling an icy shame. The woman died before he could hear her story; her, and seven others in the last few days. It is a bitter failure.

Angel, and all that she has told him—Mr Naryan wonders whether he will be able to hear out the end of her story. She has promised to set the city aflame and, unlike Dreen, Mr Naryan believes that she can.

A mendicant is sitting cross-legged on the edge of the steps down to the river. An old man, sky-clad and straight-backed. He seems to be staring into the sunset, in the waking trance that is the nearest that the Shaped citizens of Sensch ever come to sleep. Tears brim in his wide eyes and pulse down his leathery cheeks; a small silver moth has settled at the corner of his left eye to sip salt.

Mr Naryan drops a handful of the roasted peanuts he carries for the purpose into the mendicant's bowl, and walks on. He walks a long way before he realises that a crowd has gathered at the end of the long plaza, where the steps end and, with a sudden jog, the docks begin. Hundreds of machines swarm in the darkening air, and behind this shuttling weave a line of magistrates stand shoulder to shoulder, flipping their quirts back and forth as if to drive off flies. Metal tags braided into the tassels of the quirts wink and flicker; the magistrates' flared red cloaks seem inflamed in the last light of the sun.

The people make a rising and falling hum, the sound of discontent. They are looking upriver. Mr Naryan, with a catch in his heart, realises what they must be looking at.

It is a speck of light on the horizon north of the city, where the broad ribbon of the river and the broad ribbon of the land narrow to a single point. It is the lighter towing Angel's ship, at the end of its long journey downriver to the desert city where she has taken refuge, and caught Mr Naryan in the net of her tale.

Mr Naryan first heard about her from Dreen, Sensch's Commissioner; in fact, Dreen paid a visit to Mr Naryan's house to convey the news in person. His passage through the narrow streets of the quarter was the focus of a swelling congregation which kept a space two paces wide around him as he ambled towards the house where Mr Naryan had his apartment.

Dreen was a lively, but tormented, fellow who was paying off a debt of conscience by taking the more or less ceremonial position of Commissioner in this remote city which his ancestors had long ago abandoned. Slight and agile, his head shaved clean except for a fringe of polychrome hair that framed his parchment face, he looked like a lily blossom swirling on the Great River's current as he made his way through the excited crowd. A pair of magistrates proceeded him and a remote followed, a mirror-coloured seed that seemed to move through the air in brief rapid pulses like a squeezed watermelon pip. A swarm of lesser machines spun above the packed heads of the crowd. Machines did not entirely trust the citizens, with good reason. Change wars raged up and down the length of Confluence as, one by one, the ten thousand races of the Shaped fell from innocence.

Mr Naryan, alerted by the clamour, was already standing on his balcony when Dreen reached the house. Scrupulously polite, his voice amplified through a little machine that fluttered before his lips, Dreen enquired if he might come up. The crowd fell silent as he spoke, so that his last words echoed eerily up and down the narrow street. When Mr Naryan said mildly that the Commissioner was, of course, always welcome, Dreen made an elaborate genuflection and scrambled straight up the fretted carvings which decorated the front of the apartment house. He vaulted the wrought-iron rail and perched in the ironwood chair that Mr Naryan usually took when he was tutoring a pupil. While Mr Naryan lowered his corpulent bulk onto the stool that was the only other piece of furniture on the little balcony, Dreen said cheerfully that he had not walked so far for more than a year. He accepted the tea and sweetmeats that Mr Naryan's wife, terrified by his presence, offered, and added, "It really would be more convenient if you took quarters appropriate to your status."

As Commissioner, Dreen had use of the vast palace of intricately carved pink sandstone that dominated the southern end of the city, although he chose to live in a tailored habitat of hanging gardens that hovered above the palace's spiky towers.

Mr Naryan said, "My calling requires that I live amongst the people. How else would I understand their stories? How else would they find me?"

"By any of the usual methods, of course—or you could multiply yourself so that every one of these snakes had their own archivist. Or you could use machines. But I forget, your calling requires that you use only appropriate technology. That's why I'm here, because you won't have heard the news."

Dreen had an abrupt style, but he was neither as brutal nor as ruthless as his brusqueness suggested. Like Mr Naryan, who understood Dreen's manner completely, he was there to serve, not to rule.

Mr Naryan confessed that he had heard nothing unusual, and Dreen said eagerly, "There's a woman arrived here. A star-farer. Her ship landed at Ys last year, as I remember telling you."

"I remember seeing a ship land at Ys, but I was a young man then, Dreen. I had not taken orders."

"Yes, yes," Dreen said impatiently, "picket boats and the occasional merchant's argosy still use the docks. But this is different. She claims to be from the deep past. The *very* deep past, before the Preservers."

"I can see that her story would be interesting if it were true."

Dreen beat a rhythm on his skinny thighs with the flat of his hands. "Yes, yes! A human woman, returned after millions of years of travelling outside the Galaxy. But there's more! She is only one of a whole crew, and she's jumped ship. Caused some fuss. It seems the others want her back."

"She is a slave, then?"

"It seems she may be bound to them as you are bound to your order."

"Then you could return her. Surely you know where she is?"

Dreen popped a sweetmeat in his mouth and chewed with gusto. His flat-topped teeth were all exactly the same size. He wiped his wide lipless mouth with the back of his hand and said, "Of course I know where she is—that's not the point. The point is that no one knows if she's lying, or her shipmates are lying—they're a nervy lot, I'm told. Not surprising, culture shock and all that. They've been travelling a long time. Five million years, if their story's to be believed. Of course, they weren't alive for most of that time. But still."

Mr Naryan said, "What do you believe?"

"Does it matter? This city matters. Think what trouble she could cause!"

"If her story's true."

"Yes, yes. That's the point. Talk to her, eh? Find out the truth. Isn't that what your order's about? Well, I must get on."

Mr Naryan didn't bother to correct Dreen's misapprehension. He observed, "The crowd has grown somewhat."

Dreen smiled broadly and rose straight into the air, his toes pointing down, his arms crossed with his palms flat on his shoulders. The remote rose with him. Mr Naryan had to shout to make himself heard over the cries and cheers of the crowd.

"What shall I do?"

Dreen checked his ascent and shouted back, "You might tell her that I'm here to help!"

"Of course!"

But Dreen was rising again, and did not hear Mr Naryan. As he rose he picked up speed, dwindling rapidly as he shot across the jumbled rooftops of the city towards his aerie. The remote drew a silver line behind him; a cloud of lesser machines scattered across the sky as they strained to keep up.

The next day, when, as usual, Mr Naryan stopped to buy the peanuts he would scatter amongst any children or mendicants he encountered as he strolled through the city, the nut roaster said that he'd seen a strange woman only an hour before—she'd had no coin, but the nut roaster had given her a bag of shelled salted nuts all the same.

"Was the right thing to do, master?" the nut roaster asked. His eyes glittered anxiously beneath the shelf of his ridged brow. Mr Naryan, knowing that the man had been motivated by a cluster of artificial genes implanted in his ancestors to ensure that they and all their children would give aid to any human who requested it, assured the nut roaster that his conduct had been worthy. He proffered coin in ritual payment for the bag of warm oily peanuts, and the nut roaster made his usual elaborate refusal.

"When you see her, master, tell her that she will find no plumper or more savoury peanuts in the whole city. I will give her whatever she desires!"

All day, as Mr Naryan made his rounds of the tea shops, and even when he heard out the brief story of a woman who had composed herself for death, he expected to be accosted by an exotic wild-eyed stranger. That same expectation distracted him in the evening, as the magistrate's son haltingly read from the Puranas while all around threads of smoke from neighbourhood kitchen fires rose into the black sky. How strange the city suddenly seemed to Mr Naryan: the intent face of the magistrate's son, with its faint intaglio of scales and broad shelving brow, seemed horribly like a mask. Mr Naryan felt a deep longing for his youth, and after the boy had left he stood under the shower for more than an hour, letting water penetrate every fold and cranny of his hairless, corpulent body until his wife anxiously called to him, asking if he was all right.

The woman did not come to him that day, nor the next. She was not seeking him at all. It was only by accident that Mr Naryan met her at last.

She was sitting at the counter of a tea shop, in the deep shadow beneath its tasselled awning. The shop was at the corner of the camel market, where knots of dealers and handlers argued about the merits of this or that animal and saddlemakers squatted crosslegged amongst their wares before the low, cave-like entrances to their workshops. Mr Naryan would have walked right past the shop if the proprietor had not hurried out and called to him, explaining that here was a human woman who had no coin, but he was letting her drink what she wished, and was that right?

Mr Naryan sat beside the woman, but did not speak after he ordered his own tea. He was curious and excited and afraid: she looked at him when he sat down and put his cane across his knees, but her gaze only brushed over him without recognition.

She was tall and slender, hunched at the counter with elbows splayed. She was dressed, like every citizen of Sensch, in a loose, raw cotton overshirt. Her hair was as black and thick as any citizen's, too, worn long and caught in a kind of net slung at her shoulder. Her face was sharp and small-featured, intent from moment to moment on all that happened around her—a bronze machine trawling through the dusty sunlight beyond the awning's shadow; a vendor of pomegranate juice calling his wares; a gaggle of women laughing as they passed; a sled laden with prickly pear gliding by, two handspans above the dusty flagstones—but nothing held her attention for more than a moment. She held her bowl of tea carefully in both hands, and sucked at the liquid clumsily when she drank, holding each mouthful for a whole minute before swallowing and then spitting twiggy fragments into the copper basin on the counter.

Mr Naryan felt that he should not speak to her unless she spoke first. He was disturbed by her: he had grown into his routines, and this unsought responsibility frightened him. No doubt Dreen was watching through one or another of the little machines that flitted about sunny, salt-white square—but that was not sufficient compulsion, except that now he had found her, he could not leave her.

At last, the owner of the tea house refilled the woman's bowl and said softly, "Our Archivist is sitting beside you."

The woman turned jerkily, spilling her tea. "I'm not going back," she said. "I've told them that I won't serve."

"No one has to do anything here," Mr Naryan said, feeling that he must calm her. "That's the point. My name is Naryan, and I have the honour, as our good host has pointed out, of being the Archivist of Sensch."

The woman smiled at this, and said that he could call her Angel; her name also translated as Monkey, but she preferred the former. "You're not like the others here," she added, as if she had only just realised. "I saw people like you in the port city, and one let me ride on his boat down the river until we reached the edge of a civil war. But after that every one of the cities I passed through seemed to be inhabited by only one race, and each was different from the next."

"It's true that this is a remote city," Mr Naryan said.

He could hear the faint drums of the procession. It was the middle of the day, when the sun reached zenith and halted before reversing back down the sky.

The woman, Angel, heard the drums too. She looked around with a kind of preening motion as the procession came through the flame trees on the far side of the square. It reached this part of the city at the same time every day. It was led by a bare-chested man who beat a big drum draped in cloth of gold; it was held before him by a leather strap that went around his neck. The steady beat echoed across the square. Behind him slouched or capered ten, twenty, thirty naked men and women. Their hair was long and ropey with dirt; their fingernails were curved yellow talons.

Angel drew her breath sharply as the rag-taggle procession shuffled past, following the beat of the drum into the curving street that led out of the square. She said, "This is a very strange place. Are they mad?"

Mr Naryan explained, "They have not lost their reason, but have had it taken away. For some it will be returned in a year; it was taken away from them as a punishment. Others have renounced their own selves for the rest of their lives. It is a religious avocation. But saint or criminal, they were all once as fully aware as you or me."

"I'm not like you," she said. "I'm not like any of the crazy kinds of people I have met."

Mr Naryan beckoned to the owner of the tea house and ordered two more bowls. "I understand you have come a long way." Although he was terrified of her, he was certain that he could draw her out.

But Angel only laughed.

Mr Naryan said, "I do not mean to insult you."

"You dress like a . . . native. Is *that* a religious avocation?"

"It is my profession. I am the Archivist here."

"The people here are different—a different race in every city. When I left, not a single intelligent alien species was known. It was one reason for my voyage. Now there seem to be thousands strung along this long, long river. They treat me like a ruler—is that it? Or a god?"

"The Preservers departed long ago. These are the end times."

Angel said dismissively, "There are always those who believe they live at the end of history. We thought that *we* lived at the end of history, when every star system in the Galaxy had been mapped, every habitable world settled."

For a moment Mr Naryan thought that she would tell him of where she had been, but she added, "I was told that the Preservers, who I suppose were my descendants, made the different races, but each race calls itself human, even the ones who don't look like they could have evolved from anything that ever looked remotely human."

"The Shaped call themselves human because they have no other name for what they have become, innocent and fallen alike. After all, they had no name before they were raised up. The citizens of Sensch remain innocent. They are our . . . responsibility."

He had not meant for it to sound like a plea.

"You're not doing all that well," Angel said, and started to tell him about the Change War she had tangled with upriver, on the way to this, the last city at the midpoint of the world.

It was a long, complicated story, and she kept stopping to ask Mr Naryan questions, most of which, despite his extensive readings of the Puranas, he was unable to answer. As she talked, Mr Naryan transcribed her speech on his tablet. She commented that a recording device would be better, but by reading back a long speech she had just made he demonstrated that his close diacritical marks captured her every word.

"But that is not its real purpose, which is an aid to fix the memory in my head."

"You listen to people's stories."

"Stories are important. In the end they are all that is left, all that history leaves us. Stories endure." And Mr Naryan wondered if she saw what was all too clear to him, the way her story would end, if she stayed in the city.

Angel considered his words. "I have been out of history a long time," she said at last. "I'm not sure that I want to be a part of it again." She stood up so quickly that she knocked her stool over, and left.

Mr Naryan knew better than to follow her. That night, as he sat enjoying a cigarette on his balcony, under the baleful glare of the Eye of the Preservers, a remote came to him. Dreen's face materialised above the remote's silver platter and told him that the woman's shipmates knew that she was here. They were coming for her.

As the ship draws closer, looming above the glowing lighter that tows it, Mr Naryan begins to make out its shape. It is a huge black wedge composed of tiers of flat plates that rise higher than the tallest towers of the city. Little lights, mostly red, gleam here and there within its ridged carapace. Mr Naryan brushes mosquitoes from his bare arms, watching the black ship move beneath a black sky empty except for the Eye of the Preservers and a few dim halo stars. Here, at the midpoint of the world, the Home Galaxy will not rise until winter.

The crowd has grown. It becomes restless. Waves of emotion surge back and forth. Mr Naryan feels them pass through the citizens packed around him, although he hardly understands what they mean, for all the time he has lived with these people.

He has been allowed to pass through the crowd with the citizens' usual generous deference, and now stands close to the edge of the whirling cloud of machines which defends the dock, twenty paces or so from the magistrates who nervously swish their quirts to and fro. The crowd's thick yeasty odour fills his nostrils; its humming disquiet, modulating up and down, penetrates to the marrow of his bones. Now and then a machine ignites a flare of light that sweeps over the front ranks of the crowd, and the eyes of the men and women shine blankly orange, like so many little sparks.

At last the ship passes the temple complex at the northern edge of the city, its wedge rising like a wave above the temple's clusters of slim spiky towers. The lighter's engines go into reverse; waves break in whitecaps on the steps beyond the whirl of machines and the grim line of magistrates.

The crowd's hum rises in pitch. Mr Naryan finds himself carried forward as it presses towards the barrier defined by the machines. The people around him apologise effusively for troubling him, trying to minimise contact with him in the press as snails withdraw from salt. The machines' whirl stratifies, and the magistrates raise their quirts and shout a single word lost in the noise of the crowd. The people in the front rank of the crowd fall to their knees, clutching their eyes and wailing: the machines have shut down their optic nerves.

Mr Naryan, shown the same deference by the machines as by the citizens, suddenly finds himself isolated amongst groaning and weeping citizens, confronting the row of magistrates. One calls to him, but he ignores the man.

He has a clear view of the ship, now. It has come to rest a league away, at the far end of the docks, but Mr Naryan has to tip his head back and back to see the top of the ship's tiers. It is as if a mountain has drifted against the edge of the city. A new sound drives across the crowd, as a wind drives across a field of wheat. Mr Naryan turns and, by the random flare of patrolling machines, is astonished to see how large the crowd has grown. It fills the long plaza, and more people stand on the rooftops along its margin. Their eyes are like a harvest of stars. They are all looking towards the ship, where Dreen, standing on a cargo sled, ascends to meet the crew.

Mr Naryan hooks the wire frames of his spectacles over his ears, and the crew standing on top of the black ship snap into clear focus.

There are fifteen, men and women all as tall as Angel, looming over Dreen as he welcomes them with effusive gestures. Mr Naryan can almost smell Dreen's anxiety. He wants the crew to take Angel away, and order restored. He will be telling them where to find her. Mr Naryan feels a pang of anger. He turns and makes his way through the crowd. When he reaches its ragged margin, everyone around him suddenly looks straight up. Dreen's sled sweeps overhead, carrying his guests to the safety of the floating habitat above the pink sandstone palace. The crowd surges forward— and all the little machines fall from the air!

One lands close to Mr Naryan, its carapace burst open at the seams. Smoke pours from it. An old woman picks it up—Mr Naryan smells her burnt flesh as it sears her hand—and throws it at him.

Her shot goes wide. Mr Naryan is so astonished that he does not even duck. He glimpses the confusion as the edge of the crowd collides with the line of magistrates: some magistrates run, their red cloaks streaming at their backs; others throw down their quirts and hold out their empty hands.

The crowd devours them. Mr Naryan limps away as fast as he could, his heart galloping with fear. Ahead is a wide avenue leading into the city, and standing in the middle of the avenue is a compact group of men, clustered about a tall figure.

It is Angel.

Mr Naryan told Angel what Dreen had told him, that the ship was coming to the city, the very next day. It was at the same tea house. She did not seem surprised. "They need me," she said. "How long will they take?"

"Well, they cannot come here directly. Confluence's maintenance system will only allow ships to land at designated docks, but the machinery of the spaceport docks here has grown erratic and dangerous through disuse. The nearest place they could safely dock is five hundred leagues away, and after that the ship must be towed downriver. It will take time. What will you do?"

Angel passed a hand over her sleek black hair. "I like it here. I could be comfortable."

She had already been given a place in which to live by a wealthy merchant family. She took Mr Naryan to see it. It was near the river, a small two-storey house built around a courtyard shaded by a jacaranda tree. People were going in and out, carrying furniture and carpets. Three men were painting the wooden rail of the balcony that ran around the upper storey. They were painting it pink and blue, cheerfully singing. Angel was amused by the bustle, and laughed when Mr Naryan said that she shouldn't take advantage of the citizens.

"They seem so happy to help me. What's wrong with that?"

Mr Naryan thought it best not to explain about the cluster of genes implanted in all the races of the Shaped, the reflex altruism of the unfallen. A woman brought out tea and a pile of crisp, wafer-thin fritters sweetened with crystallised honey. Two men brought canopied chairs. Angel sprawled in one, invited Mr Naryan to sit in the other. She was quite at ease, grinning every time someone showed her the gift they had brought her.

Dreen, Mr Naryan knew, would be dismayed. Angel was a barbarian, displaced by five million years. She had no idea of the careful balance by which one must live with the innocent, the unfallen, if their cultures were to survive. Yet she was fully human, free to choose, and that freedom was inviolable. No wonder Dreen was so eager for the ship to reclaim her.

Still, Angel's rough joy was infectious, and Mr Naryan soon found himself smiling with her at the sheer abundance of trinkets scattered around her. No one was giving unless they were glad to give, and no one who gave was poor. The only poor in Sensch were the sky-clad mendicants who had voluntarily renounced the material world.

So he sat and drank tea with her, and ate a dozen of the delicious, honeyed fritters, one after the other, and listened to more of her wild tales of travelling the river, realising how little she understood of Confluence's administration. She was convinced that the Shaped were somehow forbidden technology, for instance, and did not understand why there was no government. Was Dreen the absolute ruler? By what right?

"Dreen is merely the Commissioner. Any authority he has is invested in him by the citizens, and it is manifest only on high days. He enjoys parades, you know. I suppose the magistrates have power, in that they arbitrate neighbourly disputes and decide upon punishment—Senschians are argumentative, and sometimes quarrels can lead to unfortunate accidents."

"Murder, you mean? Then perhaps they are not as innocent as you maintain." Angel reached out suddenly. "And these? By what authority do these little spies operate?"

Pinched between her thumb and forefinger was a bronze machine. Its sensor cluster turned back and forth as it struggled to free itself.

"Why, they are part of the maintenance system of Confluence."

"Can Dreen use them? Tell me all you know. It may be important."

She questioned Mr Naryan closely, and he found himself telling her more than he wanted. But despite all that he told her, she would not talk about her voyage, nor of why she had escaped from the ship, or how. In the days that followed, Mr Naryan requested several times, politely and wistfully, that she would. He even visited the temple and petitioned for information about her voyage, but all trace of it had been lost in the vast sifting of history, and when pressed, the aspect who had come at the hierodule's bidding broke contact with an almost petulant abruptness.

Mr Naryan was not surprised that it could tell him nothing. The voyage must have begun five million years ago at least, after all, for the ship to have travelled all the way to the neighbouring galaxy and back.

He did learn that the ship had tried to sell its findings on landfall, much as a merchant would sell his wares. Perhaps Angel wanted to profit from what she knew; perhaps that was why the ship wanted her back, although there was no agency on Confluence that would close such a deal. Knowledge was worth only the small price of petitioning those aspects which deal with the secular world.

Meanwhile, a group of citizens gathered around Angel, like disciples around one of the blessed who, touched by some fragment or other of the Preservers, wander Confluence's long shore. These disciples went wherever she went. They were all young men, which seemed to Mr Naryan faintly sinister, sons of her benefactors fallen under her spell. He recognised several of them, but none would speak to him, although there were always at least two or three accompanying Angel. They wore white headbands on which

Angel had lettered a slogan in an archaic script older than any race of the Shaped; she refused to explain what it meant.

Mr Naryan's wife thought that he, too, was falling under some kind of spell. She did not like the idea of Angel: she declared that Angel must be some kind of ghost, and therefore dangerous. Perhaps she was right. She was a wise and strong-willed woman, and Mr Naryan had grown to trust her advice.

Certainly, Mr Naryan believed that he could detect a change in the steady song of the city as he went about his business. He listened to an old man dying of the systematic organ failure which took most of the citizens in the middle of their fourth century. The man was one of the few who had left the city—he had travelled north, as far as the swampy settlements where an amphibious race lived in a city tunnelled through cliffs overlooking the river. His story took a whole day to tell, in a stiflingly hot room muffled in dusty carpets and lit only by a lamp with a blood-red chimney. At the end, the old man began to weep, saying that he knew now that he had not travelled at all, and Mr Naryan was unable to comfort him. Two children were born on the next day—an event so rare that the whole city celebrated, garlanding the streets with fragrant orange blossoms. But there was a tension beneath the celebrations that Mr Naryan had never before felt, and it seemed that Angel's followers were everywhere amongst the revellers. Dreen felt the change, too. "There have been incidents," he said, as candid an admission as he had ever made to Mr Naryan. "Nothing very much. A temple wall defaced with the slogan the woman has her followers wear. A market disrupted by young men running through it, overturning stalls. I asked the magistrates not to make examples of the perpetrators—that would create martyrs. Let the people hold their own courts if they wish. And she's been making speeches. Would you like to hear one?"

"Is it necessary?"

Dreen dropped his glass with a careless gesture—a machine caught it and bore it off before it smashed on the tiles. They were on a balcony of Dreen's floating habitat, looking out over the Great River towards the nearside edge of the world. At the horizon was the long white double line that marked the river's fall: the rapids below, the permanent clouds above. It was noon, and the white, sunlit city was quiet.

Dreen said, "You listen to so much of her talk, I suppose you are wearied of it. In summary, it is nothing but some vague nonsense about destiny, about rising above circumstances and bettering yourself, as if you could lift yourself into the air by grasping the soles of your feet."

Dreen dismissed this with a snap of his fingers. His own feet, as always, were bare, and his long opposable toes were curled around the bar of the rail on which he squatted. He said, "Perhaps she wants to rule the city—if it pleases her, why not? At least, until the ship arrives here. I will not stop her if that is what she wants, and if she can do it. Do you know where she is right now?"

"I have been busy." But Mr Naryan felt an eager curiosity: yes, his wife was right.

"I heard the story you gathered in. At the time, you know, I thought that man might bring war to the city when he came back." Dreen's laugh was a high-pitched hooting. "The woman is out there, at the edge of the world. She took a boat yesterday."

"I am sure she will return," Mr Naryan said. "It is all of a pattern."

"I defer to your knowledge. Will hers be an interesting story, Mr Naryan? Have another drink. Stay, enjoy yourself." Dreen reached up and swung into the branches of the flame tree which leaned over the balcony, disappearing in a flurry of red leaves and leaving Mr Naryan to find a machine that was able to take him home.

Mr Naryan thought that Dreen was wrong to dismiss what Angel was doing, although he understood why Dreen affected such a grand indifference. It was outside Dreen's experience, that was all: Angel was outside the experience of everyone on Confluence. The Change Wars that flared here and there along Confluence's vast length were not ideological but eschatological. They were a result of sociological stresses that arose when radical shifts in the expression of clusters of native and grafted genes caused a species of Shaped to undergo a catastrophic redefinition of its perceptions of the world. But what Angel was doing dated from before the Preservers had raised up the Shaped and ended human history. Mr Naryan only began to understood it himself when Angel told him what she had done at the edge of the world.

And later, on the terrible night when the ship arrives and every machine in the city dies, with flames roaring unchecked through the farside quarter of the city and thousands of citizens fleeing into the orchard forests to the north, Mr Naryan realises that he has not understood as much as he thought. Angel has not been preaching empty revolution after all.

Her acolytes, all young men, are armed with crude wooden spears with fire-hardened tips, long double-edged knives of the kind coconut sellers use to open their wares, flails improvised from chains and wire. They hustle Mr Naryan in a forced march towards the palace and Dreen's floating habitat. They have taken away Mr Naryan's cane, and his bad leg hurts abominably with every other step.

Angel is gone. She has work elsewhere. Mr Naryan felt fear when he saw her, but feels more fear now. The reflex altruism of the acolytes has been overridden by a new meme forged in the fires of Angel's revolution—they jostle Mr Naryan with rough humour, sure in their hold over him. One in particular, the rough skin of his long-jawed face crazed in diamonds, jabs Mr Naryan in his ribs with the butt of his spear at every intersection, as if to remind him not to escape, something that Mr Naryan has absolutely no intention of doing.

Power is down all over the city—it went off with the fall of the machines—but leaping light from scattered fires swim in the wide eyes of the young men. They pass through a market square where people swig beer and drunkenly gamble amongst overturned stalls. Elsewhere in the fiery dark there is open rutting, men with men as well as with women. A child lies dead in a gutter. Horrible, horrible. Once, a building collapses inside its own fire, sending flames whirling high into the black sky. The faces of all the men surrounding Mr Naryan are transformed by this leaping light into masks with eyes of flame.

Mr Naryan's captors urge him on. His only comfort is that he will be of use in what is to come. Angel has not yet finished with him.

When Angel returned from the edge of the world, she came straight away to Mr Naryan. It was a warm evening, at the hour after sunset when the streets began to fill with strollers, the murmur of neighbour greeting neighbour, the cries of vendors selling fruit juice or popcorn or sweet cakes.

Mr Naryan was listening as his pupil, the magistrate's son, read a passage from the Puranas which described the time when the Preservers had strung the Galaxy with their creations. The boy was tall and awkward and faintly resentful, for he was not the scholar his father wished him to be and would rather spend his evenings with his fellows in the beer halls than read ancient legends in a long-dead language. He bent over the book like a night stork, his finger stabbing at each line as he clumsily translated it, mangling words in his hoarse voice. Mr Naryan was listening with half an ear, interrupting only to correct particularly inelegant phrases. In the kitchen at the far end of the little apartment, his wife was humming to the murmur of the radio, her voice a breathy contented monotone.

Angel came up the helical stair with a rapid clatter, mounting quickly above a sudden hush in the street. Mr Naryan knew who it was even before she burst onto the balcony. Her appearance so astonished the magistrate's son that he dropped the book. Mr Naryan dismissed him and he hurried away, no doubt eager to meet his friends in the flickering neon of the beer hall and tell them of this wonder.

"I've been to the edge of the world," Angel said to Mr Naryan, coolly accepting a bowl of tea from Mr Naryan's wife, quite oblivious of the glance she exchanged with her husband before retreating. Mr Naryan's heart turned at that look, for in it he saw how his wife's hard words were so easily

dissolved in the weltering sea of reflexive benevolence. How cruel the Preservers had been, it seemed to him never crueller, to have raised up races of
the Shaped and yet to have shackled them in unthinking obedience.

Angel said, "You don't seem surprised."

"Dreen told me as much. I'm pleased to see you returned safely. It has
been a dry time without you." Already he had said too much: it was as if all
his thoughts were eager to be spilled before her.

"Dreen knows everything that goes on in the city."

"Oh no, not at all. He knows what he needs to know."

"I took a boat," Angel said. "I just asked for it, and the man took me
right along, without question. I wish now I'd stolen it. It would have been
simpler. I'm tired of all this good will."

It was as if she could read his mind. For the first time, Mr Naryan began
to be afraid, a shiver like the first shake of a tambour that had ritually introduced the tempestuous dances of his youth.

Angel sat on the stool that the student had quit, tipping it back so she
could lean against the rail of the balcony. She had cut her black hair short,
and bound around her forehead a strip of white cloth printed with the slogan, in ancient incomprehensible script, that was the badge of her acolytes.
She wore an ordinary loose white shirt and much jewelry: rings on every
finger, sometimes more than one on each; bracelets and bangles down her
forearms; gold and silver chains around her neck, layered on her breast. She
was both graceful and terrifying, a rough beast slouched from the deep past
to claim the world.

She said, teasingly, "Don't you want to hear my story? Isn't that your
avocation?"

"I'll listen to anything you want to tell me," Mr Naryan said.

"The world is a straight line. Do you know about libration?"

Mr Naryan shook his head.

Angel held out her hand, tipped it back and forth. "This is the world.
Everything lives on the back of a long flat plate which circles the sun. The
plate rocks on its long axis, so the sun rises above the edge and then reverses
its course. I went to the edge of the world, where the river that runs down
half its length falls into the void. I suppose it must be collected and redis-
tributed, but it really does look like it falls away forever."

"The river is eternally renewed," Mr Naryan said. "Where it falls is
where ships used to arrive and depart, but this city has not been a port for
many years."

"Fortunately for me, or my companions would already be here. There's
a narrow ribbon of land on the far side of the river. Nothing lives there, not
even an insect. No earth, no stones. The air shakes with the sound of the
river's fall, and swirling mist burns with raw sunlight. And there are

shrines, in the thunder and mist at the edge of the world. One spoke to me."

Mr Naryan knew these shrines, although he had not been there for many years. He remembered that the different races of the Shaped had erected shrines all along the edge of the world, stone upon stone carried across the river, from which flags and long banners flew. Long ago, the original founders of the city of Sensch, Dreen's ancestors, had travelled across the river to petition the avatars of the Preservers, believing that the journey across the wide river was a necessary rite of purification. But they were gone, and the new citizens, who had built their city of stones over the burnt groves of the old city, simply bathed in the heated, mineral-heavy water of the pools of the shrines of the temple at the edge of their city before delivering their petitions. He supposed the proud flags and banners of the shrines would be tattered rags now, bleached by unfiltered sunlight, rotted by mist. The screens of the shrines—would they still be working?

Angel grinned. Mr Naryan had to remember that it was not, as it was with the citizens, a baring of teeth before striking. She said, "Don't you want to know what it said to me? It's part of my story."

"Do you want to tell me?"

She passed her hand over the top of her narrow skull: bristly hair made a crisp sound under her palm. "No," she said. "No, I don't think I do. Not yet."

Later, after a span of silence, just before she left, she said, "After we were wakened by the ship, after it brought us here, it showed us how the black hole you call the Eye of the Preservers was made. It recorded the process as it returned, speeded up because the ship was travelling so fast it stretched time around itself. At first there was an intense point of light within the heart of the Large Magellanic Cloud. It might have been a supernova, except that it was a thousand times larger than any supernova ever recorded. For a long time its glare obscured everything else, and when it cleared, all the remaining stars were streaming around where it had been. Those nearest the centre elongated and dissipated, and always more crowded in until nothing was left but the gas clouds of the accretion disc, glowing by Cerenkov radiation."

"So it is written in the Puranas."

"And is it also written there why Confluence was constructed around a halo star between the Home Galaxy and the Eye of the Preservers?"

"Of course. It is so we can all worship and glorify the Preservers. The Eye looks upon us all."

"That's what I told them," Angel said.

After she was gone, Mr Naryan put on his spectacles and walked through the city to the docks. The unsleeping citizens were promenading in the warm dark streets, or squatting in doorways, or talking quietly from upper-storey windows to their neighbours across the street. Amongst this easy somnolence, Angel's young disciples moved with a quick purposeful-ness, here in pairs, there in a group of twenty or more. Their slogans were painted on almost every wall. Three stopped Mr Naryan near the docks, danced around his bulk, jeering, then ran off, screeching with laughter, when he slashed at them with his cane.

"Ruffians! Fools!"

"Seize the day!" they sang back. "Seize the day!"

Mr Naryan did not find the man whose skiff Angel and her followers had used to cross the river, but the story was already everywhere amongst the fisherfolk. The Preservers had spoken to her, they said, and she had refused their temptations. Many were busily bargaining with citizens who wanted to cross the river and see the site of this miracle for themselves.

An old man, eyes milky with cataracts—the fisherfolk trawled widely across the Great River, exposing themselves to more radiation than nor-mal—asked Mr Naryan if these were the end times, if the Preservers would return to walk amongst them again. When Mr Naryan said, no, anyone who dealt with the avatars knew that only those fragments remained in the Universe, the old man shrugged and said, "They say *she* is a Preserver," and Mr Naryan, looking out across the river's black welter, where the horizon was lost against the empty night, seeing the scattered constellations of the running lights of the fisherfolk's skiffs scattered out to the nearside edge, knew that the end of Angel's story was not far off. The citizens were finding their use for her. Inexorably, step by step, she was becoming part of their history.

Mr Naryan did not see Angel again until the night her ship arrived. Dreen went to treat with her, but he couldn't get within two streets of her house: it had become the centre of a convocation that took over the entire quarter of the city. She preached to thousands of citizens from the rooftops.

Dreen reported to Mr Naryan that it was a philosophy of hope from despair. "She says that all life feeds on destruction and death. Are you sure you don't want to hear it?"

"It isn't necessary."

Dreen was perched on a balustrade, looking out at the river. They were in his floating habitat, in an arbour of lemon trees that jutted out at its leading edge. He said, "More than a thousand a day are making the cross-ing."

"Has the screen spoken again?"

"I've monitored it continuously. Nothing."

"But it did speak with her."

"Perhaps, perhaps." Dreen was suddenly agitated. He scampered up and down the narrow balustrade, swiping at overhanging branches and scaring the white doves that perched amongst the little glossy leaves. The birds rocketed up in a great flutter of wings, crying as they rose into the empty sky. Dreen said, "The machines watching her don't work. Not anymore. She's found out how to disrupt them. I snatch long-range pictures, but they don't tell me very much. I don't even know if she visited the shrine in the first place."

"I believe her," Mr Naryan said.

"I petitioned the avatars," Dreen said, "but of course they wouldn't tell me if they'd spoken to her."

Mr Naryan was disturbed by this admission—Dreen was not a religious man. "What will you do?"

"Nothing. I could send the magistrates for her, but even if she went with them her followers would claim she'd been arrested. And I can't even remember when I last arrested someone. It would make her even more powerful, and I'd have to let her go. But I suppose that you are going to tell me that I should let it happen."

"It has happened before. Even here, to your own people. They built the shrines, after all . . . . "

"Yes, and later they fell from grace, and destroyed their city. The snakes aren't ready for that," Dreen said, almost pleading, and for a moment Mr Naryan glimpsed the depth of Dreen's love for this city and its people.

Dreen turned away, as if ashamed, to look out at the river again, at the flocking sails of little boats setting out on, or returning from, the long crossing to the far side of the river. This great pilgrimage had become the focus of the life of the city. The markets were closed for the most part; merchants had moved to the docks to supply the thousands of pilgrims.

Dreen said, "They say that the avatar tempted her with godhead, and she denied it."

"But that is foolish! The days of the Preservers have long ago faded. We know them only by their image, which burns forever at the event horizon, but their essence has long since receded."

Dreen shrugged. "There's worse. They say that she forced the avatar to admit that the Preservers are dead. They say that *she* is an avatar of something greater than the Preservers, although you wouldn't know that from her preaching. She claims that this universe is all there is, that destiny is what you make it. What makes me despair is how readily the snakes believe this cant."

Mr Naryan, feeling chill, there in the sun-dappled shade, said, "She has hinted to me that she learnt it in the great far out, in the galaxy beyond the Home Galaxy."

"The ship is coming," Dreen said. "Perhaps they will deal with her."

In the burning night of the city's dissolution, Mr Naryan is brought at last to the pink sandstone palace. Dreen's habitat floats above it, a black cloud that half-eclipses the glowering red swirl of the Eye of the Preservers. Trails of white smoke, made luminescent by the fires which feed them, pour from the palace's high arched windows, braiding into sheets which dash like surf against the rim of the habitat. Mr Naryan sees something fly up from amongst the palace's many carved spires—there seems to be more of them than he remembers—and smash away a piece of the habitat, which slowly tumbles off into the black sky.

The men around him hoot and cheer at this, and catch Mr Naryan's arms and march him up the broad steps and through the high double doors into the courtyard beyond. It is piled with furniture and tapestries that have been thrown down from the thousand high windows overlooking it, but a path has been cleared to a narrow stair that turns and turns as it rises, until at last Mr Naryan is pushed out onto the roof of the palace.

Perhaps five hundred of Angel's followers crowd amongst the spires and fallen trees and rocks, many naked, all with lettered headbands tied around their foreheads. Smoky torches blaze everywhere. In the centre of the crowd is the palace's great throne on which, on high days and holidays, at the beginning of masques or parades, Dreen receives the city's priests, merchants, and artists. It is lit by a crown of machines burning bright as the sun, and seated on it—easy, elegant and terrifying—is Angel.

Mr Naryan is led through the crowd and left standing alone before the throne. Angel beckons him forward, her smile both triumphant and scared: Mr Naryan feels her fear mix with his own. She says, "What should I do with your city, now I've taken it from you?"

"You haven't finished your story." Everything Mr Naryan planned to say has fallen away at the simple fact of her presence. Stranded before her fierce, barely contained energies, he feels old and used up, his body as heavy with years and regret as with fat. He adds cautiously, "I'd like to hear it all."

He wonders if she really knows how her story must end. Perhaps she does. Perhaps her wild joy is not at her triumph, but at the imminence of her death. Perhaps she really does believe that the void is all, and rushes to embrace it.

Angel says, "My people can tell you. They hide with Dreen up above, but not for long."

She points across the roof. A dozen men are wrestling a sled, which shudders like a living thing as it tries to reorientate itself in the gravity field, onto a kind of launching cradle tipped up towards the habitat. The edges of the habitat are ragged, as if bitten, and amongst the roof's spires tower-trees are visibly growing towards it, their tips already brushing its edges, their tangled bases pulsing and swelling as teams of men and women drench them with nutrients.

"I found how to enhance the antigravity devices of the sleds," Angel says. "They react against the field which generates gravity for this artificial world. The field's stored inertia gives them a high kinetic energy, so that they make very good missiles. We'll chip away that floating fortress piece by piece if we have to, or we'll finish growing towers and storm its remains, but I expect surrender long before then."

"Dreen is not the ruler of the city." Nor are you, Mr Naryan thinks, but it is not prudent to point that out.

"Not anymore," Angel says.

Mr Naryan dares to step closer. He says, "What did you find out there, that you rage against?"

Angel laughs. "I'll tell you about rage. It is what you have all forgotten, or never learned. It is the motor of evolution, and evolution's end, too." She snatches a beaker of wine from a supplicant, drains it and tosses it aside. She is consumed with an energy that is no longer her own. She says, "We travelled so long, not dead, not sleeping. We were no more than stored potentials triply engraved on gold. Although the ship flew so fast that it bound time about itself, the journey still took thousands of years of slowed shipboard time. At the end of that long voyage we did not wake: we were born. Or rather, others like us were born, although I have their memories, as if they are my own. They learned then that the Universe was not made for the convenience of humans. What they found was a galaxy ruined and dead."

She holds Mr Naryan's hand tightly, speaking quietly and intensely, her eyes staring deep into his.

"A billion years ago, our neighbouring galaxy collided with another, much smaller galaxy. Stars of both galaxies were torn off in the collision, and scattered in a vast halo. The rest coalesced into a single body, but except for ancient globular clusters, which survived the catastrophe because of their dense gravity fields, it is all wreckage. We were not able to chart a single world where life had evolved. I remember standing on a world sheared in half by immense tidal stress, its orbit so eccentric that it was colder than Pluto at its farthest point, hotter than Mercury at its nearest. I remember standing on a world of methane ice as cold and dark as the Universe itself, wandering amongst the stars. There were millions of such worlds cast adrift. I remember standing upon a fragment of a world smashed into a million shards and scattered so widely in its orbit that it never had the chance to reform. There are a million such worlds. I remember gas giants turned inside out—single vast storms—and I remember worlds torched smooth by irruptions of their stars. No life, anywhere.

"Do you know how many galaxies have endured such collisions? Almost all of them. Life is a statistical freak. It is likely that only the stars of our galaxy have planets, or else other civilisations would surely have arisen elsewhere in the unbounded Universe. As it is, it is certain that we are alone. We must make of ourselves what we can. We should not hide, as your Preservers chose to do. Instead, we should seize the day, and make the Universe over with the technology that the Preservers used to make their hiding place."

Her grip is hurting now, but Mr Naryan bears it. "You cannot become a Preserver," he says sadly. "No one can, now. You should not lie to these innocent people."

"I didn't need to lie. They took up my story and made it theirs. They see now what they can inherit—if they dare. This won't stop with one city. It will become a crusade!" She adds, more softly, "You'll remember it all, won't you?"

It is then that Mr Naryan knows that she knows how this must end, and his heart breaks. He would ask her to take that burden from him, but he cannot. He is bound to her. He is her witness.

The crowd around them cheers as the sled rockets up from its cradle. It smashes into the habitat and knocks loose another piece, which drops trees and dirt and rocks amongst the spires of the palace roof as it twists free and spins away into the night. Figures appear at the edge of the habitat. A small tube falls, glittering through the torchlight. A man catches it, runs across the debris-strewn roof, and throws himself at Angel's feet. He is at the far end of the human scale of the Shaped of this city. His skin is lapped with distinct scales, edged with a rim of hard black like the scales of a pine cone. His coarse black hair has flopped over his eyes, which glow like coals with reflected firelight.

Angel takes the tube and shakes it. It unrolls into a flexible sheet on which Dreen's face glows. Dreen's lips move; his voice is small and metallic. Angel listens intently, and when he has finished speaking says softly, "Yes."

Then she stands and raises both hands above her head. All across the roof, men and woman turn towards her, eyes glowing.

"They wish to surrender! Let them come down!"

A moment later a sled swoops down from the habitat, its silvery underside gleaming in the reflected light of the many fires scattered across the roof. Angel's followers shout and jeer, and missiles fly out of the darkness—a burning torch, a rock, a broken branch. All are somehow deflected before they reach the ship's crew, screaming away into the dark with such force that the torch, the branch, kindle into white fire. The crew have modified the sled's field to protect themselves.

They all look like Angel, with the same small sleek head, the same gangling build and abrupt nervous movements. Dreen's slight figure is dwarfed by them. It takes Mr Naryan a long minute to be able to distinguish men from women, and another to be able to tell each man from his brothers, each woman from her sisters. They are all clad in long white shirts that leave them bare-armed and bare-legged, and each is girdled with a belt from which hang a dozen or more little machines. They call to Angel, one following on the words of the other, saying over and over again:

"Return with us—"

"—this is not our place—"

"—these are not our people—"

"—we will return—"

"—we will find our home—"

"—leave with us and return."

Dreen sees Mr Naryan and shouts, "They want to take her back!" He jumps down from the sled, an act of bravery that astonishes Mr Naryan, and skips through the crowd. "They are all one person, or variations on one person," he says breathlessly. "The ship makes its crew by varying a template. Angel is an extreme. A mistake."

Angel starts to laugh.

"You funny little man! I'm the real one—they are the copies!"

"Come back to us—"

"—come back and help us—"

"—help us find our home."

"There's no home to find!" Angel shouts. "Oh, you fools! This is all there is!"

"I tried to explain to them," Dreen says to Mr Naryan, "but they wouldn't listen."

"They surely cannot disbelieve the Puranas," Mr Naryan says.

Angel shouts, "Give me back the ship!"

"It was never yours—"

"—never yours to own—"

"—but only yours to serve."

"No! I won't serve!" Angel jumps onto the throne and makes an abrupt cutting gesture.

Hundreds of fine silver threads spool out of the darkness, shooting towards the sled and her crewmates. The ends of the threads flick up when they reach the edge of the sled's modified field, but then fall in a tangle over the crew: their shield is gone.

The crowd begins to throw things again, but Angel orders them to be still. "I have the only working sled," she says. "That which I enhance, I can also take away. Come with me," she tells Mr Naryan, "and see the end of my story."

The crowd around Angel stirs. Mr Naryan turns, and sees one of the crew walking towards Angel.

He is as tall and slender as Angel, his small, high-cheekboned face so like her own it is as if he holds up a mirror as he approaches. A rock arcs out of the crowd and strikes his shoulder: he staggers but walks on, hardly seeming to notice that the crowd closes at his back so that he is suddenly inside its circle, with Angel and Mr Naryan in its focus.

Angel says, "I'm not afraid of you."

"Of course not, sister," the man says. And he grasps her wrists in both his hands.

Then Mr Naryan is on his hands and knees. A strong wind howls about him, and he can hear people screaming. The afterglow of a great light swims in his vision. He can't see who helps him up and half-carries him through the stunned crowd to the sled.

When the sled starts to rise, Mr Naryan falls to his knees again. Dreen says in his ear, "It's over."

"No," Mr Naryan says. He blinks and blinks, tears rolling down his cheeks.

The man took Angel's wrists in both of his—

Dreen is saying something, but Mr Naryan shakes his head. It isn't over.

—And they shot up into the night, so fast that their clothing burst into flame, so fast that air was drawn up with them. If Angel could nullify the gravity field, then so could her crewmates. She has achieved apotheosis.

The sled swoops up the tiered slope of the ship, is swallowed by a wide hatch. When he can see again, Mr Naryan finds himself kneeling at the edge of the open hatch. The city is spread below. Fires define the streets which radiate away from the Great River; the warm night air is bitter with the smell of burning.

Dreen has been looking at the lighted windows that crowd the walls of the vast room beyond the hatch, scampering with growing excitement from one to the other. Now he sees that Mr Naryan is crying, and clumsily tries to comfort him, believing that Mr Naryan is mourning his wife, left behind in the dying city.

"She was a good woman, for her kind," Mr Naryan is able to say at last, although it isn't her he's mourning, or not only her. He is mourning for all of the citizens of Sensch. They are irrevocably caught in their change now, never to be the same. His wife, the nut roaster, the men and women who own the little tea houses at the corner of every square, the children, the mendicants and the merchants—all are changed, or else dying in the process. Something new is being born down there. Rising from the fall of the city.

"They'll take us away from all this," Dreen says happily. "They're going to search for where they came from. Some are out combing the city for others who can help them; the rest are preparing the ship. They'll take it over the edge of the world, into the great far out!"

"Don't they know they'll never find what they're looking for? The Puranas—"

"Old stories, old fears. They will take us home!"

Mr Naryan laboriously clambers to his feet. He understands that Dreen has fallen under the thrall of the crew. He is theirs, as Mr Naryan is now and forever Angel's. He says, "Those times are past. Down there in the city is the beginning of something new, something wonderful—" He finds he can't explain. All he has is his faith that it won't stop here. It is not an end but a beginning, a spark to set all of Confluence—the unfallen and the changed—alight. Mr Naryan says, weakly, "It won't stop here."

Dreen's big eyes shine in the light of the city's fires. He says, "I see only another Change War. There's nothing new in that. The snakes will rebuild the city in their new image, if not here, then somewhere else along the Great River. It has happened before, in this very place, to my own people. We survived it, and so will the snakes. But what *they* promise is so much greater! We'll leave this poor place, and voyage out to return to where it all began, to the very home of the Preservers. Look there! That's where we're going!"

Mr Naryan allows himself to be led across the vast room. It is so big that it could easily hold Dreen's floating habitat. A window on its far side shows a view angled somewhere far above the plane of Confluence's orbit. Confluence itself is a shining strip, an arrow running out to its own vanishing point. Beyond that point are the ordered, frozen spirals of the Home Galaxy, the great jewelled clusters and braids of stars constructed in the last great days of the Preservers before they vanished forever into the black hole they made by collapsing the Magellanic Clouds.

Mr Naryan starts to breathe deeply, topping up the oxygen content of his blood.

"You see!" Dreen says again, his face shining with awe in Confluence's silver light.

"I see the end of history," Mr Naryan says. "You should have studied the Puranas, Dreen. There's no future to be found amongst the artifacts of the Preservers, only the dead past. I won't serve, Dreen. That's over."

And then he turns and lumbers through the false lights and shadows of the windows towards the open hatch. Dreen catches his arm, but Mr Naryan throws him off.

Dreen sprawls on his back, astonished, then jumps up and runs in front of Mr Naryan. "You fool!" he shouts. "They can bring her back!"

"There's no need," Mr Naryan says, and pushes Dreen out of the way and plunges straight out of the hatch.

He falls through black air like a heavy comet. Water smashes around him, tears away his clothes. His nostrils pinch shut and membranes slide across his eyes as he plunges down and down amidst streaming bubbles until the roaring in his ears is no longer the roar of his blood but the roar of the river's never-ending fall over the edge of the world.

Deep, silty currents begin to pull him towards that edge. He turns in the water and begins to swim away from it, away from the ship and the burning city. His duty is over: once they have taken charge of their destiny, the changed citizens will no longer need an Archivist.

Mr Naryan swims more and more easily. The swift, cold water washes away his landbound habits, wakes the powerful muscles of his shoulders and back. Angel's message burns bright, burning away the old stories, as he swims through the black water, against the currents of the Great River. Joy gathers with every thrust of his arms. He is the messenger, Angel's witness. He will travel ahead of the crusade that will begin when everyone in Sensch is changed. It will be a long and difficult journey, but he does not doubt that his destiny—the beginning of the future that Angel has bequeathed him and all of Confluence—lies at the end of it.

When Strangers Meet

Sonia Orin Lyris

S ONIA ORIN LYRIS IS YET ANOTHER GRADUATE OF CLARION WEST, CLASS OF 1992, WITH A NUMBER OF SHORT FICTION CREDITS. SHE HAS FINISHED HER FIRST NOVEL, A FANTASY.

HERE, WE HAVE THE BEGINNINGS OF A NEW HISTORY—COMPLETE WITH MISUNDERSTANDINGS, POTENTIAL TRAGEDY, AND GREAT IRONY . . . FOR ALL CONCERNED.

"THE VOICES FROM the sky have called again, Great One," said the One's Second.

"When strangers meet," said the One, "all benefit."

"Are they strangers," asked her Second, who happened to be an older sister, and pale green, "these new ones from the sky?"

The One sat back on her soft throne, stretching all her top limbs out to the side in a motion that said that she could wait until tomorrow to worry about tomorrow.

The Second hesitated, unsure if this meant a dismissal from the throne room or not. The One laughed, a hissing sound that relaxed the Second. The sound of the One content was always a good sound.

"I think these new ones may be strangers," the One said. "We have sent them our language books, and they have sent us theirs. They wish to come, to meet us. To understand us."

"As strangers?"

"They say they are friends, but they must study our language and then understand. I don't think they mean to be familiar."

"I am sure you are right, Great One. Shall we give them permission to join us?"

The One considered.

"Tell them to ask again, after the festival. The new year brings clarity, and strangers bring benefits."

* * *

Today the Great One's Second was younger, and nearly pink in shade, and her soft movements around the room soothed the One.

"I do not recognize you," the One said to her sister. The Second pressed her limbs to her stomach, uncertain.

"Thank you, Great One," she murmured. "I only hope to please."

"You do please. Your smell is unfamiliar. You do not distract."

It was a good day, this tenth day before the festival of the cooling time, and the One felt good. Her Second moved around the large room, cleaning away the specks of dust and dirt, replacing a few of the long sheets of odor-absorbing textile, and touching the deep sound bells so that they spun and their low hum might better soothe the One.

And it was a good day because the voices from the sky had called to say that they were happy to be strangers. Strangers always brought benefit.

The One drifted sleepily, daydreaming of the coming festival, her pastel-colored younger sisters who would soon be adults, the flower tastes her sisters would bring to tempt her to delight, and the spin dance the silks would perform. And then, later, of the days and nights she would have, secluded with the many males who had matured since last year.

She drifted, the One, filled with the calm that the bells brought, hearing only the unanticipated sounds of her Second, as she moved around the room, tidying and adjusting and turning.

"The silks have come again, Great One," the green Second said.

The One had felt herself grow euphoric and relaxed lately, and though it happened every year, she found herself surprised at how complete the change was, so complete that those who came day after day to consult with her about festival plans did not irritate her even though they were, by now, quite familiar.

"The silks," her Second said again, quite softly. Barely a breeze to remind the One that her attentions were asked.

"Yes, of course," said the One. "They want—what they always want."

"Yes, Great One."

"Then I will see them. Him. Is it a him?"

"Yes, Great One, their leaders are usually male." The Second's tone was a mild echo of the One's own amusement.

So hard to remember, the One thought. But then, so many things were hard to remember in this season before the festival. Male leaders? She shook her head.

In it came, the long, slender, warm silk, walking in on two long legs, its arms hanging down like long leaves at her—his, the One corrected—side. Every inch coated with the lush, fine cream strands that gave them their names.

Clumsy it seemed, for a silk, walking in as though uncertain, hesitant, not using the grace that his kind could so easily bring to every movement. And yet, she reminded herself, not all of them were equally talented.

But they would dance for the spin dance—how they would dance. Whirling like snow crystals in sculpted storms, this was how they would dance.

And when they had danced with every last bit of life that was in them, spurred on and on by the delight of the One and her many sisters, when blood squeezed from their poor bodies, lovely but too fragile to hold the passions poured into them, then would they be truly lovely indeed.

He stood before her, large pale blue eyes raised shyly. He did not smell bad, but musky, like the grain they were fed.

It was good that he visited now, when she was not so irritable. Another season and he would have so disturbed her that she would not be able to talk with him at all. He looked down to show his respect.

It was well that they gave respect. The One and her sisters kept the silks alive all year round, gave them shelter, planted their food, saw to the health of their young, and let them alone to live their lives as they saw fit.

The One felt deliciously relaxed. She wanted to drowse again. Just as soon as she was done with the silk. She tilted her head at the silk.

"You are strange to me," she said.

"You honor me, Great One."

"Speak."

"Great One, I fear to disturb you—"

"If you have concerns, you must speak. We care for you. You are dear to us."

The silk looked down, his large eyes sparkling.

"Great One, it is the festival. All of us were young last year, and did not see it, but—"

He glanced up at her, then away.

"Yes?" The One prompted.

"We have been told, about the dance in the cold, on the warm arena floor. Of how many hours it will go—so many hours! Great One, we were young last year, and our parents did not return to us from the dance. We owe you everything, of course; our food and water—you are so very kind to us, but—"

"But you want to know whether you will die in the dance."

He looked to the side of the room, then to the other, and then down again.

"Yes."

The Great One stretched a little, moving two of her limbs to another soft place on her throne where they might be even more comforted. The soft throne called to her to rest, to sleep, to dream.

"Yes," the One answered. "Of course you will die. All of you who dance will die."

The silk's eyes were very large now, and they sparkled quite like ice in the sun. His lovely eyes cut through the One's easy calm, and she was filled with the sharp delight of anticipation. She had seen twenty silk dances in her lifetime, and they never ceased to give her awe of the loveliness the silks could create out of their own bodies.

"But, Great One," the silk stammered, "surely you don't mean— Surely I do not understand."

He was breathing heavily, so upset that she could nearly taste it. He would upset the others if she left him unchanged, and then they would fear before they danced, and there was no need for that.

She pressed the scent out of herself, pressed it into the air and toward him, along with her reassurances, which she breathed onto him, into his large, wet eyes.

The pale blue, frightened eyes closed a little, and his breathing slowed.

"You didn't understand before, it's true," said the One. "But you do now."

Slowly he blinked, staring at her, and a crease came to his mouth, one that meant pleasure.

"What else, then, silk? Have I answered your concerns?"

The silk considered, brushing his long nails through his arm hair.

"Yes, Great One. You are kind and gracious. I regret having disturbed you over this small thing."

"We care for you. Your needs do not disturb us."

"Thank you, Great One."

"Go now and rest with your sisters and brothers, and anticipate with us the festival of the cooling time."

"It is cold," said the One's newest Second, just after dawn on the morning of the festival.

"Is it too cold?" asked the One, feeling pleasure as the ritual of the cooling time began.

"It is not too cold," said the Second, shaking leaves around the room, their sweet, sharp odor clinging to the One's throne. For the moment, in her tranquil state, the smell was simply a contrast to the calm odor that she had lived in all year.

"Is it not cold enough?" she asked her Second.

"It is cold enough," answered the Second, crumbling the leaves between her many limbs, scattering the pieces all around in a ranging disarray that would have been an outrage to the One on any other day of the year.

"When it is cold enough, but not too cold, then we must leave this place, as we leave all that we know from the year past, and go to make new life in a new place," said the One.

The odor of the leaves was becoming disturbing. The One knew she could not stay in her room much longer. Knowing this, and remembering that it happened every year this way, did not prevent her from beginning to feel irritated.

She stretched her limbs and slowly pressed herself up and out of the soft throne. How long had it been since she had last left this room? Or even her throne? The cold was a heavy blanket on her thoughts, and she could not remember.

Two Seconds were at her side, ones she did not recognize, which was good. At half her size, she could hurt them if she thought them too familiar. And the way she felt now, she might have hit them just because of the smell of the leaves, which was now so thick in the room that she wondered if she might become sick from it.

"We go," the Seconds chorused, encouraging her. She managed to step down from the throne and walk, leaning on her Seconds.

Out they went, from the room in which the One had lain comfortably all year, to the long tented hall that led to the arena. As they stepped out into the bright sunlight, the world seemed a simple, white place, every rock and plant covered in snow and ice. The One saw rainbows in the cracks of white, and deep red in the few spots of shadow.

They escorted the One to her winter throne, which was not at all soft, and this did not improve her mood. Knowing that the throne was hard for the purpose of keeping her awake through the long festival did not help.

Around her in a large circle, above the arena floor, sat all her many sisters, most of whom she would recognize if she looked closely at them, so she did not. On the ground below, at the edges of the floor, huddled the silks.

At that moment the One did not care about the silks, did not care about the snow and ice, did not even care about the males who now would be waking and beginning to call to her from inside their soft nests. What she felt more than anything was an overwhelming sense of outrage, that she should have been forced out of her soft room with terrible odors, forced into the bright sun, and for what? To discover that it was winter?

The One clicked her throat in anger and turned side to side, looking for the Seconds who had escorted her here. She had decided to kill them.

Instead, others were there now, though she did not remember them coming; they were older Seconds, ones she recognized. She was about to squeeze scent at them, to command them to die, and to bring others so that she could kill them all for having done this to her. She would breathe on them so that their bodies would decide to die; their eyes would darken and grow black and they would fall to the ground, their limbs twisting together tightly in death.

Then a scent grew from plates that her sisters held. Flower scents. The One felt sudden hunger, and she reached to take and taste the array of treats they had made for her. As she put each delightful edible in her mouth, her anger melted.

She tasted each of the flower foods, and wriggled at the ones she liked best. Other Seconds ran off and brought back more of her favorites. She tasted and ate, tasted and ate, and as she did her stomach grew full and her mood calm. After what must have been a very long time, she sat back on the hard throne.

"Let the festival of cooling begin."

One by one the many silks stepped into the ring, moving their feet slowly across the dark gray, heated floor. Some looked afraid, but the One and her sisters sent their reassurances to the silks, and the silks smiled and began to turn. Soon they were all turning, arms spread, turning and turning, cream silk fur flowing in the breeze, blurring their shapes as they danced.

As every sister watched, their heartbeats came into alignment with the One's heartbeat, their breath with her breath. Below, the silks twisted and whirled, their eyes wide, their breath steaming out into the cold air.

They met and separated in intricate patterns, held each other and released, pushing far away and coming back again. Every move was as graceful as if it had been planned and practiced for years.

The One found herself forgetting who and where she was, so entranced was she with the dance. It should go on, this dance; it should go on for many days.

When a silk fell, the others helped it to its feet, pulling it back into the dance. More fell. Each was helped to stand, to continue the dance.

When daylight failed and night came, the sisters kept breathing their delight down upon the dancers, who often faltered but never stopped. The cool white shapes moved with every bit of strength and passion they had. Those who were unable to stand lay on the heated floor, writhing, no less lovely for all their exhaustion.

The One and her sisters watched all night long as the silks danced, always breathing their reassurances and pleasures down upon the silks.

When dawn came, only two of the silks were still moving. All the silks had dark stains on their bodies; at their eyes, mouths, and dark smears across their fur. The two who moved lay on the ground, staring up at the lightening sky, their limbs trying to keep rhythm with the heartbeat of the One and her sisters. At last, these two were still as well.

The One felt a great joy. The new year had begun.

The One went to the males' nests, and there she stayed in darkness for a good number of days, until she was well-satisfied and all the males were dead.

The old throne room had been burned to the ground, as it was every year, the smell of crushed leaves having made it uninhabitable. In place of the old throne room another one had been built. She sat there now, on the new throne, which seemed softer than the old one, and smelled most reassuringly of nothing.

The Second who came to her today was very young, having only just reached adulthood at the new year with all of last year's children.

"You are strange to me," she told the Second.

"I am honored," said the Second, twitching with the awkwardness of her youth, which the One found charming.

But best was that the One felt her own clarity again. With the festival and mating over, she found she could think again, could reason, and did not feel the need to constantly drowse.

"Are the young silks healthy?" the One asked her Second.

"Yes. Healthy and growing, Great One."

"They mate next season. See to it that it is a fruitful season so that next year's dance is plentiful."

"Yes, Great One. And Great One, the voices from the sky—"

"The strangers."

"Yes. They wish to join us. They have asked again, now that the year is new. They say that they have studied our books, and that they come as strangers."

"When strangers meet, all benefit," the One said thoughtfully.

"Yes, Great One. They say that they have many hopes for mutual understanding between our kind and theirs."

The One clicked her throat. Her Second stepped away.

"Not too much understanding. There should not be too much understanding between strangers."

"No, Great One," the Second said, limbs twitching.

"They have much to learn yet."

The Second watched as the One stretched on her throne.

She was young, this Second, very young. She would learn, in time, what it was to be the One's Second. If she did not first become too familiar.

"I wonder what gifts the strangers will bring," the One said. "I wonder if they will dance."

The Day the Aliens Came

Robert Sheckley

D YING IS EASY, COMEDY IS HARD, AND HUMOROUS SF IS RARER THAN PTERANODON TEETH. ROBERT SHECKLEY HAS BEEN WRITING EXTRAORDINARY SCIENCE FICTION FOR MANY DECADES, AND HIS SPECIALTY HAS BEEN THE SHARP, SATIRICAL, AND FUNNY. A NUMBER OF HIS NOVELS AND STORIES HAVE BEEN MADE INTO MOTION PICTURES, IN PARTICULAR *THE TENTH VICTIM, THE PEOPLE TRAP,* AND *FREEJACK.*

ENRICO FERMI ONCE ASKED, "IF THERE ARE SO MANY ALIEN INTELLIGENCES IN THE GALAXY, WHY HAVEN'T THEY VISITED US?" SHECKLEY OFFERS A LIVELY WARNING ABOUT THE PERILS OF OUR PLANET BECOMING THE "IN" PLACE TO BE.

ONE DAY A man came to my door. He didn't quite look like a man, although he did walk on two feet. There was something wrong with his face. It looked as though it had been melted in an oven and then hastily frozen. I later learned that this expression was quite common among the group of aliens called Synesters, and was considered by them a look of especial beauty. The Melted Look, they called it, and it was often featured in their beauty contests. "I hear you're a writer," he said.

I said that was so. Why lie about a thing like that?

"Isn't that a bit of luck," he said. "I'm a story-buyer."

"No kidding," I said.

"Have you got any stories you want to sell?"

He was very direct. I decided to be similarly so.

"Yes," I said. "I do."

"OK," he said. "I'm sure glad of that. This is a strange city for me. Strange planet, too, come to think of it. But it's the city aspect that's most unsettling. Different customs, all that sort of thing. As soon as I got here, I said to myself, 'Traveling's great, but where am I going to find someone to sell me stories?' "

"It's a problem," I admitted.

"Well," he said, "let's get right to it because there's a lot to do. I'd like to begin with a ten thousand word novelette."

"You've as good as got it," I told him. "When do you want it?"

"I need it by the end of the week."

"What are we talking about in terms of money, if you'll excuse the expression?"

"I'll pay you a thousand dollars for a ten thousand word novelette. I was told that was standard pay for a writer in this part of Earth. This is Earth, isn't it?"

"It's Earth, and your thousand dollars is acceptable. Just tell me what I'm supposed to write about."

"I'll leave that up to you. After all, you're the writer."

"Damn right I am," I said. "So you don't care what it's about?"

"Not in the slightest. After all, I'm not going to read it."

"Makes sense," I said. "Why should you care?"

I didn't want to pursue that line of inquiry any further. I assumed that someone was going to read it. That's what usually happens with novelettes.

"What rights are you buying?" I asked, since it's important to be professional about these matters.

"First and second Synesterian," he said. "And of course I retain Synesterian movie rights although I'll pay you fifty percent of the net if I get a film sale."

"Is that likely?" I asked.

"Hard to say," he said. "As far as we're concerned, Earth is new literary territory."

"In that case, let's make my cut sixty-forty."

"I won't argue," he said. "Not this time. Later you may find me very tough. Who knows what I'll be like? For me this is a whole new frankfurter."

I let that pass. An occasional lapse in English doesn't make an alien an ignoramus.

I got my story done in a week and brought it in to the Synester's office in the old MGM building on Broadway. I handed him the story and he waved me to a seat while he read it.

"It's pretty good," he said after a while. "I like it pretty well."

"Oh, good," I said.

"But I want some changes."

"Oh," I said. "What specifically did you have in mind?"

"Well," the Synester said, "this character you have in here, Alice."

"Yes, Alice," I said, though I couldn't quite remember writing an Alice into the story. Could he be referring to Alsace, the province in France? I decided not to question him. No sense appearing dumb on my own story.

"Now, this Alice," he said, "she's the size of a small country, isn't she?" He was definitely referring to Alsace, the province in France, and I had lost the moment when I could correct him. "Yes, I said, "that's right, just about the size of a small country."

"Well, then," he said, "why don't you have Alice fall in love with a bigger country in the shape of a pretzel?"

"A what?" I said.

"Pretzel," he said. "It's a frequently used image in Synestrian popular literature. Synestrians like to read that sort of thing."

"Do they?" I said.

"Yes," he said. "Synestrians like to imagine people in the shape of pretzels. You stick that in, it'll make it more visual."

"Visual," I said, my mind a blank.

"Yes," he said, "Because we gotta consider the movie possibilities."

"Yes, of course," I said, remembering that I got sixty percent.

"Now, for the film version of your story, I think we should set the action at a different time of day."

I tried to remember what time of day I had set the story in. It didn't seem to me I had specified any particular time at all. I mentioned this.

"That's true," he said, "you didn't set any specific time. But you inferred twilight. It was the slurring sound of your words that convinced me you were talking about twilight."

"Yes, all right," I said. "Twilight mood."

"Makes a nice title," he said.

"Yes," I said, hating it.

"*Twilight Mood,*" he said, rolling it around inside his mouth. "You could call it that, but I think you should actually write it in a daytime mode. For the irony."

"Yes, I see what you mean," I said.

"So why don't you run it through your computer once more and bring it back to me."

When I got home, Rimb was washing dishes and looking subdued. I should mention that she was a medium-sized blond person with the harassed look that characterizes aliens of the Ghottich persuasion. And there were peculiar sounds coming from the living room. When I gave Rimb a quizzical look, she rolled her eyes toward the living room and shrugged. I went in and saw there were two people there. Without saying a word, I went back to the kitchen and said to Rimb, "Who are they?"

"They told me they're the Bayersons."

"Aliens?"

She nodded. "But not my kind of aliens. They're as alien to me as they are to you."

That was the first time I fully appreciated that aliens could be alien to one another.

"What are they doing here?" I asked.

"They didn't say," Rimb said.

I went back to the living room. Mr. Bayerson was sitting in my armchair reading an evening newspaper. He was about three or four feet tall and had orange hair. Mrs. Bayerson was equally small and orange-haired and she was knitting something orange and green. Mr. Bayerson scrambled out of my chair as soon as I returned to the room.

"Aliens?" I said, sitting down.

"Yes," Bayerson said. "We're from Capella."

"And what are you doing in our place?"

"They said it would be all right."

"Who said?"

Bayerson shrugged and looked vague. I was to get very accustomed to that look.

"But it's our place," I pointed out.

"Of course it's yours," Bayerson said. "Nobody's arguing that. But would you begrudge us a little space to live in? We're not very big."

"But why our place? Why not someone else's?"

"We just sort of drifted in here and liked it," Bayerson said. "We think of it as home now."

"Some other place could also feel like home."

"Maybe, maybe not. We want to stay here. Look, why don't you just consider us like barnacles, or brown spots on the wallpaper. We just sort of attach on here. It's what Capellans do. We won't be in the way.

Rimb and I didn't much want them, but there seemed no overpowering reason to make them go. I mean, they were here, after all. And they were right, they really weren't in the way. In some ways, they were a lot better than some of the other apartment-dwelling aliens we came to know later.

In fact, Rimb and I soon wished the Bayersons would be a little less unobtrusive and give a little help around the apartment. Or at least keep an eye on things. Especially on the day the burglars came in.

Rimb and I were out. The way I understood it, the Bayersons didn't do a thing to stop them. Didn't call the police or anything. Just watched while the burglars poked around the place, moving slowly, because they were so overweight, fat alien thieves from Barnard's Star. They took all of Anna's old silver. They were Barnardean silver thieves and their traditions went back a long way. That's what they told the Bayersons, while they robbed us, and while Mr. Bayerson was going through his eyelid exercises just like nothing at all was happening.

The way it all started, I had met Rimb in Franco's Bar on MacDougal Street in New York. I had seen a few aliens before this, of course, shopping on Fifth Avenue or watching the ice skaters in Rockefeller Center. But this was the first time I'd ever actually talked with one. I inquired as to its sex and learned that Rimb was of the Ghottich Persuasion. It was an interesting-sounding sexual designation, especially for someone like me who was trying to get beyond the male-female dichotomy. I thought it would be fun to mate with someone of the Ghottich Persuasion after Rimb and I had agreed that she was basically a her. Later I checked with Father Hanlin at the Big Red Church. He said it was OK in the eyes of the Church, though he personally didn't hold much with it. Rimb and I were one of the first alien-human marriages.

We moved into my apartment in the West Village. You didn't see a lot of aliens around there at first. But soon other alien people showed up and quite a few of them moved into our neighborhood.

No matter where they were from, all aliens were supposed to register with the police and the local authorities in charge of cult control. Few bothered, however. And nothing was ever done about it. The police and municipal authorities were having too much trouble keeping track of their own people.

I wrote stories for the Synestrian market and Rimb and I lived quietly with our house guests. The Bayersons were quiet people and they helped pay the rent. They were easygoing aliens who didn't worry much; not like Rimb, who worried a lot about everything.

At first I liked the Bayerson's ways, I thought they were easygoing and cool. But I changed my mind the day the burglars stole their youngest child, little Claude Bayerson.

I should have mentioned that the Bayersons had a baby soon after moving in with us. Or perhaps they had left the baby somewhere else and brought it in after they'd taken over our spare bedroom. We were never really clear on where the aliens came from, and their babies were a complete mystery to us.

The way the Bayersons told it, the kidnapping of little Claude was simple and straightforward. It was "Good-bye, Claude." "Good-bye, Daddy." When we asked them how they could do that, they said, "Oh, it's perfectly all right. I mean, it's what we were hoping for. That's how we Bayersons get around. Someone steals our children."

Well, I let it drop. What can you do with people like that? How could they stand to have little Claude raised as a Barnardean silver thief? One race one day, another race another. Some aliens have no racial pride. I mean it was cuckoo.

There wasn't anything to do about it so we all sat down to watch the TV together. All of us wanted to see the Savannah Reed show, our favorite.

Savannah's main guest that evening was the first man ever to eat a Mungulu. He was quite open about it, even somewhat defiant. He said, "If you think about it, why should it be ethical to eat only stupid creatures, or deluded ones? It is only blind prejudice that keeps us from eating intelligent beings. This thought came to me one day recently while I was talking with a few glotch of Mungulu on a plate."

"How many Mungulu make up a glotch?" Savannah asked. She's no dummy.

"Between fifteen and twenty, though there are exceptions."

"And what were they doing on a plate?"

"That's where Mungulu usually hang out. Accumulate, I should say. You see, Mungulu are plate-specific."

"I don't think I know this species," Savannah said.

"They're pretty much unique to my section of Yonkers."

"How did they get there?"

"They just pretty well showed up on my plate one night. First only one or two glotch of them. They looked a little like oysters. Then more came so we had the half dozen or so it takes to generate a halfway decent conversation."

"Did they say where they were from?"

"A planet called Espadrille. I never did quite catch where it was, quadrantwise."

"Did they say how they got here?"

"Something about surfing the light-waves."

"What gave you the idea of eating the Mungulu?"

"Well, I didn't think about it at all at first. When a creature talks to you, you don't right away think of eating him. Or her. Not if you're civilized. But these Mungulu started showing up on my plate every night. They were pretty casual about it. All lined up on the edge of my good bone china, on the far side from me. Sometimes they'd just talk to each other, act like I wasn't even there. Then one of them would pretend to notice me—oh—it's the Earth guy—and we'd all start talking. This went on every night. I began to think there was something provocative about the way they were doing it. It seemed to me they were trying to tell me something."

"Do you think they wanted to be eaten?"

"Well, they never said so, not in so many words, no. But I was starting to get the idea. I mean, if they didn't want to be eaten, what were they doing on the edge of my plate?"

"What happened then?"

"To put it in a nutshell, one night I got sick of horsing around and just for the hell of it I speared one of them on the end of my fork and swallowed it."

"What did the others do?"

"They pretended not to notice. Just went right on with their conversation. Only their talk was a little stupider with one of them missing. Those guys need all the brain power they can come up with."

"Let's get back to this Mungulu you swallowed. Did it protest as it was going down?"

"No, it didn't even blink. It was like it was expecting it. I got the feeling it was no cruel and unusual punishment for a Mungulu to be ingested."

"How did they taste?"

"A little like breaded oysters in hot sauce, only subtly different. Alien, you know."

After the show was over, I noticed a bassinet in a corner of our living room. Inside was a cute little fellow, looked a little like me. At first I thought it was little Claude Bayerson, somehow returned. But Rimb soon put me wise.

"That's little Manny," she said. "He's ours."

"Oh," I said. "I don't remember you having him."

"Technically, I haven't. I've delayed the actual delivery until a more convenient time," she told me.

"Can you do that?"

She nodded. "We of the Ghottich persuasion are able to do that."

"What do you call him?" I asked.

"His name is Manny," Rimb said.

"Is 'Manny' a typical name from your planet?"

"Not at all," Rimb said. "I called him that in honor of your species."

"How do you figure?" I asked

"The derivation is obvious. 'Manny' stands for 'Little Man.' "

"That's not the way we generally do things around here," I told her. But she didn't understand what I was talking about. Nor did I understand her explanation of the birth process by which Manny came into being. DDs, Deferred Deliveries, aren't customary among Earth people. As far as I could understand it, Rimb would have to undergo the actual delivery at some later time when it would be more convenient. But in fact we never got around to it. Sometimes it happens like that.

Manny lay in his crib and ooed and aaed and acted like a human baby would, I suppose. I was a pretty proud poppa. Rimb and I were one of the first viable human-alien intermatings. I later learned it was no big deal. People all over the Earth were doing it. But it seemed important to us at the time.

Various neighbors came around to see the baby. The Bayersons came in from their new room which they had plastered on the side of the apartment house after molting. Mrs. Bayerson had spun all the construction material out of her own mouth, and she was some kind of proud I want to tell you. They looked Manny up and down and said, "Looks like a good one."

They offered to baby-sit, but we didn't like to leave Manny alone with them. We still didn't have a reliable report on their feeding habits. Fact is, it was taking a long time getting any hard facts about aliens, even though the federal government had decided to make all information available on the species that came to Earth.

The presence of aliens among us was responsible for the next step in human development, the new interest in composite living. You got tired of the same old individualism after a while. Rimb and I thought it could be interesting to be part of something else. We wanted to join a creature like a medusa or a Portuguese man of war. But we weren't sure how to go about it. And so we didn't know whether to be pleased or alarmed when we received our notification by mail of our election to an alien composite life-form. Becoming part of a composite was still unusual in those days.

Rimb and I had quite a discussion about it. We finally decided to go to the first meeting, which was free, and see what it was like.

This meeting was held at our local Unitarian Church, and there were almost two hundred people and aliens present. There was a lot of good-natured bewilderment for a while as to just what we were supposed to do. We were all novices at this and just couldn't believe that we were expected to form up a two hundred person composite without prior training.

At last someone in a scarlet blazer and carrying a loose-leaf binder showed up and told us that we were supposed to be forming five unit composites first, and that as soon as we had a few dozen of these and had gotten the hang of morphing and melding, we could proceed to the second level of composite beinghood.

It was only then that we realized that there could be many levels to composite beings, each level being a discrete composite in its own right.

Luckily the Unitarian Church had a big open space in the basement, and here is where we and our chimaeric partners fit ourselves together.

There was good-natured bewilderment at first as we tried to perform this process. Most of us had had no experience at fitting ourselves to other creatures, so we were unfamiliar with for example, the Englen, that organ of the Pseudontoics which fits securely into the human left ear.

Still, with help from our expert (the guy in the scarlet blazer) who had volunteered to assist us, we soon had formed up our first composite. And even though not everything was entirely right, since some organs can fit into very different types of human holes, it was still a thrill to see ourselves turning into a new creature with an individuality and self-awareness all of its own.

The high point of my new association with the composite was the annual picnic. We went to the Hanford ruins where the old atomic energy place used to be. It was overgrown with weeds, some of them of very strange shapes and colors indeed. There was a polluted little stream nearby. We camped there. There were about two hundred of us in this group, and we deferred joining up until after lunch was served.

The Ladies' Auxiliary gave out the food, and they had a collection point just beyond, where everyone put in what they could. I dropped in a Synestrian bill that I had just been paid for a novelette. A lot of people came around to look at the bill and there was a lot of ooing and aahing, because Synestrian bills are really pretty, though they're so thick you can't fold them and they tend to make an unsightly bulge in your pocket.

One of the men from the Big Red composite cruised over and looked at my Synestrian bill. He held it up to the light and watched the shapes and colors chase each other.

"That's mighty pretty," he said. "You ever think of framing it and hanging it on the wall?"

"I was just about to think about that," I said.

He decided he wanted the bill and asked me how much I wanted for it. I quoted him a price about three times its value in USA currency. He was delighted with the price. Holding the bill carefully by one corner, he sniffed at it delicately.

"That's pretty good," he said.

Now that I thought about it, I realized that Synestrian money did have a good smell.

"These are prime bills," I assured him.

He sniffed again. "You ever eat one of these?" he asked me.

I shook my head. The notion had never occurred to me.

He nibbled at a corner. "Delicious!"

Seeing him enjoying himself like that got me thinking. I wanted a taste myself. But it was his bill now. I had sold it to him. All I had was bland old American currency.

I searched through my pockets. I was clean out of Synestrian bills. I didn't even have one left to hang on my wall back home, and I certainly didn't have one to eat.

And then I noticed Rimb, melding all by herself in a corner, and she looked so cute doing it that I went over to join her.

IV

WIN, LOSE, OR DRAW

Gnota

Greg Abraham

GREG ABRAHAM LIVES IN PORTLAND, OREGON, ALONG WITH A DISPROPORTIONATE NUMBER OF OTHER CONTRIBUTORS TO THIS ANTHOLOGY. HE IS WORKING "FULL STEAM AHEAD" ON A NOVEL. "GNOTA" IS ONE OF HIS FIRST FICTION SALES.

THAT BEING THE CASE, WE ALL HAVE REASON TO BE ENVIOUS: "GNOTA" IS A WONDERFUL EXAMPLE OF NEAR-FUTURE SPECULATION, QUIET YET INSISTENT, AND PERFECTLY BELIEVABLE. IT ALSO HAS AN ENDING I FIND MELVILLEAN. BEWARE: "GNOTA" MAY HAUNT YOU FOR YEARS TO COME.

BRIGHT HUNTER LOW in the west, Orion refused to be chased away by dawn over Makedonija. Pablo remembered another night, three months ago. Orion had been turning a somersault over the Andes, home. That October, full of springtime and dreams, seemed impossibly far away. But right there, like an extension of the Hunter's belt, one of the orbital colonies still beckoned.

To the east the horizon took on bands of dusky green and swarthy red. Pablo's thoughts began to drift, and he imagined the taste of cinnamon in his morning coffee.

"Marc!" he called loudly. A veteran in the Coalition Peace Force, Marc was Pablo's best friend. From Reims, Marc spoke an easy, slangy German that Pablo scrabbled to understand. He was always telling Pablo that their patrols in Skopje were a dangerous farce, that the Coalition Peace Force was just a puppet for the German Hegemony that used Makedonija as a buffer to keep the Islamic Compact at bay. But it paid better than anything back home, Marc always added, willing to bite the hand that fed him but not ready to leave it bleeding.

Pablo turned a corner, went back up a street, his stunner ready as he searched the doorways of Skopje, shrunken by the century of Terror, and before that a century of wars.

He stopped, tried to be stern as he shook Marc awake. He looked so tired, asleep in his gray service coat, the CPF insignia bright in the darkness of the doorway, like his short blond hair. Marc was small, always smirking at Pablo, always hungry, always trying to show him the ropes.

"*Morgen*," Pablo called out, laughing kindly as Marc leapt to his feet.

"Shit, I'm cold." He huddled against the wall.

"Coffee? That cafe on the way back to the base?"

"Glad to see you're corruptible. Coffee, yes." Marc rubbed his mittened hands together.

Corruption? Since Pablo had joined the CPF and left Cuzco, discipline had been next to nil. Further evidence that they were just "dogmeat," as Marc put it, there to prod Muslim fundamentalists back toward moderate Turkey, from where they'd been driven.

Sauntering toward the cafe, Pablo watched the last of the stars blink out. For all its beauty over grim Skopje, dawn made him sad. It reminded him that he was no closer to the colonies. Europe down here, so far from home, was just supposed to be a step on the way.

They slouched over coffee. Marc's eyelids were still heavy. Every blemish stood out like an injury on his pale skin. His teeth looked brittle . . . his life itself felt somehow brittle to Pablo, perhaps like all of Europe. But sometimes Marc, too, talked about the colonies. Despite his constant sleepiness, a spark would ignite that reminded Pablo of his own hopes to work and build where things might not be torn down again. Marc's eyes lit up as they imagined the tethered assemblies, immense spiderwebs full of manufacturing and invention.

As if suddenly caught by the realization of where they were, Marc straightened. "Let's go. Almost oh-seven hundred." Pablo saw it, how they both got distracted by their dreams. Marc had spent much of his adolescence laboring in the Champagne plains and had no fond memories of it. Orphaned young, he seemed to have few good memories at all, which saddened Pablo. But there were a few. Marc sometimes spoke of an abandoned church in Reims, ancient and crumbling, but full of purple twilight. "Now, if the colonies are like that, only new . . . !" Marc told him once, and the spark in his eyes had burned brightly.

As they hurried, Pablo sighed at the sun's slight warmth. The Skopje streets—battered by a history of war and plague—were gilded with a bright patina. He noticed a young woman coming up behind them, her gait brisk despite a heavy sack swinging at her side. Her baggy trousers and scarf fluttered in the morning wind, and he admired her from behind as she overtook them. She walked so happily compared to most of the sullen and frightened Muslim women. He lingered in front of a shop, in love, summoning again the quick view he'd gotten of her dark good looks.

The young woman cried out abruptly when she spotted one of her fellow nationals farther up the street. Her tone softened, but her gestures became frantic as she turned to Marc, uttered a phrase or two. Frozen where he was, a little jealous now, Pablo saw that she wanted Marc to hold her sack. For just a moment! her shoulders pleaded, slight bones tensing bird-like into a bow when Marc obliged. As the woman fled, one of the handles tore away from the sack. Easing the load downward, Marc squatted to secure it.

The explosion led with neither light nor darkness. They punched in tandem, and Pablo never heard a thing.

"He's alert. Aren't you, Mr. Mamani?" The voice called from a smear of light that coalesced into a matronly nurse. Nothing hurt, or they might have given him something, drugs could blur like this, and Pablo smiled. "Is she okay?"

"Who?" a man's voice asked from behind Pablo's head, a long way, so far it made him think of home.

"Is the girl okay?"

"We'll hold the foil here, Mr. Mamani, and you just need to sign. If I put the stylus in your hand, it won't be any trouble at all. Doctor, explain it to him again. Mr. Mamani—"

"Private Mamani," Pablo corrected her.

The doctor intruded, "We need you to sign. We've had no luck getting your files from the CPF. Contacted your home town up in Arequipa, but there's some delay. We need the release to waive litigation in the event of . . . death, complications, or violation of religious taboos. You understand? We know signed releases are already in your records. This is exactly the same thing."

"Taboo?"

"Interspecific gene transfer."

"What are you going to do? Is she okay?"

"We're not going to do anything except take a little of your tissue for some transgenic repair later."

"Transgenic?"

"Doctor, you're frightening him." The nurse touched Pablo's face and he focused on her other hand goaded the stylus into his palm. Shoving the clipboard near, the doctor fanned several layers of foil, matte and indestructible, a permanent record . . . this must be serious . . . space pitched and yawed as Pablo's hand floated toward the documents. Then the doctor's cuff encroached again. "Look at the light. Yes, like that. You won't feel a thing. Just watch the . . . there we go. Corneal tissue, Mr. Mamani, that's all we need. Thank you."

"Private Mamani," he reminded the cuff.

But the doctor was already a stream of white out the door.

"Thank you," the nurse echoed.

"Is she okay?" Pablo clutched his fear for the Muslim girl as he felt himself going to sleep.

Mamá,

Once again, please excuse this, text only, but like I said before, full-service terminals are hard to find here and much more expensive than at home. Besides, I haven't shaved and you wouldn't want to see me. There's nothing for you to worry about, but a few days ago I had a small accident and was in the hospital for a while. This may give me a chance to see a little bit of Europe. Isn't it funny how things work out? Here only a few weeks and already I get furloughed.

Pablo stepped away from the full-service terminal in Sarajevo station after it debited his card. The mag-lev would leave for Athinai in a few minutes.

Discharged from the hospital yesterday, Pablo had bought new clothes, including a baggy sweater, gray and blue that reminded him of his uniform. It looked good with his service coat.

A few days ago I had a small accident . . . it had been two weeks and his ribs still ached. Everything ached. Everything, body and soul. While he'd been signing his releases, his captain had stopped by. The officer handed him a small ivory-colored box. Plastic. From an envelope he took a sheet of official-looking foil, CPF blue. Pablo read the data: Marc Landrieux. Age: 22. Next of Kin: None. Contact in Case of Emergency: Private Pablo Mamani, Coalition Peace Force. Here was a little money and a box of ashes from a free cremation. Pablo had held it in just one hand even after the captain left, wondering where he could put such a thing.

A person. And with a passion he'd never known before, Pablo had hated. He hated the beautiful young woman who had wanted them *both* killed.

He got on the mag-lev and slouched so that nobody could see his chest pack beneath the sweater. He was always aware of the pack's light weight, awake and in his dreams, the ones that had started the night after his doctor had explained what happened. *A small accident . . .* The dreams were like reality, except the Skopje street was warm, and the beautiful Muslim woman had lingered and turned to smile at him. The bomb detonated slowly. A streak of white broke loose, hardened into a fragment of Marc's fibula that speared through Pablo's chest—just as the doctor had explained—through his heart. The dream always ended with the weight of the pack that now helped him stay alive. *You wouldn't want to see me . . .* The medics had prevented brain death until they flew him into Sarajevo. The facial burns had been easy enough to treat, so he looked fine. And the nurses assured him that nobody could see a thing beneath his clothes.

Marc had died instantly. Is that why I want to hide, Pablo wondered, because I survived, because I stopped to look, because I *wanted* her? Local police had caught the woman. A lieutenant from the base had tried to cheer him up with a story about how the cops had beat the hell out of her.

Pablo had wanted to turn away when he heard it, hide even then, but the chest pack hadn't been fitted yet, so there were too many tubes shunting in and out of his chest, arms, groin. That afternoon he'd been a monster, with fluid-filled tentacles, whispering machines, and an empty chest. The woman had looked so alive. Even now Pablo wondered . . . maybe he wasn't.

The doctors had installed a temporary artificial heart. A real heart will be better than a machine, Pablo reminded himself, especially since I'm young. But the real one won't be available for months. All of this to protect my cardio-pulmonary system. I've heard it over and over again. What it means is that part of the machine is left outside of me, so I'm saddled with this chest pack.

Not forever. But sometimes every minute is forever.

Every time he moved, breathed, tried to rest, even undid his fly to piss, the pack was there below his chin, pressing, telling him that his life depended on it, that he wasn't good for much as a soldier, either on earth or in space. The Muslim woman had taken away his dream of life in the colonies.

But maybe not forever.

The mag-lev eased above the rail and accelerated.

Why the bombing? Was it because they were just "dogmeat," pushing around "dark" people—who were lighter than Pablo himself—pointlessly pushing them back from a continent depopulated by wars and plagues? If that was true, maybe the bomb had damaged his heart in a way the doctors couldn't fix, not with an artificial one, not with a real, transgenic one. He started to breathe harder. His pulse quickened . . . after a slight delay.

Night came and eventually he dozed. Later he watched the countryside through his window. The century of Terror, with its plagues and climatic disruption, had destroyed whole peoples. Big cities, like Athinai, fell the hardest. Her skeletal suburbs, half stripped and totally overgrown, made room now for small farms. Eventually more light cheered the scene, along with full-scale demolition and reconstruction. The mag-lev pulled into Orfeos Station. Doors opened and the midnight chill had him buttoning his coat.

He'd retrieved his backpack—for all its size, so free compared to what he wore on his chest—and started in the direction where the neon looked brightest. Before he cleared the station, he heard a woman calling out.

Pablo fought back his dread, grabbed it like a bucking and impossibly quick llama, knew it must not win or it might drag him off anywhere. He stopped, turned, and saw that she was old, her gray hair tucked haphazardly beneath a scarf. Black coat, dark eyes, pockmarked skin. She'd seen the Terror, and now those experienced, yellowed eyes raked him while Greek that he couldn't understand burned his ears. He shrugged, shook his head no. Her German came much thicker, "You want to get your head bashed in? Your throat slit? Get rid of the insignia! You should have left the patches with whoever you stole the coat from . . . stupid boy!"

He tried not to respond, shook his head in another uncomprehending *no*. She cared about him, but how would she react if she knew that the coat was his? And why couldn't it be? Because he was out of uniform? Or because he was dark like her, like the Muslim girl? The Muslim . . . he didn't want to think about her beauty, because its memory increased his fear. That beauty had betrayed him, had helped him betray himself.

The woman dropped her totebag and seized him by the arm with a grandmother's anger. She rummaged in the tote for . . . a small knife. Pablo flinched; she barked at him again and cut thread on his shoulders. Such an act of friendship . . . Pablo squatted to make her work easier. But he caught her wrist when she reached for the patch on his chest. She cursed, grabbed the coat again. When her hand came to rest against the chest pack, she didn't even seem to notice.

The insignia lay in the street. She kicked them away, slapped his cheek lightly—still dissatisfied with his stupidity?—then found her tote and strode on.

Pablo stood numbly in the face of her kindness and contempt. In Makedonija, he told the darkness, a hole got torn in my chest; in Athinai for five minutes, and you tear away any evidence of my being a soldier.

You think that I'm like you, he wanted to cry, *like the past.*

His heart thudded eerily and he felt trapped, by Orfeos, by the world. Farther along signs glowed in Greek, Turkish, German, Pinyin. No hostels tonight. He needed the privacy of his own room. He entered a cheap-looking hotel with a sign that said it catered to Hegemony tourists.

The room was fairly decent. Wooden composite flexed beneath his steps. Glue had once held something down—perhaps carpet or tile—but now a clear resin strengthened the floor and that was good enough. Plumbing at one time, but everything had been removed and the pipes capped, except for a small sink. Down the hall was a bathroom.

A solar wing-and-battery unit jutted from the side of his window and powered the dim lights. In the distance rose a truncated hill, its slopes and mesa-like summit bright with clubs. "Best nightlife in Europe," the clerk had told him. *"Acropolis,"* Pablo murmured. Every name in Greek meant something. Acropolis? You could buy flatscreen or virch programs that showed ancient buildings standing there.

He left his clothes on until he returned from the bathroom. Sweater and undershirt came off last. The mirror over the dresser reflected the chest pack, not much more than a centimeter thick, no bigger than his hand. The white plastic housing made it look like the box that held Marc's ashes. And the harness only made things worse. His shoulders itched beneath the ocher fullerene weave. The pack analyzed hormone levels, respiration, adjusted heart rate accordingly, secreted hormones of its own. If his white cell count told his body to run a fever, the pack's computer understood, and he'd have a shallower, quicker pulse. He could live normally . . . and whenever the pack couldn't compensate quickly enough, it would sound an alarm to warn him.

Disgusted, he flicked off the lights and went back to the window. He could go home to Arequipa tomorrow and wait for his heart. Live out his life somewhere in the Andean Confederation, where people spoke nimble Spanish or Quechua, where things were always getting a little better. He could resume his education on the net or in realschool, and someday soon the Confederation would have its own consortia, and they, too, would build more orbital colonies. Someday. Because the earth, even the vigorous Andes, was frail. Why did home equal failure? Nobody, nothing would say it except the hole in his chest. Damn, there *wasn't* any hole, not a physical one. Still, the real hole, the one only he could measure, got bigger all the time. As if Europe wanted him to be an empty shell, maybe like Europe itself. But his emptiness—and the continent's—was paradoxically full, heavy with layers of memory or meaning that couldn't quite surface.

Urgency gripped the emptiness and made his pulse race . . . a beat too late. At the end of the hall was a public terminal. He yanked his pants and sweater back on. It was late, but hospitals operated around the clock.

In the nearly dark hall, Pablo stood at the console and touched options on the screen. Forget the vid, but he selected voice and text—that would make it seem serious. Mamá always confirmed her important calls with hardcopy. Information found the number and connected him.

The hospital's smart asked him what he required.

Pablo wondered how he could say it: confirmation that his future hadn't unraveled. "Can you tell me where you get the transgenic organs?"

The smart paused, then informed Pablo he was being connected to a lab.

"Why?" A man's voice, a real person. Machines were never that terse.

"I was just discharged yesterday. You can look up my records. My name's—"

"Right here, Pablo. System picked it up from your debit card."

"I don't know . . . I wanted . . . how's my transplant doing? Where are they going to get it?"

"Grow 'em all over. What are they fixing? Says here . . . shit . . . no wonder you're edgy." The German had a Slavic accent, humor warming the slow, broad vowels. "My dad lost his liver last year when twenty-three-LV made him start rejecting his own tissue . . . picked it up from some venison. Cardiac contract work . . . a research farm in a place called Vansbro, Svealand Autonomous State. You're looking at seven or eight more months. Those Swedes do real good work, but too bad it's not something without any moving parts. They're doing that in vats now, near Dresden. Hey, I should probably get back to work, but thanks for talking. Anything you want to know, call. Here's the lab number. That'll debit us. I'm usually here alone. Name's Dovic."

"Thanks." Pablo signed off.

Somebody to talk to . . . it helped. Was it the chest pack that frightened him most, or the loneliness? It was so easy to believe he'd never be close to anybody again.

Returning to his room, he undressed for good and got into bed. It was still hard to rest on his back. Rolling onto his stomach, he slipped the pillow down to his chest. Fatigue soon looped around him, tied him to the settling weight of sleep.

After a few days he moved to a hostel and began to acquaint himself with the poorer parts of the Acropolis district after dark.

March, brittle and often cold, gave way to April, warmer and more yielding, except for the occasional storms. He mastered Athinai's inexpensive pleasures. But the chest pack allowed loneliness—as it had allowed fear—a new point of entry.

At night it was easy to find girls who'd deal with him on his terms. Sometimes they embarrassed him, whispering that he shouldn't be afraid, not guessing what he really feared, that they'd discover the chest pack or that his own excitement would trigger a warning. The alleys, even the doorways if it was late enough, gave him an excuse to keep his coat on. The girls praised his Incan features. But afterwards the emptiness seized him, sometimes left him more afraid than when he'd started out that evening.

Tonight sex just made him more restless. He diverted down a narrow street and searched for a place to settle in to have some coffee. A boy followed, light and dark among the neon and shadows, as angular as a mountainside or rocky beach. Pablo knew this game, wasn't interested. But hustlers drank coffee, too, and Pablo's loneliness was deep tonight. When he sat down at a cafe table, open to the spring air, the boy joined him, looking bigger than he really was because of all those angles, face, elbows, knees.

Over their coffee Pablo told him, "That's all you're going to get."

"Then that's all I want. My name's Georgios." As much Turk as Greek, Georgios had bad teeth like the rest of the Europeans. His smile addressed necessity and desire all at once. "Where are you from?"

"Arequipa."

Georgios's eyes asked the question again.

"The Andean Confederacy."

"Why are you in Athinai?" Mockery—of whom?—lit up Georgios's eyes. The cuffs of his shirt were dirty.

Pablo shrugged and looked away. They drank their coffee in a silence that protected his dreams of the colonies. The quiet presence eased his loneliness more than any words could.

"You don't really belong here." Georgios's eyes focused on some middle distance as he spoke. "I've seen you before in the last few weeks . . . you're so handsome . . . and you don't belong here. The Germans come to do things they're afraid they can't do at home . . . it's the only reason me and Athinai still exist." He slouched in the chair and cradled his coffee in his lap, gazed down into the cup. "I wonder what'll happen when the Germans go broke . . . I hear the Austral-Chinese are building colonies of their own. I'd like to see them run the Germans off. Then again, it would always be somebody. I belong in Athinai. You don't."

A tightness settled at the base of Pablo's throat, just above the chest pack. "You could be a soldier," Pablo said. "The CPF will be on those Australian colonies, too."

"So that's why you wear that ugly coat sometimes! You want to be a soldier? I sell my hide by the night, thank you, not the year."

"It's not like that!" Pablo almost shouted. Doubt struck first, then the anger that came an instant late, that might have relied in some small way on the chest pack. This kid understood. Georgios's hunger made him smart. Europe was still going hungry. He'd seen it in Marc, in the girls, in all the ruins of a world improbably rich a hundred years ago . . . a terrible hunger that nobody could flee because it was the hunger of the *world* itself.

Georgios left soon after that, and Pablo stalked through the darkness. Nothing eased the doubt and the hurt, it just got later, night becoming a thick film of angry, tired moments.

He knew what he wanted when he found a public terminal in the lobby of a casino. He dropped his debit card into its slot and searched his pockets for the hardcopy from his last call to the hospital. It was like a talisman, evidence of his heart. He entered the number, got linked to the lab, voice only, but the price was right.

"Pablo Mamani! Play all night? Sleep all day? Yeah, you must be in Athinai!"

"You said to call if I had any questions." Pablo rested his head against the terminal, tried to breathe deeply. He felt his pulse racing. "What can go wrong? Right now, it's beating so fast you wouldn't believe it . . . the chest pack."

"Not much can go wrong with those units as long as you stop by a pharmacy once a month and have the cartridges replaced. See, those cartridges are full of gel blisters—"

"No," Pablo cut him off. "I mean, thanks, but the new one, the new heart in Vansbro, wasn't that it? Vansbro?"

"Scared, aren't you?" No scorn in those words. Dovic sounded like he cared. "See, there's this old part of the brain called the amygdala, and getting scared is part of its job. Your amygdala's telling the hypothalamus to crank out corticotropin-releasing hormone. That hormone tells the pituitary gland to spit out ACTH. It's like a relay race, because the ACTH tells the adrenal gland to dump a bunch of cortisol into your blood. Now, your chest pack's monitoring your blood chem, and when it tastes all that cortisol, those pumps *go to work*. Kick back. It's a great machine, but it doesn't know *why* you're scared."

I'm not sure why I'm scared either, Pablo told himself. I know I'll be good as new by the end of the year, and the colonies are waiting. The colonies that Marc never saw . . . that Georgios doesn't want to, because the Hegemony runs them like they run Europe. His fear spiraled again.

"What you need to do," Dovic told him, concern evident in that slow, Slavic accent, "is find yourself a nice Athinai girl and just curl up for a while. Physical contact does incredible things to your brain. You'll have your pack purring."

"Curl up? *I* don't even like to see myself naked." God, it felt good just to say it. Pablo felt his pulse get slower, lighter.

"Then what the hell, if you don't want to get laid, get some exercise. Maybe you *need* that pack to work overtime. Find a bike and go for a long ride."

Pablo's doctor had assured him that exertion was fine with a careful warm-up. "Maybe I will. A real long one. Thanks. Talk to you soon?"

"You've got the number. Need to sign off. The centrifuge is calling."

And Dovic was gone.

Leaning there, pocketing his card, then pulling it out and reinserting it, Pablo touched in the codes for information. A map of Europe. Overlaid now with a transportation grid. And now with elevations in color.

His account had been credited with his disability for April. Yes, a long ride. Back home he'd biked near Mt. Coropuña with his old heart. Even with this machine, he'd manage the roads he looked at now.

In the morning Pablo boarded a sleek mag-lev ferry. It glinted in spring sun, its Casimir engines silently drawing power from vacuum fluctuation. Zero point energy charged the tripole fields that let it fly free of any rail or road bed. Free. He knew his mag-lev repair, could even lay toroidal windings by hand if he had to. It perplexed him, made him angry that much larger versions of the same engines took people to the colonies, while the tiny version powering his chest pack kept him away.

Soon he was twenty meters above the Mediterranean. The ferry picked up passengers and vehicles in Kriti, arrived in Sicilia just before lunch, where the Italian transfers debarked. In the afternoon the mag-lev stopped at the southern end of Sardegna, then made Marseille just after nightfall.

The seaport was a much smaller and sleepier version of Athinai. Night sky faded a bit beneath the lights, but he could easily see Orion in the west. At home it meant the sadness and solace of autumn, but down here in Europe he felt the spring. The sea and stars bolstered his hopes as he searched for a cheap hostel.

The next day, he left Marseille on his new bike. Almost penniless, he didn't care. He knew he was alive.

In early May, Pablo stopped his bike near the town of Reims. The shadow of the Hegemony, so nearby, touched the spirit, weighed down everybody and everything—except for the cathedral, visible from all directions.

He'd spent nearly a month among the farmers in the sunny valleys of the Rhône and Saône. They were no different from those back home in Arequipa, just poorer, terribly poor as they fed the Hegemony to the east. Its presence made things harder instead of easier. The farmers struggled to replace their old generators, batteries, and photovoltaics—moody as the sun—with hydrogen tech, but they always wound up paying for propane or gasoline instead.

Pablo wondered in whose image the beautiful cathedral had been built. The Hegemony would rebuild Europe in its own image, and in its own time. While the town murmured sadly, the cathedral sang, and Pablo suddenly yearned to understand that music. Pedaling again, he drew closer to Reims.

I have survived, the cathedral told him. He felt its strength in his chest. What are dreams without the past? it asked. Before the Terror, before the wars, we wanted to reach the stars, it assured him with its towers, and it urged him to enter.

Marc had said the light was purple. And he might have called it silver.

It was both and neither. Many of the countless colored panes were missing, but afternoon sun shifted delicately amid the weightless ascent of stone, light streaking along the tracery, slowing around the piers, so that only the stars themselves might look farther away than the vault above. Pablo wandered the nave, felt himself stared at by a thousand carved faces, angelic, demonic, human, but all dreaming. This was Marc's home. In its beauty, maybe it was everyone's.

When Pablo left, the sun was very low. The song of the cathedral didn't fade behind his back. Stone, so mercifully cool and real, made all those centuries of dreaming almost bearable.

His heart—*his heart*—breaking, in the dusk amid stone and light, Pablo wanted to cry out, You make me ache for a home that doesn't exist. You take *earth* and use it to make my dream of the stars real for a moment. Here. And in that moment, I see that we're as fragile as our past, wherever we go. And as beautiful.

He found a cheap meal, which he lingered over to kill time. When he left, the night pressed close against him, insistent but gentle. Reims had none of Athinai's bright lights. Glancing up from time to time, he followed the celestial equator, marked constellations, counted the colonies. The cathedral had brought them closer. Tonight they were friends and no longer gods.

Retrieving his bike, Pablo rode to the mag-lev station, bought passage to Stockholm. He had to make the trip on a free-flyer via Flandre, because the only rail through the Hegemony was for freight. No roads, no passenger trains east. Anything to keep the poor out, Pablo supposed. The Terror had taught the Hegemony all it ever wanted to know about refugees.

He napped at the depot. It was a light sleep with sudden depths, brief dreams. He spoke to Marc in the cathedral, laughed with him among the saints and devils. The Muslim girl joined them, pleaded for their help, a look of dread in her eyes. She had been so afraid in the back of Pablo's mind, where he'd pushed her, hidden her. Now she fled the cathedral and they followed, full of desire, full of her urgency. She began to climb outside, gripped stone high above the arching portals. Finally she escaped gravity, and in her flight was peace.

Pablo awoke. Haunted by the girl and the cathedral, he found a locker for his backpack, and before he secured it, found Marc's ashes.

He got his bike and rode through the dark streets back to the cathedral, its outline looming, etched against the stars. The splendid west portals had a few lights shining on them, but that was all. Pablo found one of the doors unlocked.

He entered, smelled ancient stone, calcified, broken; a few strands of weak incandescent bulbs ran along the nave. The outdoor lights caught the blue and red of the windows and chased it in, small spears of color. Yes, earth itself had risen to become this place. But without sun, the nave spoke too much of generations forever lost.

Pablo went back out, stumbled along the south wall amid stone and lead, plastic and wood, finally found a bit of clear earth. He searched the southern sky, looked toward home, the top of the world. With his heel he dug a shallow hole.

A chunk of stone in his hand, he smashed the container open and emptied it. He let the grit and bits of incinerated bone cascade over his fingers. Despite his pain, he couldn't hate the Muslim girl. Perhaps for her all of Europe was a chest pack, letting her go nowhere, weighing against her heart. The cathedral, with its lost dreams and stubborn beauty assured him that people yearned to live—and struggle and die—for a good reason.

He pitched the container away and shoved earth back into the hole. He buried a part of himself with Marc, the part that *wanted* to hate forever. Rubbing his dusty hand against the cathedral wall, he hid his face in his palms and cried, tasting centuries of death and dreams.

Pablo was the only passenger to debark in the village of Vansbro. Stockholm had looked beautiful from the air, a mosaic of islands, docks, parks, but that was all he saw, with barely enough time to transfer to the much smaller mag-lev that brought him to Kopparbergs District.

After finding a place to stay, he got directions to the "farm," along with assurances that there was plenty of time to pedal round trip before nightfall. He set out, exhilarated until the chest pack's alarm began to hum. Finally so close to his new heart, was he tempting fate? A second warning, then a third, each higher in pitch than the last, but he didn't back off until he'd broken a sweat.

Had he arrived? It didn't look like a farm. Several buildings, low and white, spotlessly clean, glowed amber in the late sun. Pablo saw no one except a lean young woman with shimmering dark hair. Her lab coat took on the golden hues of the walls before she disappeared into a building. He hurried in her direction, leaped onto the porch and waited for the sensors to announce him.

She opened the door. A calm gaze sparkled from beneath heavy lids. Her skin was as fair as the Swedes, but the sturdiness of her features—and the nighttime beauty of her hair and eyes—suggested Turkish parentage, too. "I . . . my name . . ." and he saw that she understood the German, "is Pablo Mamani. The lab . . . it's a long story . . . they told me that a heart is being grown for me here. I wanted to see." The heat from his blushing face burned his forehead, even his ears.

She nodded as if the air was thick, as if it supported her chin when she let it drop slightly. "Mamani . . . I remember. I'm done with my work. The animals aren't really my worry, but yes, I can show her to you."

"Her?" asked Pablo.

"It'll make you no less the man." She blushed a little, too. "Luck of the draw. I create a chimeric immune system in several fertilized eggs . . . the transgenic organ contracts, I handle the engineering. The gene splicing is never perfect, but she comes surprisingly close. Almost perfect matching of the histocompatibility antigens. The other piglets will be used in research. Almost a *perfect* match!" She laughed warmly, clearly pleased, and started across the lawn.

He followed. She was perhaps twenty-five, and almost as tall as he. "My name's Pablo," he repeated.

"Pablo Mamani, Andean . . . I read the report carefully . . . interesting major histocompatibility complexes, probably because of your ancestry. It was the reason they couldn't take something off the shelf. With somebody as young as you, there's almost no tolerance for the stimulation of antibodies. You'll have that heart for a long time, so even where there's no chance of rejection, the tissues need to be matched closely enough to prevent graft arteriosclerosis. No scarring your arteries, Pablo."

His cheeks burned again because she already knew him so well. It took a minute, but he found the courage, "And what's *your* name?"

"Kristina Tornberg." Her half grin, almost hidden as she turned her head, suggested that he'd surprised her by caring.

They passed the buildings, and lawn became field, with shadows of birch and pine woven through a lazy, ruddy dusk unlike any he'd ever seen before. Kristina led him to a gray silocrete building as low and immaculate as the white ones.

They entered a brightly lit hallway. "The compound is as clean as the labs and almost as sterile. The animals have runs that get them outside, and they're very well cared for."

Pablo smelled the disinfectant and straw when Kristina opened a glass door. Choruses of squeals greeted him while he traveled down the corridor.

She ushered him up to a silocrete pen with stainless steel rails and whistled. A piglet, newborn-pink but big enough to be an armful, darted in from the yard, bouncing the rubber flap off her nose. Skidding in straw, she braced herself against the low wall and grunted. Pablo watched Kristina scratch the piglet's head, then took over.

"I guess I'm out here more than I think. I also do a lot of the lab work for the organ contracts. We're a small firm. Since she was a chimeric embryo, I had to keep an eye on her antigens, and watched maternal tolerance, too. And your little pig there's gnotobiotic . . . she doesn't have any acquired immunities that could cause problems for you."

Pablo backed away from the pen.

Kristina smiled. "Don't stop. She loves getting her back rubbed. They all do."

"I don't want to give her anything that might make her sick . . . you know?"

Kristina shook her head and laughed, brief music, a single note. "I should have been clearer, but recipients don't visit very often." She hesitated. "You're the one person in the world she can share germs with. She's *part* of you, remember? Or will be."

It caught Pablo right underneath the chest pack: the price of his dream would be this animal's death. When the doctor in Sarajevo had tried to make sure he'd understood, it had seemed so abstract. Genes coding the piglet's immune system had been replaced by his own when she'd been only a single cell, a fertilized egg. The placenta had sheltered her from her mother's "alien" antibodies, and after almost four months, she'd been delivered cesarean along with her littermates. "The heart will be ready in October?" he asked.

Kristina nodded and rummaged in a cabinet. "Near the end of the month."

Thoughts of a new heart suddenly embarrassed him almost as much as the chest pack. He rubbed the piglet's back again, finally lifted her up and cradled her against his chest—she certainly didn't mind the pack—her stiff legs jostling in the air. "What's her name?" he asked.

Kristina fed the piglet a small biscuit. "I call her Pig. But they're all Pig."

Pablo fingered the tag in the piglet's left ear, *2103-Mamani.* She grunted, happy with her biscuit as Pablo put her back down.

"What was the word?" he asked Kristina. "Gnoto . . . ?"

"Gnotobiotic?"

"*Gnota.* That's a good name for her." He wanted to cuddle the pig some more—such an important pig—but saw that Kristina had grown restless. "Well, I'd better go now?" Reluctant to leave, he made it a question.

They left the way they'd come, Pablo in the lead, sensing Kristina close behind him.

The sun had nearly set, its light redder amid the blue shadows. They crossed the fields in silence. Kristina seemed wistful, lost somewhere as she gazed downward. Eventually she pointed and told him, "The path is over there, but it's nice to walk like this, where you can hear the grass . . . I think so, anyway."

"Yes," murmured Pablo, though field had given way to the groomed lawns. He reined in his hope, summoned courage. "May I come visit again?"

"How long will you be in Vansbro?"

"I'm not sure . . . as long as I want to be. They tell me Lake Siljan is beautiful in the summer, and I have a bicycle. My time's pretty much my own until the surgery."

She paused in front of the lab. Back home in Arequipa night never fell this slowly. In the prolonged dusk, hesitant evening darkened her hair with indigo, touched her pale skin with rose.

Kristina took his hand in both of hers, almost as a doctor might . . . almost. She nodded. "Yes, come back. Whenever you can. As soon as you like."

And she slipped away from him into the lab.

He biked back to the village slowly, letting night fall on the unfamiliar road. His new heart had called him down here to Svealand, to Vansbro. Now it would hold him here. His heart . . . or Kristina? There was no point in feeling so much for a stranger. The girls in Athinai had never made him want to watch their every move and remember it forever. But Kristina wasn't a girl. She made *him* feel like a child, but in a way that wasn't bad. And what had she said? Come back whenever he could, as soon as he liked.

The stars appeared. He studied their beauty here. As if he'd never seen them before, they captured his mood, slowing him with a new yearning that was of the sky but not of space or the colonies.

In the following weeks Pablo often rode to Lake Siljan, a day away, to camp out; and summons came from both the government of Makedonija and the Coalition Peace Force. The young woman who had killed Marc would go to trial in August, and Pablo was to witness against her.

At times he forgot about her completely. At others, he imagined what a relief it would be to know that she'd get her own for what she'd done. But since he'd left Reims, she hadn't appeared anymore in his dreams.

July came and he spent more time at the lake. When in Vansbro, he made a trip every morning to feed Gnota and see Kristina, sometimes visited in the evenings, too.

Summer had spilled so much sun into the fields that they'd turned blond, whispering as he left them to cross the meticulous lawns. It was Saturday, and he'd come late. Almost lunchtime, and Kristina would have finished up her work by now. She'd talked about cycling with him to Lake Siljan, or renting one of the tiny mag-levs the Germans were making popular. He didn't find her in the lab, so he headed over to the residence where a few of the employees lived. Knocking lightly, he entered the sunny room.

Kristina greeted him with just her eyes. Closing the door behind himself, he went and sat at the table while she put down a second plate. "Gnota's growing so fast," he said, "but she always looks like a baby."

"Her strain's been juvenilized to help her organs retain the qualities of fetal tissue. Reduced antigenicity." Kristina touched his shoulder before she sat across from him, offering a piece of cheese. "Sometimes I'm jealous of Gnota."

Pablo looked into her eyes and understood part of what he'd risked in coming here to this continent, to this country with its lustrous summer, to this cool room on this warm day. It seemed simple now, this sequence that might take him as far from the colonies as anyone could be. The earth spoke in an alluring way here. Kristina's eyes glistened. He shouldn't talk about the pig, not during lunch, not today, even if Gnota was his life.

Kristina had slipped out of her lab coat before coming to the table. He admired the simple blouse, draping—but full of promise—across her lean shoulders and small breasts. Her body, like her language, was always full of purpose. After a while, nibbling a little of the cheese and fruit, sipping the afternoon coffee she'd brewed for them, he moved his plate out of the way and folded both his hands over one of hers. Resting his chin lightly atop his knuckles, he murmured, "You really do want to come to the lake with me, don't you?"

"It would be nice . . . sometime . . . before you go home." She stroked his hair, and he felt the warmth of her little finger as it slipped down to the base of his neck.

"Do you know why I don't . . ." and he couldn't imagine how a man would talk about these things.

Her hand lifted away from his neck like the geese that flew away from the huge lake north of here. She rose and came around the table, took him by the shoulders. Now the back of his neck knew the warmth of those breasts. He escaped his chair awkwardly and turned. Holding her, he felt her nudge him toward the other room.

"I don't want you to see me like this," he whispered.

"Like what? The pack? It's not important. It's only for a little while."

His arms were like springs, letting her press only so close. She stroked one of his forearms with her hand. "When I'm better." He let the words get muffled as he buried his face in her neck. But desire—and trust—already took hold of his ugliness and lessened it.

"When you're better, you'll be gone." She settled them both onto the edge of the bed, tipping back and tugging him with her. There was nothing forlorn in her tone. The words were like Gnota's body, warm though implying future pain.

His head rested near her chest, and he toyed with each of the buttons until he nuzzled between her breasts, summer to his nose, salt to his tongue that reminded him of things so long ago—so young—that he had no words for them. "I'm not sure that I'll want to go, not even when I'm better."

"There's nothing wrong with you, Pablo; and you'll be gone *before* the transplant . . . at the other end of the world." She knew he'd promised his mother that the surgery would occur in São Paulo. "And then the colonies," Kristina reminded him.

"No," he sighed as she escaped him, tugging his shoes from his feet. Then it was his turn to slip away from her, but she had hold of his trousers and shorts. He did her work for him, losing his pants.

It made them laugh. "You move like Gnota," she said, the smile dimming to a grin that still showed off the edges of her fine teeth. She slipped out of her skirt, nothing on beneath. The hair at her crotch was slight and black, another testament to her Turkish ancestors who'd come down to Sweden even before the Terror. Leaving the blouse draped about her shoulders, she began to raise his sweater over his head. She stroked his hair, pinched his ear lightly. "This is too warm . . . but we can leave the undershirt on."

Tenderly she was beside him, guided him to kneel over her. Again he nuzzled her, his back arching beneath her warm palms, his nose and his tongue running from below her navel toward her belly, along its warmth, until he had the taste of her breasts again, the taste of the salt between them. He kissed her brow that might be sleepy, her lips that might be pouting, her ear hot as the afternoon outside. He entered her with little skill and much love, drew deep breaths, letting them be a storm in her ear. The chest pack might make a noise; and he had no other language for the sun and the cool air on his back, for the warmth beneath him, more alive than the night, and more boundless than any other place that had caught his dreams.

August brought shorter evenings, warm and full of indigo shadows, like May's. The shadows were sleepy now, and twined across the straw-colored grass, turning it to silver.

Pablo went around to the back of the compound and whistled for Gnota. She'd grown so much that it was easy to stroke her white back without reaching. Dusk had its own language, made promises about the stars that would appear soon. Pablo fed Gnota an apple. Her snuffles and grunts told of her impatience and the pleasure she took in his visits. It was a language as eloquent as the evening's, full of special words for joy. Gnota shared her happiness, addressed her discontent when he was late or absent too much. The lowest of animals hungers, Pablo told himself, but you— and I—can suffer loss. You are a part of me, and you're sad when I'm gone too long . . . so I'm a part of you, too. He scratched her back as she finished her apple. "Brother and sister . . ." Dread of going to Sarajevo eased as Pablo recognized how welcome he was here.

Stroking Gnota, he understood how he needed something that would kill her. His hand stilled and she nudged him. "Sorry," he whispered, voice rough with regret. "Do you hope for things, too?" She must in some way. She could be disappointed.

And disappointment was the price of hope.

Stars in the warm evening, a palm wetted by a snout seeking another apple, that palm stroking rough bristle, warm too—the chest pack, a chilly burden—Pablo saw that death was not the imposition of pain, but the cessation of joy. The vision hurt with its message of waste.

What did the young Muslim woman in Sarajevo need so badly that she would kill? What joy had been stripped from her life that made her yearn for something at least as much as Pablo yearned to be free of his pack and go to the colonies? He remembered Athinai and Reims, remembered Marc, saw Europe turning its forgetfulness into new victims. He was one of those and sensed the terrifying bond with all the others, yesterday's . . . and tomorrow's.

He fought back scalding tears, and Gnota grew unusually still beneath his palm. Sister, he almost said aloud, I came down to Europe dreaming of some beautiful thing, the stars, and what will I do to you? How much joy's wasted here?

Pablo brought out a second apple for Gnota, and her grunts tousled the night.

Later he went to the apartment. Kristina let his silence be real, something poised between them for a while, then she played gently, made the silence smaller, urged him to love her, warm and strong, shy and still quiet in his undershirt.

A small lamp by the table turned her face to a shadowed landscape as he rested beside her. A sound, the beginning of a word . . . but she blinked, eyelids fluttering quick as a bird's wings. Finally she asked him, "Was it a mistake to come here? Should you go home after you leave Sarajevo?"

He shifted so that the bridge of his nose pressed against her jaw, and he felt his own breath trapped near her collarbone. "I don't know if it was wrong to come here, but wouldn't it be wrong not to come back?"

She sighed so deeply that it moved his thumb resting between her breast and her ribs. "Do you ever wonder what I think about Gnota?" she asked him.

With the bridge of his nose he nuzzled the side of her face.

Her hand eased him away as she laid her palm lightly on the chest pack. "I love you," she whispered, "and I want you to love yourself again." She reached for the base of the lamp. In the darkness she held him.

* * *

Kristina rode with him as far as Stockholm. There he met a military transport that took him through the Hegemony to Sarajevo. The next day another transport carried him to the courthouse's roof. As the heat stifled him, he watched the crowds gathering below. Inside the courtroom, mercifully cool, there was no public at all. His fear ebbed. He'd already lived this moment, this arrival, too many times. But it resembled none of those scenarios. The sterile courtroom made death simple.

The young Muslim woman was seated in front of him, and he didn't recognize her at first in her Eurostyle suit. But at one point she turned. Catching a better glimpse was all it took for him to know those bitter-brown eyes as seemingly innocent today as on that winter morning. Kristina's skin was much fairer, but she was no less beautiful than this woman. He saw it, suddenly, Kristina's beauty melded with all the darkness of his own people.

And in the same moment that he refused to let himself keep comparing this woman and Kristina, he remembered Gnota's brown eyes, her eager happiness. He knew that his life—as he *hoped* to live it—required Gnota's death, but he couldn't see what was to be gained by this woman's death, too. He would never forget her, and he was certain that later he'd rage at himself. But he'd lie, say he wasn't sure this was the same woman. Maybe she would live. And if she recognized that she'd been forgiven, could some joy return for her? After the beatings? He felt the terrible weight of his chest pack but couldn't blame her as he had before.

It cut into the depths of his soul: Gnota had come into existence because of this woman's violence . . . and soon Gnota would die because of his need.

No, the courtroom couldn't make right and wrong simple, nor life and death. In the end, what would the woman's execution mean? The cessation of what joy? What *dreams?*

As Pablo was led to the stand, he passed near her. She stared at him. Or had he been staring at her first? He couldn't be sure. Above her lip was a scar that hadn't been there last winter. Those eyes, the color of earth . . . they blazed with a single question, Why are *you* free?

He took a step toward her and wanted her to understand that she was a stranger; and so, of course, he couldn't make any accusations.

In harsh German she muttered, "You—pig!"

Pablo shook his head, disbelieving, staring at her.

She lunged. "Pig—you should die like!" Her own lawyer fired a stunner, and she crumpled, grabbing Pablo's arm. He staggered, and the tears he choked back became quiet, strangled laughter, full of shame for this body that she still wanted dead; full of hatred for this place, for this continent that changed him, for this hating world that swore *it* would never change. Never.

The woman's lawyer howled for a recess, better a postponement.

Pablo let himself be led from the courtroom, knowing he was part of this world and that he could never be the same.

Four days later the Muslim woman was sentenced to death, her lawyer unable to bar her confession.

Pablo never testified.

"Hey, Dovic, somebody said you moved to swing shift. Got a minute?"

"Sure. Just getting ready to have a bite to eat."

"Hang on," Pablo told him. He slipped his debit card into Kristina's terminal and coded for video. After a few seconds he saw Dovic, just slightly older than himself. Sandy-colored hair and thick downy brows—so many people our age, thought Pablo, so few who are old. He'd never seen his grandparents, and even his father had died in the last of the Plagues. The world is ours to rebuild. Does that make us poor or rich?

Dovic grinned. "You're a *kid!* Should've paid more attention to those records. No wonder you were scared. This says you're calling from Vansbro. You had to go see for yourself, huh?"

No, he wasn't a kid. "Only a couple weeks until the surgery. I called to say thanks. You're right. I was kind of scared."

"About the time they disconnect you from your box, you're gonna *really* sweat. Couple days before they split you open, they'll have you back on the tubes. Did they schedule the surgery here?"

He shook his head no.

"What the hell! Maybe a vet can do it there in Vansbro. But glad I got to see you. Hmm, a couple red lights are flashing . . . looks like the equipment needs to eat before I do. Say, when you get back up to the Andes, let's talk. The boy's gonna be old enough to travel soon, and me and my wife . . . mag-lev fares are getting cheaper every day. We're thinking about emigrating, you know? Skilled labor and everything, shouldn't be hard. *Too* skilled, sometimes! Shit, three reds . . ."

And Dovic ended it, leaving a blank screen and the afterimage of a big grin.

It faded in the apartment's twilight.

Pablo put on his jacket and left. He crossed the fields, let the cold afternoon move him to the compound's door.

With an eager squeal and a soft mouth, Gnota leaned against the wall of her pen and took the halved apple from his hand. Her snout pressed wet against his palm, whisked away as she lowered her fruit to the floor. He took the other half from his pocket, and soon he munched, too, braced against the rail and stroking Gnota's bristle. After a minute he kicked off his shoes and hoisted himself into the pen to sit on the silocrete and straw. Cool floor, warm air, the smells of disinfectant and feed mixed happily down here. He closed his eyes a while, let his sadness burn like a fever, rocked when Gnota butt-brushed him. To reach a hug around her took such a stretch now. Each time she felt the embrace, she slipped out of it, battered his arm to steal the rest of his apple.

Pablo held it between his teeth, playing as her snout met his mouth. Her saliva was as good as his, maybe better with all that gamma globulin. He reached under her belly, a hot, hard barrel, and drew her close.

She grabbed the apple, warm flesh, warmer breath, wet lips. Her grunts grew louder and part of the apple broke off, her hooves clattering on the silocrete. Pablo grunted, too, swallowed, sprang forward and tackled the pig, rolled her onto her side. She squealed, escaped from beneath him, circled, butted him.

"You're not as timid with her as with me." Kristina reached into the pen and had him by the hair. He scooted in her direction, pressed his lips against her hand. "But I love you, too," he whispered.

Gnota tried to knock him out of the way. Pulling himself up by the rail, he let himself be caught in Kristina's gaze.

Tomorrow he'd take a mag-lev to Stockholm, another to Madrid and then fly to São Paulo. He looked away. "Will they send her over, or just her . . . the heart?"

"It's not too late to have the surgery in Stockholm." Kristina helped him back across the rail. "I could be with you."

They had discussed this before. Every time they argued gently, newly. Kristina said she loved him, and he was as certain of this as of anything in his life. You must have the surgery in Stockholm, she always said. If you wanted it, Pablo, the CPF would discharge you, and you could work here, go back to school on the net or nearby.

But there were the colonies. He had wanted to help build a world with a sure future.

Had wanted. It said so much, and maybe that was why they could argue it again and again.

His arms were folded just casually enough that the chest pack hid beneath his sweater. "You'll spend time with her before she goes away?"

Kristina's nod was so brief, so dignified. It said, How can you even ask?

"She shouldn't have to die." He closed his eyes and drew a deep breath, unable to escape the images: Marc, Kristina, the young Muslim woman's face merging with all the others, until he was aware of Gnota again near the rail. He looked down at her. When all was said and done, did the Muslim woman get to choose life or death any more than Gnota? Or had race and tribe done to her what he would do now to his friend and sister?

Marc died because of the Muslim's dream of freedom. And she had died, too. Death . . . had his dream died? But the streets of Athinai, the vaulted beauty of Reims, Kristina's love: all this said that a dream is a moment, not a place. Dreams changed because time didn't pause, never hesitated.

Kristina slapped Gnota's back, then moved close, eased his arms away from his chest.

She rested her chin on his shoulder as she spoke softly, "You came here to Vansbro . . . it took a different kind of courage than soldiers imagine they'll need."

Do I want to be free of you, too, Kristina? Pablo asked himself. You're Europe, just as much as I'll be Gnota. Can I ever be free of either of you now?

Free. I left home a year ago and came down here on my way to the colonies. I was free to come . . . am *not* free to go. Gnota's death is a price, and my memories of you, Kristina, will always be a treasure with a price imposed by me, because I've seen joy . . . in the face of darkness. The colonies are bright, but Kristina is joyous. And Gnota is joy.

"I'm not sure I want the colonies anymore," he said aloud. "I've learned that the colonies wouldn't be the stars. The stars are dusk and . . . you. I can live without the colonies . . . but Europe's a dark place. With you, Kristina, even that darkness has become something beautiful, here at the bottom of the world."

And he saw it: winter is coming here; the nights will soon be too long for me to bear . . . no, too long for me to like. But space would be dark, too. Gnota will die.

It doesn't matter whether the dream is the colonies or you, Kristina, the dream is nothing unless I stop chasing it and go to work. Here? Back home in Arequipa? Or the colonies after all?

"Kristina," he said softly, "I'll have the surgery in Stockholm. That will give us two more weeks to argue. After that? Maybe the world is a colony. Maybe I belong here after all." He closed his eyes, saw the cathedral again, alone and ancient, half-wrecked, full of transfixing light and marvelous beings.

Kristina leaned over the rail and scratched Gnota's back. "Maybe you do," she said. "I'm not sure you'll know until you have your new heart." As her hand rested on Gnota's neck she said more softly, "There will always be a scar under your sweater. It's a scar that I could love." Her hand lifted from Gnota's back and folded inside her other hand as they alighted at her waist.

"You're so gentle, Pablo." She reached and touched him near the chest pack. "There's so much life here. Even if you go, I want you to remember me. Not just Gnota."

Pablo wrapped his arm around her, took the beautiful woman back for himself. "So much life *here,*" he echoed. He held Kristina tightly, burying his face for a moment against her neck, unafraid of the chest pack, only afraid to let her go too soon.

He heard Gnota's grunt. Hungry for another apple? Jealous for more attention? Or simply eager to be with people she knew and trusted?

Through a window at the end of the corridor, Pablo saw that night was bringing a skiff of snow.

Rorvik's War

Geoffrey A. Landis

GEOFFREY A. LANDIS HAS WON NEB-
ULA AND HUGO AWARDS FOR HIS SHORT FICTION. LESS THAN COINCIDENTALLY,
AT NASA HE'S TRYING VERY HARD TO PROVE THAT MANY OF HIS FELLOW SF
WRITERS ARE WRONG: HE IS CURRENTLY DESIGNING SOIL EXPERIMENTS FOR THE
ROVER ON THE UPCOMING MARS PATHFINDER PROBE. THUS, HE JOINS THAT IN-
TERESTING BREED, THE WORKING SCIENTIST WHO WRITES FINE SCIENCE FIC-
TION.

THE LAST THING WE WANT IS TO BE CAUGHT IN THE GRINDING MILL OF HIS-
TORY. BIG EVENTS, BIG TRENDS, NOT ONLY SCARE US: THEY CAN KILL US AND
DESTROY EVERYTHING WE'VE EVER LOVED AND LABORED FOR.

THE FIRST CASUALTY OF WAR IS TRUTH. THE SECOND CASUALTY IS FREEDOM.
LOST SOMEWHERE BETWEEN THESE, SOMETIMES EVEN BEFORE A WAR BEGINS, IS
A NATION'S HONOR.

1.

A SPAZ LAUNCHER lies beside Private Rorvik, broken in the lee of a crushed
building. The air is crisp with the tang of smokeless powder.

He is dying. The hole in his belly leaks blood around his clenched fingers, around the spike of crimson pain that shoots through the core of his
being, turning dry Boston dirt into red-brown mud. There is a lot of mud;
hours' worth. Try to ignore the pain, try to forget you're dying.

He is tired, so tired, but he can't sleep. The pain won't let him move.
Each breath stabs like a bayonet into his stomach. His fear is gone, along
with hope, and he is left with only pain.

The sky is blue, impossibly blue for a day so gray, brilliant burnished
blue, the blue of boredom, babbling burning broken blue, bright baking
burning bleeding . . . Stop it. Stop it stop it stop it. Think of something
else. There is a taste of copper in his mouth. Maybe he would be rescued.
The sounds of battle as the Russians are driven back, the rumble of mi-

crotanks. The purple glint of sunlight off a video lens, peeking around the corner, the shout of discovery: "Hey! There's somebody alive here!" Soldiers—Americans, thank God! Scurrying people all around, a ripping sound as someone pulls the tab of a smoke grenade and tosses it into the clear area behind him, boiling red smoke twisted like an insubstantial genie to guide the helicopter into the hot zone. "You all right there? Hang on, we've called for medics. Help is coming. You'll be okay, just hang on." Whop whop whop as the chopper comes in, and a stab of pain as the medevac team lifts him up, the pain is there but it's distant because it's going to be all right. He grins stoically and the men cheer at his bravery. The chopper takes off, Russian stingers swarming after it but the decoys and the door-gunner get them all, it's going to be all right, it's going to be all right, it's going to be . . . Stop it.

You're dying. There will be no rescue. The American forces are in retreat. The best you can hope for is the Russian advance.

Think of something else. Think of your family. Think about Lissy. He tries to recall his daughter's face, but can't. Brown hair, freckles, pixie nose. It means nothing to him. How she used to beg him for rides on his knee, pretending it was a pony, no, a *horse,* Daddy, ponies are for *children* and suddenly he sees her there, right in front of him, she is really there and he tries to smile for her and tell her it is all right and that he loves her more than anything but his smile turns into a grimace and all he can do is croak. When he tries to reach out to her the pain hits him in his belly like fifty millimeter cannon fire. He clenches his jaw to keep from screaming, then spits the blood out of his mouth. She isn't there, she has never been there at all and he will never see her again.

And then he can hear them, a low rumbling throbbing of the dirt beneath him, treads and six-legged walkers rumbling across the broken pavement of the city. But this isn't a hallucination; this is real. God! Could it be?

He tries to move, to look, but the pain is too much. Something winks in the corner of his vision, and he slowly turns his head. Indicators on the broken spaz launcher suddenly glow to life. The IFF light flickers, on and off, red. Foe. And another light insistently green: targets acquired and locked, warheads armed and ready.

The spaz launcher is still working! Somehow the advancing Russians have missed it; the broken building must have shielded it from their surveillance drones. Guessing from the rumbling in the distance, the advancing mechs must be a whole division. He could put a big hole in their advance, if he gives the launch command.

And then their drones will home in on him and blow him away.

Or he could wait, he could disable the launcher, he could wait for them to find him. Surely they take prisoners of war? They would bring him to a hospital, fix him up, and maybe someday in a POW exchange he'll be sent home, disabled but still alive. A hero. Nobody would have to know about the launcher. Nobody would ever know . . .

He looks at the launcher. Go away, he thinks. I don't want you. I didn't ask for you. I never asked to be a soldier.

He could go home a hero, but inside he would know. And the Russians would advance, they would take Boston, and Worcester, and Springfield. Lissy would grow up speaking Russian, she would go to Russian schools, and after a while she would learn to hate him.

He can hear scrabbling, something coming up the hill. A lens pokes around the corner, just as he'd imagined it, but it is a Russian lens, attached to a camera on six spidery metal legs, an unarmed battlefield surveillance unit. It looks at him, humming softly to itself.

They've found him. It is now or never.

He pulls his hand away from the wound in his belly and tries to sit up. The hole opens up afresh, and a new flow of blood wells into his lap. He tries not to look at it. He tries to ignore the pain. The drone—unarmed, thank God!—continues to watch him.

He reaches out to the panel and hits *actuate.* The launcher shudders and vibrates like an epileptic having a seizure, as armor-piercing hunter-seekers chuff from the aperture. The hum of the drone watching him changes pitch and he knows that the Russians are zeroed in, but it is too late; too late for them, too late for him. He leans back and gasps. For a moment, the world goes purple-black. Far away, he can hear the *chumpf* of explosions as his missiles find their targets, and closer, much closer, the rising whistle of incoming shells.

The first shell explodes a few meters away, and the ground swells up like a wave and tosses him casually against the broken building. He opens his eyes, and after a moment, they focus. In a frozen moment of perfect clarity, he sees the shell that will kill him swell in an instant from a speck into an absolutely perfect circle, deadly black against the blue, blue sky.

And then there is nothing at all.

2.

Rorvik remembered the day his draft notice had come as clearly as if it had happened yesterday. It had been seven-thirty in the morning, and Angela was about ready to head for work. As she kissed him, promising to hurry home, there was a knock on the door.

Angela pulled away from him and turned. "Who could that be, at this hour?"

"Probably a salesman." The knock came again, three measured raps. He was annoyed. The few minutes in the morning while Lissy was still asleep and before Angela went off to work was about the only time he had Angela to himself. "I'll get it." He jerked open the door, ready to give somebody an earful. "Yes?"

It was a balding man in a plain blue suit. Standing just behind him, flanking him on either side, were two larger men. The man looked at a piece of paper. "Mr. Davis C. Rorvik?"

"What do you want?"

"Excuse me. You *are* Mr. Rorvik?"

"Yes, but—"

The man glanced toward Angela, and then back. "May we speak to you alone for a moment, Mr. Rorvik?"

"You may not," Angela said sharply, coming up behind him. "If you have something to tell him, you can say it right here." She made a show of looking at her watch. "And quickly."

The man shrugged, and addressed Rorvik. "Mr. Rorvik, as a duly authorized agent of the United States Selective Service, it is my duty to inform you that as of this moment, you are a member of the United States Armed Forces."

"Wait one moment—"

The man opened a folder and removed a stack of photocopied papers. He ran his finger down the top page to the signatures, and then showed it to Rorvik. An ancient student loan application. "This is your signature?"

He didn't remember the particular document, but the signature was clearly his. It had seemed a good bargain at the time: tuition money for college in return for a promise to serve if needed, and they probably wouldn't even need him anyway. With the collapse of communism across the globe, there was no prospect of war in sight. "Yes, but . . ."

The man nodded at one of the goons, who pulled something out from under his jacket.

"I'm too . . ." There was a hiss, and Rorvik felt a cool sting at the back of his neck. ". . . too . . . ." His knees suddenly buckled, and he slid slowly to the ground. Inside the house, Angela screamed.

He couldn't move. His muscles felt like warm pudding; his head felt as if somebody had swathed it in lint. The man continued to speak; presumably to Angela. "Under the provisions of Emergency order 09-13A, you are forbidden under penalty of law to discuss this draft notice or to divulge any information concerning the whereabouts of Mr. Rorvik." One of the men wrapped his arms under Rorvik's armpits. The other picked up his legs. "This includes discussing the matter with any agents of the press." Angela had stopped screaming, and was, as far as he could tell, listening in silence.

"The provisions of the Emergency order allow for full compensation for any inconvenience occasioned by Mr. Rorvik's service." The two men picked him up and started to take him away to the gray station wagon idling at the curb. As the two men swung him around, he could see his nextdoor neighbor Jack on his way to the subway stop, briefcase in hand. He was taking an intense interest in the weeds poking out through the cracks in the sidewalk. He didn't once look in Rorvik's direction.

As they bundled him into the car, Rorvik managed to complete the phrase he had started, hours ago ". . . too old to be drafted. I'm thirty-eight years old . . . . "

3.

"It's the Eff-En-Gee. What's your name, FNG?"

"Rorvik."

"That Swedish?"

"Close enough. It's Norwegian."

"Wrong answer, FNG." The big corporal tapped him on the chest. "Start counting. I'll tell you when you can stop."

Rorvik dropped down and began doing push-ups. "One! Two! Three!"

"Either you're an American or you're meat. Got it?"

"Heard and understood."

The corporal—Driscott, his name-tag had said—watched him for a few moments. "You may think your name's Rorvik, but I think your name is FNG. You mind that, FNG?"

"No, sir."

"Good. You learn fast, FNG. You know what FNG stands for?"

"No, sir."

"Stands for Fuckin' New Guy. Means you're dangerous, FNG. You're going to get us all killed. Forget yourself, go outside. Feel good to get outside for a few minutes, wouldn't it, FNG?"

"No, sir."

"Good answer. Get yourself specced by a flying bear eyeball, and you realize you made a fuck-up when you get pounded to dust by arty. One tremendous ker-powie is the last thing you're going to hear. Now, that wouldn't bother me a bit—nobody much cares if the Army's got one FNG more or less—but that same arty fire is gonna spread *me* across a few acres of landscape too, and I wouldn't like that very much, no.

"—Count real quiet there, Private FNG, I want you to hear me and hear me good.

"Reason we call you FNG is so that we don't forget, even for a moment, that you're not to be trusted. One FNG is as dangerous as a dozen bear-eyes.

Live 'til the next new guy comes in, maybe you deserve a name of your own, and *he's* the FNG."

Driscott put his foot on Rorvik's back and pressed him against the ground. " 'Til then, you don't do nothing outside of rules, and maybe we all live a little longer. Got it?"

"Heard and understood."

"Good. I think I'm gonna get along with you, FNG. I think we're gonna get along fine."

There had been no air travel, of course—Russian microsats could spot an airplane and their SAMs would blow it out of the sky from a thousand miles away. Rorvik, along with half a dozen other draftees, dazed and scared, had been taken across the interdiction zone in an armored convoy that dashed from hardpoint to hardpoint, screened with chaff, decoys, jammers. At first he wondered why it was necessary to get to the battle zone at all; later he was taught that radio relays were weak links in a battle, and that a critical half of their communications was by line-of-sight microwave and laser links that required proximity. No communications link was entirely secure, but the shorter the link, the more reliable it was.

Later yet he realized that it didn't matter where the soldiers were actually located. The fire zone could move a hundred miles in the blink of an eye when the Russian computers made a new guess at the American command location. The front lines were everywhere.

Driscott took his foot away and reached down a hand. It took a moment before Rorvik realized that Driscott was offering him a hand up. "You're gonna learn about this war fast, FNG. First thing you gonna learn, we don't get the information here. They don't tell us nothing."

"Yes, sir."

"You married, FNG? Got a family?"

"Yes."

"Too bad. Forget 'em. War first started, the soldiers stayed back from the lines and let the metal take the fire. Sometimes even got to go home on weekends. That got stopped real quick. Fuckin' Russkies didn't know the rules; too many civvies killed when the Russkies targeted the ops. You're here for the duration, got it?"

"Understood." The funny thing was, he could barely even remember the war starting. He was old enough to remember watching CNN with his parents by the hour during the breakup of the Soviet Union, remembered the sense of relief as the world stood down from the brink of nuclear annihilation. But the rise of the Russian junta and the new cold war had seemed to occur in the blink of an eye when he hadn't been paying attention. In hindsight, it was inevitable—though nobody had predicted it at the time—that a strong-man would take over control from the ruins of the Soviet system. It was funny how something so important could seem so distant. He had been too busy marrying, trying to start a family, trying to keep a job in an economy going sour year by year. He knew it intellectually, could quote the headline statistics, but the threat of war had never seemed real to him, even as the cold war turned into a war of hot steel.

And the new threat of war wasn't like the old. It was to be a war of computers, not missiles. "I don't even understand why we're here," Rorvik said to Driscott. "They'd told us that the computers made war obsolete. That battlefield simulations can predict the outcome of every battle, so nobody would actually fight anymore."

"Yeah?" Driscott seemed amused. "Tell me about it, new guy."

"If our battlefield simulations say the same thing the Russian ones do, and they know the outcome of a battle before the first shot is fired, why are we fighting? They said that whoever was going to lose would know, and back down. What happened?"

"You got sold a bill of goods, FNG. Lissen to too many of those TV commentators." Driscott shook his head. "Just goes to show. Nah, them computers don't know everything. Ya can't predict the psy-fucking-cology of the guys in the field. You can put in the numbers, but can you put in morale? Can you put in fuckups?" He tapped Rorvik's chest. "It's you and me, buddy, you and me make the difference. We aren't just fighting a war. No, what we're doing is showing them Russian computers that they don't got a clue about just how tough the American soldier really is. No matter what they throw at us, no matter how tough things get, even if all we have left is rocks, we just keep coming. We never give up. Never. Got it?"

"Got it."

4.

For a moment after he wakes, his dream of being a civilian seems like it had been only yesterday, the memories of civilian life stronger and more alive than those of the war. The feeling fades. It was just that the war had started so *fast,* and his life had changed so quickly and completely, it sometimes feels like he had been a civilian just hours before.

Rorvik is a tactical operator on the fly-eyes, one of the best. A fly-eye is a tiny infrared-visible camera with an encrypted radio transmitter, hung under a plastic flex-wing with a miniature propeller and motor, the whole thing folding up to a streamlined package about the size of a pencil that fits into a rifle. It is up to him to find targets for the artillery, located somewhere in a secured hiding place fifty miles or more distant.

The war is a huge game of hide and seek. When the enemy is found, the smart shells pound cracks through his armor to incinerate the meat within.

Somewhere in the city below, a grunt hiding in the deserted city fires him into the sky. Rorvik knows nothing about the soldier who launches him, nor cares, but waits with a rising sense of anticipation until he hits apogee and spreads his wings. Deployed, silent, nearly radar invisible, he soars over darkened buildings looking for movement, flying in slow zigzags to present a less predictable target. His motor gives him about five minutes of power, but it is a point of pride with the fliers not to use it, but to soar the tiny flexwing on thermals and on the ridge lift from rooftops, prolonging his flights for hours before he has to return to the drab world of concrete and first sergeants and smelly underwear and MRE packages eaten cold to avoid unnecessary IR signature. He hates cold water shaves and the endless pinochle game the E-5 sergeants play in their den; he hates the smell of stale piss that washes over the room whenever one of the men opens up the latrine canister to take a leak, and the rotten-fruit smell of unwashed bodies the rest of the time. (There is a perennial rumor that the enemy is developing an odor-sensitive homing bomb, and that when it is developed the field troops will be subject to a smell discipline as strong as the IR discipline is now. God, he wishes they'd hurry.)

But, flying his eye, he is far from all that. He flies above the city, the flier's electronic eyes becoming his own, heedless of his body controlling the flier far below.

He soars over the darkening city. It is spring, but the few trees left in the city provide scant obstruction to his cameras. A flutter of movement attracts his attention, and he wheels around. Nothing. No, there! He zooms in. A piece of paper blowing in the wind. He circles for a minute, hoping to catch something else, but nothing moves. MI will examine his snapshot of the paper, he knows, trying to determine where it came from, if it is ours or theirs.

"Little Eagle? Word from Uncle Henry that they've seen Bear footprints north in sector Tiger three-niner. They want you to eyeball it for them. Do you need a new bird?"

Tiger 39. He flashes up a map. About a kilometer north of him, in the area that once used to be north Cambridge. "Negative, unless they're in some real rush about it. I can get there in five minutes."

"Roger. We're standing by."

He can see the pink warmth of a thermal off to his left, and banks around. He increases speed until his wings begin to ripple and lose lift, then backs off a hair.

Four minutes later he is circling the area.

The sky is muddy brown in the falsecolor of his IR display. "It's an evac zone," the voice in his earphones says. "Anything you see will be bears."

He hears the slight riffle of air behind him. He snap-rolls instantly, and the diving hawk misses him by inches. He pushes into a dive to gain airspeed, with one eye watching the Russian hawk pull up to come around at him again, with the other flashing to his map to find if he is near a sector where he has fire support from the ground. Negative. He flips his mike on.

"Load up another birdy, Wintergreen. I've drawn a hawk."

"No can do, Little Eagle. A couple of bear eyes moved in too close to our guys on the ground. Advise you run for the green in sector X-ray niner."

The Russian hawk, abandoning stealth, has lit its tiny pulsejet and is coming at him from below. "Negative, negative. It's too far. Blow the eyes away."

"Sorry, Sport. Too many eyes. We don't want to risk the bears getting a fix on our artillery. You're on your own."

"Fuck you very much, Wintergreen." He starts an evasion pattern. No way he can outrun a hawk; he pushes the stick forward to the edge of flutter and heads in zig-zags toward the turbulence of a fragged building.

He'd been hoping he could ride the turbulence, but the gusty wind is too much for him. The wind-rotor grabs him, flips him upside down. He rolls out inches away from smashing against the concrete, pulls out hard, and stalls. Hanging dead in the air for the instant before falling, he feels more than sees the hawk coming at him. He is dead meat.

And in the next instant the hawk flies apart, ripped to shreds by gunfire. He pushes forward, regains flying speed, and hightails down-wind, at the same time keying his mike. "What the hell was that? Flechette?"

"Birdshot. I found a grunt dumb enough to step outside to take a shot. You owe me one, Sport. Can you make it now?"

"Affirmative."

"Keep your eyes peeled. Local support arty is pinned down, but we have some long-range shoot'n'scoot that can wipe the Bear HQ if you happen to find it in your travels."

"Rog." He finds some lift, gains altitude, and heads for Tiger.

He flies over territory that is familiar to him. He had worked near here once, before he was married. For a moment he wonders why the Russians had invaded. Arming for war had shored up a failed economy, but did it make any sense for the Bears to actually hold territory? They must have had a reason, or at least a pretext for one, but for the moment Rorvik can't remember what it was. But then, who could ever psych out the Russians? Leave that to the professionals, with their super-computers and tactical models. Not to the soldiers.

Tiger three-niner. Circling the area, he finds a cluster of relatively undamaged buildings, apparently the remains of an old housing project. A bit exposed for a fire base, but still . . . He circles lower, looking for signs of habitation. Nothing. There! Traces of body heat lingering in the still air, a yellowish fog in the IR. He zooms out and follows the heat trace across the city as it brightens into lime green and then the pale blue of recent passage. There, under an overhang, the scarlet flash of a warm body. He checks his map. This is an evac area; a free-fire zone. A flash of movement. "Think I got something here. Hold five." He banks around.

"Standing by to fire."

He comes in low, stalls, fights the building's turbulence. Another flash of movement; a foot. "Got it! Bogeys, could be a Bear fire-control post." He flashes his IR range finder. "My coords plus five at twenty-two surface, mark. I'm coming around to guide your fire." He rides out and into some slope lift from the breeze flowing up over the facade.

A different voice, the slight echo of multiple radio relays. "Roger. Outgoing, one, two, three." His vision flickers static for a moment from the EM pulse used to dazzle any Bear radars from tracing back the rising shells. It takes a moment for the shells to clear far enough to aero-maneuver, a moment in which he is suddenly aware of sitting in a concrete bunker with a flickering television helmet on his head, and then his vision sharpens back to normal and he is flying again.

The fire support base is miles away; it will be a minute before the shells came in and need his terminal guidance. Something about what he's seen bothers him. He flicks back to his last photo. A foot shows in the shadow of an overhang. He zooms in, enhances contrast. Barefoot. The Russians are that far out of discipline? He circles back, penetrating upwind slowly, searching for a good view. There. He hovers for a moment into the wind, panning his eye around behind him. Shapes move, but the shadow is too deep to distinguish them in visual. He turns up contrast and sharpens his gain. There.

The instant before he stalls out, he gets a good shot.

Three children circle around a suspended object. The oldest is perhaps fourteen, the youngest perhaps nine. One, blindfolded, holds a broken mop handle like a club. In a corner a scruffy yellow dog watches them. He looks closer at the suspended object. He recognizes it as the throw-away cardboard transport tube for an 80-mm Russian antiaircraft missile. It has been decorated, painted bright colors, given old buttons to serve as eyes, four painted cardboard legs and long floppy ears. A crude caricature of a donkey. A piñata.

The voice in his earphones says, "Twenty seconds to incoming. Ready for terminal guidance."

"Abort your rounds! Abort!"

"Say again, Eagle?"

"Abort your rounds! Civilians!"

"Roger." Three sharp cracks in the air above him as the lifting bodies detonate. "Rounds aborted." There is a pause, and then, "Do you have a vector on the target that can avoid the civilians?"

He feels like ash, like he had been burned and there is nothing left. Shooting at shadows is common enough, but it won't endear him to his superiors. "Negative. False alarm. Sorry, guys."

There is a long pause, and then, "Operations wants to talk to you, Rorvik."

Using his name instead of his code is a bad sign. "Acknowledged."

"That means now, Private."

"Roger." He scrambles and finds some lift, prolonging the flight, knowing it might be his last. "I'll be there as soon as I'm down."

Another pause. "Negative, Rorvik. Ops wants to talk to you pronto. Advise you blow the bird and get your butt down here before you get marks for insubordination."

"Heard and understood." No help for it. The critical chips on his bird are set to melt when they lose the carrier wave for more than a few seconds, or if he gives the coded signal. The rest of the bird is just sticks and plastic; no more than a toy. He flicks the cover off the toggle, caresses it for a second, and then presses it with his thumb. His eye-screens flash black for an instant, and then there is nothing left of the world but the whisper and swirl of static.

He pops his helmet, and is in a grimy concrete bunker crammed with equipment and stinking of sweat and hot electronics. Next to his contoured seat, two other fliers sit, faceless in the white plastic of surround helmets, oblivious to him and the rest of the world, except for their birds. His muscles ache from the body English he gave his bird while flying, but the bunker is too cramped for him to stretch. He unpins the throat mike, and goes to explain.

5.

They are kept in the dark about the overall course of the war, but from the consistent, slow retreat, and the way that replacements—men and materiel both—are getting scarcer and scarcer, by the end of the summer Rorvik knows that the war is not going well.

Some of the men from Rorvik's unit keep a Russian lieutenant tied up in a remote bunker, nominally an auxiliary command post but actually just an abandoned garage that hasn't been shelled, with a roof thick enough to mask IR signature. They call her Olga—nobody knows her real name; it had been written on her uniform way back when she'd had one, but none of the gang could read Cyrillic, and she either can't or won't speak English.

Rorvik's unit is all male. Equality be damned, the Army is still segregated by sex. Only Headquarters units and reserves mix genders; every operational unit Rorvik has served in has been all male. There are all-female units too, the subject of a good deal of unlikely stories and rude speculation, but Rorvik's unit rarely meets them, except on the field, where the drones are sexless and the operators invisible, hidden behind labyrinths of encrypted radio relays. The Russian lieutenant is the only female any of them has seen for weeks—some of them, months.

And they know that there is little chance that they will survive the war anyway.

As Rorvik passes by, one of the boys yells out an invitation for him to join them. Rorvik walks faster, and they snicker. "Ol' Davey's too good for us." "No, it's just that he's waiting until we capture a *boy*." "Maybe he's got his own nookie stashed away somewhere, some pretty Russky major."

Their lieutenant pretends not to notice, but he knows. No way he could miss it. They are supposed to turn prisoners over to the authorities—they desperately need Russians for their simulations—but, for the moment, that is impossible. No doubt as soon as they rejoined their Battalion the prisoner would be "found," and rescued from the civilian "partisans" who had so cruelly mistreated her.

Could he do anything? Informing headquarters about the prisoner would result in her disappearance, and possibly his own, long before any inspection might get to them. Still, the thought that there could be something he might do chews at Rorvik's conscience and worries him at the odd moments when battle duty or his eight-hour watch leaves him free to think.

As the battle eddies and stalls, with movement by lightning air deployment and half the battle fought by remotes, it is almost pointless to mark battle lines. Most of the Boston area is controlled by neither the Russians nor the American forces, but watched by both. To the extent that anybody can say, though, Rorvik's unit is temporarily behind enemy lines. Or at least, they are cut off from support.

Their control bunker is buried under Dorchester. When the battle moved closer, his unit had to stay inside; but now, with the battle line off in Roxbury, some outside mobility is possible. At work, of course, he is right in the thick of battle, wherever it is.

Rorvik was taken off of tac surveillance to become a drone runner. He alternates with Drejivic, six hours on, six off, controlling four robot warriors. The warriors are intelligent; if the coded remote signal is jammed, they will keep fighting until the interference clears, and their IFF (identify, friend or foe) signals—changed hourly—keep them from shooting each other. But remotes work best if an actual human watches over them to make decisions. In a hard fire-fight, it is best to let them on their own; human reaction time only slows them down. He'll interfere only when indecision about a questionable IFF threatens a gridlock. Occasionally he'll have to call in Rick, who runs another four, to take one of his drones; or Rick will call him in. It is a point of pride not to do this too often.

Angie, Lissy, Gumby, and Pokey, he calls them. Drejivic has other names.

He hooks into the computer. When he runs drones, his body stays in the bunker, but *him*—the important part of him—is the drone. He flits back and forth from one viewpoint to another. When he wears one body, the views from the other three cameras are always visible in the edge of his vision.

When he concentrates on one drone, the others fight on their own initiative.

Angie and Lissy, the fliers, he likes best. These aren't the disposable surveillance flexies he flew when the war was young; these are armed fighting drones. The fliers are pigs for energy use, though, and have to conserve their time aloft. On the ground they are clumsy. More than once he's had to use his rocket-assisted take-off to haul ass out of fire too hot for them to handle. The rasstos are one-shot units; use one up and you have to bring the drone home and wait for a replacement. Like everything else, they are running low. He's been chewed out several times, the sarge drilling in that we are *not* to get into situations where we have to rassto out.

Unfortunately, Angie is waiting for a replacement rassto, and Lissy is out of action. She's taken a couple of rounds of small-caliber fire. The maintenance tech has her now, trying to scrounge parts to put her back together.

Gumby and Pokey are his two bipedal walkers. Running them feels almost like wearing a robot suit. Gumby is the most flexible of his drones. His problem is that they long ago ran out of ammo for the 3-mm skittergun that is Gumby's utility weapon. He still has the 10-mm armor piercers and rockets, but on his own, Gumby's first move in a firefight is still to bring up the skittergun. The slight hesitation it takes for Gumby's tiny processor to remember it didn't work could be fatal. The unit is supposed to be adaptable enough to remember, but Rorvik guesses that that part of his programming has been shot out.

Pokey is operational, but weaponless until parts become available, after the unit rejoins the main army. Mostly Rorvik stays out of Gumby's viewpoint and lets the drone move around on auto while he scouts from Pokey.

What the drones fight, mostly, are other drones. There are human infantry in the field, on both sides, but they tend to be dug into stealth emplacements, mobile and heavily protected, only popping out for missions too delicate to be run by drones.

In the distance, the heavy overcast glows orange with reflected light as the ruins of Boston burn.

The status bulletin has given them a clear for an hour. It is rare that their computers can predict a clear for that long; somewhere far away one side or the other must have ferreted a major command center, and a battle must be drawing all of the resources available. For now, Rorvik's area is clear of Russian eyes, and they can move around outside. Drone runners have to take rest shifts of a minimum of three hours to stay at peak effectiveness; the regulations demand it, and so he knows he won't be called back except for a serious emergency.

A block from their bunker is a square that still has a few trees in it; the closest thing to a park within the defense perimeter. He decides to go there for as long as the clear lasts.

Someone else has gotten there before him.

The woman in the park has a SISI gun grafted right to her shoulder, and the eye-shaped barrel turns to aim at him at the same time she raises her head. He takes an involuntary step back; the gun unnerves him. See it, shoot it: he could be dead with a single thought. She must have volunteered to have the gun grafted into her nervous system; the regulations don't allow them to modify you without consent. It means that she is from a live-combat unit, and that is unusual as well, especially for a woman. Women have to volunteer for front-line duty.

He was in a live-combat unit once, during the first battle for Boston. He remembers—but that was early in the war; there is no point in dredging up those memories.

Her insignia shows her to be a Spec-4. He has heard that a female infantry company had temporarily moved in to an area south of them, but hadn't realized that their clear areas would overlap. The gun moves like something alive on her shoulder, pivoting minutely as she shifts her eyes, jerking from target to target with the unblinking attention of a snake.

She watches him eyeing her gun. "It's no safer behind the lines, soldier. I'd rather have it be up front, where I can fight back, than where you are, buried in some concrete bunker and never hear it coming, you know?"

"Doesn't the gun make you a target?"

"Makes me dangerous." She smiles. "I like to be dangerous."

She is too tall, too many muscles and too few curves, and wears a wrinkled jumpsuit made of fireproof fabric that masks what feminine lines she has. She is desirable as all hell.

She can tell he is thinking about that, too, and she laughs. "Soldiers think any woman out here is sex-crazed, you know it? I'm not like that. I've got a husband, and two kids. They're what I'm fighting for."

"I know."

"You married, soldier?"

He nods.

"Happily? Got any kids?"

"A girl."

She nods. "Then you do know." As she unzips the jumpsuit, she says, "They're back at home, and we're here." She runs the tip of one finger along the gun barrel for a second, then does something to it with the other hand, and it stops tracking her gaze. "This didn't happen, you know? It's the war. No commitments, no promises, no looking each other up, after."

"No." He doesn't believe there will be an after, not anymore. He has seen the craters where houses once were, the lines of refugees, miles long, trudging endlessly out of the cities toward areas they believed might be safe. He has seen the ruins of the area where his house had been, where his wife and girl once lived.

But he still believes in now.

Her name is Westermaker, she whispers. She kneels to unzip his pants. He strokes her hair—short, dark and very slightly curled—as she runs her lips along the underside of his cock.

A confused jumble of thoughts crowds through his head all at the same time. He feels himself already beginning to dribble, and wonders if he will be able to hold back, or if he will come the instant she takes him in her mouth. Wonders if he will ever be able to tell Angela about this, and whether she could possibly understand. Wonders if the Army issues female grunts birth control. Wonders if she will stay long enough for him to take her twice.

He reaches down to slide his pants off. She cups his buttock in a palm as she delicately touches the end of her tongue to the tip of his cock, and the burst of machine-gun fire takes her low in the chest. Her mouth opens to scream as her lungs spatter out the side of her shredded uniform and across the jagged ends of her splintered ribs. An instant later, without a sound, she dies.

He staggers back, his ears ringing with the report, tries to turn around, and trips on the pants tangled around his knees. He rolls over and looks right into the lens of a Russian walker. With the soft whirr of servos, the machine gun tracks to his face.

He squeezes his eyes shut. The smell of blood is very strong.

Nothing happens.

After a long moment he opens his eyes. The machine is still there, unblinking; the gun still aimed right for him. It is heavier and clumsier than the American units Rorvik is familiar with, all angles and graceless ceramic armor-plate, and very deadly. Surreptitiously, he reaches behind him and gropes for a rock. The machine does nothing. It takes an eternity to find a rock loose enough to pull out of the ground. When he finally pries one loose he waits for an instant, gauging the distance, and then, with a quick, smooth motion, hurls it at the machine.

It dodges easily, still watching him, still tracking him with the gun, still holding back its fire. The gun must have jammed, he thinks, and then, an instant later, God, it's already called in artillery on me.

But the gun killed Westermaker easily enough, and the remote is making no effort to get clear of incoming artillery.

He should have never gone out, not even to a clear zone, without his sidearm. But he is a drone runner; he isn't supposed to fight face to face. Holding his pants up with one hand, he scrambles to his feet, preparing to make a run for it, and hears the hydraulics start up behind him. He freezes. Suddenly he realizes what the remote is up to.

Where can he go?

It had shot Westermaker. Westermaker had been armed, though her SISI gun had been useless against a threat she never saw. He is no threat. The operator—somewhere miles away—can shoot him anytime he wanted. But his very presence means that there must be a command post somewhere nearby. Why not let him go, and watch where he went?

The tell-tale on his wrist has started to blink urgently red: return to secure area immediately. A warning that does him no good at all.

A block of ice forms in his lungs. It is suddenly impossible for him to breathe. He doesn't dare go back, it would lead the bears right into his post.

There is no way he can warn his unit, but if he doesn't return they will know, and take measures. Either way, it is too late for him.

The smell of blood has vanished, but the acid smell of spent powder etches his nostrils, fills the entire world. Slowly, slowly, he turns and starts to walk, then run. Crosswise and down hill; in a wide loop away from his bunker, away from safety, away from hope.

6.

In the ruins of Worcester, the triumphant Russian troops are coming up Belmont Street from Boston. The resistance waits for them. Rorvik's unit has managed to find a gas station that was shelled to rubble early in the war; its buried storage tanks are almost untouched. They have filled a Dumpster with gasoline, poured in five dozen bags of nitrate liberated from an old greenhouse supply, and then melted in styrofoam to make it gel. At the bottom of the Dumpster is a pound of black powder, with a detonator made from a lightbulb filament.

The Dumpster is hidden inside the bricked-up front of an abandoned apartment block, just another forgotten piece of debris in a city full of rubble.

Russian air cover is too complete and the computer triangulation and jamming too swift for Rorvik's unit to trust a radio link, even with encrypted relays. They lost two men learning that lesson. Rorvik was odd man out on the coin toss. He has found a concealed niche, across the street from the bomb, and waits, nervous, sweat dripping down his back. Through a tiny hole drilled in the wall, he watches the enemy as it walks, crawls, rolls up the street on jointed steel legs and armor-plated wheels.

Wondering if he will be able to get away, after.

Now.

The explosion is huge, an orgasm in orange and black and glorious rolling thunder. The blast picks up one of the ceramic-armored high-mobility one-man tanks and flips it against the wall. It struggles to right itself, but the move is pointless. As planned, the blast has undermined the stone façade of the building, and a slow-motion avalanche of Fitchburg granite rumbles down over the column. Five tanks and about a dozen mechanicals are swept up in the river of boiling stone, then tossed aside and buried by rubble.

The Russian commander is sharp, and in control. Before the dust has started to settle, Rorvik hears the amplified voice booming out in clipped Russian. "They left a man behind to detonate it! Find him! Squadron A, left side of the street! B, right!"

He should have scrambled the instant he pressed the button, not stayed to see what he accomplished. He could hide forever from ordinary eyes, but to infrared sensors the plume of his breath must glow like a beacon. He has only moments. He dashes through the streets, and can hear the clatter of armored soldiers entering the street behind him.

He dodges down an alley, hoping to stay out of sight of the sky for a few more moments, and only after he enters it sees that the shelling has completely blocked it with rubble. It is too late to turn back the way he came; troops are too close behind him. He spots a window into the basement of a dime store, and miraculously the iron grille over the window has been shaken loose, but the glass is still intact. He smashes the glass with a piece of asphalt and drops into the darkness.

He lands awkwardly, bruising his leg. In a few moments his eyes adjust to the dimness. The basement is empty save for rubbish; the cement floor damp and glistening. Across from the window a stairway once rose to the main level. It is now just a pile of splintered wood. The door hangs above empty space, and through bullet holes he can see sky.

This, then, will be his last stand. There is nowhere left to run.

Turning, he sees the shadow of an articulated leg fall across the empty window. He limps away from the window, crouches against the wall and pulls out his automatic. The remote stops, hesitates by the window while the operator queries for directions, and then a lens pokes in through the window.

It swivels left, the wrong way. Rorvik aims, but holds his fire, waiting for a better shot. The body of the remote starts to press in through the window at the same time the camera pans right, and an instant before it fixes on him, Rorvik fires.

His shot is aimed at one of the vulnerable hydraulic lines, and the spray of hot fluid tells him he damaged it. Before he can shoot again, two more shatter the door above. He hears the shot an instant after he feels it hit him in the chest. The second shot, an instant later, he never hears: the one that blows apart his skull.

7.

Then he awoke. The memory of being drafted was fresh in his mind, as it always was when he awoke from a long sleep. All that had been long ago. He'd been captured; the US had fallen. He was, like many others, in a re-education camp. Since he'd been drafted, not volunteered, the camp bureaucracy had considered him a victim of the imperialist aggressors, rather than a war criminal. That fact had earned him a chance at reeducation, instead of the bullet in the back of the head that had awaited most of his fellow soldiers.

As he stood in the line for the "voluntary" evening reeducation lecture, a man behind him put a hand on his shoulder and whispered.

"Resistance meeting tonight. Strike a blow for freedom!"

How crazy were they? Didn't they know that the bears had stoolies and paid informants everywhere? Hey, he could even earn brownie points—maybe even a chance to see Angela and Lissy—by passing along what he'd heard.

The lecture was about economics and simulation war. Very little of the war, he discovered, had actually been fought; most of it had been simulation. Both sides' tactical computers could model the outcome of every battle, and the side that would have lost would always withdraw without actually fighting.

In theory.

"What the capitalist computers failed to take into account," said the lecturer, a tall Hispanic man with a Stalin moustache and a habit of nervously looking over his shoulder, "was that the loyal soldiers of the Hegemony have the force of history with them. Citizens of a democracy are by nature unable to act in harmony. Knowing that history is invincible, the soldiers of the Hegemony are unswerving. Purity of ideology gives them strength. How could the computers of an obsolete political system calculate this? Only with the data from actual battles, showing the staggering battlefield superiority of Hegemony troops. Victory of the Hegemony was inevitable. Even now, with algorithms bolstered with actual battle data, the computers of the aggressor capitalist governments have correctly calculated their inevitable defeat. The capitalist government has surrendered unconditionally to the provisional government, and asked all its soldiers to lay down arms. Resistance of any sort is treason, and will be dealt with as such."

Rorvik listened to it sleeping with his eyes open, automatically noting phrases to parrot back in the group-reeducation sessions the next morning. Attending the lecture would earn him points, maybe a second piece of toast at breakfast the next time supplies came to the camp.

Later, after the official lecture, the lecturer—who had been a high-school history teacher before the war—casually gathered interested parties for the second talk, this one quite unofficial. The Americans had a clandestine school system of their own in the camps, and whenever the Russkies' lecturers gave any information from the disputed territories or talked on how the resistance was going, they tried to sort out the kernel of truth from the shell of propaganda. The resistance was still alive, they said, and the Russians were having a tough time trying to govern the territory they had captured. If they could hold out, frustrate their captors at every turn, soon the alleycats would . . .

"Resistance" was a forbidden word, and anyone caught using it could be shot without hesitation. The slang for the day was to call the remnants of the armed forces who had escaped capture "alleycats."

But nothing changed, and if there really were alleycats, he'd heard plenty of talk but seen no real signs of them in the camp. Until now.

As the man spoke, barely loud enough to hear, Rorvik's attention drifted. The talk was about the necessity for computer models to be grounded in data, something Rorvik had no need to be taught again. His mind was running on another track. He couldn't actually remember being captured, and suddenly that had struck him as odd. Surely that was an important moment in his life; he ought to have vivid memories, or at least some recollection of how it had happened. He must have blacked out, that was it. The time he had been wounded, bleeding to death in the rubble . . . but no, he hadn't been captured then, he remembered it vividly, remembered the artillery, remembered dying.

No, that was impossible, he had survived, joined the resistance, set off the bomb and been chased into . . . no, that couldn't be. He had died then, too. There was something wrong with his memory. Had he hallucinated it? But it had been real, he was sure of it, as real as the barbed wire and concrete surrounding him.

One of the other men in the camp, Povelli, brushed past him on the way to the latrine. Rorvik looked up, and Povelli, without looking at him, bent over, untied his shoe, and then carefully retied it. "Wait a few minutes, then get up and make like you gotta go to the crapper," Povelli said softly. Rorvik glanced around. No one was paying attention to them. "Past the crapper, you know the tool shed? Ten minutes. Whistle once when you approach."

Rorvik nodded slightly, as if agreeing with something the professor said, and Povelli finished tying his shoe and got up.

The lecture was breaking up anyway; it was dangerous to gather in groups of more than two or three for very long. Rorvik stretched and looked around. Nobody was paying particular attention to him. He strolled toward the latrine.

Before he got halfway to the meeting, just outside the prefab, Khokhlov stopped him. They had two reeducation counselors to assist them in learning correct political thought. Khokhlov was the nicer of the two, and spoke British-accented English with a bare trace of gutteral Slavic vowels.

He offered Rorvik a cigarette. The Russians all smoked heavily. Rorvik accepted it, but only puffed on it enough to show that he appreciated the courtesy.

"You have come very far in your thinking, Mr. Rorvik," Khokhlov said. "I believe you are one of my best students."

Rorvik nodded and gave him a wide smile. "Thank you. I have been doing my best."

"Are you dissatisfied at all?" Khokhlov waved his hand. "Of course, I know that food here is not as plentiful as it could be. I assure you that we all are under the same conditions, even guards."

Rorvik wondered what Khokhlov could be after. Did he know about the meeting? "No, no—everything is fine," he said. He knew quite as well as Khokhlov that complaining was a sure sign of regressive-thinking. "Really."

"Perhaps we could chat a bit?" said Khokhlov. He took Rorvik by the arm. "I have been very disturbed by something I heard, my friend. One of the people I have been chatting with—you won't object if I don't mention his name?—said that he believed you were sympathetic to the resistance. I, of course, told him this could not be correct, but he quite insisted on the point."

"No, no," Rorvik said hastily. "Absolutely not. I steer clear of them, let me assure you."

Khokhlov looked interested. "Really? Then you know who they are?"

He wanted to kick himself for speaking without thinking, but tried to keep his expression innocent and candid. "Well, no—that is, not really. I've heard rumors, of course—"

"I am quite interested in rumors."

"It wouldn't be fair—"

Khokhlov cut him off. "I am judge of fairness in this camp, Mr. Rorvik. Please, we are not barbarians here. Let me give you my assurance that I am here to help people adjust to scientific society, not to punish them for retrograde thinking. If you are hearing rumors, I should be aware of them. If people are spreading tales—gossips, this is correct word?—spreading the gossips without foundation, I should know this, in order to better guide people to correct thinking. Please, do not hesitate to speak completely candidly with me."

Rorvik smiled ingratiatingly, trying to assume the puppy-dog expression of a convert to correct-thinking. "I don't know any specific names."

"I am afraid that you are not being completely open with me, Mr. Rorvik," Khokhlov said, his face expressing deep sorrow mixed with sternness, the expression of a teacher with a willfully disobedient pupil. "Perhaps I have been overly hasty in evaluating your progress toward objective political thought. You are aware, I am sure, that this camp is quite the luxury dacha. You are guests here, not prisoners. In other places food is not quite so plentiful, and discipline is a bit more . . . severe. Please, I beg of you, tell me some names." He smiled. "I do believe that we could . . . work together."

"I'm afraid not, sir."

Khokhlov frowned. "I am not stupid, Mr. Rorvik. Let me point something out to you. I know that there are resistance sympathizers in this camp, and I know something is going on. I can feel it in the air, and I also have my . . . sources. I suspect that you know what is going on. Now, consider. We have been talking for quite the while. Ten minutes? Don't think we haven't been noticed. Now, what are these resistance sympathizers to think, as they watch us talk? Even if you assure them you told me nothing, how can they trust you? Talk to me, and I will see to your safety—I have my means in this camp, I assure you—or else . . ." He shook his head. "It is not me you should be afraid of. You are tagged for being a pigeon whether you talk or not."

Khokhlov was right, he realized. Even though he hadn't joined the resistance, he knew too much. Had there been any way he could have avoided talking to Khokhlov? No; the reeducation counselors were all-powerful within the boundary of the camps. Even the guards feared them, and a prisoner who deliberately refused to talk when asked politely could expect to be denounced, or even shot. But it was the wrong night to be talking to him. He wouldn't survive the night without Khokhlov's protection.

His muscles were knotted up, and he had to force himself to breath normally. He knew the feeling intimately; it was the feeling of having hostile, invisible eyes watching from the sky, the feeling of being a target for inevitable death.

But just what, really, did he have to live for? If he talked, other people would die. It wasn't fair—he'd never even joined the camp resistance!—but he understood war very well by now. He shook his head slowly. "I'm sorry. I really am."

The muscles in his neck didn't loosen, but he realized that he could breathe again.

"I am, too, Mr. Rorvik." Khokhlov waited for one more moment, then shook his head and strode briskly away, as if he wanted to have nothing more to do with Rorvik, abandoning him to his fate. "I am, too."

Rorvik knew that his one chance was to find Povelli—or somebody, anybody with a line to the resistance—and try to explain. There was a bare possibility that they might take a chance on him, if he went to them immediately, showing he had nothing to hide.

He didn't move.

There was something wrong. He desperately needed to find somewhere to think. There was nowhere; standing here by the barbed wire was as good as anywhere.

He squeezed his eyes tightly shut. Where the hell was he?

In a camp.

Was he?

The memory of the draft was still fresh in his mind. His biceps still ached from the pushups that Driscott had made him do, back when he was still a FNG, what, two years ago?

That was impossible.

He had died. Unambiguously, totally. Shot in the chest, shot in the head, blown to pieces by artillery.

That was impossible, too.

Simulations. That was the key. He remembered that from his civilian days, as the superpowers of Europe and Japan and America jockeyed and maneuvered for position, watching their simulations of what would happen in every possible attack scenario, each waiting until they found one where they'd have the advantage. Much of battle was mathematical, a matter of strategy and tactics, faceless forces fighting other faceless forces.

But in some situations, the people mattered. They would need to know how real troops react in battle before they could believe the computer models. God, Driscott had told him that, right out; Driscott had told him everything, and he had been too dumb to understand.

He opened his eyes, and tried to disbelieve what he saw. There was no camp; no war. When he'd been drafted, there had been no war. How long ago was that? A few days? A month? It was ridiculous to think that the Russians would invade the United States; what would they get out of it? The whole war made no sense, not unless it was a scenario, an elaborate set-up to probe how soldiers would act in wartime.

He even knew the technology; it wasn't that much more sophisticated than what he had used to run his drones, except that the resolution would be higher. *Was* higher.

It looked real. There would be micro-lasers somewhere, rastering the image directly onto his retina. If the resolution was high enough, there would be no possible way to tell the difference between real and simulated. He would be drugged, strapped into a contour-couch somewhere, maybe in Washington? Paralytic drugs certainly, to keep his motions from causing problems, while SQUID pickups read the nerve impulses to his muscles. Maybe hypnotics to make him suggestible, make it easier for him to mistake the simulation for reality.

He pinched himself, then punched his arm as hard as he could. It hurt, but that proved nothing. That could be simulated.

There must be other real people in the simulation, too. Who? Westermaker? Driscott? Who was real, and who simulated? Westermaker, he thought. She had to be real. Somewhere she was still alive. Someday she would go back to her husband, back to her kids. In a few days she would be wondering if he had been real or a simulation. And an incident that had been innocent and decent would turn into a pornographic sideshow for some Washington desk-jockeys.

It took him a moment to realize that if this was true, then somewhere—maybe not even far away—Angela and Lissy were alive too, waiting patiently for him at home, oblivious of the nonexistent war. Not starving to death in a relocation camp, not buried in unmarked graves hidden under mountains of rubble. Alive.

God, now he knew what he had been drafted for. Not to be a real soldier, but to play out simulations, perfect computer simulations of possible battle scenarios. The people he'd fought, the ones he'd fought with, weren't real. They needed to know how he'd hold up under stress, how any average American would hold up. They needed the data to make their computer simulations work. He was fighting this war so that, in real life, no one would ever have to fight a war.

He was a pawn.

But was he a pawn of the Americans? Or the Russians? What if the Russians needed to know the reactions of American soldiers, too? What if they really were planning an invasion?

That was ridiculous.

He started to shake his head, first left, then right, watching for a time-lag in the video response. It started making him dizzy, but he refused to stop. "Let me out!" He shook his head harder, faster. The other prisoners stared at him. "Stop the simulation! I quit, I tell you! I'm quitting!"

His head hurt, and the world was no less real. He clenched his teeth and slapped himself on the side of the head, ignoring the pain. Blood started to flow down his cheek on the third or fourth punch, but now he thought he could see something, a blur of black-anodized aluminum, out of focus in front of his eyes, the raster-head of a retinal laser-scanner. He shook his head more violently, left and right, up and down, and he could see it more clearly, with the lenses and sensors that kept it focused on his eyes. It had slipped slightly off to the side, and the reeducation camp was the part out of focus now, two-dimensional, the view from each eye skewed. He tried to pull it off his head, but his hands felt nothing. He shook his head harder. The moment before he passed out, the head-mounted display slipped entirely away, and he could see the room, and the computers, and the figures of three doctors bending over him with expressions of alarmed concern.

8.

The man from the Selective Service thanked Rorvik, reminded him of the penalties for talking to any person at any time about his service experiences, and then shook his hand. Rorvik could see Angela waiting for him at the door. The house looked different; smaller, the paint dingier than he remembered. He'd only been gone a week.

Stop that. If it were a simulation, they would have used photographs of the house; it would be perfect in every detail.

He scanned the bushes automatically, looking for the glint of sun from drone lenses, wishing he had his IR augmented vision. Then he caught himself, forced his muscles to relax. There was no war, no hiding drones.

The government car drove off, and Lissy darted from behind Angela and scampered out to greet him. He spread his arms to receive her, and she almost knocked him over with her enthusiasm. "Daddy! You're home! I missed you!"

He picked her up and swung her around. She was bigger than he remembered. Could she have grown so much in a week? Her hair was darker, her face thinner and more ordinary than in his memories.

"I missed you too, Tiger-cub," he said.

She looked up at him, growling like a tiger but with a wide smile, and he hugged her. Then he nuzzled his face up under her ponytail, and purred at her as loud as he could. She giggled and purred back.

They couldn't possibly simulate that. He opened up his arms. Angela joined them, and he hugged them both at the same time. "I missed you, too, Daddy-cat," Angela whispered.

It was real this time.

He was home.

Real.

Radiance

Carter Scholz

ARTER SCHOLZ HAS NOT PUBLISHED
FICTION IN A GOOD MANY YEARS; HIS RETURN IS CAUSE FOR CELEBRATION.

THE COLD WAR PRODUCED ANY NUMBER OF CULTURAL WONDERS, OR DIS-
TORTIONS, DEPENDING ON YOUR POINT OF VIEW. (FROM MY OWN POINT OF VIEW,
BOTH WONDERS AND DISTORTIONS.) THE PRESSURES PLACED ON NATIONS, CUL-
TURES, INDIVIDUALS, HAVE BEEN HORRENDOUS. WITH THE BIRTH OF THE NU-
CLEAR AGE, PHYSICS KNEW SIN; CHEMISTRY HAS KNOWN IT AT LEAST SINCE HIGH
EXPLOSIVES AND POISON GAS IN WORLD WAR I.

AND YET . . . THERE HAS NOT BEEN A WORLD WAR SINCE 1945. HOW WILL
HISTORY JUDGE THE COLD WARRIORS? PERHAPS MORE IMPORTANT, HOW WILL
THEY JUDGE THEMSELVES?

1.

QUINE APPROACHED THE Labs on a road that led nowhere else. The morning light was thick, corpuscular. Behind the razorwire of the perimeter
fence, cranes and water towers and incinerator stacks rose above the fortress
city's sprawl of buildings. Construction vehicles moved on the roads.
Beyond, grassland stretched to hillsides yellow from drought and spotted
with dark stands of live oak.

Soon he saw the protesters blocking the gate. Cars in both lanes were
stopped. Blue lights and red lights flickered atop patrol cars on the road's
shoulders. Blackclad police formed a line between the protesters and the
gate. Over chanting, rhythmic but unintelligible, rang a bullhorn's clipped
commands, and the protesters fell back from the roadway to the shoulders,
the rhythm of their chant stumbling. A few remained kneeling before the
gate. Three police holstered their batons and moved respectfully among
them, like acolytes among devouts, helping them one by one to their feet
and leading them within the gates to a waiting bus. The sequence of block-
ade, arrest, and release was by now ritual. The arrested chatted with their
captors.

As the cars edged forward Quine saw once again the darkhaired young woman in the crowd and once again felt the hollowing of his heart. Her resemblance to Kate, any reminder of Kate, still lanced him.

Two cars ahead, Leo Highet's red convertible sounded its horn as Highet leaned out to heckle—Get a life! The woman flinched and Quine's eyes locked on Highet's head, the bald spot, the wedge of features visible in the rearview mirror, the broad nose and dark glasses. Past the gate Highet's car sped into a right turn to the administration building while Quine drove on to the second checkpoint, then through a desert of broken rock, buried mines, and motion sensors on metal stalks like unliving plants. Past this moat he stopped at a third checkpoint, then parked in the shade of a concrete building with its blank walls and horizontal slits of embrasured windows, nervously thumbing the car radio—traffic and weather together, while he watched two younger scientists cross the lot and enter the building. Then he stilled the car and went in.

In his office one high horizontal window framed a blank oblong of sky. On the walls, left by the prior occupant and by Quine untouched, hung seismographs of bomb tests, the branched coils of particle decay, a geological map, electron micrographs of molecular etchings, a fractal mountainscape, all overlaid by memos, monthly construction maps, field test schedules, Everyone Needs To Know About Classification, cartoons, Technology Is What Sets Man Apart, and nearby a whiteboard thick with equations in four colors so long unwiped that Quine's one pass with a wet rag had left the symbols down one edge ghosted but not eradicated, and a second desk, loose papers cascaded across its surface, the computer monitor topped by a seamsplit cardboard carton BERINGER GREY RIESLING and buttressed by books, manuals, folders, xeroxes, Autoregressive Modeling, Rings Fields and Groups, Leonardo da Vinci Notebooks, Numerical Solution of Differential Equations, Selling Yourself and Your Ideas! and under the desk banker's boxes DESTROY AFTER, and D NULL in black marker. Devon Null, the prior occupant, was "on indefinite leave." But when Quine had moved in, Highet had insisted that he leave Null's half of the office untouched, either against Null's return, or, as Quine was coming to believe, as a monument to disappearance.

Quine checked his computer mail. Most of the messages were notices, chaffing, power plays, trivia.

A memorial service will be held Nov. 1 for Al Hazen who died Oct. 27 following a lengthy illness. He was 51. Hazen worked with the Weapons Test Group at Site 600. Donations in his memory may be made to the American Cancer Society.

One message could not be ignored:

Date: Thu 31 Oct 12:10 EST
From: Leo Highet <sforza@milano>
To: Philip Quine <quine@styx>
Subject: Radiance
Cc: dietz@styx, szabo@styx, kihara@dis, huygens@aries, lb@dioce
　　Gentlemen:
　　As you know, the Beltway boys are coming and it is CRUCIAL that they go home awed. I want confidence, energy and style. There are unanswered questions and we will take hits on those. Meeting at noon today to brainstorm our approach, bldg 101, rm 210.
　　Highet

"To apply and direct this vast new potential of destructive energy excited the inventive genius of Leonardo as had few other enterprises."

More galling than the message was Highet's new computer log-in *sforza* and his closing quote. This inspirational conceit, that they were all Renaissance *maestri* under the gentle patronage of Prince Leo the High, had come ironically from Quine, who was reading about da Vinci's eighteen years as military engineer under Ludovico Sforza, Duke of Milan. Leonardo had written, "I hate war, as all rational men hate it, but there seems no escape from its bestial madness." Not while men of genius bend their talents to it, Quine had added. Here was Highet's response.

Highet. What a piece of work. Builder and destroyer of his own legend. A fecund theorist but a distracted experimenter, an indifferent administrator but a champion politician. Most Lab scientists considered themselves above the funding process, but Highet tracked it as carefully as any experiment. From the start of his career he had traveled often to the capital, made himself known and available to congressmen and their staffs. In reward for such attentions he was at a young age appointed technical representative to a disarmament conference. His conduct was impeccable until one afternoon, goaded by the other side's mendacious presentation and by his own ungovernable need to occupy the center of every situation, he let slip classified data.

Highet made allies sooner than friends, and enemies sooner than either. His allies were silent while his enemies leapt to break him. But Highet made the first of the hairsbreadth escapes on which his legend was built. A paper published a year before, cosigned by the President's science advisor, had exposed the same secret. The hearings were dropped and Highet was exiled to an underfunded oubliette of the Labs housed in temporary trailers: J Section.

Anyone else would have languished there. But Highet built by inches a power base, using his charisma to attract the brightest, most driven graduate students he could find, forming in the meantime new political alliances. When Congress at last funded Radiance, all the necessary talent was in J Section, and fiercely loyal to Highet. Soon he was associate director.

Radiance's charter was to develop energy weapons of all types, but Highet's hope and pet was the Superbright: an orbiting battle station of hairthin rods webbed round a nuclear bomb. The bomb's fireball would excite the rods, focusing its energy into beams that would flash out to strike down enemy missiles, all in the microsecond before the station consumed itself.

So far the beams flashed out only in theory. The theory, originated by Null, seemed to Quine sound, but the more he studied the computer model, the less he understood why Null's last test had produced even the ghost of a beam. No subsequent tests had shown it. Yet the farther tests fell behind expectations, the more strident became Highet's public claims. Warren Slater, in charge of testing, at last resigned in protest. His letter of resignation was classified and squelched. Bernd Dietz had taken interim charge of testing, and to Quine had fallen the task of finding in disappointing test data any optimism about the promised results.

With the showpiece of his career vulnerable, Highet had grown more reckless than ever. He began showing up at high profile, high tech conferences and seminars, on neural nets, genetic programming, nanotechnology, virtual reality, cold fusion, artificial life, making no discriminations between the cutting edge, the speculative, and the snake oil, as if the force of his character could remake physical law. He spoke in banquet halls at Red Lion Inns, he passed out abstracts, offprints, videotapes, he painted futures brighter and more definite than the present, with himself and his visions at the center of them, inviting the wise and the bold to sit with him in the prosperity and rectitude of that inner circle, outside which was darkness, barbarism, and chaos.

And many have made a trade of delusions and false miracles, deceiving the stupid multitude. Again the voice. Quine recognized the line from Leonardo's *Notebooks.* In the mind's shadows were countless voices, dead, living, unborn. Since working on Radiance he had dreamed them. Now they irrupted into his waking life.

On his second computer, secure in steel shielding, waited Quine's simulation of the rods. Abstract figures gyred in bright colors on the screen. The bland satisfactions of programming. The self-contained machine worlds. It was near to pornography, gaudy and without nuance. Any halfbright notion could be simulated, the simulation tweaked to success, and the success conjured as proof for funding. Realization was, as Highet might put it, a "materials" problem, an exercise left to minions. Bend your backs, men, to prove this golden turd of an idea.

The display glitched and broke into the debugger. Lines of code filled the screen, void qelem, malloc (xarray), atof (nptr), an arcane pidgin halfway to madness. He ceased to see the words, his eye grasping instead the pixels, the shards of contained light the characters comprised.

What is light? The great mystery. Surfaces boil with quantum fire. How comes this dumb swarming to write beauty, alarm, or desolation on our souls? Eyes are the questing front of the brain, and channel to the heart. The eye may not, as Archytas thought, emit illuminating rays, but our modern understanding is no surer.

Mind's eye and heart's channel presented him now Kate's russet hair, full mouth and cheeks, dimpled chin, dark eyes framed by wire glasses. Like a key those features fit his heart. Her flexed shoulder blades under a leotard's scooped back. In a yoga class they'd met. Flirting, lunch, a few dates. She was twenty-three, he thirty-four. Hence his reticence, and paradoxically his faith that the years between them were his to reclaim at will. Her attention augured it. But when at last he bared his need for joy and hope, so long put by, it came out a bitter plea. Save me. Who wouldn't flee from that? She regarded him kindly. Oh, Philip, the moment's passed. It just didn't happen for us. There's someone else.

That the moment could pass. That he had let it. Had not seen it passing. Almost two years since and still it pained. His hand sought his carotid artery. Sixteen in ten seconds: ninety-six. Everything now cause for alarm: gas pains, headaches, shortness of breath, specks in his vision. The blue pills with their excised triangle. Not at work. Certainly not with a meeting.

The morning was gone to no end. Since failing with Kate he seemed to fail at everything, and he saw in all his life only patterns of failure and emptiness.

Quine avoided that part of the building where Highet's young theorists worked, X Section, or, as the older men called it, the Playpen. But today his customary exit was blocked by a tour group of weary adults and bored children in facepaint, their guide saying, —tiny robots that actually repair human cells, as he swerved past a sign WARNING TOUR IN PROGRESS NONCLASSIFIED CONVERSATION ONLY to the swell of the Brahms Requiem in full clash with The Butthole Surfers and a rapid din of simulated combat followed by the admiring exclamation, —Studly! Big win! and laughter fading as he passed an open room in which three refrigerators stood flanked floor to ceiling by case upon case of soda, and veered into a stairwell clattering down metal steps to a metal door held open by a wastebasket and silent despite EMERGENCY EXIT ALARM WILL SOUND and emerged onto a loading dock between brown Dumpsters NOT FOR DISPOSAL OF HAZARDOUS WASTE stepping down onto a paved path then jumping back to dodge a white electric cart DAIHATSU jouncing onto a debris of torn asphalt and treadmarked dirt past chainlink CREDNE CONSTRUCTION and three blue PORT-O-LET stalls to vanish behind three glossy cylindrical tanks COMPOSIT PLASTEEL CONTAINMENT DO NOT INSTALL WITHOUT READING PLASTEEL KIT B IN-STRUCTIONS, on past temporary trailers holding his mouth and nose against the stench of bright green flux oozing from an open pipe into gray earth, until he regained the main road and passed the checkpoint, showing his badge, to enter Building 101, passing through the lobby in which for the edification of visitors and the inspiration of employees were displayed models of bombs, lasers, satellites, boosters, and photos of the celebrated Nobelists who'd devised them, and on to the conference room where all but Highet had arrived.

—He was one of these, shall I say, Marxist radical types. He was so radical his mother cut him out of the family money. Hello, Philip. We're waiting for Leo as usual. So he's in Prague now selling laptop computers to the Czechs. Ah, the man himself.

—Who's this you're talking about, sounds like he's figured out that free markets are diplomacy by other means. Everyone, this is Jef Thorpe, postdoc from the University of Utah, he's here to look us over. Jef worked with Fish and Himmelhoch on cold fusion, and I just want to say don't believe everything you read in *Nature,* something's happening there, someday we'll look into it ourselves. Jef, Aron Kihara, our new press officer, takes the heat for my excesses. Bernd Dietz, materials and research. Frank Szabo, systems integration. Phil Quine, our X-ray focusing guru. Philip, Jef's done interesting work in your area, you should talk to him. All present? Let's do it.

Highet seated the young man opposite Quine, jeans, dark jacket over T-shirt, black hair, high color, a small gold stud through his left nostril, his presence a breach of protocol and probably security, though the others knew better than to say so.

—You all see the news last night? About the protest? We won. We won because we got to go last. First the protesters, out on the street, wind noise, harsh lighting, then our rebuttal from our respectable office. They put us last because we provided closure. So that's our model for the presentation: beginning, middle, end. Begin with our successes, footage of tests. Middle: video simulation, highlighting potential problems. By defining the problems we control the questions. End with entirely new approaches and spinoffs. Aron's running the show, but I may break in at any point.

—Leo, can we skip the last part, the science fiction?

—No, Bernd. Past, present, future. Closure. Without this you leave people ready to ask questions.

—We're avoiding questions?

—Not if they're intelligent and informed but we have a few critics and wise guys on this panel and I'd like to keep it simple.

—Leo, I have more respect for the intelligence of Senators. Congressmen are not always so bright but

—Bernd, it's simple courtesy. We inform them at a level that's neither condescending nor technical, we assure them their money is being well spent, show them how, say thanks so much.

—Salesmanship.

—Grow up, Bernd, a couple times a year I ask you to do this. Is the money well spent? Yes or no.

—Yes, yes.

—I'd ah, feel better if we could discuss the middle part in detail, there are just some questions that I'm not comfortable to address without ah, just a little more input. For example the focusing data . . .

—Aron, only Slater has questioned that data, and he's gone. Discredited. Focus is now Philip's baby.

—So, ah, focus is our main problem?

—Yes, it's one, said Quine. —Focus, brightness . . .

—But we're within an order of magnitude?

—I don't see any quantitative agreement with theory. The tests have shown a few bright spots. That's all I'm willing to commit to.

—That's all you've committed to for what is it ten months now Philip?

—I don't see any fundamentals. I'm beginning to wonder

—Are you pulling a Slater on me, Philip? Because I want to tell you something, all of you. Some people in the lower echelons are making Slater out to be some kind of hero. To me this man was a menace to every one of us because he didn't care about winning. He didn't know what he wanted out of life and wouldn't have been able to get it if he had known. I have no respect for parasites like that.

—Leo, Null had a brilliant notion and we should pursue it, but that's all it is so far, a notion. We

—No one's questioned Null's theory, no one, not even critics.

—Sure but it's a long way from there to even a prototype

—We have supporting test data

—which may or may not mean qualitative agreement may or may not, but never quantitative, we have no understan

—well you're the one with the models Philip lo these many

—and you're the one who said this was a long term project, your words, long term, now suddenly

—oh sure, and if we all had seven lives

—now there's a little pressure it's

—what I'm hearing

—it's suddenly urgent

—what I'm hearing from you Philip is that we need more shots. Convey that necessity to our guests when they're here, think you can do that?

—I won't pretend there's focus

—You're not going to give me an inch are you?

—Not on the basis of spotty data I can't interpret.

—I tell you what. There's an eighty kiloton shot next Saturday. That's your baby, Bernd? Philip, piggyback it. Get yourself some better data.

—In what, a week? Design and fabricate apparatus in a week?

—Nine days. Jef can help you if he sticks around.

—Now hold on

—Get off the pot. Let's move to Frank's contribution. You've all read it?

—Leo

—We're moving on.

There was a brief silence in which papers rustled.

—Nothing new here, said Dietz.

—That's its strength. We've taken heat on pre-production technologies. This is a simple, viable off-the-shelf option, an element of the overall system. It's an easy sell. Contractors are lining up.

—It's also good show-and-tell, said Szabo. We can point to a card cage, this is the guidance system a year ago, then hold up a wafer, here it is today. Tangible progress.

Dietz continued to study the paper. —These are Baldur anti-satellite missiles in a smaller package.

—Close enough.

—These were shelved over ten years ago as a violation of the ASAT treaty.

—That toilet paper? Let that worry us we might as well pack it in.

—These are not by any stretch of the imagination directed energy weapons. You want to put, what does it say, five thousand of these in orbit . . .

—We're pursuing many options, Bernd. These would be one layer of an overall shield. It's a long way to deployment. Oh and we get something else totally for free with Frank's idea. Always think dual use. Put a warhead on these guys they're earth penetrators, aim them downward get a thousand g impact, three k p s terminal velocity, earth-coupled shock waves destroy hardened shelters. We have a friend in the Pentagon who's hard for that and the Beltway boys know it.

—Wait just, you mean, this, these ah interceptors are for the presentation? But it's, we need to address the existing problems, that's what they're coming for, we can't feed them something totally new! And with this Slater thing

—Aron, trust me, it's the best possible thing to do. As far as Slater goes, he's history, a blip, not even an incident. This visit was scheduled long before he had his snit. Sure we'll get closer scrutiny than we would in the average dog-and-pony but call it an opportunity. Remember NORAD's well-publicized false alarms and screwups, they got a billion-dollar facelift out of it. You up to speed now?

—Well yes, I mean, no not on the interceptors but . . .

—Just put Frank's paper in the kit, I'll step in. Oh, and make sure everyone gets a souvenir.

—A, I'm sorry?

—A souvenir. What are you giving the kids for family day today?

—Ah, some laser-etched aluminum disks . . .

—Good. Run off half a dozen make it a dozen more etched with the Radiance logo, can you do that? And glossies of the new artist's renderings.

Highet was out the door before anyone else had left their seat. Thorpe, abandoned, stood but did not move quickly enough to follow the older man out. As the seated men studied him incuriously he blushed and exited.

The others then rose. Szabo went out singing under his breath, —It's a long way, to deployment, it's a long way, I know. In the meantime, we have employment, it's the stick that makes us go . . .

At the doorway Dietz said to Quine, —Outrageous that he should bring a boy into that meeting and criticize you this way. Easy for him to make promises, but when the promises are not so easy to deliver we suffer for them.

—I don't think the boy knew what he was getting into.

—Tell me what you want added to this test as soon as possible. He has put our asses on the line, both of us.

—I'll send you e-mail.

—Souvenirs! He gives senators souvenirs.

Quine had come to the Labs at Réti's invitation, Réti, the legend, intimate of Einstein, Heisenberg, Schrödinger, founder of the Labs. Impossible to refuse. Réti had for one semester graced Quine's university with his presence, where he'd sat on Quine's doctoral committee. Quine must have made an impression, for two years later Réti called him. I hear you are working hard on some good ideas. How would you like unlimited resources for this work? Come for the summer, work on what you will.

Quine and Sorokin, a fellow postdoc, had isolated the emission of a single photon from a calcium source in order to determine whether a lone quantum displayed wave-particle complementarity. They'd refined their approach for two years, paring it to essentials, designing an experiment they had a hope of realizing with the school's meager resources. Elegance born of need. In one month at the Labs Quine designed and built a detector acute enough. The experiment came off on the first try. Both tunneling and anticoincidence were evident. They had touched the central mystery. Even a single photon is both particle and wave.

Quine stayed; after that there was never a question of it. Not till much later did he guess that he'd been played. That Réti had waited two years before approaching him for a reason. That by then his work was ripe for plucking, and the Lab's resources had little to do with its fruition apart from giving them the juice of it.

His paper brought him a celebrity almost grace. Unlimited time to think. No assigned duties. And the mysteries ceased to open to him. Idle, he took on a Lab problem, quantum optics of X-ray mirrors. He welcomed the work, as though it paid some tithe of the mind to the practical. And it was interesting science, but finally it was, as the pioneers had with exact irony called their first bomb, a "gadget." A solution that laid bare first principles was useless if it couldn't kill missiles. So his mirrors never passed a design review, but he was left alone to fiddle with quantum optics for telescopes and such. Then Radiance geared up, and his modeling software proved flexible enough to accommodate the next idea: the bombpumped Superbright. Opportunistic as a virus, the Labs exploited any evident skill. And so he was out of quantum optics and into weapons modeling. He became busy. Still he kept silent faith with the mysteries. He would return to them when the pressures of the moment were past. Programming took only the surface of his mind; its capital he held in reserve. But Quine could feign reserve, even to himself, while reserving nothing, and he came at last to understand that he did well at programming precisely because he brought his all to it. Nothing was left over.

When he left the building the sun was low. The air was warm, and as he started the car the radio blurted —record temp, before he silenced it.

Through the gate traffic slowed. Demonstrators in costume paraded in the road. Quine edged forward through skeletons and spooks with signs and props, TECHNOLOGIES OF DEATH, a longrobed mantis-headed figure towering on stilts above the crowd, tambourines jangling, EL DÍA DE LOS MUERTOS, and lab security herding the crowd off the road. As he cleared the crowd a klaxon blared. The mantis swayed, tugging at robes snagged on the perimeter razorwire as the entrance gates slid shut, alarm lights strobing. On the inner perimeter road security vehicles appeared racing. Then he saw standing by his passenger window the woman who resembled Kate. She wore black spandex bicycle pants and a blue chambray shirt. She was staring at the gate. Quine hesitated, then rolled down the window.

—You want a ride out of here? They're going to start arresting people.

She looked at him, then back at the gate. On the main road Quine saw a flurry of approaching lights. City police.

—I can't wait.

Whoops blasts squeals cut the crowd noise. She saw the vehicles approaching and with something like annoyance got into Quine's car. Quine sped away shutting his window against the shriek of the passing vehicles.

—I'm Philip.

—Lynn. Did you see what happened?

When he looked at her all resemblance to Kate fell away. Same body type, same round features, but hair almost black with just a russet tinge, cropped close to the neck. No glasses. Dark penetrating eyes. Tanned calves darkly downed, lithe as a huntress's. No key turned in his heart, just a faint echo of loss.

—The one on stilts, his costume caught on the fence. It must have set off the alarm.

—Were you there for the demo?

—No. I work there.

His ID was still clipped to his jacket. She had been looking at it, and now she smiled slightly.

—What do you work on?

He turned onto a road parallel to the freeway where earthmovers were parked in debris-filled lots between emporia of sporting goods, fast food, auto parts, videotapes, computers, discount carpets. Sun flashed through the struts of a half-finished retaining wall.

—Defensive weapons. Where can I take you?

—You mean Radiance. Do you believe in it?

And those in the anterooms of Hell demur, saying, I do not approve of what goes on inside.

—It's what I do.

—Do you know what Einstein said? That you can't simultaneously prepare for war and prevent it?

—Where can I take you.

—Drop me at the corner of Mariposa.

—We didn't hear about the evening protest. The organizers usually let us know.

—Maybe they're tired of playing your game.

—It's not my game.

A green sign with white letters MARIPOSA hung over the intersection. Quine pulled to the curb by a bus stop bench placarded FAST DIVORCE BANKRUPTCY. She turned to him with sudden vehemence.

—But isn't it a waste now that the cold war

—Look, and hearing annoyance in his voice he immediately stanched it, —even if I, it's classified and I work, I only work on a small part of it, I don't even know . . .

—These demonstrations won't stop, you know. Until you do. You don't know how angry people are.

—Then I'll probably see you again out there, he said.

—You will.

She unbuckled her seatbelt. Suddenly he wanted to know her.

—Would you have lunch with me some day?

She looked at him incredulously. —Lunch? With you? But why?

—Because I'd like to talk to you.

—Do we have anything to say to each other?

—Maybe not. But if even you and I can't talk, what hope . . .

—You're the enemy. Her eyes fixed on him.

—Oh well if you feel that way

—I do!

—Then there's nothing, squeal of brakes obscuring his words as a bus pulled to the curb ahead of him. She was out the door before he felt the protest of his heart. So even now he had not relinquished some forlorn hope of starting over.

When he reached home Nan's car was in the lot. Most Tuesday nights she spent here at Quine's. He went to her place Friday nights and some weekends. But he'd worked late Tuesday, so they'd shifted it to tonight. He'd forgotten.

Nan worked in another section of the Labs, handling personnel files. He had met her after failing with Kate. He had never told her about that. She was so unlike Kate. Her features were sharp and fine, her skin pale, her straight auburn hair just starting to show gray, her slight body always dressed with a style that in its impeccability read as a brave front.

—Lo, she called as he entered, —In the kitchen. I picked up some tortellini at Il Fornaio and a salad, is that okay?

—Fine.

—Some bread in the oven, can you get that?

She chattered about her day, a seniority conflict in her department. Quine's patience wore. When, setting the plates down, she bent to kiss his neck, he stiffened and pulled away.

—What's wrong?

—Highet's going mad again. A Congressional visit's coming up, it should be routine, but he acts like the program's at stake.

—Is it?

—First he drops Null's work in my lap, then today he starts pimping some lunatic idea of Szabo's, and assigns me a postdoc like, like some kind of chaperone . . . and the protesters.

—What about them?

—They're getting on my nerves.

—Have you made any progress?

—No I haven't made any progress. There's no progress to be made!

—Please don't snap at me, Philip.

—I can't even discuss it, you don't have the clearance.

She carried dishes into the kitchen without speaking.

—Look, I have an insane deadline. I won't be able to see you for a week or so.

—We're seeing Ginny and Bill on Sunday, I thought.

—I can't. I'm sorry I just can't.

She sighed and left the kitchen. In the living room the television came on. When after a moment he entered the room he heard her in the bedroom speaking on the telephone. Remote control in hand he viewed a cool panoptic tumble of war famine catastrophe enormity larded with a fantastic plenty of goods caressed by smiling tanned models, to pause on the logotype of Martin Marietta, —a proud supporter for twenty-five years of science programming on public television, his impulse to switch again frozen by the worn, imposing face of Horatiu Réti, saying, —There is now a cult of the beautiful theory. But how beautiful is reality? These so-called beautiful theories, these elegant mathematics are not verified by experiment. Experiment shows us a mess of a universe with over a hundred basic particles and three irreconcilable forces. We would like to unify them all, just as we would like to smooth over all the political differences in the world. But experience shows, in physics and in politics, that this is not always possible.

Abruptly the screen blanked then cleared to the involute radiance of the bomb. Sun's heart. Cosmic ground. Siva and Devi coupling. A thin roar issued from the set and the waspish voice rode over it, —The duty of science is to pursue knowledge even if it leads to the unbeautiful. Or to the evil. How else learn about evil?

Nan returned to sit beside him. —Isn't that Réti?

The camera returned to the physicist facing an interviewer. Quine remembered. Though emeritus director, Réti was rarely at the Labs; the office he kept there served him solely as a clubroom or a set. Six months ago a film crew had come to the Labs. He had heard Réti shouting behind the closed door.

—Watch, this is what Highet calls the liberal bias of the media, said Quine as the camera went to the interviewer.

—Many of your colleagues turned away from weapons design for ethical reasons. Some of them, your schoolmates, your collaborators, have won Nobel Prizes. Do you ever feel that your work with weapons has cost you credibility or respect within the scientific community? Has it compromised you as a scientist?

—Never.

—You're closely connected to Radiance. What about recent charges that test results have been faked?

—This is a lie. First, I am not closely connected . . .

—You've lobbied extensively for the system in Washington.

—I am no lobbyist! I am a private citizen with some scientific expertise, and when I am asked to testify about technical matters I do so . . .

—But for over forty years you've been an advocate of nuclear weapons, your authority and influence are well known.

—You listen to me. It is an imperfect world, a dangerous world, even an evil world. All ends, even the best, are reached by impure means. Reason is supposed to be the hallmark of science, but no one is swayed by reason. A theory, an idea, does not make its own way. It was Einstein who said merit alone is very little good; it must be backed by tact and knowledge of the world. I know of many cases, maybe the data does not quite agree with your theory, no, the carpers will question, your case is clearer if you discard *this* set of data, if you report only *these* results. And who are these frauds? Ptolemy. Galileo. Newton. Bernoulli, Mendel, Millikan. What matters in the long run is not your scruples, but whether you have driven your knowledge home!

A man has no wealth nor power but his knowledge, Réti had once said to Quine. But now he said that if power did not lead, knowledge could not follow. Quine saw behind the fury in Réti's eyes a bright and open wound: more illustrious for his influence than his work, Réti had failed at everything but success. And Quine's life, he suddenly saw, was bent to Réti's influence. Quine stood up, ignoring —Philip? what is it? and went to the bathroom. He clutched the sides of the sink, heart racing. In the cabinet he found the pill bottle.

The spirit is radiant, yet there are two principles of radiance: that of light, and that of fire. Fire comes to the use of those who go not the way of light. And the difference is, that fire must consume its object.

Quine swallowed the pills and his nausea subsided as he returned and sat, to Réti's angry voice, —So I have no Nobel Prize, that accolade of *pure* science. But Alfred Nobel would understand me well. Yes, I have the ear of presidents. And history will be my judge, not you.

—What is it? What's the matter?

Quine turned to Nan, her face in the phosphor light bleak as a rock outcrop. He reached to touch her neck. Unsmiling she leaned against his hand. His fingers cupped her nape and he draw her mouth to his.

In the bedroom they undressed on opposite sides of the bed. The television droned on. Between her legs he felt the string of a tampon, and as he touched it she bent double and enclosed him in her mouth. Above the activities of their bodies his spirit hovered sadly regarding the terrain of his life. Lightly his hands cradled her head. He began to pump semen. Deep inside him a talon drove home and brought forth, impaled, his soul, writhing. A minute later he was awash in sleep. Waiting at a counter to pick up xeroxes. Quick tap at his shoulder. Kate. She smiled, her eyes upon him, and he knew it was a dream, and he was happy, and he slept.

2.

The morning sky, pallid with haze, conveyed yet enough sun to cast through his high window a faint rhombus which crept along the wall toward the doorway relentless as a horologe. Quine gazed at it half hearing the radio, —ildfires in three counties, when his phone rang.

—Quine.

—Is this Philip?

—Yes, who's this.

—Lynn. From the demo yesterday?

—Oh yes. How did you . . .

—I behaved badly. I'd like to apologize. Are you free for coffee?

—Well, not this morning, I . . .

—Later this afternoon?

—Well I

—I can get off work at four. Do you know the Café Desaparecidos? In the central mall. I work near there, I don't have a car.

—Sure I, okay, I'll see you there about four.

As he hung up Jef Thorpe knocked on his open door. Black jacket, blue shirt, jeans. A faint pock where yesterday the nose stud had been.

—Come in.

—I guess we'll be working together.

—You're staying.

—Never a question of that. Listen, that meeting yesterday, I didn't belong there, I'm sorry if . . .

—Not your fault. As you see, Dr. Highet has his way of doing things.

—Yeah. Before we start I want to tell you, the single-photon experiment you did with Sorokin was really elegant. I was surprised to find you here, I thought you'd be somewhere more theoretical.

—I thought everyone had forgotten that experiment by now.

—Oh no. It was very sweet work.

—The detector was critical. We worked on it for two years and couldn't get the resolution we needed. We got it only after I came here, they could mill the beryllium to micrometer tolerances.

—You didn't follow it up.

Sorokin had said, you don't leave an infant like this to fend for itself. But Sorokin had always been inflexible. He had refused even to visit the Labs during the experiment.

—Sorokin thought I was wrong to come here. He said it would be a black hole. He may have been right. Of course things look different from inside.

—Black hole, yeah, I've thought of that. But you know where I come from. That limits my options in the straight academic world.

—You don't have any qualms about defense work?

—What's this, a background check?

—No, I just, you might want to consider your position while you can. I came in neutral about defense work, and before long I was in the thick of it. It's especially easy to slip into it from nuclear science.

—I'll keep that in mind. I'm kind of apolitical.

—Let me show you what I have, turning to the computer which glowed with:

Date: Fri 1 Nov 09:05
From: Leo Highet <sforza@milano>
To: Philip Quine <quine@styx>
Subject: Upcoming J Section Tests
11/4 23:00 PDT, Building 328, Codename "Stelarc," groundbased laser guide star, R. Grosseteste, sup.
11/9 18:00 PDT, Site 600, Codename "Taliesin," 80 kiloton, B. Dietz & P. Quine, sup.

"Mechanics are the Paradise of mathematical science, because here we come to the fruits of mathematics." LdV

—Looks like we're real, said Thorpe.

—You're lucky. It was years before I was directly associated with a shot.

—Is that luck?

—It's a bit of prestige. A merit badge.

Quine cleared the screen and brought up the Radiance test data.

—You see. Intense brightness here, and here. Very erratic pattern. Agrees with the theory to a point, but when we increase power, we don't get the expected increase in beam, we get less in fact. We've talked about trying different metals in the rods, we've used gold till now, but mercury . . .

—Yeah, elements seventy-two through ninety-five would be good to try but with our time constraints I checked with Fabrication, they have gold rods ready to go, maybe we should stick with those and put our efforts into sensor configuration, keep it simple, don't you think?

—Sounds reasonable.

Thorpe continued to stare at the screen. —Could this be an annulus? This pattern I mean, could the sensors be picking up an imperfect focus, the edge of a ring? If we move them in . . .

—I've tried, no luck.

—Can I look at your focusing code?

—Yes, sure, all the files are in this directory.

—That's great. Mind if I work here? pointing to Null's desk.

—Ah, sure. Sure, go ahead. I'm going for lunch and maybe a swim. I'll see you later.

We read of the beaver that when it is pursued, knowing that it is for the medicinal virtue of its testicles and not being able to escape, it stops; and it bites off its testicles with its sharp teeth and leaves them to its enemies.

Gaunt, saturnine, Bran Nolan in a corner of the cafeteria looked up unsmiling from scattered papers to raise a hand in greeting.

—How's our new boyo Kihara?

—Well enough. Weren't you in line for that position?

—It's my Tourette's syndrome. Terrible liability in a press officer, you never know what he might blurt out in public.

—Seems you should have been asked.

—Do you know, I'm happier, if that's the word I want, where I am. Kihara is a little lamb, a kid. The last man, Vessell, didn't outlast Slater. And we're not through with all that, no indeed.

—Getting some work done? Quine indicated the papers.

—"The Labs have a longstanding commitment to developing new methods and technologies to protect the environment," the most effective of which to date has been the press release. Do you know we have a toxics mitigation program now. Seems some chemical seeped into the ground water under a vineyard off the north boundary. Vines died, soil went gray, the whole field stinks like sepsis. I'm writing an upbeat report about it. And yourself? How's the death ray coming?

—We can maim small insects at a meter. The new concept is interceptors. Small flying rocks.

—Do you know, da Vinci invented shrapnel. He'd have been right at home here with all these advanced minds.

—Yes, that's Highet's conceit.

—Throwing rocks at things. We should be proud, thinking about these old impulses in such an advanced way. Years ago Réti had some harebrained flying rock scheme, these things never die, just get recyc

—Bran, Bran, Bran. What must I do to get you to use a font other than Courier? Nolan pulled back from the sheaf of papers brandished in one plump hand beneath his nose.

—Bob, how's the gout? I don't like this business of tarting up manuscripts. You get enchanted by the beauty of it all. You start to think you're writing the Book of Kells.

—A few attractive fonts, tastefully applied, can spice up a presentation so. A little humanitas, you know. Why else, Bran, did we get you that powerful and costly workstation?

—Jeez, Bob, I don't know, why did you? I'm still figuring out the type balls on my Selectric.

The sheaf of papers fell fanning from their clip onto the table. Shaking his head and chuckling grimly, Bob withdrew.

—Humanitas, yes, that's what we need, isn't it, Highet with his Renaissance, and Aldus Manutius there, need a few more particle men who've read the Tao Te Ching, couple more managers who've studied Sun Tzu, lend these binary views a little tone, dress up the winners and losers, the Elect and the Preterite, the screwers and the screwed, each man in his station. Keep your distance from the Preterite, can't have just anyone winning, because if you let the rabble win, if they can rise, you can surely fall.

Nolan folded back pages, —Listen to this lovely bit, "the support of this tight-knit community," support is it now? I'd have said the goading, the ambition, the *Schadenfreude,* that's what gets the work done. Look around you, these are people without lives, the wife walked out six months ago with the kid, they're eating Campbell's soup cold out of the can, they haven't got a clean shirt, but after a few months of eighteen-hour days they've got *data* that everyone wants to see. They *win big.*

—Bran, you keep working here.

—What should I do then, write novels? Or maybe journalism, that's it, *investigative* journalism. Have you met the journalist from Cambridge? Right over there with his tape recorder, name's Andrew Steradian. He's researching the belief systems of those who work on weapons of mass destruction, I think was his phrase. Quite the charmer. He's published one book on scientific fraud, and a paper highly critical of what he calls the defense establishment. You probably don't watch TV but there was an antinuclear program on PBS last night, Steradian was in it abusing Réti.

—Does Highet know all this?

—Highet invited him.

Quine headed for the door, passing as he did Andrew Steradian, holding a small microphone before a J Section technician, saying, —you're so goldang busy every day you just put off thinking about it, though in Quine's view pressure was a tool well used to put off thinking.

Black cottonwoods around the pool throve despite the drought. Catkins littered the water. A jet moved in the sky, stitching a contrail across the thin lace of cloud drifting eastward through which a hot sun struggled to assert itself. Quine sat on a towel on the grassy verge and watched a portly bearded swimsuited man enter through the gate, barrel chest glossed with sunbleached hair, and behind him a woman in a white halter top and shorts, the heads of three men turning to follow. The pool was crowded this Friday afternoon; unlike Quine, most worked a five-day week, most would depart hence into a forgetfulness. In the shallows of the pool two young girls splashed. One opened her mouth to show her companion a bright penny on her outstretched tongue. A young mother in a black maillot gripped a ladder to raise herself half from the pool and wave at her infant in a nearby stroller, glisten and shadow in the cords of her back, and Quine suffered a pang for a life now beyond his knowing: to be wed, with child, so young. On thermals a blackwinged bird, *Cathartes aura,* rocked and banked. Jet's thunder fell like muffled blows. The warmth and the sound of water churned by swimmers and the spray tossed up by their passing lulled Quine into a lethargy from which he woke with a start to consult his watch. On the pool's floor danced cusps of light.

When he parked at the town's central mall the high cloud had passed and the sky was pale blue overhead and scum brown near its horizons. Quine walked sweating between pastel columns under a pediment that alluded to no place or time through smoked glass doors into an atrium so chill and disjunct it might have been another planet. Outside methane and ammonia storms might blow. Shops, granite benches, low fountains, and climbing plants ringed a pool in which stood a steel sculpture of crippled symmetry, as if a Platonic solid had ruptured.

The cafe's high walls rose past exposed beams and ducts to the nacre of frosted skylights. Lynn sat at a glass table in a wireframe chair, face downcast at papers before her. In the moment before she looked up, Kate's face glowed before him. In this cafe they'd first talked. What do you do, Philip?

—Hoy es el día de los muertos, Lynn said in greeting, banishing Kate's image. Angularities all her own moved in her flesh; a small gap showed between her teeth as she smiled.

Quine seated himself and said gravely, —I should tell you I'm involved with someone.

—Jesus, I said I wanted to apologize, not start an affair.

—I, sorry I . . .

—And maybe pick your brain about Radiance.

—I'm sorry, what did you say? El día . . .

—The Day of the Dead. All Saints' Day. All this used to be Mexico, you know, they called it Aztlan. Once my law firm shuts you people down, we're going to reclaim all of Aztlan for the native peoples. Don't look that way, I'm joking, that's the kind of thing the far right says about us.

—You're a lawyer?

—Paralegal.

—What's that you're reading?

—Your press releases. She held a sheaf set in unadorned Courier font.

—God you people have fingers in a lot of pies. When I started my concern was the bombs, but now I find out about the supercomputers, the lasers, the genetics, the chemicals, it's a separate world in there, isn't it.

—You probably know more about it than I do.

—Your cover stories are so creative. Every one of. Oh, go ahead, order, she's waiting.

—Cappuccino. What you do mean, cover stories?

—I'll have an espresso, please. Every one of these quote benign technologies has a pretty easy-to-imagine military use. Laser X-ray lithography for etching microchips, uh huh, and here's one about kinder gentler CBW, "less virulent" tear gas for "crowd control," heavier specific gravity for controlled delivery, if this is the stuff you're public about one can only imagine the rest.

—You're wrong, there's a genuine effort to convert to peacef

—Dual use, I know all about it. Genuine effort to blur the line is what it is, and it goes beyond the Labs, people in physics and comp sci departments across the country lining up at the same trough, the grants are there and if they don't take the money someone else will. What a waste of resources.

—It's more complicated. I won't defend it, but the people I work with, they're not cynical, not

—Oh, I know how people get caught up in their work. I have a friend there, not in Radiance, in another section. He's a Quaker, he calls it "being in the world." I can respect that, at least he's thought about it. How did you get into it?

—I'm, well, a lapsed theorist. But I'm not typical . . .

Was he not? Réti, Highet, Dietz, Thorpe, all had failed in some subtle way that in such a place could be denied. But where was there not failure and denial?

—Do your people pay any attention at all to our demonstrations?

—In J Section? Not much.

—We seem to get to your boss, at least.

—You mean Highet?

—In his little red sports car. What about you? What did you think about yesterday's?

—It seemed, I don't know, festive, almost a costume party, I didn't realize at first it was Halloween . . .

—It was a ceremony. An exorcism.

—Oh come on, what, you mean we're possessed

—By arrogance if nothing else.

—That's absurd, you can't convince anyone with supersti

—It's no different from your rituals, your bomb tests, just as absurd and ritualistic, but really dangerous!

—Not my tests, and he remembered *Dietz, Quine, sup.* —I'm no good talking about this.

The set of her features, so poised and eager, softened and her voice lowered. —I don't mean to attack you. I'm sure you

—But I'm not sure! Because what if it is a waste, the billions and decades and lives and talents, then it's not just me, not just my mistake, but something wrong at the root . . .

—If it is a mistake, you can face it, call a stop.

—But there's never any stopping. It's almost as if these things we work on . . . they use us to get born. Could use anyone.

—I'm sorry Philip . . .

—No it's not your fault. I just, I need to get back. Her face was so concerned that he almost cried out with self-pity. He abruptly rose and walked away stolid with loathing of his own erratic heart, and of her for stirring it.

In the night he woke sweating with a pulse of ninety, reached for the pill-bottle next to the small box DREAMLIGHT Unlock Your Inner Potential and its plastic headset. The pills opened a plain of timelessness and haze in which it seemed a lost part of himself dwelled. All then was fine. As he lay gazing at the grainy darkness of the ceiling his fluency returned, wonderful problems enticed and yielded to his insight, wisdom depended from the sky like fruit. As he began to drowse he roused himself to attach the headset like a blindfold around his temples. When he dreamed, a red strobe in the headset, sensing his eye movements, flickered and roused him enough to observe but not to wake.

The battle station shines in the void of space. Arms pivot as targets rise in swarms, bright points on the black hollow of a crescent Earth. They blur in a silver mist of chaff. Above the crescent distant stations ignite in globes of light and their beams lance out, targets crumpling, but swarm follows swarm, breaching the atmosphere, too many to destroy, and the dream begins again with different stations, Mylar skin of mirrors rippling, missiles coming on as earth-based beams strike up and the mirrors twitch to focus . . .

The world has changed, the enemy has collapsed into ruined republics. Yet despite this consummation of all the Labs has worked for, the work goes on unabated, the mood is spiritless, the shots in the desert continue, as though it is some ritual of penance, some black and endless propitiation of forces that by losing their fixed abode have gained in menace. Now effort must redouble to keep those forces from finding a new abode, from tenanting, aye, the Labs.

Vertigo of waking. Tearing of Velcro as the headset falls free. Wan dawn light. Stillness, faint whistle of tinnitus, first sounds of birdcall. And he realizes this dream is true. The enemy is gone. And the work does go on, and on.

3.

In the next days Lynn was not among the protesters. Their numbers had diminished to a small group in daily vigil by the main gate holding a drooping sheet painted DIABOLIS EX MACHINA. Quine in his machine slowed through the gate and stopped, valves in the engine ticking, for a backhoe lurching across the main road to a dirt track that wound behind a building, and closed his window against the dust billowing toward him as he went on past an air hammer chiseling a sidewalk to rubble, overtones of its chatter following him across the rock moat and into the building where, too late to retreat, he saw Thorpe seated at Null's computer tapping rapidly without letup at Quine's entrance.

—Morning, said Quine.

—Is it still? I've been here all night. Something there for you to read.

Atop Quine's stack of journals, a year's unread accumulation, colored slips in their pages flagging articles that at an earlier time would not have waited a day, was a xerox topped with a yellow sticker SEEN THIS? *Physical Review Letters 1954.* A joke? A dig at his age?

—I know it's old, said Thorpe. —But I think it applies. See, I started with an EE from a hick school, taught myself quantum mechanics by reading Dirac, things don't change that much. Lots of ideas have been left hanging. That's how I, I mean, stumbling in embarrassment at having carelessly touched as he thought Quine's sensitive point, —not to say, it's just, if you're a student like me, not well connected, not seeing the latest preprints and hearing all the gossip, you need another way up. This is my way, looking for old forgotten stuff to build on.

—So tell me about this.

—I came across it working for Fish and Himmelhoch, looking for a nuclear model to explain the cold fusion reaction. Okay I know, the current wisdom is, there's no reaction, it's bogus, or if anything is happening it's electrochemical, fine. But you can model the process in a nuclear way, the phenomenon's called superradiance. The equations are quite similar. Highet saw the connection.

—To this? Highet told you about Superbright?

—Very sharp guy.

—That's quite a breach of classification.

—He kind of hinted around, citing the open literature. Anyway it's moot, I'm cleared now. What do you think?

—I'll read it when I get a chance, dropping it back atop the stack of journals.

—But, I mean, we don't have much time. Should I pursue it?

—What have you been doing?

—Well, here, let me show you, I started modifying your code but I had a couple of quest

—You've changed my files?

—No no I made copies, all changes made to my copies and I was just wondering about a few things like here where you've got this array of reals here, what's that?

—That's the rod array, angles lengths diameters densities

—Okay, because see I was thinking if you make that something like ten to the minus ten here

—That's the thickness, we can't make rods that thin it's imposs

—But if we play what-if with these numbers . . .

—Wait what are you

—then the beam, oop that's a little extreme but you see what I

—But there's no, I mean sure, you can make the model do anything, but it has to correspond to reality!

—I'm just getting the feel of the system. But, oh here I wanted to know what this function does, this hyperbol

—Yes that's the response curve of the sensors we're using, it . . . look, can this wait? and without pausing Quine was out of the office as from speakers overhead a pleasant female voice advised, —Attention all personnel. Starting at midnight, tiger teams will conduct exercises in this area using blank ammunition, and he turned into the restroom where at the far end, past a row of sinks and urinals opposite metal stalls, a gym bag hung on a hook with a towel and steam billowed forth in a pelting rush of noise and Quine, elbows braced on a basin, looked up sharply from the laving of his hands at a bass voice echoing against the hard tile, —*bist du ein Thor und rein,* to see in the mirror not his own eternally surprised features but fogged void, turning from the hiss of his faucet to glimpse through dispersing mist a hard white nude male body emerging to towel itself still singing, —*welch Wissen dir auch mag beschieden sein.*

In the cavernous building where Dietz supervised, Quine watched long metal tubes welded one by one to the great monstrance in which the bomb, a quarter mile underground, would rest. From sensors at the ends of each tube hundreds of cables would run to the surface. Dietz displayed a blueprint of the cylinder.

—We are already welding. I cannot wait to know.

—Can you hold off a day or two? If I had any idea where to put the damn things I'd tell you if I had any idea even how to find what I'm looking for . . .

—All right, we can go ahead with other things for just a little while. Now the rod configuration . . .

—Unchanged. I'm not touching that.

—Make sure, please, that Highet knows all this. Sometimes he wanders through here and if things are not what he expects he is most unpleasant.

Outside Highet's office Quine, arm raised to knock, from within heard Highet's insistent rasp, —like Kammerer, you know, it's not who makes the mistake it's who takes the blame, and at Thorpe's voice barely audible, —sorry for the poor son of a bitch stuck in his position at his age, barely shows his face, and Highet, —never passed a design review, Quine's ears flared with heat, the door before him turning flat and insubstantial as he lowered his hand and proceeded down the hall unseeing, guided by a familiarity more the prisoner's than the adept's around a corner to a water fountain, studying a bulletin board and its overlapping notices O Section, programmer needed to model underground plumes, K Section, LASS expert needed, Z Section, multimedia guru sought, B Section, materials engineer, while two young men passed, one saying, —I have no special loyalty to OOP, and on to a further junction where a convex mirror above him presented an anamorphic view around the corner. There Nan emerged from a cross corridor with a wiry black-haired man in a blue knit shirt, his biceps and forearms hard and tanned. The two spoke briefly. The man put a hand on Nan's neck and bent forward to kiss her mouth. Quine turned back the way he had come, slowing only when he found he had nearly circled the building. He backtracked to Highet's door and entered without knocking. Highet was alone.

—Get Thorpe out of my office.

—What's your problem now, Philip?

—He's so important give him his own space, I don't want him hanging around me.

—Thought you'd appreciate the company, thought he might be useful to you.

—What's that supposed to mean?

—Thorpe handles himself well, you could learn from him. Show some team spirit. Poor boy's feeling abandoned by you.

—I'll work with him, but I don't have to like him or share office space with him. It's bad enough Null's stuff is still there.

—Thorpe has his own space. You want him out, you tell him so. By the way, Réti's here for a visit, you might want to pay your respects. Instead of running around down in Fabrication with Dietz.

—Someone has to tend to those details.

—Let me tell you something, Philip, I'm a smart guy but to be brutally honest I'm a second-rate physicist. I have the ideas but not the persistence, I've known that for twenty years. But I have learned to position myself and to use other people to get what I want. Win win, you know, we help each other look good.

Voices approached in the corridor as Highet went on in a lower tone, —One path in the world is up. There's also a path down. What there isn't is standing still. Now you, friend, have been standing still for quite a little while. I'd say you need to make some career decisions soon, before they're made for you.

Flanked by two Lab factotums, Horatiu Réti came slowly, stamping his cane, into Highet's office. His eyes, azure behind thick lenses, peered without recognition as Quine greeted him.

—Ah, my young friend, how are you?

—You remember Philip Quine, Horatiu. That beautifully sweet photon detector he built for us.

—Of course, of course.

—So here we are, three generations of first-rate physics talent.

—Yes yes, the torch is passed.

—I really must be

—No, stay. Horatiu, Philip's going to get us the data we need to silence the critics.

—The critics, there is no need to mind them.

—From your eminence perhaps not, but I have to deal with these fools and dupes almost daily. Do you know what a senator, a United States senator, said to me the other day? He called this place a scientific brothel.

—I know the man you mean. Brothels I am sure he knows well, but of science he is ignorant.

—Well unfortunately this ignoramus chairs a committee that oversees our funding, so I have to deal with him.

—Speaking of influence, this left-wing journalist, I see him here again, why do you let him in? Six months ago he abused my trust with gutter tactics of the worst sort.

—You mean Steradian? He's a useful idiot. He's so cocksure I let him hear things I want to see in print, look here . . . Highet lifted from the desktop a folded newspaper, —"Radiance Research Forges Ahead," see, this is solid gold. He's so excited when he hears something that may be classified, his critical sense shuts off. You can see him quiver like a puppy dog from the excitement.

—Keep him away from me, I want nothing to do with him. What is our testing status?

—We need more. As always. Classifying them has helped deflect criticism but we're still being nickel and dimed.

—What do you need?

—An additional three hundred million over the next year.

—I will talk to the President. This is for Superbright?

—Yes. We can definitely show quantitative agreement with theory. It's only a matter of time and money.

—What isn't?

—Excuse me, Leo about that agreement we're

—Philip will tell you how close we are. He and his new assistant have made tremendous headway, just tremendous.

—So? Tell me about this, my young friend.

—Well, I think it's premature to say so. There's a shot next Friday. We'll know better then.

—Philip's too modest, that's always been his problem.

—No, I just think we need a lot more

—More funding. Basically it's a matter of funding. In the long run we see coherent beams striking out a thousand miles and diverging no more than a meter. We see a single battle station downing every missile any enemy can launch.

—That is excellent, I can tell the Preside

—But

—Horatiu, we're also going ahead with your interceptors. As part of the overall system.

—Baldur?

—Smaller, faster, smarter, cheaper. Less than thirty billion to deploy. That's dirt cheap.

—Even twenty years ago I thought that this idea only needed the technology to catch up. It is good we have a history, a tradition, a culture here.

—Like Ulysses, we're never at a loss.

—Oh, is that so, never at a

—Philip

—unless we're trying to produce a thousand mile beam where no test has ever shown

—Philip

—Well how long do you think we can keep it up! this this

—As long as it takes.

—And you, Dr. Réti?

—My young friend, I am an optimist.

—Philip, I want a word. Excuse us Horatiu. One arm clutched Quine in tight embrace and steered them into the hallway, Highet saying in low controlled tones, —One day soon, very soon, I'll stop giving you second chances. Come up empty this time and you're through. Clear?

—Meaning what? You'll what?

—I don't know. I don't know but it will be terrible and final and I promise you'll never forget it. Highet raised his voice to hearty amiability, —Good man! You let me know, and went back into his office.

With the darkening of the sky the life of the building went to X Section, the Playpen, where the younger men worked on schemes even more speculative than Superbright, and Quine returned for the thousandth time to theory with the sinking heart of a man returning to a loveless home. Entrapment. As if fine wire had threaded his drugged veins, and now, as feeling returned, any movement might tear him open. He fidgeted the radio on to, —fades to a reddish color as it enters the Earth's shad, and off as he saw again the tilt of Nan's head, the man's hand cupping her neck. The ridge of her collarbone, the warm pulse of the vein across it.

On Null's whiteboard deltas sigmas omegas integrals infinities in variegated ink still wove like fundamental forces their elegant pattern around a void. From the clutter on the desk he lifted CENTURY 21 LABS QUARTERLY. Changing world betokens larger role for science. Acceptable levels of social risk. Public does not fully understand. World free of threats too much to ask. Revolutionary new technique. Major improvement. Important to a variety of national goals. Unique multidisciplinary expertise. Two young men, one poised to hurl something, caromed past his doorway. He shut the door on guffaws and —teach you some hydrodynamics!

Paper atop his stack, 1954, by Black. He turned to the citations, then read from the start, stopping often to reread with a doggedness that made shift for his halt sense, once so fine, of the rhythms of thought and confirmation, their probe and test and parry and clinch that now required his slow and remedial attention to be seized. As he read, his respect for Thorpe grew even as an emptiness opened within him. When he was finished he stared into space before reaching across the desk to snap off the lights.

The phone chattered. On the second ring he lifted it, holding silence to ear for a moment before speaking. In the darkness the computer screen, phosphors charged by the room's vanished light, was a dim fading square.

—Quine.

—Hi, it's Lynn. I'm hiking up Mount Ohlone with some friends tonight, want to come?

—Well . . .

—I know it's short notice.

—No I mean sure, why not.

—Good! Meet us at the park gate about nine. It's ten miles north on Crow Canyon Road.

In the hallway a length of surgical tubing, knotted at both ends, lay ruptured and limp in a film of water. As he left the building sprinklers came on in a silver mist and rainbows shimmered in the floodlit air. He drove out past parked vehicles and armed men in fatigues.

He was early. The sky was starry. Seldom was he this far from the valley's lights. Orion, Taurus, Canis Major. Eyes reaching into interstellar void. Where in this blackness is the seed of love? of meaning? Or is corruption inherent in Being itself, wrong at the root?

A car approached, lights snagging in the trees, then came around the last bend lightless and rolled to a stop.

—Mark, Jackie, this is Philip.

—Why're we whispering?

—Park's closed.

They went round the closed gate and past a building set back among trees. In a second-story window a dim line flickered, a fluorescent tube not on nor off, stuttering between states. Fifty yards farther they left the road for a broad path that rose winding under black oak, then bay. An owl called.

Ahead Jackie laughed and touched Mark's arm, not a lover's touch, but a gesture of intimacy with the world, the same hand caressing air and underbrush. They talked softly about people they knew, hes and shes darting in and out of audibility like moths in the dark. Next to him Lynn pulled at a low branch. Leaves popped free and she crushed them under Quine's nose, carrying to him a strong waft of mint and resin.

—Sweet bay, she said, —is sacred to Apollo, but this is not European bay, *laurens,* it's California bay, *umbellularia.* Her tongue lingered on the liquids.

They climbed until they broke from the woods onto an open slope. A path through long dry grass led to another dark grove. The moon, not yet risen, rinsed palely the eastern sky. The valley to the south was filled with glittering points. At its verge was the floodlit terrain of the Labs.

—And this is *Artemisia tridentata,* Lynn said, inhaling as she broke from a sagebrush a twig of gray leaves. —Smell it. I wonder what god loves this.

—How do you know all this?

—This is where I grew up. This is the smell of my home. This is how I know I belong.

—Look! Jackie called, —a green star! Is that a planet? and finding the pale disk straight up in the Ram, a handbreadth from Mars near the Sisters, Quine knew it was no star, but the beam of a laser ten miles south stabbing sixty miles to the edge of space where sodium atoms glowed in its heat, and he said to Lynn, —not a planet, but some miracle of strange device, and she laughed before dropping the pungent twig and running to the next grove, and he ran after, the path dipping as seductively as the sweet hollow at the base of the spine, until he tripped and went sprawling, heart thudding, hackles alive. What was he outrunning? A presence, almost, was in the grove. He feared it though it was benign. It was not death, but it would change his life if he allowed it.

Three figures stood before him laughing. —You okay? and a flash of shame, not for his fall but for the falseness of his position before these children. The errors of his life were irrevocable; as yet theirs were not. He had wanted to borrow the grace of their youth, that was the shame. Mark held out his hand. Quine grasped it and was pulled to his feet and followed them out of the grove.

Jackie opened a backpack and brought out bread, cheese, fruit, a plastic bottle of water. On the grass they sat eating. The ridgeline was hard black against the sky and pieces of the rising moon glinted in the trees.

—You from around here, Philip?

—From the East. Isn't everyone? I've been here five years.

—Practically a native. What do you do?

—Computers. I write software for Taliesin Systems.

—Friend of mine worked for CodeWin, maybe you know him.

—It's a big industry.

—Getting bigger by the day, said Lynn dryly.

—Ah, look, look at the moon. It cleared the ridge, swollen, no goddess remontant but an airless world already mapped, trodden, and projected for division into satrapies of mining, manufacturing, and defense, occupancy lapsed only until these scenarios could enrich their planners at a margin of return greater and more reliable than what current technology assured.

—We're contracting with an aerospace company, Quine went on, to control low-orbit balloons a couple of miles across, apparent size of the moon, sunlit, carrying messages.

—Messages?

—Commercial messages, logos. Advertising.

—But that's, Jackie began and Mark cut in, —Didn't I read about this, the Sierra Club's bringing suit . . .

—Maybe so, we're just the contractors, I don't really know, and Jackie glancing at Lynn seemed to lose interest, resuming with Mark in a low voice their conversation of hes and shes while Lynn walked away, obliging Quine to follow at a distance, leaving behind—she doesn't see you as a friend she sees you as more and that's scary, to overtake her on a knoll where she faced the valley lights with crossed arms.

—Philip, these are my friends. Don't lie to them.

—I was trying it on. That's a Lab phrase. You don't like me as a software mogul?

—You do this a lot? Jerk people around?

—No, it's . . . look it's just a bad habit. Defensive. Sometimes you have to, there, to advance your goals, lying's almost a game, see if the other guy's smart enough to catch it.

—And Mark wasn't smart enough for you. You take his good faith for foolishness.

—No, it's . . .

—I'm trying to understand you. You repay friendship with falsehood?

—It's . . . you don't know what's happening there, what I'm up against right now . . .

—Tell me, then.

—I can't.

—They really have their hooks in you.

—I know that.

—Can't you quit?

—And do what! Turn from the one place where my, my talents have meaning, from everything that defines me?

—What do you want, Philip?

—Want? I want five years back. Before them I was a scientist.

—They haven't robbed you of that.

—Yes, that's so, I gave myself over, and now I'm on the line for something I don't care about. That's the way, yes, you're going to get screwed regardless, so you should make sure it's for something that matters to you . . .

—But you, I don't believe this, you don't engage with people, you stand off, you get angry and defensive when you think they don't approve, and then you think you're screwed?

—Lynn . . .

—I don't know what to say, I really don't. I understand if you're bitter, but not flaunting it, this almost pride in it . . .

—Pride! . . . I have an insoluble problem, data that's no good fraudulent predictions a Congressional visit next week a few days to vindicate what isn't, and I'm taking a walk in the moonlight because I don't know what to do! Not pride that's desperation . . .

—It's that bad? Face hidden in moonshadow, she stepped toward him. His need to be touched and take comfort welled up, but some stricture unknown yet dreadful held him still. After a moment's wait she stepped back.

They returned to where Jackie was packing the picnic, still talking to Mark, —so I'm going wait, stop, this is it, these are the boundaries and he's like, what did I do? She handed the pack to Lynn, —take this? and embraced Mark from behind, her whiteclad arms around his chest, straps of her shortlegged overalls a dark X on her back, bare calves duckwalking the pair down the slope.

In the lot Lynn said to Jackie, —Get a ride with you guys?

Quine called out, —Mark, just joking about the balloon.

Mark looked up, fumbling with his keys, smiling. —Oh yeah?

—Thanks for inviting me. He got in the car, opened the glovebox, found a tablet, felt the excised triangle, brushed lint from it, swallowed it dry.

In the apartment was a smell. It was like stale smoke and rotting food, edged with something fouler, like the metallic stench of the bright green flux from the open pipe. At first he thought it came from outside, where earlier they'd been roofing. But on the deck the air was fresh. He knelt to the carpet and smelled nothing. In the kitchen he bent to the drain and smelled nothing. From a bottle he squeezed a pearl of soap onto a sponge, ran hot water in the sink, scrubbed and rinsed it. He scrubbed the stove top. The ceiling fan was silted over by grease and spiderweb. He fetched a chair and reached to touch it. A black gobbet fell from it to the stove top. He fetched pliers and freed the nuts holding the shield, banging with the handle to break the dried paint around the rim. In both hands he bore the shield like a chalice to the sink.

In its concavities had pooled a glossy tar. He scrubbed it for minutes, smutch washing slowly into the sink. Then he spooled off yards of paper toweling, wet and soaped it, and climbed the chair to wash over and again the sleeve of the fan, the blades, the hub. A viscous brown residue clung to the towels and his fingers. Farther into the recess, beyond his reach, was more tar.

Sweat soaked him. He went onto the deck. The moon was dim, its fullness lurid, as if behind smoke. He stared in wonder and fear until the knowledge that it was an eclipse broke upon him banishing fear and wonder alike.

When he went back in the smell was waiting. He understood that from now on everything would smell like this. For a while he sat at the table with his eyes shut, then opened the newspaper for the memory of CARPETS CLEANED but it parted to 24 HRS OUTCALL DAWNA and LOVE TALK $2/MIN and he stared bleakly at the sullen pout, circleted forehead, hair as wild as if fresh risen from the sea, under a shiny black cloak linen garb pleated in most subtle fashion. His hand found the telephone, and after a distant chirrup a small insinuating voice flicked like a tongue in his ear, and he stepped sharply back from the uncradled receiver, switched off the lights, leaving the voice breathing unheeded into the darkness and the reddish moonlight pooled on the floor.

He showered. In the steam lust swelled in him like nausea. Joylessly he seized its nexus. Hot spray lashed him. Incoherent images and broken geometries flashed upon him. Runnels nudged moonwhite globs toward the drain. Depleted he toweled. On the sink were Nan's toothpaste, hairbrush, lipstick, mascara. On the toilet tank a travel kit of quilted cotton gaped, displaying diaphragm, jelly, tampons, vitamins, ibuprofen, hairpins, barrette, lens wetter, a glass jar of face cream. A towelend snagged the open zipper as Quine scrubbed dry his hair. Items hailed on the tiled floor. He dropped the towel, then swept his hand across the sink top. He grabbed the kit and hurled it. The jar flew out and smashed against the wall.

4.

Dry sycamore leaves scraped over pavement in a hot wind drawn west from distant desert by a stalled offshore low. Over the ridge east of town dust and the smell of manure from the farmlands and a haze of smoke blew fitfully into the valley. As the sun rose through layers of pollution Quine, driving to the back gate of the Labs so as to avoid the protesters, passed the dead vineyard by the north boundary. He pulled over, stilling the engine and the radio's—ty thousand acres ablaze.

The gate was closed but unlocked under a bright new sign bearing the biohazard trefoil and DANGER TOXICS MITIGATION PILOT SITE ALPHA KEEP

OUT. The drone of flies rose and fell like a turbine. Inside the gate the flies abated. A stubble of dry vines clung to irrigation uprights. Underfoot a chromegreen film glazed cracked gray silt. Bark from a withered vine sloughed like white ash on his fingers. Then from deep in the vineyard a warm moist flatus perfused the air. A stink like the chyme of a dying beast. He ran back to the car choking and drooling. At a roadside faucet he rinsed his mouth, his face, his hair, his hands, yet the foulness, as of corroded metal, lingered. What god loves this?

At Null's desk Thorpe worked.

—Bernd Dietz called. He has to know where to put the sensors. Today.

—I'm tempted to leave them where they were in the last shot.

—We can't do that, Highet would

—That's why I'm tempted.

—Yeah, he can be a prick can't he.

—Not if you play by his rules. He always has a carrot handy.

—Well I have quite a few ideas but you need to look them over, tell me where they're out of line, you know we're really down to the wire here and

—Okay, let's assume Black's right . . .

—Oh then you've read

—Assume we're looking at quanta as localized particles guided by a physically real field . . .

—Highet, you know he really grilled me on this stuff when he came out to Utah, put me through the wringer, made me prove every assumption, but after an hour I had him convinced, and I though he really respected . . .

—Typical Highet slap and stroke.

—Now suppose we . . .

—You're good at this. And very fast.

—Commercial software you know, those eighteen hour days tone you right up.

—Don't touch that, we can't change the rod array, I've already told Dietz.

—Can we reorient it?

—Maybe. I'll check.

Under Thorpe's shaping the model gradually began to show correlation. After several hours one run produced an annulus. Then nothing for hours more. They ate dinner in the cafeteria, not speaking, then returned to work. Thorpe coded for a hour, then ran the model. The annulus. He rotated the rods; power jumped and the annulus closed to a point. They stared at the screen. Thorpe bit his thumb. —What do you think?

—It looks all right.

—It *looks* fantastic. It's a hundred times brighter than the last shot's data. But the model's tweaked to hell and gone.

—I don't see anything wrong.

—No . . . so we would put the sensors here . . . see, this is how I work. I'm not a theorist, I don't have your background, I need the machine, to immerse myself in the code, feel the system . . .

—Well, it's a remarkable job. I couldn't have done this. I've tried for months.

—But the thing is, at some level it's all just pushing numbers around. I don't know if the code is saying anything real.

—We'll know soon enough.

—Do you think something's wrong?

Quine shrugged. —Nothing I can see.

—You're not convinced.

—I don't have to be. It's what Highet wants, isn't it?

—Yeah but, that's not what you think I'm doing, is it?

—No . . .

—Because I would never do that.

—I'm sure you

—Since Fish and Himmelhoch I have to be very careful. They were crucified, just crucified, they're pariahs, their careers are finished. Anything to do with cold fusion is tainted, you may as well say you're working on perpetual motion. And I was on that team, I was in that lab.

—Perpetual motion, you could probably sell that to Highet. At least as a talking point.

—It's not funny to me. I had nothing to do with that debacle, just so we're clear on that.

—Sure. I understand.

—I'm sorry I'm touchy. Just tired. You've been generous, letting me work with your code and all, I really thought you'd stick me with the scut work but you've done it haven't you all the test details and let me do the interesting part. This could take me a long way and I won't forget it.

—Why don't you go home, get some sleep?

—Yeah, I'm whipped.

—Take tomorrow off. I'll tell Highet.

—No no, I'll be in. We have to make up a work order.

—I'll do it, don't worry about it.

—Are you staying longer?

—God no, what is it, midnight?

—Two.

—No, I'm leaving in five minutes. I'll write the work order tomorrow.

—Oh I meant to, here's something else for you to read . . . and, hesitating a moment, Thorpe placed a stapled xerox atop Quine's stack, held his gaze, and departed.

It was a new paper by Sorokin. At a prestigious school now. Tenured. Quine skimmed it as if reading news from a distant galaxy or a remote epoch. It solidified and extended the work they'd done together, the experiment that had separated them. It was clear that it was a field now and that Sorokin owned it. He stanched the welling of envy and self-pity. Good for Sorokin.

But instead of going home Quine broke apart Thorpe's code and studied the changes closely. He gave the model a new set of energies: points clustered around the focus. Again, with different energies, the same focus emerged. Something was wrong, he could smell it; oh yes, his instinct was not yet dead.

Near dawn he found it. Along with the sensor positions, Thorpe had tweaked the sensor response function. Quite incidentally it now emphasized certain wavelengths, exactly as the beryllium sensors themselves did when struck by the bomb's radiation. No wonder it matched the test data so well. Now that he saw it, the flaw jumped out like a figure from an optical illusion. Glue in a house of cards. And down in a corner of Null's whiteboard, half erased, was it? yes, the same function, same tweak. It had been in the corner of Quine's eye for months. Wasted months. Wrong from the start. Error or fraud? No way to know. Maybe started as one, became the other. Sleep soon. Faint light outside. But wait. If you removed the tweak, if you stopped trying for a beam, chaff fell from the problem and the expressions said something else entirely.

A presence entered the room. Air gravid and light adance. Instead of the battle station there appeared to his mind's eye a congruent tide of radiance, all the universe's light at wavelengths and colors beyond mere vision, streaming in intricate brocade, weaving and mediating between matter and energy, wave and particle, the phenomenal and the noumenal. Here was the central mystery, laid open for his knowing, and at the very gate of revelation he knew he was unprepared to pass into this realm of light, and he drew back. The presence, like a roebuck in forest, startled and was gone.

Cold rage at aspirations dashed and traduced. In compensation, then, knowledge reborn as an instrument of power. Though mystery elude, information is sure. *Thus angels must feel, radiant with the certainty that flows from might.*

—Bernd, I need some sensors.
—For Taliesin.
—Yes.

—I have a work order already, this morning, from Thorpe.

—I need more.

—We do not have time to add

—Find the time. I want sensors on there made of something other than beryllium.

Dietz was silent. He began leafing through a logbook. —Do you know, try as we might we cannot keep traces of oxygen out of the beryllium. I have told Highet this. Long ago.

—Really.

—I have proposed hydrogen in the past.

—You have? Why haven't we tried it?

—"Don't mess with success."

—I see. I'd like to try it.

—Does Highet know?

—I'll take responsibility.

—Without his approval I can do little.

—Bernd. This is what Slater thought, isn't it. That the beryllium sensors were giving false brightness. And Null knew it too, didn't he.

—I did not see Slater's report.

—Make some hydrogen for me. Cable them separately from the beryllium.

Dietz shut the book. —Send me a work order. I will have to send a copy to Highet.

Kihara came through the doors with a following of suited men. —Won't be a minute, gentlemen, don't let us disturb you, you can see here the precision engineering we're capable of, bang-up job of inventiveness, maximum return on investment, the answer to reversing the balance of trade deficit, innovative federally generated technology transfer to industry, improves the nation's economic competitiveness as we work deliberately and consciously to build partnerships, a new class of information with commercial value, very creative cooperative efforts, freedom to negotiate intellectual property rights, fees and royalties, cover the technological waterfront, take for instance these fine-grained superplastic steels, not to mention X-ray lithography . . . and Quine returned to his office rummaging through CENTURY 21, Rings Fields and Groups, Computer Addict Wholesale Microcenter, TeX Technical Reference, to come upon WORK ORDER Form 4439A Authorized Use Only, and sat for a minute holding a pen above it suddenly frozen at the sound of Thorpe's approaching voice, —you have to invoke the world control option from the command line, relaxing as the voice receded, pen moving to spell SECONDARY SENSOR ARRAY.

*　*　*

From Highet's open door he heard, —You want less pressure, try the Institute for Advanced Salaries, it's a fucking retirement village for the reality-impaired! and a lower voice unintelligible in response, then —I don't care, I want results! the lower voice growing sharper: —is cheap. My people have to make it happen, as the door opened and Dietz, pale and shaking, came out past Quine glancing at him without a word and stormed down the hall, Highet following to the door, calling out, —A beard without a mustache, does that make you an honest man? and to Quine, —You. I don't want to talk to you now. Send me e-mail.

—I think you'll want to hear this. We can show quantitative agreement.

Highet looked at him with loathing. —You want to change the sensors. The day before the shot.

—I want to try hydrogen.

—That's an incredibly bad idea, that's totally braindead, to introduce a new measurement technique at this stage. You have to calibrate, you have to

—If Slater's right, if the beryllium shows false brightness, it's only a matter of time until we know it. It might as well be now. Or do you want to spend fifty million on another shot?

—I'd love to. Who told you Slater said that?

—It's common knowledge. We'll have to address the issue eventually.

—Common knowledge. My ass.

—It might be wise to preempt questions about it. The shot's so close to the presentation, we can't be expected to have formal data that quickly. But we could say we're investigating. If we have to.

—You're sure about the quantitative agreement?

—The simulation's excellent. I won't take credit for it. Jef Thorpe did the work.

—Did he now. Well, we're a team. Good results show good management.

—I'd like Jef to give the presentation.

Highet's eyes fixed in calculation on Quine as the phone rang and Quine waited for the dismissive wave with which Highet ended audiences, but instead he spoke a moment, then covered the mouthpiece and said, —want to make some money Philip, Devon Null's taking on investors, and uncovering the mouthpiece, —yes, application's outside the envelope no problem there, keep me briefed, and in another moment hung up, leaning back and clasping his hands over his thinning crown, gazing at the ceiling.

—Well that's fine, that's very fine. Wonder if we could work up a little something. I could invite some key people to the ranch for the shot, some unnamed sources, goose the process a little, can we get Thorpe in on this?

—He's probably in my office.

—You may work out yet Philip, Highet grudged as one thick finger stabbed the phone. —Jef? Leo. Get your ass over here, rising to pace past framed and signed photos of three presidents, another of Réti and himself with the current president, artist's renderings of the Superbright and of a fusion-driven spaceship, cartoon of a mushroom cloud WHEN YOU CARE ENOUGH TO SEND THE VERY BEST, certificates from professional societies, a length of cable, a circuit board. He stopped at the window, gaze caught by something, and parted the vertical slats of the blind with his fingers, speaking softly, almost to himself.

—Do you know the darkness that's out there? Do you realize how tenuous this all is? Twenty thousand years of civilization, and only in the last five hundred has rationality begun to displace superstition. I tell you I would sup with the devil, I would court armageddon, not to lose that. When I think of those fucking tree huggers out there . . . and turning back to Quine, voice low and insistent, —Think the ills are in a system, think it's that simple, Réti with his anticommunism, your new girlfriend and her peacenik buddies, wonder why's she drawn to you?

Quine said nothing.

—Darkness and malady is in the human heart, Philip, you can't eradicate it, don't you know that? The enemy is the heart. And all you can do is propitiate the darkness there . . . as Thorpe arrived in black linen jacket, red T-shirt, nose stud, eyes eager, and Highet's demeanor switched to the cheerful, —Jef, my man. I want to wow the rubes when we go to the desert. We have a ranch out there with a data feed from the test site. What can you do that's portable and fantastic? I want flash that makes you reach for your checkbook.

—Hey, I've got an interface toolkit from my CodeWin days, I can throw something together overnight. Just tell me what kind of data I have to work with.

—I'll e-mail the details. Shot's tomorrow evening, you'll have to get a plane out by noon to set up. Not too much for you, is it?

—Demo or die, I know the drill, said Thorpe, grinning.

The evening wind whipped dust across the flat stretch of highway, slowing traffic and shuddering the shells of cars backed up across three lanes behind flashing lights at EXIT NLY CODOR IC S as Quine punched —illion in property loss, over to —noninjury accident being cleared at the Codornices Road exit not blocking lanes for you, drowned in a siren blaring up the shoulder OHLONE VALLEY RESCUE ECNALUBMA as Quine edged against horns and unheard curses into the exit lane and cut back on a commercial strip to loop up behind the central mall the reverse of whose colonnaded and pedimented facade, raw concrete stained by long ago rains, caught with a sort of wounded dignity the sun's last rays as they lanced past Estancia Estates An Adult Community where Quine parked and for a moment held in his gaze a prospect of bungalows arrayed on lawns billiardgreen out to their surveyed boundary of dry pasture before ascending the walk and ringing the bell.

—Oh! Philip. Come in. I wasn't expecting you.

—Well it's Friday night, I thought

—Oh I'm glad you, but just, if you'd called I would have made dinner . . .

—I wasn't sure I was coming.

—Your work is done?

—There's a test. I fly out tomorrow afternoon. And there's a presentation Monday.

—Can you stay tonight? We can go out for . . . is something wrong?

—Can I ask who's the guy with the curly black hair and the good tan?

—The, what?

—I happened to see you both the other day. In a hallway. He was acting pretty proprietary.

—Proprie . . . Nan's face flushed.

—How long has this been going on?

—His name's Ben and he's a good friend, and it's been . . . we've been friends for years. Five years at least. Since before I knew you.

—You still see him?

The flush darkened, and her mild features contorted into an anger he'd never seen in her. —You mean, do I sleep with him? Yes, I have, once or twice since you and I have been together.

—Once or twice. You've lost count.

—Oh, Philip! Why are you, this is hateful!

—It hurts me, Nan.

Her face was a mask of plain misery. —We never—

—Never what, laid down rules? No, I didn't think we had to, I thought some things went without saying.

—Without saying what! that I'm yours alone when you don't give me anything, not even a word of love, for God's sake Philip I didn't turn to Ben for sex, just for, for kindness, to feel that I *mattered* to someone! A year, almost two years of my life Philip, I'm no longer a young woman, do you want to know when it was I saw Ben, when it was I went to him after you and I were together?

The coldness, the absolute coldness of the moment.

—You don't even care do you. When we met, at the Labor Day picnic two years ago, and I was so charmed by you, your intelligence, your modesty, your reserve. Do you remember, there was a thunderstorm? I hadn't seen one since moving West. And you took me home, we were drenched, and I loaned you clothes. Oh Philip, it was over between Ben and me he was like a brother, I just wanted to, I don't know, say good-bye, tell someone close to me how happy I thought I'd be.

—And the second time?

—Yes, a year later, when you didn't come to dinner, didn't call, and I waited and waited so it was only an anniversary just a date on the calendar that's all but I called Ben and he came over to be with me, and he didn't, didn't even *want* . . . cut off by her sobs, jagged and piercing.

—But I, you knew I was in a meeting, you could have

—And you call him proprietary! When you come here and, and sulk for hours, barely acknowledge my existence, don't call for days on end, and then expect, how do you think that makes me feel . . . cut by sobs, —and you've never, never asked me what I want, how I feel, I would have told you about Ben if you'd asked if you'd shown any interest at all in my past. I don't think you know who I am!

Within him a stone fell and fell, soundlessly turning.

—Philip, talk to me! Don't turn off like this!

—I have nothing to say, and he was out the door, where streetlights had come on, knowing that his leaving was a catastrophe more final than anything gone before, a withdrawal he could never make right. Don't tell me, don't tell me we don't feed the emptiness in each other. Betrayal is an aether through which an energy moves.

5.

One hundred miles from Mesa Encantada, whose tracts of waste and infecund desert had been reclaimed for science as Site 600, was the Advanced Research Institute of the Eastern Sierra, a ranch at the edge of the Owens Valley, a black facility whose funding appeared in no budget. Deeded to the government by a conservative rancher, it served as a layover site for Lab personnel on their way to the desert. It nestled in the broad base of a canyon near a creek's loud runoff through lateral moraine. To the west the ground rose in the space of a few miles from six thousand feet to a twelve thousand foot crest of granite crags. Below, to the east, the highway lay like a ribbon dropped across the wrinkled valley floor, and a hundred miles farther across desert dotted with sage under a flotilla of thunderheads was Mesa Encantada.

Even before the Labs, Quine had seen ARIES. On his first trip west, while switching planes at Phoenix, he'd been paged and diverted to a single-engine craft bound for a Kern County airstrip, where a sheriff's four by four awaited him. The first Radiance shot had just gone off and at the ranch they were celebrating. Quine met Highet there as he beat a twelve-year-old at chess, telling the boy, I'll trade a bishop for a knight anytime, I love knights, they leap barriers, they face eight ways at once.

A month after that he was at the Mesa. Rank smell of sage hovered in the predawn cool, immensities of desert air quivered to the horizon. They drove upcanyon with the sun rising behind them, the young initiates joking, group leaders and guards and observers in DoD hardhats silent and grim. Roadways of cables led from instrument trailers over desert pocked with the collapsed craters of previous tests to the distant borehole. Above it a red crane pointing straight up. The count reached zero. And the earth rippled. A wave rushed toward them and the ground shook as if a train were passing and passing and passing. When it stopped the air was a clear plasma of exaltation. To know that the binding forces of matter were yours to break, the wealth of nations yours to drive into such sublime force, this was a deep and secret sweetness known only to the few.

At the ranch now Thorpe was joking with some grad students from X Section. Others were there from J Section, and some stern faces he didn't know, military or intelligence, and Steradian alert as a corrupt deputy. Highet arrived in black Western shirt with red and white embroidery across the yoke, blue jeans, and tooled leather boots, carrying cases of soda, chanting in a false twang, —Twaace the sugar, twaace the caffeine . . . followed by a Western senator, cadaverous and grinning in white Stetson, and his young aide plump and groomed to a sheen, with the zealous black eyes of a pullet.

—Look at em, young, brilliant, confident, said the senator. —That's how I felt at their age. They own the world.

—The world? retorted Highet. —They own their genitals. The rest of them's mine, raising his voice to introduce, —Gentlemen, the right honorable Howard Bangeter, R-Utah . . .

The aide asked if physics had yet succeeded in finding in the traces of Creation the fingerprints of God, and Highet nodded, a slow smile spreading and his tonguetip darting as his hands rose to conjure, —Not God exactly . . . as Quine walked onto the deck where three barbecue grills sizzled, and a keg of Coors Lite sat amidst greasy paper plates bearing the ruins of meals, and the sun had long since chased the waning moon, itself pursuing Venus, behind the mountain wall. Although the sky retained day's blue a chill came down from the remote snowless peaks.

—This young man, Highet's voice carried out from within, won last year's Heinrich Hertz Fellowship in Physics, a prestigious award I happen to administer . . . and Quine stepped down from the deck, crossing dry grass to the creek's rockstrewn willowed bank where it trickled through small pools and clumps of rotting leaves. Quine followed it up, breath laboring. He stopped at a large boulder long ago frostwedged and tumbled from a higher place, and sat. No residue of warmth. The western ridge was a great dark wave. In the east a glamour of rosetint clouds swept up from the horizon. The ranch was small below him. A wind came down the great wall of rock. Into this chaos he might ascend and be lost.

But he did not. He returned to the ranch, Thorpe's voice coming as he slid open the glass doors, —background, trucks on the highway, that sort of thing. Other side of the spool you can see some small temblors we had this afternoon. When the shot goes off we'll definitely see more than a wiggle. But the real action's on screen. At the site they're recording everything for later analysis but data's also piped to this workstation where autocorrelation software I wrote gives us an immediate window on what's happening. Red is intense energy, blue less intense. We're looking for a red ringlike structure.

Quine watched the stylus quiver as about him others conversed. Without warning the stylus jerked. The screen of the workstation came to life, numbers flowing down its right edge. Colors coalesced fitfully on screen. The senator and his aide leaned in enrapt. A minute passed. Blue and green surrounded a corona of yellow and a jagged red core flecked with white.

—We have brightness, Thorpe said. —A hundred times the last test. More. Maybe a thousand times.

—Three orders of magnitude improvement in six months, declared Highet. —At this rate we'll have every enemy missile on Earth neutralized in a few years, and raising his tone with his glass, —To Team Radiance! Leonardos of the age. You people are the best in the world.

Grunts and howls of triumph went off like rockets.

—Do you all know what we've done? We've broken the back of Communism. And that's only so far.

More applause. The senator's aide leaned smiling to whisper in the senator's ear.

—Need now's a nice little war where we can demo this stuff. Feed some tinhorn tyrant some antiquated missiles and provoke him to use them.

A second wave of guests arrived, a dozen men in suits adorned with MAMMOTH CONVENTION CENTER NAME COMPANY and a few women packaged as brightly as new software, and Quine moved off through the manic younger men hopped up by caffeine and sugar and the shot.

—PDP downstairs running spacewar

—thought Malibu was bad but Acapulco's about three inch waves

—blasts wheat into stubble in a shock tube at mach ten, that's his study, eighty k a year

—maybe the moon's changed its orbit or

—translate the project into terms attractive to DARPA

—well Mazatlan then or Valparaiso

—think I'll propose rye

—dup rot swap drop

—corn smut

—know better than to say that in public with troops on the border

—shell game

—call it Virtual Wilderness

—I hear Sara squeezed it out

—boy or girl?

—people make money on it they're more likely to go along

—girl, I think that's what Mo said

—why leave home to get away

—he didn't go deep enough

—photo and topo database with fractal interpolation software to smooth the animation

—get ourselves into a quagmire like Viet

—substantive working relationship with at least six major US companies

—get USGS or Interior onboard

—hell why not go worldwide

—translate the project into terms attractive to DoE

—not this time, this is South*west* Asia

—get on your Nordic Track put on the goggles you're up in the Cordillera

—and somebody from the insurance company's selling records of who owns what where to thieves

—take out the infrastructure of the whole frigging country if we have to

—smells sounds good weather get up close to extinct animals

—everybody makes out, homeowner's paid off, insurance company raises rates, thieves fence the stuff, fence makes a profit

—ought to get the Basil Zaharoff memorial award

—as defined in paragraph R of section 11 of the Atomic Energy Act of 1954

—guy shot by on a bicycle, sliced the damn finger right off for the ring

—knowingly and with intent

—living things probably get wiped out in a pretty thorough fashion every few million years

—better than real

—so cool cause like the program's working but you don't know what it's doing so there's these emergent properties

—sophisticated encryption algorithms deserving of patent protection

—control the flow of information, do it by classification do it by misdirection principle's the same

—incorporating certain aspects of prior art such as multiplication

—translate the project into terms attractive to Disney

—object oriented

—get this straight, if I say nine times six is seventy-two I'm infringing?

—yes but when your story comes back it has your fingerprints on it then you know where it's been

—I have no special loyalty to DNA

—must have misjudged my audience

—value intellectual autonomy over anything

—fifty-four, no of course not but if you codify your knowledge that nine times six is sev, ah, fifty-four in any machine-executable formalism

—sometimes the envelope pushes back

—women at that high energy conference in Tsukuba

—held research positions at four universities published thirty papers before anybody realized

—won't impact the users of the algorithm, or affect the multiplication market, only the vendors of such algorithms

—kinbakubi kenkyu kai?

—lineal descendant of ibn-Musa al-Qarizmi that being the first publication

—no PhD not even a BA all his papers copied from obscure journals

—seme-e?

—Go for it, Bruno, do the meat thing.

Quine edged into a hallway and down a narrow flight of stairs as behind him music began pounding, catching as he turned a last glimpse of Thorpe, cheeks flushed, smiling at a circle of admirers the impartial smile of triumph.

Nature is more ready in her creating than time in his destroying, and so she has ordained that many animals shall be food for others.

He continued downstairs toward a light. In the cellar seven or eight young men from X Section were gathered around an old rackmounted minicomputer and a pool table.

—so he goes, learn to hassle people and lie with a straight face.

—Excuse me, I need to get back. Does anyone know the arrangements?

—Excellent advice, dude.

—Excuse

One glanced up.—There's pool cars outside somewhere.

Full dark. A dozen cars. E108637. DEPARTMENT OF ENERGY OFFICIAL

USE ONLY. Key in the column. The seat harness slid up and drew in over his chest and waist as a chime sounded and dash lights blinked red then glowed teal. The car swayed and bounced for a mile down the dirt road. There the highway stretched north and south into void, under stars like chips of ice. He could go anywhere. But time was a field that moved with him, inescapable, close as the blue light in the cabin. He drove for hours without stopping, radio for company, wash of noise, hollowness in his being. Mountains that a century ago killed emigrants with their rigors fell to his vehicle. Descending to the flats, he saw brushfires crawling brightly on far ridges like luminous protolife, like the fitful colors on Thorpe's screen from the bad sensors, and the fires fell away behind him and the farm cities loomed on the ancient seabed, their lights and capillary highways glowing with perfervid intensity in the unnatural warmth persisting from this arid summer long past its term, its heat bonded to the earth like some toxin to a susceptible organ, and booming through the car's windows when he opened them was the smell of dust, manure, smoke, exhaust, chemicals, and he crossed the last ridge to arrive in his valley of a million souls, of all the places he might go, for all the freedom he had, here again.

In the dark apartment he stripped, trailing damp rank clothes to the bathroom. The mirror's sudden light showed him, before selfhood interposed its protective assurance, the face of a stranger, aging and vulnerable. The soft flesh of his body was without tone or color. Lowering his eyes from the harsh brightness he stood voiding for long seconds. A ribbon of urine twisted along the axis of its arc as it splashed into the bowl. Standing thus he blinked, faded, woke. The gates of sleep stood open and he was through them, uncleansed, as soon as he lay down.

On a moonless night at the edge of a forest there is the slap and sizzle of rainfall. A moist breeze springs up. Yet where he stands, in long grass, all is dry. Only in the forest is it raining. A figure in the forest shadows stands regarding him. It holds an offering of some kind, a gift. He does not move to take the gift, and shortly the figure recedes into the forest.

6.

Gathering before dawn the crowd set out for the main gate, to be met by police as unceasing arrivals swelled it further, until Lab workers began to show up in their vehicles and county and city police were called to divert traffic to the north gate against the columns of people still coming, and the south road was closed to vehicles and state police summoned, and still the spectacle slowed traffic to walking speed, so that Quine was late to Highet's office where Highet stared out his window at the south road.

—Those people out there will never understand. It could be so much worse. On the other side, entire cities, entire regions have no civilian industry at all, it's all military. Here we cut our deals as needed but we still do real science. We bring in people like you. We roll back the darkness.

—There's a problem.

Highet turned. —What.

—The beryllium and hydrogen sensors were cabled separately. Thorpe's analysis at the ranch used only the beryllium. I looked at the hydrogen data yesterday. No brightness. No beam. Nothing there.

Nodding, Highet turned again to the window. —I see. The hydrogen sensors which I asked you not to use. You know, I almost stopped that work order, came that close. But I wanted to see what you had in mind.

—As supervisor it was my decision.

—On your head be it. Where's your quantitative agreement now?

—You saw at the ranch. The beryllium shows it. Spectrum peaks as predicted. But that's not a focused X-ray, that's oxygen in the beryllium glowing at just the right wavelength. It looks exactly like the new model's predictions for focus.

—And where did this new model come from?

—Thorpe's been modifying my code. I found a routine where just this set of frequencies is amplified. You'll find that my copies of the files haven't been modified for ten days.

Highet came from the window, pacing past the photos of presidents and artists' renderings, touching the length of cable.

—I see. Well, this is bad for him, you know. Especially after Fish and Himmelhoch. He has a history.

—I wouldn't call it intentional. The ideas he brought were good. I worked with him, I didn't see this, it could have happened to anyone.

—It doesn't matter. He has a history, voice sharpening, —quackery or carelessness, you think it matters? You think you can ever walk away from your history?

Quine said nothing.

—Now those hydrogen sensors, you piggybacked your own little test onto the piggyback, that was very cute. Did Thorpe know about that?

—You saw the work orders.

—He knew he was getting feed from the beryllium only?

—It was his demo.

—Yes, you saw to that. All right. We'll keep him on for a while. Then you'll write him a letter of recommendation. Down the road we'll issue a report on the false brightness. You'll be group leader on that. Highet's voice was tight with controlled fury. —You begin to interest me, Philip. I thought I knew what to expect from you.

—At least we caught this now.

—Oh no we haven't. We haven't caught a thing yet.

—I don't want to sound naive, you're not going to mention this at the presentation?

—Today? I think not. I think I will not at this time give the enemies of reason grounds sufficient to bury an entire body of knowledge and aspiration. Highet lifted from his desk a small device etched with a craft undreamed of even a decade before, raising it before him like a talisman, then replaced it and gazed at Quine implacably. —I believe not.

The telephone rang and Highet lifted it in midring, —No I can't see anyone right now, as Nolan came through the door bearing a red folder, acknowledging Quine with a minute change of expression.

—Very clean data from your shot, said Nolan.

—no damn it Senator Chase is coming in an hour

—Oh, you've seen it?

—We prepared the overheads. A match with theory unparalleled since Mendel's peas. Kid's a barn burner is he?

—what do you mean here now? We're not set up

—He'd like to be.

—damn it keep him down there

—You're taking him under your wing.

—fucking lantern-jawed hero of the people can just wait

—My political skills are legendary, Quine joked.

—don't care! Do whatever it takes! I'll call you when we're ready.

—I've noticed, Nolan said, turning to Highet as he put down the phone.

—have to do everyone's job, what's this?

—Overheads of the Taliesin data.

—Fine, just leave them. Bernd there you are find the rest of the team will you get them up here we have a little problem god damn senator from the liberal east arrived just a little ahead of schedule he's downsta, Aron where the hell have you been we've got a PR . . . Nolan!—

—Oh! I just, sorry, didn't see your foot

—Jeez sorry Aron let me help you up . . .

—Nolan will you get the hell

—my slides! here don't step on

—Nolan!

—just put these back in order, with the ah integrated twenty-four-bit color TGIF animations and music in standard MIDI files

—Aron

—little problem with the synthesizer all the instruments stuck on the cowbell patch so when we played the *Apocalypse Now* music, the Wagner Valk, rather intriguing actually but hardly

—Aron, will you

—then our Silicon Graphics machine couldn't read the TGIFs so we converted them to Video Postscript but somehow they came out black and white one inch square so

—Aron, will you please

—go low tech instead, keep it simple, four synchronized slide projectors overheads eight-track digital tape

—Aron, get up! Leave the, will you leave the slides on the floor. Go to the lobby. Keep Senator Chase busy down there.

—But I

—Go! and pacing to the window, parting the blind, —Fuck's this going to play like, must be a thousand of them in the road.

—The news said two thousand, said Dietz.

—They'll claim five. Supposed to keep these assholes away from the main gate put them up in the north corner, I want to know how this got out! glaring at Quine, —I want to know who's been talking to these people, who let them know Chase was coming today.

—Leo, it's symbolic. Today's Armistice Day, you know?

—Shit on that, it's to embarrass us. All for Chase. Man keeps calling me up about twenty kilos of plutonium gone missing, I keep telling him we don't stockpile plutonium here.

—But we do, Leo.

—Well, Bernd, Chase doesn't have the clearance to know that, and picking up the phone midring, —Yes? Damn it, Aron, just, look, take him to the downstairs conference room think you can do that? . . . no will you forget the fucking slides, thumbing the phone's button, —Where's Szabo? You all go down, I'm right behind you.

—Senator, glad you could make it. This all? Expecting more of your colleagues . . .

—Doctor Highet. These two gentlemen are from the General Accounting Office. You'll be seeing more of them.

—Why don't you all take a seat and we'll begin.

—There's just one thing I want to know, Doctor Highet. Is the Superbright going to work?

—I believe our presentation will address any

—I don't want a presentation, I want a yes or no. At the present moment, judging from everything you have to date, is it a workable weapon, within the budget and timeframe we have?

—Beyond question. In fact we have new results that show

—A new Radiance test? When?

—I can't discuss that in open session.

—Then maybe you can discuss claims of exaggeration and fraud from Warren Slater.

—Those are lies. Slater sabotaged my teams repeatedly. He had reasons of his own to derail this program.

—Such as?

—I can't discuss that in open session.

—Slater's not the only critic. Some of your own people

—Those are not my people. Those are people who've made up their minds that certain technical problems are too hard to solve. They're wrong. They could be making a contribution, but instead they find fault.

—So why are you behind schedule?

—We're not.

—According to your own timetable

—Senator, we have brilliant, creative people together here doing important work. Leave them alone and they accomplish miracles. But if you put limits on them . . .

—You're not answering me. I didn't ask about miracles.

—I am answering you if you'll let me. You cannot nickel and dime a program like this in the research phase, not if you exp

—Research? I thought you were engineering phase.

—Very nearly.

—You sent the President a letter claiming engineering phase.

—I do not acknowledge that. If such a letter were to exist it would be top secret, and you lack the clearance to see it or the competence to evaluate it.

—Doctor Highet I'm getting tired of this, you have oversold this program to the tune of thirty bill

—Senator

—you have stonewalled, you have defied

—Senator

—gress, you have hidden behind classifica

—Senator, you're an asshole. You might even be a traitor.

—I will not take that from you, sir!

—You don't have a clue what's at stake here, one look at the masses out front you're ready to cave, sell out this nation's security its technological edge its, breaking off for the figure in the doorway who bowed his head in apology.

—Gentlemen, we have had a bomb threat. We need to clear the building.

—Good God.

—What the hell?

—Your peacenik constituency, Chase. Good work.

—I'm not through with you, Highet.

—Fine, I'm willing to sit right here play Russian roulette.

—Gentlemen please, the security forces will be coming through, you can move to Building 101.

Harsh urgent clipped static blurted in the hallway. Gallop of many feet approached.

—Clear this area!

Outside the building a security squad came running in a wedge, helmeted and visored, booted in horseskin, only the flesh of their hands visible holding batons at port arms. Leather creaking, heels clattering, radios jabbering, they divided the exiting crowd and Quine was swept the wrong way, out past an unmanned checkpoint before he broke clear onto a lawn where men in blue jumpsuits trailed strips of yellow CAUTION tape on two then three sides of him and he dashed through the diminishing gap as behind him shouts were raised. Between windowless walls a stair dropped him to where two burly men rounding a corner dealt him a blow with lumber they carried, —Jesus watch it! hurling him to his knees against a chainlink fence vibrating at the lip of a great pit. In this excavation five, seven, ten vehicles labored grinding and roaring in desperate intensity, beeping hollowly as they reversed or clanking furiously forward over a terrain of pale mud. Vast as it was it would not bury a millionth of the dead should the bombs created here detonate. Quine pulled free of the fence with a tearing of fabric and went down a walkway of plywood sheets, pausing before a trailer CREDNE CONSTRUCTION in whose doorway two T-shirted men eating lunch regarded him with dispassion as with a handkerchief he rubbed dirt and blood from his palms, temple, and knee visible through ripped pants, then down a long stair of raw wood stained with mud, glancing back at concentric terraces gouged from the hillside, *the city is built on two levels, lords and palaces above, common workers below,* and rounding a corner to where a stream of people hurried past guards at a checkpoint.

—Look I need to

—Move on, there's been a bomb threat.

—Yes but I'm in an important meeting I need to get back to

—This is a secured area.

—I'm cleared dammit! clapping his breast where no photo ID, but a torn flap of pocket, depended, —oh Christ, look my name's Philip Quine can't you call

—Keep moving! The guard pushed him back into the stream of people advancing slowly toward the main gate. He made his way through it and broke free, starting to jog on a rough track that led to the perimeter road, where he doubled back to approach the entry kiosk from its far side passing and passing close on his left the unending mass of protesters, just beyond a row of trees and the perimeter fence, only to stop short of the entry road where cars were stalled by the leading edge of the crowd inside coursing around them like a stream around rocks, while bullhorns blared —personnel, do not exit by this gate repeat do not, and outside the gate protesters swirled in place like debris at a confluence of cataracts, held back by a skirmish line of county police. Quine stood sweating and panting until sirens turned him to face four cars slewing to a stop on the perimeter road and discharging blackvested Lab security forces one of whom leveled his club at Quine and cried, —You!

Quine ran for the kiosk. More Lab police had arrived inside, forming a line to divert Lab personnel from the gate, then quickly moving forward to the gate. Quine was suddenly between two police who linked arms to bar his passage.

—I belong inside. For a moment their visors, opaque, bronze, iridescent, mirrored twin Quines, elongated, battered, dismayed. Then he was seized and pushed through the gate into the street.

A helicopter swept overhead. He held his ears.

Let us now speak the truth as we know it. Say that the sun is round, and bright, and hot. The sun fires its acolytes, darkens their skins, elevates their wormridden souls, the sun rises in our birth and sets in our death, its writing is in the spots upon its face and in the spots it prints upon our skins. It is in us whether we labor under it or hide from it, it strikes through our souls, it ignites the light of our being, or limns the shadow of our denial.

In the crowd he saw Lynn, her dark head appearing and vanishing among others, lithe nape and shoulders bare and tanned below the cropped marge of hair, sun blazing on the straps and back of a white tank top.

Light is a wave and we are carried upon it, light is a particle to pierce us with revelation. Light is sun or moon, a heat that tempers or a gentleness that silvers with love.

He pushed toward her. At the end of its circuit the helicopter turned.

Here in the crowd are fools, innocents, knaves, here we are jostled, in hazard, we can do nothing but strive against currents, knowing how slight is our power to reach any shore we set out for.

He called her name and the call was lost in noise. The surge of the crowd pushed them together and she turned to him, eyes wide and surprised. It was not Lynn. Against their will they embraced. He clung to her until another push felled him. The cut on his knee opened and he bent to stanch it. When he rose she was gone and he was among figures wearing skulls of papier-mâché and skeletons painted on black tights. Tambourines jangled, clattered.

Say what you know, that love is lost. That light is lost. But see, loveless our souls still blaze. Our sun has not gone out, for fire comes to those who go not the way of light. What's lost is well lost. See, we blaze and are not consumed.

Around him people tied kerchiefs across their faces. Overhead the helicopter roared. Its black belly glistened like a spider's thorax, then it rocked and moved off, vanishing behind a silver mist that fell onto the crowd as gently as the first rain of spring. Tears sprang to Quine's face and he dropped to his knees gasping and blinded, clinging to the nearest figure, saying over and over, —I belong inside, his voice unheard even by himself.

Old Legends

Gregory Benford

S CIENCE FICTION IS ABOUT DIALOG. SCIENCE ITSELF IS A CONTINUOUS, SOMETIMES RANCOROUS DIALOG ABOUT OBSERVATIONS AND EXPERIMENTS, WITH A NUMBER OF ESSENTIAL AND OH-SO-USEFUL RULES: FALSIFIABILITY, REPEATABILITY, UNIVERSAL IMPLICATIONS, AND REMOVAL OF SELF FROM THE FINAL EQUATION. SOMEHOW, THIS HAS LED TO THE MISTAKEN IMPRESSION THAT SCIENTISTS—OR AT LEAST SOME SCIENTISTS—ARE MORE OR LESS THAN HUMAN: COLD, PRECISE, UNCARING. THOSE WHO HAVE MET A LOT OF SCIENTISTS KNOW HOW WRONG THIS IS. GREGORY BENFORD, A HIGHLY REGARDED PHYSICIST HIMSELF, HAS MET A LOT OF SCIENTISTS; SOME OF THEM, THE MOST INFLUENTIAL OF OUR TIME.

THIS ARTICLE—ESSAY BY WAY OF MEMOIR—SERVES TO ILLUMINATE THE QUESTIONS ASKED BY CARTER SCHOLZ, AND TO CONNECT SCIENCE FICTION INTIMATELY WITH MODERN SCIENCE. IS IT POSSIBLE THAT SCIENCE FICTION KNOWS SIN, AS WELL?

LONG BEFORE I became interested in science itself, I was a science fiction reader. The Space Age changed that in 1957. At the time it seemed that the central metaphor of science fiction had become real, foggy legend condensing into fact.

I read about Sputnik on the deck of the *S.S. America,* sailing back from Germany, where I had lived for three years while my father served in the occupying forces. The one-page mimeographed ship's newsletter of October 4 gave that astonishing leap an infuriatingly terse two sentences.

By the time I re-entered high school in the U.S., just emerging from years when the Cold War seemed to fill every crevice of the world, the previously skimpy curriculum was already veering toward science, a golden, high-minded province. Suddenly I found that I could take a full year of calculus and physics in my senior year. This was quite a change. I put aside my devoted reading of the sf magazines and launched myself into science, the real thing.

I began to think seriously that a career of simply studying the physical world, which I had often read about in fiction, could be open to such as me. I had done reasonably in high school up until Sputnik, getting Bs and As, but not thinking of myself as one of the really bright members of the class. I imagined that I would probably end up as an engineer, but I really wanted to be a writer. When I scored high in the national scholastic exams of 1958 nobody was more surprised than I. But those scores opened the advanced classes to me in my senior year, and a whole new landscape.

This fresh path led directly to an early afternoon in 1967, when two physicists and a clerk from the personnel office at the Lawrence Radiation Laboratory ushered me into a large office without preamble, and there sat a distracted Edward Teller behind a messy desk piled high with physics journals.

To my surprise, the other physicists quickly excused themselves and left. Teller was scientific director of the Laboratory then, fabled for his work developing the A-bomb and H-bomb, and his epic split with Robert Oppenheimer.

They sprang Teller on me without warning. I had gone up to Livermore to discuss working there as a research physicist, following my doctoral thesis at the University of California at San Diego. Nobody told me that Teller insisted on taking the measure of every candidate in the program. "We didn't want you to be nervous," one said later. It worked; I was merely terrified.

He was the most daunting job interviewer imaginable. Not merely a great physicist, he loomed large in one of the central mythologies of modern science fiction, the A-bomb. In the next hour no one disturbed us as Teller quizzed me about my thesis in detail.

Attentively he turned every facet over and over, finding undiscovered nuances, some overlooked difficulty, a calculation perhaps a bit askew.

He was brilliant, leaping ahead of my nervous explanations to see implications I had only vaguely sensed. His mind darted as swiftly as any I had ever encountered, including some Nobel Laureates. To my vast surprise, I apparently passed inspection. At the end, he paused a long moment and then announced that he had "the most important kvestion of all." Leaning closer, he said, "Vill you be villing to vork on veapons?"

Unbidden, images from Stanley Kubrick's film *Dr. Strangelove* leaped to mind. But Teller had impressed me as a deep, reflective man. I said I would—occasionally, at least. I had grown up deep in the shadow of the Cold War. My father was a career army officer, and I had spent six years living with my family in occupied post-war Japan and Germany. It seemed to me that the sheer impossibility of using nuclear weapons was the best, indeed the only, way to avoid strategic conventional war, whose aftermath I had seen in shattered Tokyo and Berlin. Paralleling this direct experience was my reading in science fiction, which had always looked ahead at such issues, working out the future implied by current science.

That afternoon began my long, winding involvement with modern science and fiction, the inevitable clash of the noble and imaginary elements in both science and fiction with the gritty and practical. I have never settled emotionally the tensions between these modes of thinking. Growing up amid the shattered ruins of Germany and Japan, with a father who had fought through World War II and then spent long years occupying the fallen enemy lands, impressed me with the instability of even advanced nations. The greatest could blunder the most.

I quit Livermore in 1971 to become a professor at the University of California at Irvine. In novels such as *In the Ocean of Night,* written after my "Rad Lab" days, I see in retrospect that I was thrashing out my mixed feelings. I often turned to other scientists to fathom how my own experience fit with the history of both science and fiction in our time. I did not see then how intertwined they were and are, and how much we face the future using the legends of the past.

SIXA VS. SEILLA

"Veapons" called immediately to mind the central fable of sf in those days—the event which seemed to put the stamp on John Campbell's *Astounding* magazine. In the spring of 1944 Cleve Cartmill published a clear description of how an atomic bomb worked in *Astounding,* titled "Deadline." Actually, Cartmill's bomb would not have worked, but he did stress that the key problem was separating non-fissionable isotopes from the crucial Uranium 235.

This story became legend, proudly touted by fans after the war as proof of sf's predictive powers. It was a tale of an evil alliance called the Axis— oops, no, the Sixa—who are prevented from dropping the A-bomb, while their opponents, the Allies—no, oops, that's the Seilla—refrain from using the weapon, fearing its implications.

In March 1944 a captain in the Intelligence and Security Division and the Manhattan Project called for an investigation of Cartmill. He suspected a breach in security, and wanted to trace it backward. U.S. security descended on Campbell's office, but Campbell truthfully told them that Cartmill had researched his story using only materials in public libraries.

A Special Agent nosed around Cartmill himself, going so far as to enlist his postman to casually quiz him about how the story came to be written. The postman remembered that John Campbell had sent Cartmill a letter several days before the Special Agent clamped a mail cover on Cartmill's correspondence. This fit the day when agents had already visited Campbell's office. Campbell was alerting his writer, post-haste. Soon enough, Security came calling.

Sf writers are often asked where they get their ideas. This was one time when the answer mattered. Cartmill had worked for a radium products company in the 1920s, he told the agent, which had in turn interested him in uranium research. He also fished forth two letters from Campbell, one written ten days short of two years before the Hiroshima bombing, in which Campbell urged him to explore these ideas: "U 235 has—I'm stating fact, not theory—been separated in quantity easily sufficient for preliminary atomic power research, and the like. They got it out of regular uranium ores by new atomic isotope separation methods; they have quantities measured in pounds . . ." Since a minimum critical mass is less than a hundred pounds, this was sniffing close to Top Secret data.

"Now it might be that you found the story worked better in allegory," Campbell advised, neatly leading Cartmill to distance the yet unwritten tale from current events. Plainly Campbell was trying to skirt close to secrets he must have guessed. Literary historian Albert Berger obtained the formerly secret files on the Cartmill case, and as he points out in *Analog* (September, 1984), Campbell never told Cartmill that wartime censorship directives forbade *any* mention of atomic energy. Campbell was urging his writer out into risky territory.

Cartmill was edgy, responding that he didn't want to be so close to home as to be "ridiculous. And there is the possible danger of actually suggesting a means of action which might be employed." Still, he had used the leaden device of simply inverting the Axis and Allies names, thin cover indeed. Campbell did not ask him to change this, suggesting that both men were tantalized by the lure of reality behind their dreams.

The Office of Censorship came into play. Some suggested withholding *Astounding's* mailing privileges, which would have ended the magazine. In the end, not attracting attention to the Cartmill story and the magazine seemed a smarter strategy. Security feared that ". . . such articles coming to the attention of personnel connected with the Project are apt to lead to an undue amount of speculation." Only those sitting atop the Manhattan Project knew what was going on. "Deadline" might make workers in the far-flung separation plants and machining shops figure out what all this uranium was for, and talk about it. The Project was afraid of imagination, particularly disciplined dreaming with numbers and facts well marshaled. They feared science fiction itself.

All this lore I already accepted, but I was curious about those at the top

of the Project, such as Teller. Self-cautious, a mere, fresh postdoctoral physicist, I did not at first ask him about any of these legendary events. I was
busy, too, learning how science works in such lofty realms.

I discussed both physics and politics with Teller while at the Lab, finding him delightfully eccentric and original. One hammering-hot summer
day in Livermore, we continued well into the lunch hour. Teller wanted to
go swimming, but refused to break off discussions. "Ve must not be all in
our minds, all the time." I went with him. He cut an odd figure as he
threaded among the muscular sunbathers, mind fixed on arcane points of
theoretical physics, his skin pale as the underbelly of a fish. He sat at the
pool edge and shed his suit, tie, shirt, the works right down to—instead of
underwear—a swim suit. This man plans ahead, I thought.

As a boy in Budapest he had come in second in a contest with a street-
car, losing a foot. Beside the pool he unfastened his artificial foot, unembar-
rassed. (In *Dr. Strangelove,* I couldn't help recalling, it was an artificial
hand.) He kept talking physics even as he wriggled over to the edge. He
earnestly concluded his point, nodded earnestly, satisfied, and then seemed
to realize where he was. I could almost hear him think, *Ah, yes, next problem.
Svimming. Vere iss . . . ?* "Edward," I began—and Teller instantly flung
himself like an awkward frog into the water, obliviously comic.

Moments like these led me to finally see through the cultural aura that
obscures figures like Teller. They are more vast and various than we think,
funnier and odder and warmer. Dr. Strangelove doesn't exist. Teller had
made a name for himself at Los Alamos by thinking ahead. He proposed the
hydrogen fusion bomb, the Super, while the A-bomb was under development—and lobbied to skip the A-bomb altogether, leapfrogging to the
grander weapon.

With his penchant for problem-solving, Teller was a symbol of the
"techno-fix" school of warfare, and by the 1960s the times were running
against him. At one Livermore lunch, an arms control negotiator furiously
said to me, "He's the Satan of weapons! We've got to stop him." Many
scientists felt just as strongly.

H. Bruce Franklin's *War Stars: The Superweapon and the American Imagination* made the case that sf, particularly in the pulp magazines, strongly
influenced U.S. foreign policy. In the 1930s Harry Truman had read lurid
pulp magazine sf yarns of super weapons settling the hash of evil powers.
Often they were held in readiness after, insuring the country against an
uncertain future.

Truman wasn't alone. Popular culture's roots run deep. Time and again
at Livermore I heard physicists quote sf works as arguments for or against
the utility of hypothetical weapons. As I came to know the physics community more widely, this complex weave deepened.

BEEPS

At Livermore I got involved with the theory of tachyons, the theoretically possible particles which can travel faster than light. Not the sort of thing one imagines a "weapons lab" allowing, but Teller allowed the theorists a wide range. When the tachyon idea popped up in the physics journals, I discussed it with Teller. He thought they were highly unlikely, and I agreed, but worked on them anyway out of sheer speculative interest. With Bill Newcomb and David Book, I published in *Physical Review* a paper titled "The Tachyonic Antitelephone." We destroyed the existing arguments, which had avoided time-travel paradoxes by re-interpreted tachyonic trajectories moving backward in time as their anti-particles moving forward in time. It was simple to show that imposing a signal on the tachyons (sending a message) defeated the re-interpretation, so the causality problem remained. If sending a tip-off about a horse race to your grandfather made him so rich he jilted your grandmother and ran off to Paris, that was just as bad a violation of cause and effect.

Teller invoked a different argument against tachyons, which recalled the casual lunchtime discussions at Los Alamos, which were legendarily fruitful. At one, Enrico Fermi asked his famous question, "Where are they?"—and raised the still fiercely contentious issue of why aliens, if they are plentiful in the galaxy, haven't visited us by now. (That question undoubtedly inspired the proposal that radio listening might turn up alien broadcasts, made by Giuseppe Cocconi and Philip Morrison in 1959—the same Morrison who had worked in the Manhattan Project.) Using similar logic, Teller noted that tachyons could be used to send messages backward in time. "Vhy haven't they been sent? Vere are our messages from the future?"

Our answer was that nobody had built a tachyon receiver yet. Neat, perhaps, but a bit too neat. Surely somehow nature would not disguise such a profound trick. There had to be a way of seeing from theory why such disturbing things could not occur.

I was so intrigued by these hypothetical particles that I wrote papers investigating their consequences. That drew me into a distant friendship with Gerald Feinberg of Columbia University, who had introduced some of the ideas of tachyonic field theory. He was an amiable, concentrated man, always thinking through the broad implications of the present. He was also a first-class physicist who had edited a science fiction fanzine in high school with two other upstart Bronx Science High School students, Sheldon Glashow and Steven Weinberg—who later won the Nobel prize for their theory which united the weak and electromagnetic forces. Titled ETAOIN SHRDLU for the frequency of letter use in English, the only fanzine ever edited by Nobel Prize winners stressed science with earnest teenage energy. (A generation later Stephen Hawking spent most of his free time reading sf paperbacks. Enthusiastically discussing them decades later with me, he was like most readers, able to recall plots and ideas easily, but not titles or authors.)

Tachyons were the sort of audacious idea that comes to young minds used to roving over the horizon of conventional thought. Because of Feinberg I later set part of my tachyon novel at Columbia. By the late 1970s I thought tachyons quite unlikely, since several experiments had failed to find them (after an exciting but erroneous detection in 1972). Still, the issue of how physics could *prove* that time communication is impossible remained—the primary issue for all of us, including Teller. Tachyons seemed a better way to address this than the more exotic beasts of the theorists' imaginations, such as space-time wormholes.

So I framed the issue using tachyons, exploring how people in the future might get around the problem of having no receiver: by using energetic tachyons to disturb a finely tuned experiment in a physics lab in the past. Gerry chuckled when he heard this notion, pleased that his theoretical physics had spawned a novel about how scientists actually worked. He was rather bemused by the continuing cottage industry of tachyon papers, now numbering in the several hundreds. When an Australian experiment seemed to find cosmic rays moving over twice the speed of light, the field had a quick flurry of interest. Gerry was intrigued, then crestfallen when the results weren't confirmed.

He told me years later that he had begun thinking about tachyons because he was inspired by James Blish's short story, "Beep." In it, a faster-than-light communicator plays a crucial role in a future society, but has an annoying final *beep* at the end of every message. The communicator necessarily allows sending of signals backward in time, even when that's not your intention. Eventually the characters discover that all future messages are compressed into that *beep,* so the future is known, more or less by accident. Feinberg had set out to see if such a gadget was theoretically possible.

This pattern, speculation leading to detailed theory, I encountered more and more in my career. The litany of science is quite prissy, speaking of how anomalies in data lead theorists to explore new models, which are then checked by dutiful experimenters, and so on. Reality is wilder than that.

No one impressed me more with the power of speculation in science than Freeman Dyson. Without knowing who he was, I found him a like-minded soul at the daily physics department coffee breaks, when I was still a graduate student at the University of California at San Diego. I was very impressed that he had the audacity to give actual department colloquia on his odd ideas. These included notions about space exploration by using nuclear weapons as explosive pushers, and speculations on odd variants of life in the universe. He had just published a short note on what came to be called Dyson spheres—vast civilizations which swarm around their star, soaking up all available sunlight and emitting infrared, which we might study to detect them. (This was a direct answer to both Fermi's question and the Cocconi-Morrison proposal—more links in a long chain.) Dyson had read Jules Verne while a child, and at age eight and nine wrote an sf novel, *Sir Phillip Roberts's Erolunar Collision,* about scientists directing the orbits of asteroids. He was unafraid to publish conjectural, even rather outrageous ideas in the solemn pages of physics journals. When I remarked on this, he answered with a smile, "You'll find I'm not the first." Indeed, he descended from a line of futurist British thinkers, from J. D. Bernal of *The World, the Flesh and the Devil,* to Olaf Stapledon to Arthur C. Clarke. In *Infinite in All Directions,* Dyson remarked that "Science fiction is, after all, nothing more than the exploration of the future using the tools of science."

This was a fairly common view in those burgeoning times. In my first year of graduate school in La Jolla I noticed Leo Szilard at department colloquia, avidly holding forth on his myriad ideas. Szilard had persuaded Einstein to write the famous letter to Roosevelt explaining that an A-bomb was possible, and advocating the Manhattan Project. He had a genius for seizing the moment. Szilard had seen the potential in nuclear physics early, even urging his fellow physicists in the mid-1930s to keep their research secret. I had read Szilard's satirical sf novel *The Voice of the Dolphins* in 1961, and his sf short stories, and decided to wait until I had time from a weathering round of classes to speak to him. I was just taking some difficult examinations in late May 1964 when Dyson told me that Szilard had died of a heart attack that morning. It was a shock, though I had scarcely exchanged a dozen words with him. (Of his rather cerebral fiction he had said, "I am emotionally moved by extraordinary reasoning.") I had not seized the moment.

Szilard was obsessed with nuclear dangers, and Dyson carried some of Szilard's thinking forward. A student of Dyson's made headlines in 1976 by designing a workable nuclear weapon using only published sources. I recalled the Cartmill episode. When I remarked on this, Dyson said, "The link goes back that far, yes." At the time I didn't know what he meant.

Throughout all this, politics was not an issue. I was a registered Democrat, others were Republican, but our positions did evolve from our politics.

Scientists often read sf at an early age and then drift away, but many maintain a soft spot in their hearts for it. Some, like me, bridge the two communities.

So it was no surprise to me when Teller enlisted sf allies in his policy battles. Especially effective in the 1980s was Jerry Pournelle, a rangy, technophilic, talented figure. With a .38 automatic he could hit a beer can at fifty yards in a cross wind. As needed, he could also run a political campaign, debug a computer program or write a best-selling science fiction novel—simultaneously. When he asked me to serve on the Citizens' Advisory Council on National Space Policy in 1982, at first I didn't realize that Jerry wasn't proposing just another pressure group. This was a body which had direct lines to the White House, through the National Security Advisor. Teller, too, was "in the loop."

Pournelle dominated the Council meetings with his Tennessee charm, techno-conservative ideas and sheer momentum. An oddly varied crew assembled: writers, industrial researchers, military and civilian experts on subjects ranging from artificial intelligence to rocketry. The Council, a raucous bunch with feisty opinions, met at the spacious home of science fiction author Larry Niven. The men mostly talked hard-edge tech, the women policy. Pournelle stirred the pot and turned up the heat. Amid the buffet meals, saunas and hot tubs, well-stocked open bar, and myriad word processors, fancies simmered and ideas cooked, some emerging better than half-baked.

Blocking nuclear weapons had always appealed to me. My misgivings about military involvement in the space program and other areas, which had surfaced in my novels repeatedly, vanished in matters which clearly were the military's province. Never, in all the policy and technical consulting I did while a professor at UCI, did I doubt that solving the immense problem of nuclear war lay somehow outside the province of the physicists who had started it all. But physicists could contribute—indeed, they had to try.

I favored as a first goal defending missiles and military command centers, using ground-based systems of swift, non-nuclear-tipped rockets. Technically this was small potatoes, really, not much beyond the capacity already available under existing treaties, which after all had allowed the Soviets to ring Moscow with a hundred fast defensive rockets, nuclear-tipped and still in place today.

The more ambitious specialists talked of war stars—great bunkers in the sky, able to knock down fleets of missiles. I doubted they could deal with the tens of thousands of warheads that could be launched in a full exchange. Still, to me that fact was a better argument against the existence of those thousands of warheads, rather than an argument against defense.

Finally, we settled on recommending a position claiming at least the moral high ground, if not high orbits. Defense was inevitably more stabilizing than relying on hair-trigger offense, we argued. It was also more principled. And eventually, the Soviet Union might not even be the enemy, we said—though we had no idea it would fade so fast. When that happened, defenses would still be useful against any attacker, especially rogue nations bent on a few terrorist attacks. There were plenty of science fiction stories, some many decades old, dealing with that possibility.

The Advisory Council met in August of 1984 in a mood of high celebration. Their pioneering work had yielded fruits unimaginable in 1982— Reagan himself had proposed the Strategic Defense Initiative, suggesting that nuclear weapons be made "impotent and obsolete." The Soviets were clearly staggered by the prospect. (Years later I heard straight from a senior Soviet advisor that the U.S. SDI had been the straw that broke the back of the military's hold on foreign policy. That seems to be the consensus now among the diplomatic community, though politically SDI is a common whipping boy, its funding cut.)

None of this was really unusual in the history of politics, policy and science fiction. H. G. Wells had visited with both presidents Roosevelt, Stalin, Churchill and other major figures. In 1906 Theodore Roosevelt was so dismayed by the Wellsian portrait of a dark future that he asked him to the White House for a long talk about how to avoid drifting that way. Wells's attention to war as the principal problem of the modern era found a ready audience among world leaders. Jules Verne had not commanded such respect in the corridors of power, and no writer since Wells has, but in the late twentieth century it seemed that science fiction's grasp of possibilities was once more called forth, this time by the same government which had fretted over Cleve Cartmill.

In the summer of 1984 all things seemed possible. I was not surprised that Robert Heinlein attended the Advisory Council meetings, dapper and sharp-witted. And out of the summer heat came a surprise visitor—Arthur C. Clarke, in town to promote the opening of the film made from his novel, *2010*. Clarke had testified before Congress against the Strategic Defense Initiative, and regarded the pollution of space by weapons, even defensive ones, as a violation of his life's vision.

Heinlein attacked as soon as Clarke settled into Larry Niven's living room. The conversation swirled around technical issues. Could SDI satellites be destroyed by putting into orbit a waiting flock of "smart rocks" (conventional explosives with small rockets attached)? Would SDI lead to further offensive weapons in space?

Behind all this lay a clear clash of personalities. Clarke was taken aback. His old friend Heinlein regarded Clarke's statements as both wrong-headed and rude. Foreigners on our soil should step softly in discussions of our self-defense policies, he said.

It was, at best, bad manners. Perhaps Clarke was guilty of "British arrogance."

Clarke had not expected this level of feeling from an old comrade. They had all believed in the High Church of Space, as one writer present put it. Surely getting away from the planet would diminish our rivalries? Now each side regarded the other as betraying that vision, of imposing unwarranted assumptions on the future of mankind. It was a sad moment for many when Clarke said a quiet good-bye, slipped out and disappeared into his limousine, stunned.

In that moment I saw the dangers of mingling the visionary elements of sf with the hard-nosed. The field welcomed both, of course, but the world chewed up those of such ample spirit.

Behind much of this was Teller, close advisor to Reagan. He got involved with exotica such as X-ray lasers, which I thought beside the point. The answer lay not in vastly different, new technology, but using tried-and-true methods with a different strategic vision.

I was naive about what would follow. While the Soviets got the message quite clearly—because they watched what we did, and didn't merely listen to the public debate—and began thinking about throwing in the towel altogether. Meanwhile, over the Strategic Defense Initiative issue Nobel laureates ground their axes, techno-patter rained down, politicians played to the gallery—ships passing in the night, their fog horns bellowing.

Our present had become, for that sf fan reading a newspaper report of Sputnik, completely science fictional. Even in the 1980s, though, I did not know how deep the science and science fiction connection went.

OLD LEGENDS

I had always wondered about Teller's effectiveness at influencing policy. In the 1940s, as James Gleick remarks in *Genius,* a biography of Richard Feynman, Teller was as imaginative and respected as Feynman. He was the great idea man of the Manhattan Project. So it was natural for me to ask him finally about science fiction's connection with both scientific discovery (tachyons) and science policy (the Manhattan Project).

"For long range thinking I trust in the real visionaries—the ones I prefer to read, at least. The science fiction writers. I haf always liked Mr. Heinlein, Mr. Asimov, of course Mr. Clarke—they are much more important in the long run than any Secretary of Defense."

So we talked on about how he had read magazines in the 1940s in Los Alamos, bought similar hardbacks as they began to appear in the 1950s, and eventually from the press of events kept up with only a few favorites—the hard sf types, mostly but not exclusively.

He pointed out to me an interesting paragraph in an old paperback.

We were searching . . . for a way to use U 235 in a controlled explosion. We had a vision of a one-ton bomb that would be a whole air raid in itself, a single explosion that would flatten out an entire industrial center . . . If we could devise a really practical rocket fuel at the same time, one capable of driving a war rocket at a thousand miles an hour, or more, then we would be in a position to make almost anybody say "uncle" to Uncle Sam.

We fiddled around with it all the rest of 1943 and well into 1944. The war in Europe and the troubles in Asia dragged on. After Italy folded up . . .

That was Robert A. Heinlein as "Anson MacDonald" in "Solution Unsatisfactory," in the May 1941 *Astounding*. It even gets the principal events in the war in the right order.

"I found that remarkable," Teller said, describing how Manhattan Project physicists would sometimes talk at lunch about sf stories they had read. Someone had thought that Heinlein's ideas were uncannily accurate. Not in its details, of course, because he described not a bomb, but rather using radioactive dust as an ultimate weapon. Spread over a country, it could be decisive.

I recalled thinking in the 1950s that in a way Heinlein had been proved right. The fallout from nuclear bursts can kill many more than the blast. Luckily, Hiroshima and Nagasaki were air bursts, which scooped up little topsoil and so yielded very low fallout. For hydrogen bombs, fallout is usually much more deadly.

In Heinlein's description of the strategic situation, Teller said, the physicists found a sobering warning. Ultimate weapons lead to a strategic standoff with no way back—a solution unsatisfactory. How to avoid this, and the whole general problem of nuclear weapons in the hands of brutal states, preoccupied the physicists laboring to make them. Nowhere in literature had anyone else confronted such a Faustian dilemma as directly, concretely.

Coming three years later in the same magazine, Cleve Cartmill's

"Deadline" provoked astonishment in the lunch table discussions at Los Alamos. It really did describe isotope separation and the bomb itself in detail, and raised as its principal plot pivot the issue the physicists were then debating among themselves: should the Allies use it? To the physicists from many countries clustered in the high mountain strangeness of New Mexico, cut off from their familiar sources of humanist learning, it must have seemed particularly striking that Cartmill described an allied effort, a joint responsibility laid upon many nations.

Discussion of Cartmill's "Deadline" was significant. The story's detail was remarkable, its sentiments even more so. Did this rather obscure story hint at what the American public really thought about such a super-weapon, or would think if they only knew?

Talk attracts attention. Teller recalled a security officer who took a decided interest, making notes, saying little. In retrospect, it was easy to see what a wartime intelligence monitor would make of the physicists' conversations. Who was this guy Cartmill, anyway? Where did he get these details? Who tipped him to the isotope separation problem? "And that is vhy Mr. Campbell received his visitors."

So the great, resonant legend of early hard sf was, in fact, triggered by the quiet, distant "fan" community among the scientists themselves. For me, closing the connection in this fundamental fable of the field completed my own quizzical thinking about the link between the science I practice, and the fiction I deploy in order to think about the larger implications of my work, and of others'. Events tinged with fable have an odd quality, looping back on themselves to bring us messages more tangled and subtle than we sometimes guess.

I am sure that the writers of that era, and perhaps of this one as well, would be pleased to hear this footnote to history. Somebody really was listening out there. I suspect today is no different. Perhaps the sf writers are indeed the unacknowledged legislators of tomorrow.

V
REDEMPTION

The Red Blaze Is the Morning

Robert Silverberg

R OBERT SILVERBERG'S SHORT FICTION
AND NOVELS HAVE WON MANY AWARDS, AND HAVE TAUGHT ME A LOT ABOUT
WRITING. HE IS A CONSUMMATE PROSE CRAFTSMAN, YET NEVER NEGLECTS
DRAMA OR IDEA. HIS MOST RECENT PUBLISHED NOVEL IS *HOT SKY AT MIDNIGHT;*
IN 1995, BANTAM WILL PUBLISH *MOUNTAINS OF MAJIPOOR.*

ONE OF THE PECULIARITIES AND STRENGTHS OF ALL FICTION, HOWEVER AD-
VANCED, IS THAT IT MUST ENGAGE ANCIENT EMOTIONS, TICKLE ANCIENT INTER-
ESTS, OR IT IS EMPTY. WE HAVE ALWAYS BEEN FASCINATED BY THOSE THINGS
THAT WE OURSELVES EXPERIENCE, OR FEAR, OR HOPE FOR, THINGS ESTABLISHED
(IN OUTLINE IF NOT REFINEMENT) TENS OF THOUSANDS OR EVEN MILLIONS OF
YEARS AGO. STORYTELLING IS A KIND OF ARCHAEOLOGY OF THE HUMAN SPIRIT.

SILVERBERG HAS LONG HAD A FASCINATION WITH THE PAST AND ARCHAEOL-
OGY, AS WELL AS THE FUTURE, AND HERE TELLS OF A DEDICATED MAN ABOUT TO
LOSE EVERYTHING HE HAS LIVED FOR, WHO IS GIVEN ONE LAST CHANCE—AN UL-
TIMATE DIALOG BETWEEN PAST AND FUTURE.

> *The Red—Blaze—is the Morning*
> *The Violet—is Noon—*
> *The Yellow—Day—is falling*
> *And after that—is none—*
> —Emily Dickinson

DAY BY BLAZING day Halvorsen stretched himself across a blistering abyss,
patiently searching in recalcitrant rock and hot sand for morsels of the useless past, even though he has begun to doubt the meaning and value of his
own work. By chilly night, soaking his damaged and aching leg in a shallow basin of tepid sea-water—in this arid part of Turkey, fresh water is a
luxury—he feels seductive fingers tickling the membranes of his mind.

Something is trying to get in: perhaps already has. Something keeps nestling down alongside his consciousness and whispering fantastic, tempting things to him, visions of far-off times, mighty civilizations yet unborn. Or so it often seems.

What is actually going on, Halvorsen suspects, is that he is beginning to go crazy. The fascination of what's difficult, he thinks, has not merely dried the sap out of his veins, as old Yeats feared it would, but has parched his brain beyond the bounds of sanity. And yet he can still speak six languages, including Turkish and Hebrew and modern Greek, and he can read Latin and classical Greek besides. He can recite the names of the Roman emperors from Augustus to Romulus Augustulus without missing one. Yes, his mind still functions well enough. Something else, something equally intangible and even harder to define, is what has become impaired. And then there is the sore leg, too, which mended inadequately after last summer's accident on the rocky slope and is painful all the time. The leg is really in very bad shape. He ought not to be out here on the summit of the hill with a pick and shovel. He should be sitting in his tent, supervising the work of others. But Halvorsen has always been a hands-on kind of archaeologist: a point of great pride for him.

This is the fifth week of the third season of the dig. It is high summer, when the blue cloudless sky reflects the light of the swollen sun like a hot metal plate, and the *meltem,* the dry, hot, unrelenting wind out of the inland plateau, sends fifty-mile-an-hour blasts of brown dust into your nostrils and eyes and mouth and every cranny of your clothing for four or five days without halting. Halvorsen's site is on a ragged little peninsula in southwest Turkey, overlooking the Mediterranean coast. It is an unimportant place that does not even have a paved road running to it, nor running water or electricity, and yet it has a long history. There is a tiny fishing village here now; before that, there was a Byzantine naval base; before that, Romans; before them, a Greek trading outpost; before that, a Minoan trading outpost; before that, Halvorsen thinks, a proto-Hittite encampment. And before that—ah, nobody knows what was here before that. But Halvorsen has a hypothesis, based on a few scattered and questionable bits of evidence. For three summers, now, he has been trying to find more satisfactory proof to support that hypothesis.

At mid-morning on this blazingly hot day Halvorsen is working alone on high, extending the trench that runs along the proto-Hittite side of the hill. Nobody he knows believes that the Hittites ever lived here, or anywhere else along this coast; and he himself has nothing to go by in that direction except the presence at the highest point of the site of a double line of mud-brick walls, two courses high, that feel more or less Hittite to him. But he is not particularly concerned with the Hittites, anyway: they are a

Bronze Age folk, and he is looking for something much more ancient. Still, it would be helpful to prove that the Hittites had passed this way, too. And this is his dig. He can call this wall proto-Hittite if he feels like it, at least for the time being.

The site where he is working is a difficult one, steep and precarious. A rainstorm of unprecedented ferocity for this dry coast, six winters back, had carved away half the western face of the hill, laying bare the very finds that had brought Halvorsen here in the first place; but the angle of the lie is practically vertical, the soil crumbles easily, and Halvorsen's budget will not allow him to put proper bridging across the worst of the gaps. So he hobbles around up here, walking lopsided as it is because of his torn-up leg, testing the ground as he goes in order to make sure it will bear his weight, and fearing at every moment that he will hit a weak spot and go tumbling down in a black cloud to land on the fanged rocks below.

He knows that he ought to be letting his Turks extend this trench for him. But he feels that he is on the brink of a major discovery. How would the workmen be able to detect the place where the terrain changes, and the proto-Hittite stratum gives way to an even older one?

"They'll know," Jane Sparmann says. She's the graduate student from Columbia who has been working with him out here for three years, now. "They may be illiterate laborers, but they've spent their whole lives digging in these mounds and they have a sixth sense about any kind of shift in the matrix."

"Even so," Halvorsen has replied whenever this comes up. "I want to do this myself. I have a *seventh* sense."

Sparmann laughs. Halvorsen knows that she thinks he is stubborn to the point of irrationality. Very likely Sparmann believes that too many summers under the Mediterranean sun have addled his brain, grand old figure of the field that he is. Well, so be it: she's probably right. But he intends to do his own digging up here, even so. Moving slowly along the stone base of the mud wall, looking for the precise spot at the end of the proto-Hittite wall where the soil darkens into virginity and then the place just beyond it where, he hopes, the Neolithic occupants of this site had erected their primordial acropolis.

It's a fine place for an acropolis. No enemies can come upon you un-aware, if you have watchmen posted up here. The hill runs athwart the pe-ninsula for five hundred meters, a sharp rocky ridge. Look to the west and you see the smooth blue sea. To the east, you have a long view of the baking dusty plain.

Halvorsen pokes with his pick, scrapes, peers, brushes the dirt aside, pokes again. Nothing. It's dull work, but he's used to it. Steady toil, un-relieved boredom, sweat and dust, one clump of dirt and rock after another, poke and sift, move along. He thinks enviously of Schliemann unearthing rooms of golden treasure, Howard Carter shining his flashlight beam into the tomb of Tut-ankh-Amen. But of course they had put in their months and years of dusty boredom, too.

"*Müdür Bey!*" calls a loud rasping voice from below. "*Müdür Bey!*" His title: "Mr. Director." The Turks can't or won't learn to pronounce his name. With difficulty Halvorsen levers himself upright, leaning on his shovel, and peers down the eastern slope of the hill to the place where Sparmann and three of the diggers are working, over at the edge of the Greek settlement. Ibrahim, his foreman, is standing in the trench, triumphantly holding up a crude buff-colored pot.

"What is it?" Halvorsen asks.

Jane Sparmann, at Ibrahim's elbow, cups her hand and calls, "It's full of coins! Athenian owls, some Corinthians, something from Syracuse."

"Fine," Halvorsen says, without enthusiasm. "Give him his bonus."

"You don't want to see them?"

"Later," he says.

They always pay the diggers extra for any easily marketable artifacts, to keep them from taking them on their own behalf. The expense is trivial, a hundred lire per coin. Sparmann is excited by the find—she's still young—but to Halvorsen the coins, and indeed the whole Greek settlement, are merely an irritating distraction. Dozens of Greek coins turn up wherever you put a spade in the ground. As for the stumps of a little temple, the hazy outlines of a marketplace: who cares? The Mediterranean world is full of Greek temples. They bring no news. Halvorsen is looking beneath such things, beyond, behind, searching for the secret from which all this Mediterranean splendor sprang. The unknown progenitor-race, the pivot, the fulcrum on which the magnificence turned as it began the centrifugal outreach of its grandeur.

He returns to his digging.

But almost immediately comes another booming cry from Ibrahim: "*Paydos! Paydos!*" Time to quit for the lunch-break.

Halvorsen would just as soon go on working while the others knock off. That would be bad form, though: you mustn't let your workmen think you're lazy, but it's not good to seem maniacally compulsive, either. He hobbles down the hill and over to the workshed, where the usual meal of olives, eggs, canned tuna fish, and warm beer is being dispensed.

"How'd things go, Dr. H?" Sparmann asks. She smiles pleasantly—she's very pretty, actually, though Halvorsen would never dream of laying a hand on her—but her subtext is fundamentally malevolent. She knows damned well how it has gone up there, how it goes all the time. But she is politely maintaining the pretense that he may eventually find something on the hill.

"Starting to look promising," Halvorsen says. Why not? Hope costs nothing.

This season's dig has four weeks to go. And then? Will he spend the off season, as usual, raising money for next year's work, the grant applications, the lecture series, the endless begging among the well-heeled? Not to mention the interminable business of renewing the digging permit, a hassle that was always complicated in unpredictable ways by the twists and turns of Turkish politics. How much easier it would be simply to give up, retire from field work, write some books, find a soft curatorship or chairmanship somewhere. But that would be an admission of defeat. It had been a calculated risk to propose his theory as openly as he had; if the notion had come from a forty-year-old, the eventual failure to produce substantiation would be accepted by his colleagues simply as a case of a young man's reach exceeding his grasp, but at Halvorsen's age any such failure would be an irrevocable mark of decline, even senility, a regrettable third act to such a brilliant career. He didn't dare abandon his field work. He was condemned by his own insistent hypothesis to stay out here under this glazed blue sky until he found what he was looking for, or else die trying.

"Beer?" someone asks him.

"Please," says Halvorsen, taking the bottle, though he knows that it will be weary, stale, flat, unprofitable. No surprises there. It is Efes Pilsen, the terrible Turkish beer. Halvorsen would have preferred a Carlsberg; but Copenhagen is a long way away. So he guzzles it, wincing a little, and even has a second one. Warm and weary, yes. Stale. Flat. And definitely unprofitable.

The nights are always strangely cool here, even in summer, with a sharp autumnal edge on them, as though the sun's intense heat has burned a hole in the atmosphere by day and the place is as airless as the moon after dark. Halvorsen sits apart from the others, reads, broods, sips *raki,* soaks his sore leg. The archaeologists' compound consists of two whitewashed cinderblock storage buildings, a work-shed, and six little tents down by the sandy beach where they sleep. Most of the Turkish workmen make their camps for the night on the shallow slopes just back of the dig, covering themselves with leafy branches or threadbare blankets, though some go home on donkeyback to their village five or six miles up the road.

Halvorsen's assistants—two women, three men, this year—sit outside their tents, waiting for him to go inside and fall asleep. During the season they have coupled off in various spasmodic patterns, as usual, but they try to hide that from him as though he were some sort of chaperone for them. For most of the summer, Halvorsen is aware, Jane Sparmann has been sharing the tent of Bruce Feld of the University of Pennsylvania, and the Chicago girl, Elaine Harris, has been shifting her affections between Martin Altman of Michigan State and the other boy—Riley, O'Reilly, Halvorsen can never remember which—from that university in Ohio. Let them have their fun, Halvorsen thinks: what they do at night is no business of his. But still they wait for him; and at last, though he isn't sleepy yet, he rises and waves goodnight and limps into his tent.

His body aches, his mind is terribly alert. He stretches out on his cot and prays in the clammy darkness for sleep to take him.

Instead the night-voice, that insinuating, tickling voice in his head that has been so insistently frequent of late, comes to him again and says:

—*Here. I want you to see this. This is the Palace of the Triple Queen.*

Every word is perfectly distinct. He has never heard the voice with such clarity before.

And this time the words are followed by an image. Halvorsen beholds on the screen of his mind the facade of a many-columned three-terraced structure that might almost be Hatshepsut's temple at Deir al-Bahri, except that the colonnades fold back upon themselves in topologically implausible ways, as if they were pivoting into some adjacent dimension, and the glowing bas-reliefs along the pediment are utterly alien in style, a procession of slender angular figures interlocking and bending out of focus in the same incomprehensible twisting way. Behind the columns of the topmost terrace lurks some filmy, shadow-cloaked being, barely perceptible except as huge eyes and a ripple of shimmering light, whose frail silvery form nevertheless emanates immense strength and power.

"Who are you?" Halvorsen asks. "What do you want with me?"

—*And this, this is the courtyard of the Tribunal of the People in the time of the Second Mandala.*

Halvorsen sees a sort of marble beehive, fifty or sixty hexagonal tanks out of each of which rises the face of a huge-eyed hairless figure, more or less human in general outline. They are submerged from their shoulders down in a radiant luminous fluid. Halvorsen is given to understand that these creatures are a single entity in fifty bodies, that in their own era they exerted some kind of high governmental function, that they spent lifetimes of unimaginable length standing in these six-sided pools of nutrients.

—*And what I show you now, says the voice, are the ruins of the building known as the Concord of Worlds, which also is of the time of the Second Mandala, and above it the outlying precincts of the City of Brass, constructed thirty cycles later.*

Scenes of confused splendor flood his mind. Marble pillars, shining metal slabs inscribed in unknown languages, obelisks of chalcedony, all strewn about as though by a giant's hand; and, overlying them with a casual disdain, the streets of some rigidly geometrical later city, gleaming with a cruel metallic sheen.

"This is madness," Halvorsen mutters. He sits up, gropes in the darkness for his sleeping-pills. "Leave me alone, will you? Get out of my mind."

—*I mean no harm.*

"Tell me who you are, then."

—*A friend. A colleague.*

"I want to know your name."

—*It would mean nothing to you.*

This is a new development, actually to be holding a conversation of sorts with this phantom: with himself, to be more accurate. It seems to mark a dismaying advance in his mental deterioration and he finds it terrifying. Halvorsen begins to tremble.

"What do you want with me?" he demands. Shouting out loud, now. Careful, he thinks. The others will hear you and come running, and the secret will be out. Poor old coot has lost his mind. He will beg them to cover it up, and they will promise, but of course gossip travels so quickly in academic circles—

—*I want to offer you—to offer you—*

Sputter. Hiss. Static on the line. Then silence.

"Come on, damn you, finish your sentence!"

Nothing. Nothing. Halvorsen feels like weeping. He finds a pill. Looks for the water pitcher, finds the *raki* bottle instead. What the hell. He washes the pill down with a shot of straight *raki*. Getting suicidal now? he asks himself. The Turkish whiskey burns his throat. Almost at once he feels groggy. He wonders, as the drug and the *raki* hit him simultaneously, whether he will live to see morning.

But of course he does. After breakfast everyone assembles, Jane Sparmann calls the roll of workmen, a new day's toil begins. Sweat, dust, sunscreen, bug repellent. And the tools of the trade: picks, shovels, sifting screens, brushes, tape-measures, envelopes, tags, dust-goggles, sketch-pads, cameras. Jane continues to work in the Greek-era trench; Bruce and Martin will be photographing the Minoan level, this season's central focus, which now has begun to emerge from its overburden; the other two have projects of their own in the Byzantine strata. And Halvorsen painfully ascends the hill for another attempt at unearthing some trace of his long-sought prehistoric civilization.

Business as usual, yes. Another day under the dazzling sun. That fierce light bleaches all color out of everything. Nor is there much in the way of sound: even the surf makes merely a faint snuffling noise here. Two dark puffs of dust to the east are the only blemishes on the brilliant dome of the sky. A stork appears from somewhere and hovers for a long while, wings scarcely moving, surveying the busy archaeologists skeptically from aloft.

Halvorsen, down on his knees, nose to the ground, reaches the end of the brick wall, jabs a probing-fork into the soil, feels the change in texture. It was around here somewhere that the handful of scraggly, badly eroded artifacts of apparent Neolithic origin that had lured him into this project in the first place had been exposed by the storm: a crude bull's-head in baked clay, a fragment of a double-ax amulet of distinctly un-Minoan style, a painted snippet of what he is convinced was a mother-goddess amulet. Year after year he has cut his way toward this point—delayed for two whole seasons by the discovery of the Hittite wall—and now, almost afraid of the answers he is about to get, he is ready to strike downward into the hill to see what lies five or ten meters beneath the surface. He will need the workmen to do that for him, he realizes. But he will be over them like a hawk, watching every shovelful they lift.

This afternoon—maybe tomorrow—

An unexpected interruption comes just then. From the east, a throbbing sputtering sound, a cloud of dust, a dirt bike chugging down the rough little road that leads to the site. The workmen wave at him from below, calling out, *"Müdür Bey! Müdür Bey!"* A messenger has arrived, bringing him a letter from Ankara. Perturbed, Halvorsen makes his way uneasily down from his hilltop. The envelope, soiled and creased, bears the insignia of the Ministry of Education. His fingers quiver a little as he opens it: the Department of Antiquities of the Ministry of Education has jurisdiction over all archaeological digs. Some change must have occurred; and in Turkey all change involving the bureaucracy is change for the worse.

There's been a change, yes. But perhaps not a problem. Halvorsen scans the letter, purple typescript on manila stock, translating quickly. Hikmet Aytul, the Department of Antiquities official who has charge of all archaeological work in this part of the country—Hikmet Pasha, Halvorsen calls him, because he is so vast and self-important—has resigned. The new superintendent of excavations is a certain Selim Erbek, an assistant curator of a provincial museum farther north along the coast. He is making the rounds of his new responsibilities and intends to pay a visit to Halvorsen's dig in the next two or three days.

"Trouble?" Bruce Feld asks.

Halvorsen shrugs. "I'm not sure. Bureaucratic reshuffling. Hikmet Pasha's out, somebody named Selim Erbek's in. He'll be dropping in to get acquainted with us later in the week."

"Should we take any special action?" Jane Sparmann wants to know.

"You mean, hide yesterday's coins?" Halvorsen laughs. "No, no, we play by the rules here. When Selim Bey gets here, we show him everything we've found. Such as it is." He has already debated, briefly and silently, whether he ought to get started on his own penetration of the hill before the new man arrives. Significant finds might produce unpredictable reactions; it might be wiser to take a reading on this Selim Erbek before plunging in. But Halvorsen rejects the idea. He is here to dig and, if possible, find. No sense wasting time trying to outguess the inscrutable bureaucrats.

After lunch he picks Ibrahim, Ayhan, and Zeki as his workmen and finally begins peeling back the hill, after years of anticipation. Halvorsen has worked with these three men over many seasons and trusts them totally, though he watches them closely all the same. They dig carefully and well, using their picks with surgical delicacy, running their fingers through the clods of earth in search of tiny overlooked artifacts before letting the wheelbarrow man carry the sifted dirt away. But there is nothing to find. This part of the hill, despite the fact that a few anomalous artifacts had been found in one corner of it after that monster storm, seems in general never to have felt the imprint of human use. Wherever you dig, around this site, you turn up something, be it Turkish, Byzantine, Greek, Roman, Minoan, whatever. Except here. Halvorsen has magically located the one corner of the place that nobody in the last ten thousand years has seen fit to occupy. It is the utter opposite of his expectations.

Still, there's always tomorrow.

"*Paydos! Paydos!*" comes the call, finally, at dusk. Another day gone, less than nothing to show for it.

Lying in the darkness of his tent, Halvorsen waits for the voice to come, and soon enough it is with him.

—*I will show you more, if you allow it.*

"Go on. Anything you like."

Halvorsen strives to be calm. He wants to attain numbness in the face of this absurdity. He knows that he must accept the fact of his own unfolding insanity the way he accepts the fact that his left leg will never function properly again.

—*These are the ruins of Costa Stambool.*

Into Halvorsen's mind springs the horrific sight of vast destruction seen at a great distance, an enormous field of horror, a barren and gritty tumble of dreary gray fragments and drab threadbare shards that would make a trash-midden look like a meadow, and all of it strewn incoherently about in a willy-nilly chaotic way. He has spent his life among ruins, but this one is a ruin among ruins, the omega of omegas. Some terrible catastrophe has taken place here.

But then the focus shifts. He is able to see the zone of devastation at closer range, and suddenly it appears far from hideous. Even at its perimeter, flickers of magic and wonder dance over the porous, limy soil of its surface: sprites and visitations, singing wordlessly to him of Earth's immense history and of futures already past, drift upward from the broken edge-tilted slabs and caper temptingly about him. A shimmer of delicate golden green iridescence that had not been visible a moment ago rises above everything and surrounds it.

—*This was the City of Cities.*

The broken shards are coming to life. The city of Costa Stambool begins to rise into view like a whale breaching the surface of the sea, or like a vast subterranean tower emerging from its hiding-place in the bowels of the earth. It is an irresistible force as it heaves itself out of the rubble and climbs with a roaring rush to a height Halvorsen can barely calculate.

It is less a city than a single enormous building, incredibly massive at its base and tapering to a narrow, impossibly lofty summit; and it is skinless, wholly without walls, its exterior peeled away on all sides to reveal the layered intricacies of its teeming core. Halvorsen can see a myriad inhabitants moving about within, following the patterns of their daily lives from level to level, from street to street, from room to room.

Bizarrely, the building seems to be standing on edge, its floors at right angles to the ground. But how can that be? It makes no sense. Then Halvorsen realizes that he is being granted a double perspective: somehow he is able to see the interior of the great structure from the side and top at once, a four-dimensional view, piercing downward and upward and backward and forward through the thousands or perhaps even millions of years of the city's existence. That puts him at ease. He understands how one reads the multifarious layers of a long-occupied site.

The voice in his mind guides him along.

—*The walls you see down there, glowing with scarlet phosphorescence, are the oldest levels. On top of these are the structures of the Second Mandala, and then the Third. Here you will recognize the Concord of Worlds and the City of Brass. This is Glissade, the pleasure-city of the Later Third. Here is the Palace of the Triple Queen; here, the courtyard of the Emperor of All; down here, the cells of the Tribunal of the People.*

Everything is as perfect as the day it was built; and yet simultaneously every layer reveals signs of the destruction wrought by builders of later eras, and over everything else are the brutal marks of some climactic onslaught of vandals: the work, Halvorsen is told, of the bestial invaders who at the dawn of the climactic Fourth Mandala brought fire and death to this place.

In awe Halvorsen tours the temples of unknown gods and the palaces of dynasties yet unborn but already forgotten. He stares at a vast marble slab proclaiming some empire's grandeur in an incomprehensible script. He enters the Library of Old Stambool, and sees iron-bound chests overflowing with what he understands to be books, though they look more like rubies and emeralds. The guiding voice never ceases, identifying for him the Market of All Wonders, the Gymnasium, the Field of Combat, the Tower of the Winds.

Halvorsen has never seen anything like it. He has never so much as *imagined* anything like it. It is Rome and Babylon and Byzantium and Thebes all at once, raised to the fiftieth power. In this single crushing vision Halvorsen feels that he has experienced an entire great civilization, that he has been buried beneath the totality of its immensity.

Then it is gone. As suddenly as it erupted from the ground, the great building subsides into it again, not with a crash but a sigh, a gentle cadence of descent. It falls like a feather on the wind, shrinking down on itself, and within moments Halvorsen sees nothing but the gray field of rubble again.

After a time he says, "Very impressive. I didn't know I had such powers of invention."

—*They are not inventions. They are the reality of our age, which I freely make available to you.*

"And who are you, may I ask?"

—*I will tell you. I am an inhabitant of the Fifth Mandala, which is the last epoch of the world you call Earth, very close to the end of all things.*

Halvorsen shivers. The lunacy deepens and deepens.

"You live in the future and are reaching back across time to talk to me?"

—*The very distant future, yes.*

Halvorsen contemplates that for a moment.

Then he says, "Why? What do you want from me?"

—*Simply to give you an opportunity to see my world. And to beg you to allow me to see yours. A trade, my time for your time: your body for mine, our minds to change places. I want that very much. I want it more than life itself.*

By day none of what he has heard or seen in the night seems real. There is only the brown sandy site, and the unrelenting red blaze of the sun, and the blue sea, and the different blue of the sky's rigid vault. From the white tents come his young assistants. The workmen have already breakfasted and are waiting for their assignments. "*Gün aydin,*" they say, grinning, showing big white crooked teeth. "Good morning." For them this job is a bonanza, the best pay they will ever see. They love it. "*Gün aydin, gün aydin, gün aydin.*"

The morning's work begins. Sunscreen, bug repellent, sweat, dust. Picks, shovels, brushes, tape-measures.

So the madness seems to overtake him, he thinks, only by night. Halvorsen wonders about that. Perhaps the power of his quest for understanding the buried past, here in the remorseless brightness of the day, drives off these phantoms of the imaginary future. Or perhaps it is that the monkish solitude and close atmosphere of his dark, stifling little tent invite hallucinations, especially to a tired man who tends to drink too much *raki* when he is alone. Either way, he is grateful to leave it behind, the craziness, as he stomps toward this new day's work.

He believes passionately in archaeology as metaphysics. Without true knowledge of the past, how can one comprehend the present, how can one begin to triangulate the future? Of course *true* true knowledge is impossible, but we can attempt partial truths: we can skin the earth's surface looking for clues, we can sift and sort, we can postulate. Halvorsen has spent most of his life doing this. What has it gained him? He can recognize the varying soils of differing layers of occupation. He can name the Emperors of Rome from Augustus to Romulus Augustulus, remembering even to include Quintillus and Florianus. He has—what? Five years left? Ten?—to master all the rest of it, to solve all the pieces of the riddle that he has arrogated to himself. Then he will be gone. He will join the vastness of the past, and the work will belong to others. But for the moment it is his responsibility. And so the work goes on, today for him, tomorrow for the Jane Sparmanns, the Bruce Felds. Will they see it as he does? Or will it merely be a job for them, a highway toward the comforts of tenure? How can you be an archaeologist at all, except out of love, an insatiable desire for the truth, the willingness to give yourself up to quests that may all too easily become obsessions?

Halvorsen's obsessive notion is that Asia Minor and not Mesopotamia was the cradle of civilization. Fertile, with easy access to the Mediterranean, rich in mineral ores, forests, grasslands for grazing, a reasonably benign climate, the peninsula seems to him to have been an ideal site for the transition from Neolithic life to the splendors of the Bronze Age. The flow of conceptualization could only have been down out of Anatolia's rocky spine, he is convinced: to Sumerian Iraq on one side of the cultural watershed, to proto-Minoan Crete on the other, and onward also to Egypt in the south. But there is no proof. There is no proof. Mere smudges and traces remain, where he needs walls and pillars, inscribed tablets, potsherds, idols, weapons. Time has erased it all here in Anatolia, or at least has erased what he needs to provide a foundation for his bold thesis, leaving only confusion and conjecture.

Still, he is certain that this is where it all began. The Çatal Hüyük findings tell him that, the engraved pebbles in the Karain Cave, the rock paintings of Beldibi: this is where the first canto of the great epic was written. But where is the proof? He knows that he is working from *a priori* hypotheses, always a great peril for a scientist. This sort of thing is the antithesis of the scientific method. He has allowed himself to seem to be a fanatic, a nut, a Schliemann, an Evans, obsessed with obfuscatory special pleading in defense of his *idée fixe*. Schliemann and Evans, at least, eventually delivered the goods. But he has nothing to show, and soon they will be laughing at him in the halls of academe, if that has not begun already.

Still, he digs on. What else can he do?

It's a long day. The new trench gets deeper and longer and it's still absolutely virgin. Thinking incorrectly that he has spotted something significant jutting from its side, Halvorsen jumps eagerly down into it and wrenches his bad leg so severely that he almost bursts into tears, though they are tears of rage rather than pain. Halvorsen is a big, strapping man whose physical endurance was legendary in the profession, and now he is little more than a cripple. If he could, he would have the leg cut off and replaced with something made of steel and plastic.

The *raki* helps a little. But only a little.

Lying on his back and massaging the throbbing leg with his left hand with the *raki* bottle in his right one, Halvorsen says into the dense clinging darkness, "How did you find me? And why?" He is somewhat tipsy. More than somewhat, maybe.

There is no answer.

"Come on, speak up! Have you been in touch with others before me? Twenty, fifty, a hundred, a hundred thousand different minds, every era from First Dynasty Egypt to the fortieth century? Looking for someone, anyone, who would go for your deal?"

Silence, still.

"Sure you did. You've got a million-year lifespan, right? All the time in the world to cast your line. This fish, that one, this. And now you have me on the hook. You play me. Trade bodies with me, you say, come see the marvels of the far future. You think I'm tempted, don't you? *Don't* you? But I'm not. Why should I be? Don't I have enough on my plate right here? You think I want to start over, at my age, learning a whole new archaeology? You suppose I need to worry about identifying the strata that signify the fucking Second Mandala?"

No answer. He knows that he is losing control. He never uses obscenities except under extreme stress.

"Well, go fish somewhere else," Halvorsen says. "I reject your deal. I piss on your crazy deal. I stay here, you stay there, the way God intended it to be. I go on digging in the dirt of Turkey until my brains are completely fried and you sit there amidst all your fucking post-historic apocalyptic miracles, okay? Costa Stambool! You can take Costa Stambool and—"

At last the voice out of distant time breaks its silence.

—Is your refusal a final one?

And, almost in the same moment, another voice from closer at hand, from just outside his tent, in fact:

"Dr. Halvorsen? Are you all right, Dr. Halvorsen?"

Bruce Feld's voice.

My God, Halvorsen thinks. I'm bellowing and ranting at the top of my lungs, and now they all finally know that I've gone nuts.

"I'm—fine," he says. "Just singing, a little. Am I too loud?"

"If you need anything, Dr. Halvorsen—"

"Maybe another bottle of *raki,* that's all." He laughs raucously. "No, no, just joking. I'm fine, really. Sorry if I disturbed you." Let them think I'm drunk; better than thinking I'm crazy. "Good night, Bruce. I'll try to keep it down."

And then, again:

—Is your refusal final?

"Yes! No. Wait. I have to consider this thing a little, all right? All right?"

Silence.

"God damn it, I need some time to think!—Hey, are you still there?"

Silence.

Gone, Halvorsen thinks. He has given his answer, and the being from the far end of time has broken off the contact, and that is that. Even at this moment the offer is being made to someone of the thirtieth century A.D., or perhaps the thirtieth century B.C., or any of a million other years along the time-line between prehistory and the Fifth Mandala of Costa Stambool. *A trade, my time for your time: your body for mine, our minds to change places.*

"Listen," Halvorsen says piteously, "I'm still thinking it over, do you know what I mean? Although I have to tell you, in all honesty, you'd be getting a bum deal. I'm not in really good physical condition. But I want to discuss this proposition of yours a little further before I give you a definitive answer, anyway."

Nothing. Nothing. An agony of regret.

But then, suddenly:

—Let us discuss, then. What else would you like to know?

The promised visit of the new superintendent of excavations does not occur on the second day after the receipt of the letter from the Ministry of Education, nor on the third. Halvorsen is unsurprised by that. Time moves differently in different cultures; he lives on the Turkish calendar here.

The work is now going so badly that he actually has begun to regard his nightly bouts of madness as comic relief. His leg has swollen, practically immobilizing him; it is so difficult for him to get around now that he is unable to reach his excavation site at the top of the hill, short of being hoisted up there with a sling and pulley. So he supervises fretfully from below. But that makes no difference, because Ibrahim, Ayhan, and Zeki are still digging through virgin soil. Elsewhere all around the site, nice little things are turning up for the others: Riley and Harris have found some bits of Byzantine mosaic in association with coins of the Emperor Heraclius, Feld and Altman have struck an interesting layer of early Minoan sherds, Jane Sparmann has found a cache of glass and terra-cotta beads that may indicate the presence of a previously unsuspected zone of late Greek occupation. The hilltop work, though, is plainly a bust. Hittites, or somebody who built walls in Hittite style, undoubtedly had had a fortress up there four or maybe five thousand years ago, but what Halvorsen is after is some sign of civilization two or three thousand years older than that—some deposit that will convincingly link this coastal outpost to the known Neolithic settlements far to the east at Çatal Hüyük—and he has not had the slightest luck. The three anomalous artifacts that that storm had laid bare remain perplexing enigmas, tantalizing, inexplicable.

He consoles himself with conversations in the darkness. The visions of the Fifth Mandala grow ever more baroquely detailed.

Halvorsen, who still believes that he is spinning these fantasies within the walls of his own tortured mind, is bemused by the discovery that he has such lavish qualities of imagination within himself. He has thought of himself all along as a prosaic drudge, a plodding digger in musty, dusty ancient realms. Evidently there is more to him than that, a rich vein of fabulist locked away somewhere. The realization makes him uneasy; it seems to call into question the integrity of his scholarly findings.

He wants to know about the inhabitants of the remote eon of which his informant is a denizen.

—There are very few of us. I may be the only one.

"You aren't sure?"

—Contact is very difficult.

"It's easier for you to speak with someone who lived a million years in your past than it is to pick up the phone and call someone who lives around the corner from you?"

Apparently so. There has been a great cataclysm, an invasion of some sort, a climactic battle: the last and ultimately futile stand of the human race, or rather the evolved and vastly superior successors to the human race, against an inexorable enemy so terrible that its nature seems beyond the abilities of Halvorsen's informant to communicate. This, it seems, occurred as the closing act of the epoch known as the Fourth Mandala, when humanity, after having attained a supreme, essentially god-like height, was thrust down irreparably into the dust. Now only a few lurkers remain, scuttling through the heaped-up ruins of previous glorious civilizations, waiting for their final hours to arrive. Halvorsen gets the impression that they are not even creatures of flesh and blood, these last few humans, but some kind of metallic mechanisms, low spherical beetle-like housings, virtually indestructible, in which the souls of the remaining inhabitants of Earth have taken refuge.

Some resonant chord in Halvorsen's Nordic soul is struck by the revelation that there will be a Ragnarok after all, a Götterdämmerung: that all gods must have their twilight, even the supernal beings of humanity's final epoch. He is saddened and exalted by it all at once. They were beings of a magnificence and power beyond comprehension, a race of glorious heroes, demigods and more than demigods, and yet they fell, even they. *Will* fall. It is the myth of myths, the ultimate saga. Odin and Thor and Heimdall and Tyr and all the rest of the Aesir will die in the Fimbulwinter of the world, when Fenrir the Wolf breaks his chains and the Midgard Serpent rises and the fire-demons of Muspelheim come riding forth upon the world. So it has been, over and over, and so it must and will be, to the end of time, even into the days of the great Mandalas yet to come.

"Why come here, though?" Halvorsen asks. "We're only smelly primitives, hardly more than apes. We live in ignoble times. Why not just stay where you are, up there in the grand and glorious final act of the human drama, and wait for the curtain to come down?"

—The curtain has already come down, and it happens that I have lived on beyond it. Where is the nobility in that? I want to close the circle; I want to return to the starting point. Come: take my body. Explore my world, which to you will be full of wonders beyond belief. There will be much for you to study here: our immense Past is your immeasurable future. Spend a million years, two million, as long as you like, roaming the ruins of Costa Stambool. And let me take your place in your own era.

"It won't be a fair trade," Halvorsen warns again. "You won't be getting as good as you give."

—Let me be the judge of that.

"No. Listen to me. I need to have you realize what you'd be getting. Not only are we mortal—do you really understand what that means, to be mortal?—but I'm not even an especially good specimen of my race. I'm getting to be old, as old goes among us, and I feel very tired and my leg, if you know what a leg is, was badly damaged in an accident last year and I can barely hobble around. Besides which, I've painted myself into a corner professionally and I'm about to become a laughing stock. You'd be walking into a miserable situation. The way I feel now, even the end of the world would be preferable to the mess I'm in.

—Is this a refusal of my offer, or an acceptance?

Halvorsen is baffled for a moment by that. Then he understands, and he begins to laugh.

But of course he is aware that the game he is playing with himself, out there along the borders of sanity, is a dangerous one; and he is glad when sleep at last frees him of these fantastical colloquies. When morning comes, he knows, he must rid his mind of all such nonsense and turn his full attention to the trench on the hill. And either find in it the things that he hopes will be there, or else abandon this site at last, confess his defeat, and make his choice between letting himself be pensioned off and humbly petitioning the Turks to allow him to hunt for traces of extreme Anatolian antiquity someplace else. But he ought not to go on diverting himself with these wishful and fundamentally unhealthy dreams of an escape to the Fifth Mandala.

And eventually morning comes, bringing the usual blast of dry heat, the usual clouds of little black flies, and the usual breakfast of hard-boiled eggs, processed cheese, canned sardines, and powdered coffee. Morning also brings, a couple of hours later, the Department of Antiquities' new superintendent of excavations for this district, Selim Erbek: Selim *Bey,* as Halvorsen calls him, since in Turkey it's always a good idea to bestow formal honorific titles on anyone who holds any sort of power over you.

Not that Selim Bey seems particularly intimidating. He is very young, thirty at most, a slender man, almost slight, with sleek black hair. He is clean-shaven except for a narrow mustache and is wearing khaki slacks and a thin green shirt already stained with sweat. And—Halvorsen finds this very strange—Selim Bey's demeanor, right from the start, is extraordinarily diffident, almost withdrawn. His voice is almost inaudible and he can barely bring himself to make contact with Halvorsen. The contrast with Hikmet Pasha, his big-bellied, swaggering predecessor, could not be more marked.

Halvorsen offers him breakfast. Selim Bey shakes him off.

"May we speak?" he asks softly, almost timidly.

What the hell is this? Halvorsen wonders. "Of course," he says.

"The two of us, only. Man to man, apart from the others."

Of his assistants, only Jane Sparmann is within hearing range. Does Selim Bey want privacy, or is he simply uncomfortable around women? Halvorsen shrugs and signals to Jane that she should return to her dig. Selim Bey smiles faintly, a quick crinkling of the corner of his mouth. This is all quite odd, Halvorsen thinks.

He says, "Shall we begin with a tour of the site?"

"You may show me later. We must have our talk first," says Selim Bey.

"Yes. Certainly."

The slender little man gestures from the shoreline to the top of the hill. "You have not found, I take it, any additional Neolithic artifacts here, is that correct?"

"Not as yet, no. I've only recently begun trenching along the original find site—the proto-Hittite wall up there needed a careful excavation first, you see—and although the work thus far hasn't been especially rewarding, there's every reason to expect that—"

"No," says Selim Bey. "There is no reason to expect anything."

"Sorry. I don't follow what you're saying."

Selim Bey shifts his weight from one foot to the other. His gaze rests on Halvorsen's left cheekbone. His prominent Adam's apple moves up and down like an adolescent's. He seems about to burst into tears.

He says, after a little while, "I must tell you that the previous superintendent of excavations, Hikmet Bey, did not in fact resign. Hikmet Bey was dismissed."

"Ah?"

"There were many reasons for this," says Selim Bey quietly, digging the tip of his boot into the sand as an embarrassed child might do. "His behavior toward his superiors on certain occasions—his failure to file certain reports in a timely way—his excessive drinking—even his handling, I am sorry to say, of his official financial responsibilities. It is a very unfortunate story and I regret to be telling you of such deplorable things. He needs help, that man. We must all hope that he finds it."

"Of course," says Halvorsen piously. "The poor man." He has to choke back laughter. The fat old tyrant, unseated at last! Caught with his hand in the till, no doubt. Pocketing the fees that the tourists pay to get into the museum at Bodrum and pissing the money away on *raki* and little boys.

"The reason I tell you this," Selim Bey says, "is that examination of Hikmet Bey's records, such as they were, brought forth certain revelations that it is necessary to share with you, Dr. Halvorsen. They concern the Neolithic artifacts that were found at this site after the great storms of some winters ago."

"Yes?" Halvorsen says. He feels some pressure in his chest.

"A small clay bull's head, a double-ax amulet, a female figurine, all in the Çatal Hüyük style."

"Yes? Yes?"

"I deeply regret to say, Dr. Halvorsen, that it appears that these were authentic Çatal Hüyük artifacts, which Hikmet Bey obtained at their proper site many hundreds of kilometers from here through illegitimate channels and planted on this hill so that they would be discovered here by a shepherd boy and eventually brought to your attention."

Halvorsen makes a husky sound, not quite a word.

Selim Bey rushes onward. "Hikmet Bey knew of your theories, of course. He thought it would be a proud thing for Turkey if they could be proven to be sound. He is correct about that. And so he sought to entice you to return to our land and carry out researches in his area of supervision. But the method that he used to attract your attention was very wrong. I am extremely sorry to inform you of this, and on behalf of my government I wish to offer our profound apologies for this unfortunate if well-meaning deception, for which no justification can possibly be found that can in any way negate the tremendous injury that has been done to you. Again, my deepest apologies, Dr. Halvorsen."

The young man takes half a step back, as if he expects Halvorsen to strike him. But Halvorsen simply stares. He is without words. His mouth opens and closes.

A hoax. A plant. His head is swimming.

"*Pardonnez-moi,*" he says finally, unable for the moment to remember how to say "Excuse me" in Turkish. He lurches forward, sending Selim Bey skittering out of his way like a frightened gazelle, and stumbles like a wounded ox down the path that leads to the tent colony along the beach. He moves at a terrible speed, heedless of his injured leg, virtually unaware that he has legs at all: he might have been moving on wheels.

"Dr. Halvorsen? Dr. Halvorsen?" voices call from behind him.

He enters his tent.

I am extremely sorry to inform . . . I wish to offer our profound apologies . . . no justification can possibly be found . . . the tremendous injury that has been done to you . . .

Right. Right. Right.

The *raki* provides a kind of quick palliative. He takes a deep pull straight from the bottle, exhales, takes another, takes one more. Good.

Then he kicks off his boots and stretches out on his cot, facing upward. The day's work is well along, out there on the dig, but he can't bring himself to return to it. There is no way that he can face the others, now, after what he has just learned.

The impact of Selim Bey's words is still sinking in. But there is no escaping the fact of his destruction. His theory is empty; he has wasted his time and expended the last of his professional capital on a foolish quest spurred by fraudulent clues.

As the lunch hour nears and Halvorsen still has not emerged from his tent, Feld and Martin Altman and Jane Sparmann come to him to see if he is all right. Even without knowing what it is that Selim Bey has told him, they evidently have guessed that it was highly upsetting news of some sort.

He tries to bluff it through. "There were some little questions about our permit application," he tells them. "Trivial stuff, nothing to worry about. The usual bureaucratic nonsense."

"If we can help in any way, sir—"

"No need. No need at all."

Halvorsen realizes from the way they are looking at him, that they don't believe a word he has said. They must be able to see the outward manifestations of the shock wave that has coursed through his body, the visible signs of his inner demolition. They can have no doubt now that he has heard something shattering from this morning's visitor and that he is struggling to conceal it from them. There is a look of deep concern on their faces, but also, so it seems to him, sympathy verging on pity.

That is more than he can bear. He will not let them patronize him. Feld makes one more stammering offer of assistance, and Halvorsen replies brusquely that it is not necessary, that everything is all right, that he can handle the problem himself. His tone is so blunt that they are startled, and even a little angered, maybe, at this rejection of their solicitude. But he has left them no choice but to go. Jane Sparmann is the last to leave, hovering at the door of his tent an extra moment, searching for the right words but unable to articulate them. Then she too withdraws.

So, then. He is alone with his anguish. And the central issue remains. His occupation is gone. He has made himself something pitiable in the eyes of his colleagues, and that is intolerable.

Contemplating his options now in the face of this disaster, he sees that he really has none at all. Except one, and that is an even greater foolishness than the one that has brought him to this sorry shipwreck on the Turkish shore.

Nevertheless Halvorsen voices it, more out of rage than conviction.

He stares at the roof of the tent. "All right," he says savagely. "It's daytime here, now, but maybe you can hear me anyway. Are you there? Are you listening? I call your bluff. The offer is accepted. You can take over my life back here, and I'll take over yours. Come and get me, if you can. Get me right now."

Nothing happens. Of course not, Halvorsen thinks. What madness.

He remains motionless, listening to the wind. He hears voices outside, but no words, only faint, indistinct sounds. Perhaps that's the wind, too. He feels the faintest of tremors in the tips of his fingers, and perhaps the twitch of a muscle in his cheek, and a certain mild and quickly passing queasiness in the pit of his stomach. That is the *raki*, he thinks.

"Well?" he says. "No deal, eh? No, I didn't really think there would be. You were just a fucking hallucination, weren't you? Weren't you?"

What else could it have been? he wonders. What else but an old man's lunatic fantasies? Thoughts of a dry brain in a dry season, nothing more. It was shameful to have made the attempt, even in bitter jest. And now he must get up and go back outside, and formally accept the apologies that Selim Bey has come here to deliver, and explain to the others what has happened, and then go on to pick up the pieces of his life somehow, after all. Yes. Yes. Somehow. He will have to be strong in the face of the humiliation that will be his, but there is no choice. Up, then.

He rises to go outside.

But he discovers as he sets about the process of rising from the cot that he is no longer lying on it, nor is he in his tent, and that in fact he has been utterly changed: in a moment, in the twinkling of an eye. His aging, aching body is gone, and he is a gleaming metallic sphere that moves in a wondrously frictionless way, as if by magic; and when he emerges into the open air from the airless vaulted place in which he has awakened, he enters into a realm of mighty silence, and it is the apocalyptic glories of the Fifth Mandala that he sees under the thin yellow light of evening, the immense tumbled many-layered ruins of the great City of Cities, Costa Stambool, at the end of time.

One

George Alec Effinger

D ESPITE CONSTANT HEALTH PROB-
LEMS, GEORGE ALEC EFFINGER HAS MAINTAINED A STEADY SENSE OF HUMOR
AND (MORE SIGNIFICANTLY) PRODUCED A LARGE AND DISTINGUISHED BODY OF
WORK. HIS BEST KNOWN NOVEL IS *WHEN GRAVITY FAILS.*

THERE HAVE BEEN MANY DANGEROUS IDEAS IN SCIENCE FICTION—AND, OC-
CASIONALLY, IDEAS SO DANGEROUS EDITORS HAVE REJECTED THEM REGARDLESS
OF LITERARY MERIT. (ONE EDITOR, READING A STORY BY THEODORE STURGEON,
"THE WORLD WELL LOST," IN THE 1950S, IS ALLEGED TO HAVE CALLED OTHER
EDITORS, RECOMMENDING THAT THEY, TOO, REJECT THE STORY. NEVERTHELESS,
IT WAS PUBLISHED, AND TODAY IT SEEMS TAME.)

"ONE" HAS GONE THE ROUNDS FOR A NUMBER OF YEARS NOW, REJECTED BY
ALL AND SUNDRY, WITNESS ITS YELLOWING MANUSCRIPT . . . AND YET, I IMMEDI-
ATELY FOUND IT FASCINATING, AND THEN, DEEPLY MOVING. "ONE" DOES IN-
DEED CONTAIN A DANGEROUS IDEA, YET IT QUESTIONS NOT THE OLDEST
PHILOSOPHIES OF WESTERN CULTURE, BUT THE MOST DEEPLY HELD WISHES AND
BELIEFS OF SCIENCE FICTION ITSELF.

IT WAS YEAR 30, Day 1, the anniversary of Dr. Leslie Gillette's leaving
Earth. Standing alone at the port, he stared out at the empty expanse of null
space. "At eight o'clock, the temperature in the interstellar void is a negative two hundred seventy-three degrees Celsius," he said. "Even without
the wind chill factor, that's cold. That's pretty damn cold."

A readout board had told him that morning that the ship and its lonely
passenger would be reaching the vicinity of a star system before bedtime.
Gillette didn't recall the name of the star—it had only been a number in a
catalogue. He had long since lost interest in them. In the beginning, in the
first few years when Jessica had still been with him, he had eagerly asked
the board to show them where in Earth's night sky each star was located.
They had taken a certain amount of pleasure in examining at close hand

stars which they recognized as features of major constellations. That had passed. After they had visited a few thousand stars, they grew less interested. After they had discovered yet more planetary bodies, they almost became weary of the search. Almost. The Gillettes still had enough scientific curiosity to keep them going, farther and farther from their starting point.

But now the initial inspiration was gone. Rather than wait by the port until the electronic navigator slipped the ship back into normal space, he turned and left the control room. He didn't feel like searching for habitable planets. It was getting late, and he could do it the next morning.

He fed his cat instead. He punched up the code and took the cat's dinner from the galley chute. "Here you go," said Gillette. "Eat it and be happy with it. I want to read a little before I go to sleep." As he walked toward his quarters he felt the mild thrumming of the corridor's floor and walls that meant the ship had passed into real space. The ship didn't need directions from Gillette; it had already plotted a safe and convenient orbit in which to park, based on the size and characteristics of the star. The planets, if any, would all be there in the morning, waiting for Dr. Gillette to examine them, classify them, name them, and abandon them.

Unless, of course, he found life anywhere.

Finding life was one of the main purposes of the journey. Soon it had become the Gillettes' purpose in life as well. They had set out as enthusiastic explorers: Dr. Leslie Gillette, thirty-five years old, already an influential writer and lecturer in theoretical exobiology, and his wife, Jessica Reid Gillette, who had been the chairman of the biochemistry department at a large middle-western state university. They had been married for eleven years, and had made the decision to go into field exploration after the death of their only child.

Now they were traveling through space toward the distant limits of the galaxy. Long, long ago the Earth's sun had disappeared from view. The exobiology about which both Gillettes had thought and written and argued back home remained just what it had been then—mere theory. After visiting hundreds and hundreds of stellar systems, upon thousands of potential life-sustaining planets, they had yet to see or detect any form of life, no matter how primitive. The lab facilities on the landing craft returned the same frustrating answer with soul-deadening frequency: No life. Dead. Sterile. Year after year, the galaxy became to the Gillettes a vast and terrifying immensity of insensible rock and blazing gas.

"Do you remember," asked Jessica one day, "what old man Hayden used to tell us?"

Gillette smiled. "I used to love to get that guy into an argument," he said.

"He told me once that we might find life, but there wasn't a snowball's chance in hell of finding intelligent life."

Gillette recalled that discussion with pleasure. "And you called him a Terran chauvinist. I loved it. You made up a whole new category of bigotry, right on the spot. We thought he was such a conservative old codger. Now it looks like even he was too optimistic."

Jessica stood behind her husband's chair, reading what he was writing. "What would Hayden say, do you think, if he knew we haven't found a goddamn thing?"

Gillette turned around and looked up at her. "I think even he would be disappointed," he said. "Surprised, too."

"This isn't what I anticipated," she said.

The complete absence of even the simplest of lifeforms was at first irritating, then puzzling, then ominous. Soon even Leslie Gillette, who always labored to keep separate his emotional thoughts and his logical ones, was compelled to realize that his empirical conclusions were shaping up in defiance of all the mathematical predictions man or machine had ever made. In the control room was a framed piece of vellum, on which was copied, in fine italic letters and numerals:

$$N = R_* f_p n_e f_l f_i f_c L$$

This was a formula devised decades before to determine the approximate number of advanced technological civilizations man might expect to find elsewhere in his galaxy. The variables in the formula are given realistic values, according to the scientific wisdom of the time. N is determined by seven factors:

R_* or the mean rate of star formation in the galaxy (with an assigned value of ten per year)

f_p or the percentage of stars with planets (close to one hundred percent)

n_e or the average number of planets in each star system with environments suitable for life (with an assigned value of one)

f_l or the percentage of those planets on which life does, in fact, develop (close to one hundred percent)

f_i or the percentage of those planets on which intelligent life develops (ten percent)

f_c or the percentage of those planets on which advanced technical civilization develops (ten percent)

L   or the lifetime of the technical civilization (with an estimated
     value of ten million years).

These figures produced a predictive result stating that N—the number
of advanced civilizations in the Milky Way galaxy—equals ten to the sixth
power. A million. The Gillettes had cherished that formula through all the
early years of disappointment. But they were not looking for an advanced
civilization, they were looking for life. Any kind of life. Some six years after
leaving Earth, Leslie and Jessica were wandering across the dry, sandy surface of a cool world circling a small, cool sun. "I don't see any advanced
civilizations," said Jessica, stooping to stir the dust with the heavy gauntlet
of her pressure suit.

"Nope," said her husband, "not a hamburger stand in sight." The sky
was a kind of reddish purple, and he didn't like looking into it very often.
He stared down at the ground, watching Jessica trail her fingers in the lifeless dirt.

"You know," she said, "that formula says that every system ought to
have at least one planet suitable for life."

Gillette shrugged. "A lot of them do," he said. "But it also says that
every planet that could sustain life, will sustain life, eventually."

"Maybe they were a little too enthusiastic when they picked the values
for their variables."

Jessica laughed. "Maybe." She dug a shallow hole in the surface. "I keep
hoping I'll run across some ants or a worm or something."

"Not here, honey," said Gillette. "Come on, let's go back." She sighed
and stood. Together they returned to the landing craft.

"What a waste," said Jessica, as they prepared to lift off. "I've given my
imagination all this freedom. I'm prepared to see anything down there, the
garden variety of life or something more bizarre. You know, dancing crystals or thinking clouds. But I never prepared myself for so much nothing."

The landing craft shot up through the thin atmosphere, toward the orbiting command ship. "A scientist has to be ready for this kind of thing,"
said Gillette wistfully. "But I agree with you. Experience seems to be defy-
ing the predictions in a kind of scary way."

Jessica loosened her safety belt and took a deep breath. "Mathematically
unlikely, I'd call it. I'm going to look at the formula tonight and see which
of those variables is the one screwing everything up."

Gillette shook his head. "I've done that time and time again," he said.
"It won't get you very far. Whatever you decided, the result will still be a
lot different from what we've found." On the myriad worlds they had visited, they never found anything as simple as algae or protozoans, let alone
intelligent life. Their biochemical sensors had never detected anything that

even pointed in that direction, like a complex protein. Only rock and dust and empty winds and lifeless pools.

In the morning, just as he had predicted, the planets were still there. There were five of them, circling a modest star, type G3, not very different from Earth's Sun. He spoke to the ship's computer: "I name the star Hannibal. Beginning with the nearest to Hannibal, I name the planets: Huck, Tom, Jim, Becky, and Aunt Polly. We will proceed with the examinations." The ship's instruments could take all the necessary readings, but Gillette wouldn't trust its word on the existence of life. That question was so important that he felt he had to make the final determination himself.

Huck was a Mars-sized ball of nickel and iron, a rusty brown color, pocked with craters, hot and dry and dead. Tom was larger and darker, cooler, but just as damaged by impacts and just as dead. Jim was Earthlike; it had a good-sized atmosphere of nitrogen and oxygen, its range of temperatures stayed generally between $-30°C$ and $+50°C$, and there was a great abundance of water on the planet's surface. But there was no life, none on the rocky, dusty land, none in the mineral-salted water, nothing, not so much as a single cyanobacterium. Jim was the best hope Gillette had in the Hannibal system, but he investigated Becky and Aunt Polly as well. They were the less-dense gas giants of the system, although neither was so large as Uranus or Neptune. There was no life in their soupy atmospheres or on the igneous surfaces of their satellites. Gillette didn't bother to name the twenty-three moons of the five planets; he thought he'd leave that to the people who came after him. If any ever did.

Next, Gillette had to take care of the second purpose of the mission. He set out an orbiting transmission gate around Jim, the most habitable of the five planets. Now a ship following in his path could cross the scores of light-years instantaneously from the gate Gillette had set out at his previous stop. He couldn't even remember what that system had been like or what he had named it. After all these years they were all confused in his mind, particularly because they were so identical in appearance, so completely empty of life.

He sat at a screen and looked down on Jim, at the tan, sandy continents, the blue seas, the white clouds and polar caps. Gillette's cat, a gray Maine coon, his only companion, climbed into his lap. The cat's name was Benny, great-grandson of Methyl and Ethyl, the two kittens Jessica had brought along. Gillette scratched behind the animal's ears and under his chin. "Why aren't there any cats down there?" he asked it. Benny had only a long purr for an answer. After a while Gillette tired of staring down at the silent world. He had made his survey, had put out the gate, and now there was nothing to do but send the information back toward Earth and move on. He gave the instructions to the ship's computer, and in half an hour the stars had disappeared, and Gillette was traveling again through the darkness of null space.

He remembered how excited they had been about the mission, some thirty years before. He and Jessica had put in their application, and they had been chosen for reasons Gillette had not fully understood. "My father thinks that anyone who wants to go chasing across the galaxy for the rest of his life must be a little crazy," said Jessica.

Gillette smiled. "A little unbalanced, maybe, but not crazy."

They were lying in the grass behind their house, looking up into the night sky, wondering which of the bright diamond stars they would soon visit. The project seemed like a wonderful vacation from their grief, an opportunity to examine their lives and their relationship without the million remembrances that tied them to the past. "I told my father that it was a marvelous opportunity for us," she said. "I told him that from a scientific point of view, it was the most exciting possibility we could ever hope for."

"Did he believe you?"

"Look, Leslie, a shooting star. Make a wish. No, I don't think he believed me. He said the project's board of governors agreed with him and the only reason we've been selected is that we're crazy or unbalanced or whatever in just the right ways."

Gillette tickled his wife's ear with a long blade of grass. "Because we might spend the rest of our lives staring down at stars and worlds."

"I told him five years at the most, Leslie. Five years. I told him that as soon as we found anything we could definitely identify as living matter, we'd turn around and come home. And if we have any kind of luck, we might see it in one of our first stops. We may be gone only a few months or a year."

"I hope so," said Gillette. They looked into the sky, feeling it press down on them with a kind of awesome gravity, as if the infinite distances had been converted to mass and weight. Gillette closed his eyes. "I love you," he whispered.

"I love you, too, Leslie," murmured Jessica. "Are you afraid?"

"Yes."

"Good," she said. "I might have been afraid to go with you if you weren't worried, too. But there's nothing to be afraid of. We'll have each other, and it'll be exciting. It will be more fun than spending the next couple of years here, doing the same thing, giving lectures to grad students and drinking sherry with the Nobel crowd."

Gillette laughed. "I just hope that when we get back, someone remembers who we are. I can just see us spending two years going out and coming back, and nobody even knows what the project was all about."

Their good-bye to her father was more difficult. Mr. Reid was still not sure why they wanted to leave Earth. "A lot of young people suffer a loss, the way you have," he said. "But they go on somehow. They don't just throw their lives away."

"We're not throwing anything away," said Jessica. "Dad, I guess you'd have to be a biologist to understand. There's more excitement in the chance of discovering life somewhere out there than in anything we might do if we stayed here. And we won't be gone long. It's field work, the most challenging kind. Both of us have always preferred that to careers at the blackboards in some university."

Reid shrugged and kissed his daughter. "If you're sure," was all he had to say. He shook hands with Gillette.

Jessica looked up at the massive spacecraft. "I guess we are," she said. There was nothing more to do or say. They left Earth not many hours later, and they watched the planet dwindle in the ports and on the screens.

The experience of living on the craft was strange at first, but they quickly settled into routines. They learned that while the idea of interstellar flight was exciting, the reality was duller than either could have imagined. The two kittens had no trouble adjusting, and the Gillettes were glad for their company. When the craft was half a million miles from Earth, the computer slipped it into null space, and they were truly isolated for the first time.

It was terrifying. There was no way to communicate with Earth while in null space. The craft became a self-contained little world, and in dangerous moments when Gillette allowed his imagination too much freedom, the silent emptiness around him seemed like a new kind of insanity or death. Jessica's presence calmed him, but he was still grateful when the ship came back into normal space, at the first of their unexplored stellar systems.

Their first subject was a small, dim, class-M star, the most common type in the galaxy, with only two planetary bodies and a lot of asteroidal debris circling around it. "What are we going to name the star, dear?" asked Jessica. They both looked at it through the port, feeling a kind of parental affection.

Gillette shrugged. "I thought it would be easier if we stuck to the mythological system they've been using at home."

"That's a good idea, I guess. We've got one star with two little planets wobbling around it."

"Didn't Apollo have . . . No, I'm wrong. I thought—"

Jessica turned away from the port. "It reminds me of Odin and his two ravens."

"He had two ravens?"

"Sure," said Jessica, "Thought and Memory. Hugin and Mugin."

"Fine. We'll name the star Odin, and the planets whatever you just said. I'm sure glad I have you. You're a lot better at this than I am."

Jessica laughed. She looked forward to exploring the planets. It would be the first break they had in the monotony of the journey. Neither Leslie nor Jessica anticipated finding life on the two desolate worlds, but they were glad to give them a thorough examination. They wandered awe-struck over the bleak, lonely landscapes of Hugin and Mugin, completing their tests, and at last returned to their orbiting craft. They sent their findings back to Earth, set out the first of the transmission gates, and, not yet feeling very disappointed, left the Odin system. They both felt that they were in contact with their home, regardless of the fact that their message would take a long time to reach Earth, and they were moving away too quickly ever to receive any. But they both knew that if they wanted, they could still turn around and head back to Earth.

Their need to know drove them on. The loneliness had not yet become unbearable. The awful fear had not yet begun.

The gates were for the use of the people who followed the Gillettes into the unsettled reaches of the galaxy; they could be used in succession to travel outward, but the travelers couldn't return through them. They were like ostrich eggs filled with water and left by natives in the African desert; they were there to make the journey safer and more comfortable for others, to enable the others to travel even farther.

Each time the Gillettes left one star system for another, through null space, they put a greater gulf of space and time between themselves and the world of their birth. "Sometimes I feel very strange," admitted Gillette, after they had been outbound for more than two years. "I feel as if any contact we still have with Earth is an illusion, something we've invented just to maintain our sanity. I feel like we're donating a large part of our lives to something that might never benefit anyone."

Jessica listened somberly. She had had the same feelings, but she hadn't wanted to let her husband know. "Sometimes I think that the life in the university classroom is the most desirable thing in the world. Sometimes I damn myself for not seeing that before. But it doesn't last long. Every time we go down to a new world, I still feel the same hope. It's only the weeks in null space that get to me. The alienation is so intense."

Gillette looked at her mournfully. "What does it really matter if we do discover life?" he asked.

She looked at him in shocked silence for a moment. "You don't really mean that," she said at last.

Gillette's scientific curiosity rescued him, as it had more than once in the past. "No," he said softly, "I don't. It does matter." He picked up the three kittens from Ethyl's litter. "Just let me find something like these waiting on one of these endless planets, and it will all be worthwhile."

Months passed, and the Gillettes visited more stars and more planets, always with the same result. After three years they were still rocketing away from Earth. The fourth year passed, and the fifth. Their hope began to dwindle.

"It bothers me just a little," said Gillette as they sat beside a great gray ocean, on a world they had named Carraway. There was a broad beach of pure white sand backed by high dunes. Waves broke endlessly and came to a frothy end at their feet. "I mean, that we never see anybody behind us, or hear anything. I know it's impossible, but I used to have this crazy dream that somebody was following us through the gates and then jumped ahead of us through null space. Whoever it was waited for us at some star we hadn't got to yet."

Jessica made a flat mound of wet sand. "This is just like Earth, Leslie," she said. "If you don't notice the chartreuse sky. And if you don't think about how there isn't any grass in the dunes and no shells on the beach. Why would somebody follow us like that?"

Gillette lay back on the clean white sand and listened to the pleasant sound of the surf. "I don't know," he said. "Maybe there had been some absurd kind of life on one of those planets we checked out years ago. Maybe we made a mistake and overlooked something, or misread a meter or something. Or maybe all the nations on Earth had wiped themselves out in a war and I was the only living human male and the lonely women of the world were throwing a party for me."

"You're crazy, honey," said Jessica. She flipped some damp sand onto the legs of his pressure suit.

"Maybe Christ had come back and felt the situation just wasn't complete without us, too. For a while there, every time we bounced back into normal space around a star, I kind of half-hoped to see another ship, waiting." Gillette sat up again. "It never happened, though."

"I wish I had a stick," said Jessica. She piled more wet sand on her mound, looked at it for a few seconds, and then looked up at her husband. "Could there be something happening at home?" she asked.

"Who knows what's happened in these five years? Think of all we've missed, sweetheart. Think of the books and the films, Jessie. Think of the scientific discoveries we haven't heard about. Maybe there's peace in the Mideast and a revolutionary new source of power and a black woman in the White House. Maybe the Cubs have won a pennant, Jessie. Who knows?"

"Don't go overboard, dear," she said. They stood and brushed off the sand that clung to their suits. Then they started back toward the landing craft.

Onboard the orbiting ship an hour later, Gillette watched the cats. They didn't care anything about the Mideast; maybe they had the right idea. "I'll tell you one thing," he said to his wife. "I'll tell you who does know what's been happening. The people back home know. They know all about everything. The only thing they don't know is what's going on with us, right now. And somehow I have the feeling that they're living easier with their ignorance than I am with mine." The kitten that would grow up to be Benny's mother tucked herself up into a neat little bundle and fell asleep.

"You're feeling cut off," said Jessica.

"Of course I am," said Gillette. "Remember what you used to say to me? Before we were married, when I told you I only wanted to go on with my work, and you told me that one human being was no human being? Remember? You were always saying things like that, just so I'd have to ask you what the hell you were talking about. And then you'd smile and deliver some little story you had all planned out. I guess it made you happy. So you said, 'One human being is no human being,' and I said, 'What does that mean?' and you went on about how if I were going to live my life all alone, I might as well not live it at all. I can't remember exactly the way you put it. You have this crazy way of saying things that don't have the least little bit of logic to them but always make sense. You said I figured I could sit in my ivory tower and look at things under a microscope and jot down my findings and send out little announcements now and then about what I'm doing and how I'm feeling and I shouldn't be surprised if nobody gives a damn. You said that I had to live among people, that no matter how hard I tried, I couldn't get away from it. And that I couldn't climb a tree and decide I was going to start my own new species. But you were wrong, Jessica. You can get away from people. Look at us."

The sound of his voice was bitter and heavy in the air. "Look at me," he murmured. He looked at his reflection and it frightened him. He looked old; worse than that, he looked just a little demented. He turned away quickly, his eyes filling with tears.

"We're not truly cut off," she said softly. "Not as long as we're together."

"Yes," he said, but he still felt set apart, his humanity diminishing with the passing months. He performed no function that he considered notably human. He read meters and dials and punched buttons; machines could do that, animals could be trained to do the same. He felt discarded, like a bad spot on a potato, cut out and thrown away.

Jessica prevented his depression from deepening into madness. He was far more susceptible to the effects of isolation than she. Their work sustained Jessica, but it only underscored their futility for her husband.

"I have strange thoughts, Jessica," he admitted to her, one day during their ninth year of exploration. "They just come into my head now and then. At first I didn't pay any attention at all. Then, after a while, I noticed that I was paying attention, even though when I stopped to analyze them I could see the ideas were still foolish."

"What kind of thoughts?" she asked. They prepared the landing craft to take them down to a large, ruddy world.

Gillette checked both pressure suits and stowed them aboard the lander. "Sometimes I get the feeling that there aren't any other people anywhere, that they were all the invention of my imagination. As if we never came from Earth, that home and everything I recall are just delusions and false memories. As if we've always been on this ship, forever and ever, and we're absolutely alone in the whole universe." As he spoke, he gripped the heavy door of the lander's airlock until his knuckles turned white. He felt his heart speeding up, he felt his mouth going dry, and he knew that he was about to have another anxiety attack.

"It's all right, Leslie," said Jessica soothingly. "Think back to the time we had together at home. That couldn't be a lie."

Gillette's eyes opened wider. For a moment he had difficulty breathing. "Yes," he whispered, "it could be a lie. You could be a hallucination, too." He began to weep, seeing exactly where his ailing mind was leading him.

Jessica held him while the attack worsened and then passed away. In a few moments he had regained his usual sensible outlook. "This mission is much tougher than I thought it would be," he whispered.

Jessica kissed his cheek. "We have to expect some kind of problems after all these years," she said. "We never planned on it taking this long."

The system they were in consisted of another class-M star and twelve planets. "A lot of work, Jessica," he said, brightening a little at the prospect. "It ought to keep us busy for a couple of weeks. That's better than falling through null space."

"Yes, dear," she said. "Have you started thinking of names yet?" That was becoming the most tedious part of the mission—coming up with enough new names for all the stars and their satellites. After eight thousand systems, they had exhausted all the mythological and historical and geographical names they could remember. They now took turns, naming planets after baseball players and authors and film stars.

They were going down to examine a desert world they had named Rick, after the character in *Casablanca*. Even though it was unlikely that it would be suitable for life, they still needed to examine it firsthand, just on the off-chance, just in case, just for ducks, as Gillette's mother used to say.

That made him pause, a quiet smile on his lips. He hadn't thought of that expression in years. That was a critical point in Gillette's voyage; never again, while Jessica was with him, did he come so close to losing his mental faculties. He clung to her and to his memories as a shield against the cold and destructive forces of the vast emptiness of space.

Once more the years slipped by. The past blurred into an indecipherable haze, and the future did not exist. Living in the present was at once the Gillettes' salvation and curse. They spent their time among routines and changeless duties that were no more tedious than what they had known on Earth, but no more exciting either.

As their shared venture neared its twentieth year, the great disaster befell Gillette: on an unnamed world hundreds of light-years from Earth, on a rocky hill overlooking a barren sandstone valley, Jessica Gillette died. She bent over to collect a sample of soil; a worn seam in her pressure suit parted; there was a sibilant warning of gases passing through the lining, into the suit. She fell to the stony ground, dead. Her husband watched her die, unable to give her any help, so quickly did the poison kill her. He sat beside her as the planet's day turned to night, and through the long, cold hours until dawn.

He buried her on that world, which he named Jessica, and left her there forever. He set out a transmission gate in orbit around the world, finished his survey of the rest of the system, and went on to the next star. He was consumed with grief, and for many days he did not leave his bed.

One morning Benny, the kitten, scrabbled up beside Gillette. The kitten had not been fed in almost a week. "Benny," murmured the lonely man, "I want you to realize something. We can't get home. If I turned this ship around right this very minute and powered home all the way through null space, it would take twenty years. I'd be in my seventies if I lived long enough to see Earth. I never expected to live that long." From then on, Gillette performed his duties in a mechanical way, with none of the enthusiasm he had shared with Jessica. There was nothing else to do but go on, and so he did, but the loneliness clung to him like a shadow of death.

He examined his results, and decided to try to make a tentative hypothesis. "It's unusual data, Benny," he said. "There has to be some simple explanation. Jessica always argued that there didn't have to be any explanation at all, but now I'm sure there must be. There has to be some meaning behind all of this, somewhere. Now tell me, why haven't we found

Indication Number One of life on any of these twenty-odd thousand worlds we've visited?"

Benny didn't have much to suggest at this point. He followed Gillette with his big yellow eyes as the man walked around the room. "I've gone over this before," said Gillette, "and the only theories I come up with are extremely hard to live with. Jessica would have thought I was crazy for sure. My friends on Earth would have a really difficult time even listening to them, Benny, let alone seriously considering them. But in an investigation like this, there comes a point when you have to throw out all the predicted results and look deep and long at what has actually occurred. This isn't what I wanted, you know. It sure isn't what Jessica and I expected. But it *is* what happened."

Gillette sat down at his desk. He thought for a moment about Jessica, and he was brought to the verge of tears. But he thought about how he had dedicated the remainder of his life to her, and to her dream of finding an answer at one of the stellar systems yet to come.

He devoted himself to getting that answer for her. The one blessing in all the years of disappointment was that the statistical data were so easy to comprehend. He didn't need a computer to help in arranging the information: there was just one long, long string of zeros. "Science is built on theories," thought Gillette. "Some theories may be untestable in actual practice, but are accepted because of an overwhelming preponderance of empirical data. For instance, there may not actually exist any such thing as gravity; it may be that things have been falling down consistently because of some outrageous statistical quirk. Any moment now things may start to fall up and down at random, like pennies landing heads or tails. And then the Law of Gravity will have to be amended."

That was the first, and safest, part of his reasoning. Next came the feeling that there was one over-riding possibility that would adequately account for the numbing succession of lifeless planets. "I don't really want to think about that yet," he murmured, speaking to Jessica's spirit. "Next week, maybe. I think we'll visit a couple more systems first."

And he did. There were seven planets around an M-class star, and then a G star with eleven, and a K star with fourteen; all the worlds were impact-cratered and pitted and smoothed with lava flow. Gillette held Benny in his lap after inspecting the three systems. "Thirty-two more planets," he said. "What's the grand total now?" Benny didn't know.

Gillette didn't have anyone with whom to debate the matter. He could not consult scientists on Earth; even Jessica was lost to him. All he had was his patient gray cat, who couldn't be looked to for many subtle contributions. "Have you noticed," asked the man, "that the farther we get from Earth, the more homogeneous the universe looks?" If Benny didn't understand the word homogenous, he didn't show it. "The only really unnatural thing we've seen in all these years has been Earth itself. Life on Earth is the only truly anomalous factor we've witnessed in twenty years of exploration. What does that mean to you?"

At that point, it didn't mean anything to Benny, but it began to mean something to Gillette. He shrugged. "None of my friends were willing to consider even the possibility that Earth might be alone in the universe, that there might not be anything else alive anywhere in all the infinite reaches of space. Of course, we haven't looked at much of those infinite reaches, but going zero for twenty-three thousand means that something unusual is happening." When the Gillettes had left Earth two decades before, prevailing scientific opinion insisted that life had to be out there somewhere, even though there was no proof, either directly or indirectly. There had to be life; it was only a matter of stumbling on it. Gillette looked at the old formula, still hanging where it had been throughout the whole voyage. "If one of those factors is zero," he thought, "then the whole product is zero. Which factor could it be?" There was no hint of an answer, but that particular question was becoming less important to Gillette all the time.

And so it had come down to this: Year 30 and still outward bound. The end of Gillette's life was somewhere out there in the black stillness. Earth was a pale memory, less real now than last night's dreams. Benny was an old cat, and soon he would die as Jessica had died, and Gillette would be absolutely alone. He didn't like to think about that, but the notion intruded on his consciousness again and again.

Another thought arose just as often. It was an irrational thought, he knew, something he had scoffed at thirty years before. His scientific training led him to examine ideas by the steady, cold light of reason, but this new concept would not hold still for such a mechanical inspection.

He began to think that perhaps Earth was alone in the universe, the only planet among billions to be blessed with life. "I have to admit again that I haven't searched through a significant fraction of all the worlds in the galaxy," he said, as if he were defending his feelings to Jessica. "But I'd be a fool if I ignored thirty years of experience. What does it mean, if I say that Earth is the only planet with life? It isn't a scientific or mathematical notion. Statistics alone demands other worlds with some form of life. But what can overrule such a biological imperative?" He waited for a guess from Benny; none seemed to be forthcoming. "Only an act of faith," murmured Gillette. He paused, thinking that he might hear a trill of dubious laughter from Jessica's spirit, but there was only the humming, ticking silence of the spacecraft.

"A single act of creation, on Earth," said Gillette. "Can you imagine what any of the people at the university would have said to that? I wouldn't have been able to show my face around there again. They would have revoked every credential I had. My subscription to *Science* would have been canceled. The local PBS channel would have refused my membership.

"But what else can I think? If any of those people had spent the last thirty years the way we have, they'd have arrived at the same conclusion. I didn't come to this answer easily, Jessica, you know that. You know how I was. I never had any faith in anything I hadn't witnessed myself. I didn't even believe in the existence of George Washington, let alone first principles. But there comes a time when a scientist must accept the most unappealing explanation, if it is the only one left that fits the facts."

It made no difference to Gillette whether or not he was correct, whether he had investigated a significant number of worlds to substantiate his conclusion. He had had to abandon, one by one, all of his prejudices, and made at last a leap of faith. He knew what seemed to him to be the truth, not through laboratory experiments but by an impulse he had never felt before.

For a few days he felt comfortable with the idea. Life had been created on Earth for whatever reasons, and nowhere else. Each planet devoid of life that Gillette discovered became from then on a confirming instance of this hypothesis. But then, one night, it occurred to him how horribly he had cursed himself. If Earth were the only home of life, why was Gillette hurtling farther and farther from that place, farther from where he too had been made, farther from where he was supposed to be?

What had he done to himself—and to Jessica?

"My impartiality failed me, sweetheart," he said to her disconsolately. "If I could have stayed cold and objective, at least I would have had peace of mind. I would never have known how I damned both of us. But I couldn't; the impartiality was a lie, from the very beginning. As soon as we went to measure something, our humanity got in the way. We couldn't be passive observers of the universe, because we're alive and we're people and we think and feel. And so we were doomed to learn the truth eventually, and we were doomed to suffer because of it." He wished Jessica were still alive, to comfort him as she had so many other times. He had felt isolated before, but it had never been so bad. Now he understood the ultimate meaning of alienation—a separation from his world and the force that had created it. He wasn't supposed to be here, wherever it was. He belonged on Earth, in the midst of life. He stared out through the port, and the infinite blackness seemed to enter into him, merging with his mind and spirit. He felt the awful coldness in his soul.

For a while Gillette was incapacitated by his emotions. When Jessica died, he had bottled up his grief; he had never really permitted himself the luxury of mourning her. Now, with the added weight of his new convictions, her loss struck him again, harder than ever before. He allowed the machines around him to take complete control of the mission in addition to his well-being. He watched the stars shine in the darkness as the ship fell on through real space. He stroked Benny's thick gray fur and remembered everything he had so foolishly abandoned.

In the end it was Benny that pulled Gillette through. Between strokes the man's hand stopped in mid-air; Gillette experienced a flash of insight, what the oriental philosophers call *satori,* a moment of diamond-like clarity. He knew intuitively that he had made a mistake that had led him into self-pity. If life had been created on Earth, then all living things were a part of that creation, wherever they might be. Benny, the gray-haired cat, was a part of it, even locked into this tin can between the stars. Gillette himself was a part, wherever he traveled. That creation was just as present in the spacecraft as on Earth itself: it had been foolish for Gillette to think that he ever could separate himself from it—which was just what Jessica had always told him.

"Benny!" said Gillette, a tear streaking his wrinkled cheek. The cat observed him benevolently. Gillette felt a pleasant warmth overwhelm him as he was released at last from his loneliness. "It was all just a fear of death," he whispered. "I was just afraid to die. I wouldn't have believed it! I thought I was beyond all that. It feels good to be free of it."

And when he looked out again at the wheeling stars, the galaxy no longer seemed empty and black, but vibrant and thrilling with a creative energy. He knew that what he felt could not be shaken, even if the next world he visited was a lush garden of life—that would not change a thing, because his belief was no longer based on numbers and facts, but on a stronger sense within him.

It made no difference at all where Gillette was headed, what stars he would visit: wherever he went, he understood at last, he was going home.

VI

CIPHERS

Scarecrow

Poul Anderson

I T MAY OR MAY NOT BE IMPORTANT TO
POINT OUT THAT POUL ANDERSON IS MY FATHER-IN-LAW. WE'RE ALSO FRIENDS,
AND I'VE ADMIRED HIS WRITING SINCE I WAS A KID. WHAT CHARACTERIZES
POUL'S WORK, FOR ME, IS A CLEAR-EYED, DEEPLY FELT, INTELLIGENT VIEW OF
LIFE, HIGHLY COLORED BY A STRONG SENSE OF BOTH FUN AND TRAGEDY. FOR
POUL, THE STRUGGLE OF HUMANS AGAINST NATURE IS OF PROFOUND CONCERN;
BUT THE STRUGGLE OF HUMANS AGAINST EACH OTHER, TO DISCOVER EACH
OTHER, IS EQUALLY PROFOUND.

SCIENCE AGAINST FAITH. RATIONAL THOUGHT AGAINST IMPONDERABLE MYS-
TERIES. THESIS, ANTITHESIS, SYNTHESIS . . . NECESSARY TO SOLVE THE GREAT
PROBLEMS OF ALL.

THIS WAS NOT real. It must not be.

It was.

Loren Heath stared through his faceplate and fumbled for understanding. Darkness gaped before him, rimmed with ragged metal. No, below
him. The sense of it was slight, but as the ringing in his head died away he
could feel that he pressed forward in his chair, against the safety harness,
toward the dead pilot console. The spacecraft lay at a steep slant, nose
down, crushed against the ground. Light sifted wan through several rents
in the hull. *What a smashup*, trickled across his awareness. *If the shock uptakes
had failed, I'd have my ribs caved in at least.* Wary of pain, he stirred. Nothing
worse than bruises, it seemed. *I didn't actually pass out, no concussion, just
dazed by the suddenness of this, I'll be thinking straight again in a minute.*

Bronya!

His wife's cry reached his earphones even as he sucked in a breath to call
to her. "Loren, *ukochany,* are you all right?"

"Yes," sobbed from him. "You?"

He heard another Polish word or two, then she went to the English they
had in common. "God b-be thanked. What has happened?"

"We've crashed. Total wreck, air gone, what else?"

Silence hummed for a moment. When Bronya spoke, it was flatly and fast. "We must get out at once. The radiation gauge here is climbing off the scale. Cracked fire chamber, I think, and reaction mass spills out, slowly in this gravity, but—"

"Christ, come on!" Even as he twisted his harness locks, Loren remembered she didn't like him using that name for an exclamation, when that was all that it was to him, and he'd promised her not to. Well, if she noticed now, she'd forgive. He writhed from his chair and climbed aft, up the canted deck, catching what handholds he saw among the glooms. Bronya met him at the starboard airlock. Spacesuited, her figure was as bulky and sexless as his, the air tank and powerpack making her look hunchbacked; but the meager light gave him her fair skin, high cheekbones, a loose yellow lock halfway down the brow. He wondered flashingly, idiotically, whether she made out his own lean dark features and shared his wish that they could kiss.

The servos didn't respond to their controls. He threw his strength at the manual wheel. "You go out first," he panted. "Jump as far as you can. I'll come right after you."

"Why me?" He recognized that rebelliousness.

Well, you're a woman, my woman, and I'm a Minnesotan, and—"You're the engineer. I'm only the pilot and, uh, theory jack. You might spot something we need to know about at once." He knew she'd see the speciousness, but somebody had to lead the escape, and to waste time arguing was ridiculous.

She grinned a bit. "Actually, the radiation is not so bad that a few extra seconds make any difference." Sober again: "But the fluid keeps oozing into this section. We had better not return."

The valves had swung half open. Loren saw a black full of stars. Bronya blocked the view when she squeezed past. He had a moment to rest. His heart thudded. She disappeared. He followed, poised on the verge, doubled his legs, straightened them in a leap.

Bronya was already down, a blue doll-figure in a dun rockscape. Pieces of wreckage lay amidst scattered boulders. Loren got time to behold. On Hyperion he and his space gear weighed less than a kilo. He soared far and descended with ghostly slowness. The sun was behind him, which was fortunate. Though shrunken tiny, it remained fierce enough to blind him, especially shining through airlessness. On his right, Saturn hung low, a crescent some two and a half times the size of the moon above the farmlands he remembered, its rings like a royal diadem. It would wax; Hyperion was swinging around to the dayside. Much more rapidly would planet and sun move through the sky. *But we no longer know how rapidly,* said grimness.

Descending, he saw a crag cut across the lower part of Saturn, one of several that thrust sheer from a high hill. Light and shadow limned cruel edges. Yes, and the several small craters in view, within an irregular narrow horizon, were equally fresh. Some great infall had formed this, perhaps a few centuries ago; there had not been time for gusts of gravel to erode it smooth. Loren's gaze searched for Chicago, but the hill was in the way.

He struck ground and felt regolith grit beneath his boots.

Bronya sped to him in long kangaroo leaps. They clasped hands—gloves—and again looked at one another.

The single thing that came to him to say was, "You're alive. Unharmed. We are."

Her laugh sounded forlorn. "This day is St. Severin's. The first boy we have, we should name him Severin." Loren had already agreed that the first girl would be Maria.

"Okay," he said. Never mind, now, if that was anything to saddle a kid with. "Supposing we get home to groundside jobs and start that family." He stiffened. "No, when we do."

Together, they turned and looked at what had been their ship.

La Vedette rested as if a giant had hurled her, as a boy playing mumblety-peg would throw his knife. The after section kept most of its beautiful curves, but smoke-wisps of reaction mass drifted from two jets, dispersed into a haze before it fell. That meant energy seething, spitting stuff out. "Probably impact collapsed the fusion generator into a mass that melted," Bronya said dully. "It will not cool off soon."

And the material, turned radioactive by free neutrons, was also inside the hull. To go back for food, water, anything would be to commit unnecessarily nasty suicide. Loren forced a shrug. "Makes no difference. The front end's kaput anyway."

Equipped with sensors as well as power joints, spacegloves weren't too unlike hands. How good to feel hers squeeze his. "I confess," she said, "I was not happy at being encumbered with a suit. If you had not insisted, we would be dead. Did you have . . . foreknowledge . . . a hunch?"

"No, of course not." He heard that he had snapped at her. Nerves in shreds. She didn't resent his show-me positivism; he had no right to let her attitude irritate him, ever. It was simply religious belief, plus a notion that perhaps he was mistaken in labeling certain other concepts absurd. She was gifted at her profession, and at everything else important. That was enough.

He softened his tone. "It was just, uh, cheap insurance against an unlikely contingency. And the dice did happen to roll wrong for us."

"How? In what way?"

He squinted against the glare off the metal. Clarity had come to his mind, the sort of cold calm that danger to life can bring. "At the moment, all I can do is guess. We'll know for sure when we've taken some measurements. However, I think that as we were backing down, this wretched moon suddenly changed rotation again. The axis shifted or the spin increased or whatever. Not very many meters per second, but taking us by surprise. I was close to yonder peak because the one decent landing spot near Chicago is—hell, you know that as well as I do. What I spied was . . . all at once, the damned hill coming at us. I punched for high boost but obviously couldn't react fast enough. See how the port rear jet is crumpled? That must have unbalanced the thrust. *Vedette* bounced off the hillside, turned end for end, and rammed into the ground."

"So fast." She sighed. "We were too proud." She lifted a hand as if to forestall a protest from him. "No, no, I do not imagine God decided to teach us a lesson. It was merely chaos at work. Bad luck, as you say. But I think we should take the lesson to heart."

"First we should get over to Chicago," he replied, "hole up, and scream for help. Then while we wait, we can investigate as best we're able. Maybe the robots will help us, maybe not, but at least we'll have our base."

"Right. A hot drink, a hot bath, ten or twenty hours of sleep, paradise. . . . M-m, do you know where Chicago is from here?"

"No, but I know where the North Pole is." He pointed across the level ground to a ridge. Behind it loomed a cliff, somewhat curved, grayish, faintly sheening, which made it oddly hard to discern what lay in front—an ice cliff. Like most minor satellites of the outer planets, Hyperion was ice and rock jumbled together. *"Jumbled" is the right word, oh, very much, in this case,* flitted through Loren's thoughts. A rough lump, some 205 by 130 by 100 kilometers, tumbling around yonder monster—

"Certainly," Bronya said. "We will see Chicago from the top. I must still be stupid from shock, to forget."

"No, sweetheart, you've just had a lot dumped on your mind, all at once. Me, too. Come on."

As they skim-skipped over ashen, rock-strewn soil, Loren found himself estimating. How long must they survive here? Well, a radio call would take about an hour to reach Mission Centrum on Luna. Depending on the exact positions of the planets, a relief ship could make passage in eight to ten days, torching at maximum sustainable boost. However, first the crew must be assembled and briefed, their vessel inspected, fueled, and supplied. Such a craft was definitely in the vicinity; doctrine required backup capability; but she might well be off on assignment, so that recalling and re-outfitting would consume several days more. The Service was short of everything, like the rest of civilization, crawling back into space after the Accidental War. Otherwise two or three ships would have come to Saturn to find out what went wrong during the ten-year hiatus.

Chicago should be well-stocked, though. When the last humans left the bases they had established on Hyperion in charge of the robots, they expected their kind would return, look in, make hands-on evaluations, now and then. Supplies, equipment, quarters must be in readiness for them. Naturally, they hadn't anticipated it would be this long, or that meanwhile the robots would go crazy—

Bronya's voice exploded in his earphones. "Loren! Look!"

They jarred to a halt. Having crossed the flat stretch and commenced their bounding ascent, they were halfway up the ridge and had a clear view of its top. Silhouetted against the ice cliff beyond stood the North Pole. While they knew it only from images, they could never mistake that gaunt shape. It was tilted from the vertical, perhaps ice in the rubble had crept or a cosmic pebble had struck it a glancing blow, but the signposts at the top of the scrapped neutrino antenna still pointed in their half-dozen different directions. The whole work of whimsy seemed peculiarly stark.

Loren forgot it. Close by stood a human form.

"What—who—?" He caught his breath. "Hello!" he shouted, as if he were calling through air. "Hello, do you copy us?"

"He . . . he does not stir," Bronya whispered.

A mummified corpse? Whose? How? For a moment Loren was a child again on the farm, night huge around the house, wind skirling, fallen leaves blown with a click and rattle as of hooves swift across gravestones, and he gone to bed after hearing a ghost story told. . . . He stamped the qualm down. It had no business in him. Okay, his folks were Agrarian Revival, fine people, he loved them, but he'd left their ways far behind. "Maybe too far," Bronya said once. "Maybe that is why you are so determined an unbeliever." Very well, let him live by his unbelief.

He led the way onward. The figure abided, motionless, back toward Saturn. It was his size, somewhat shorter than the Pole. Spacesuit—No, by . . . by Gauss, it wasn't. Whatever might be inside had never been human.

He confronted it. Bronya joined him. Slowly, she reached out and fingered a sleeve. Fabric wrinkled in her grasp.

The thing wore a coverall, Service blue. Boots were on its feet, if it possessed feet. A couple of tubes were secured at the chest and draped over the shoulders, but they led to no air tank or anything else. Wires were attached here and there, as if to simulate circuits. A carrier pouch and a calculator hung at the belt. The arms terminated not in gloves but in grapple claws such as men used to handle dangerous objects. On top was neither head nor space helmet. Metal, it vaguely suggested the dome of an early Earthside observatory. After a moment, Loren identified it as the cut-off end of a protective container for an optical system.

Emboldened, Bronya prodded and stroked. "It has support inside, some rods joined together." Her laugh rattled. "I do not wish to say, 'Skeleton.' "

"Scarecrow," Loren mumbled.

She gave him a startled glance. "What?"

"I guess you never heard of scarecrows." He spoke automatically. "Long forgotten in Europe, like most places. People put them in their fields or gardens where I grew up. I don't know if they always had or if this was something else the early Revivalists took to doing, another tradition resurrected. Stuff an old set of clothes with straw and hang it on a frame; set it out to frighten off crows and other birds that raid crops."

His attention was on the North Pole. No reason for that—yes, there was, he admitted to himself. Comfort. A reminder of sanity, of the humor that is a basic part of sanity. While they were here, the original expedition had amused themselves by erecting this.

Was the North Pole on the actual axis of rotation, even then?

Perhaps not. That shifted about as Hyperion wavered. From time to time, unforeseeably, the change was swift and radical; *no, don't dwell on that, not yet, you know it too damn well.*

In twenty-odd Earth years, radiation and micrometeoroids had only slightly eroded the pointers and the legends on them. New York 12, this way; London 4, that way; Cairo 17, a third way: the unit always 100 kilometers, the distances approximate and fractal, measured along the rugged surface by robots crawling over it, the names bestowed on conspicuous natural features or, in the cases of Chicago and Madrid, bases. The captain had been Rita Dooley, the second in command Hernando Alvarez . . .

As if from afar, he heard Bronya: "Who raised a scarecrow here?"

"Huh?" Hauled back to himself, he yelped, "The robots! Who else? They've gone insane, you know. As mad as this whole moon." He swallowed. "I'm sorry. That was babyish of me."

"We both need rest." Her gentleness hardened. "Are the robots truly insane? What may they be trying to frighten off?"

"Nothing. Can't be anything. Scarecrows don't work. Never did."

"Then why do people make them?"

"Why, well, it's something they do. Something they've done since time out of mind. Why is Christmas in December? That doesn't square with the Gospel as I recall it. But people needed a winter solstice festival." Loren snapped after air. "I'm babbling again. Let's get to shelter." He peered and pointed. "There's Chicago."

Down across the flats, beyond a crater and the hill that had destroyed *La Vedette,* twin domes caught sunlight and Saturnlight, shining like a promise.

Bronya turned her look from the faceless thing toward him. Her smile illuminated the desolation. "Yes, let us. And when we have rested, we will have a little time for our own, no?"

First we'd better send our distress call, he refrained from saying. *And while we wait for relief, our duty is to use whatever resources we find, trying to get some hint as to what has possessed the robots on Hyperion.* She understood it as fully as he did. It was simply that, besides being a cosmonaut, she was a loving woman. *After we'd met, I realized how bleak my life was before. Mathematics and physics are wonderful, the same as your interest in history and anthropology are to you, darling; but by themselves, studies soon become hollow. Like that scarecrow.*

The remembrance sent his eyes skyward, which was careless of him when he was picking his way back down the ridge. The sun dazzled most stars out of vision, but he spied some elsewhere in heaven, and a minute crescent along Saturn's rings, an inner moon. Probably one or two other light-points were also satellites. Huge Titan must be on the far side of the primary, or he'd have found it. At closest approach to Hyperion, that orange disc swelled to twice the size of a harvest moon rising over plowed Earth.

Why did no nightmares flit in its unbreathable air and poisonous swamps, when they did across this bare stone and ice and emptiness? The robots on Titan, and elsewhere throughout the Solar System, continued their research quite capably. Databases at home overflowed with information they had sent during the hiatus; scientists wouldn't catch up for another decade. Meanwhile the machines continued exploring, mapping, measuring, analyzing, reporting. They offered interpretations—hypotheses, theories—when they could, or confessed it in rational wise when some phenomenon baffled them. Narrow minds, yes; you might well say monomaniacal; but in those fields for which they were made and programmed, brilliant, actually creative. Of course, it took humans to see things in a larger context. Equally of course, the machines were neither infallible nor invulnerable. They made their mistakes, they suffered their losses. Yet on the whole, isolated, eventually left marooned, they had kept the great endeavor going.

Except on Hyperion, Hyperion of the chaos.

Useless, this wondering. The Service dispatched *La Vedette* to find answers. Questions had been plentiful already, shot across space after the hiatus, during which communications from Hyperion turned into gibberish. Responses were as bewildering.

"Why did you report the moon standing still for one orbital period? That's physically impossible."

Following two hours of radio lag: "The light knows it is necessary. One-one-six. Twenty-zero-eight—" A string of meaningless numbers went on for minutes before transmission ended.

"We are keeping telescopic watch now. We know Hyperion did not turn sideways yesterday as you told us. Furthermore, your time signals indicate you have reset your clocks to incorrect rates."

"It is the false truth that is of the light, the true falsity that is of the dark. Seven-zero-three-nine—"

And long, capricious silences. One was by chance discovered to be due to a change in the beamcast band. Its contents were totally unintelligible, save for four words, "—send us your messengers—"

Loren broke the surface of perplexity. He and Bronya had reached the low ground, skirted the crater, were approaching the base.

Emptiness pressed in on all sides. "Where are the robots?" she wondered.

"They seem to have abandoned this site," he answered. His mouth was dry. "Maybe temporarily. But if any were hereabouts, they'd have noticed us and come on the double. Wouldn't they?"

"To be honest, I am relieved. Best we get well prepared before meeting them. Quick, darling!"

Eager, she sprang ahead of him to the airlock of the habitation unit. He lingered, peering around. Maybe a machine lurked watchful. Or maybe not. The many tracks he saw could be years old.

Bronya choked back a scream.

He sped to her. Mutely, she pointed to the niche where the servo motor had been. The manual opener was missing, too.

"My God," he blurted. "Locked out."

"They, they removed this—*Why?*"

The scarecrow knows. "If we can get into the workshop section, we should find stuff for improvising a gadget to let us in." His voice was as harsh as the fear-smell of his sweat. "Let's go see."

The other dome was likewise denied them. Only an outlet for recharging powerpacks from the minireactor within remained available.

Bronya looked at a wristband gauge. "I have air for three hours yet," she said. "It must be about the same for you. I would trade half mine for a jug of water that we could share."

"This way." He led her around the wall to the rear.

They stopped. A whoop broke from him.

Roofs at the back sheltered two paved squares. The robots had left the moon buggies parked there. For a short while the humans clung to one another and trembled.

Loren's hands still shook when he opened the toolbox of the nearer vehicle. Within lay hollowness. "It is empty here, too," said Bronya from the second one. She had heard him groan. "They made sure nobody shall get into Chicago without their leave."

"That doesn't make sense," he protested. "If we hadn't crashed, we'd've had the means."

"I do not think they have people from Earth in mind." Her gaze sought the ridge. The Pole was visible as a bright streak. "Something else walks this moon." She crossed herself.

Practicality cracked through desperation. "What did they leave us?" They raised the lids of the rear lockers.

She sprang high. "Air bottles! Full!" For the first time, tears escaped. He recognized the stammered Polish. *"Blessed Maria, thank you."*

"And water," he breathed. "Field rations." Again they embraced. They heard themselves shout. *A joyful noise unto the Lord,* he recalled from the church of his childhood.

Plugging nipples into helmets and avidly sucking, they quenched thirst and, faintly surprised, noticed hunger. Synthetics pushed through a chowlock weren't a bad stand-in for a T-bone smothered in onions, Loren decided. The sanitary attachments on the vehicles were intact as well; whatever happened, his dear and he need not die befouled.

Calm, then, they took inventory. Together the buggies offered them air for a week or so—food and water for longer, but that was irrelevant. Fuel cells and accumulators were fully charged. If they transferred everything from one vehicle to the other, they could drive for about 2,000 kilometers, with power to spare for their suits. The controls included an excellent built-in computer with graphics capability; people traveling across this worldlet might need to solve complex problems in a hurry. The database included maps.

"You know," Loren said, "maybe we can bash our way into the shop and get what we need to fix the airlocks."

Bronya considered before she shook her head. "I suspect we would only ruin a car. These buildings were made to withstand meteoroids of up to three kilos' mass."

"Well, you're the engineer."

"Besides, if we could break in like that, the robots would have removed the cars."

"You understand what this means, don't you?"

"Yes. We must go to Madrid."

"I guess that's where the robots have their headquarters now."

"I pray you be right."

"Why?"

"When they see us, they won't leave us locked out. Surely not. They cannot be so deranged." He almost heard her add, *Can they?*

"We'd better get started. It's a long ways."

They boarded, a single jump to the seats. She took the steering, he keyed for maps and studied the displays. "West-southwest from Chicago," he directed. "Not that that means anything much. But for our purposes, we assume the North Pole really is what it claims to be."

"Is it?"

He lifted a hand to screen off the sun. His eyes picked out the brighter stars. "Not anymore."

"We have no compass, only a, hm, goniometer. How can we navigate?" She had never expected to fare like this.

Neither had he, but the basic problem had appealed to his mathematical talent, back home, and he had inquired. "We steer by landmarks. Let me find out how—Okay, I've got it. I'm setting the computer to give us the proper bearing and image of each one ahead, in succession, as we pass the previous one. First make for yonder tall needle-like rock sticking above the horizon."

Independently mounted and powered, the wheels went smoothly over stones, gravel, dust, hillocks, cracks, ice surfaces grimy and scarred. Speed varied with terrain, but the database declared that normal driving time between Chicago and Madrid was 27 hours.

The riders could not help looking back. The domes, the wreck, the remnants shone a while in sight, until the buggy crossed the ridge at a low point and they were blocked off. Vision went to the height. The North Pole stood askew, the scarecrow black athwart Saturn. Bronya shivered. "I will be glad when we cannot see you," she said to it.

That happened soon, upon this tiny, grotesquely configured body. Within an hour, the sun was also down. For a while an arc of rings glimmered above a glacier, a mythic bridge, then only the stars remained. Their light unhindered, it seemed they would crowd the darkness out of heaven. The Milky Way cataracted frost-white. On the ground, ice spread sheets of pallor amidst murk. The humans traveled as if through an early dusk on Earth.

Bronya's speech was slurred. "My eyes keep crossing. I am too tired to hold this two-gram head of mine up."

"No wonder, after what you've been through." Loren stroked her faceplate, behind which was her cheek.

"We had better stop and rest."

"No, you lie down. I'm not sleepy yet. Let's make all the distance we can."

"Yes. Thank you." She rose and went back to the flatbed. Gravity varied according to location, but nowhere did you need a mattress. He heard a brief murmur of Polish, a prayer, before he was alone with the sound of her breathing. *Why am I not wiped out? I'm no tougher than she is. Too keyed up, I guess.* Having taken the driver's seat, he found scant employment. With its sensors and internal computer, the vehicle steered itself most of the time, deftly adapting to conditions and picking ways around obstacles. He need only redirect it occasionally toward the next landmark. As little as he weighed, even steep slopes demanded no particular effort to keep his seat.

Twilit crags and craters, hills and hollows, rilles and ridges, lava levels, broken boulders, iron-gray ice, windless, lifeless, beneath a welter of un-winking stars, and he himself nearly afloat—his mind drifted from the dreamscape, sought elsewhere.

It was, again, to analysis. He was not ignorant of the arts and humanities nor uninterested in them, any more than Bronya was as regarded mathematics and theoretical physics. However, he knew that in most respects he was a prosaic sort, compared to her. His keenest appreciation was of the abstract, the austere grandeurs and elegant beauties created when imagination wielded rigor. From Hyperion to chaos in general was no far journey of the mind.

He began with the particular. Into what new state had the satellite been swinging precisely when his ship was setting down? The buggy carried basic observational equipment. A main purpose of traveling in it had formerly been to take sightings from different areas and thus determine how the mass behaved and how that behavior changed from cycle to cycle. Eventually the robots were programmed, tested, ready to take over this job as well as all the other probings—geological, chemical, topographical, anything that might lead toward deeper comprehension; and the humans went home. They left their equipment for those who would someday return.

After familiarizing himself, Loren spent several hours using it, in between his piloting tasks. He measured and clocked the progression of stars across heaven, entering into the computer the point on the surface at which he obtained each datum. Thus he accumulated a store of information, rough, incomplete, but sufficient for preliminary study. The vehicle was then traversing level ground. He could safely switch off the map function and devote the computer to finding out what the facts implied.

He put fingers to keyboard, and truth grew from them. It was he who guided the electronics, queried, directed, aimed the numbers and released them to do their work, criticized, pondered, tried this or that variation, walked around in his head and saw how close to rightness his concept had gotten. The exhilaration of a Michelangelo hewing forth a Moses was upon him.

In the end he knew. Although his understanding was a crude approximation, the rest would merely be refinement. The motion of Hyperion had flipped over, as so often before, but this time it had been toward an entirely new attractor.

No wonder *La Vedette* suffered shipwreck. There was no way in the universe that he or anyone else could have allowed for such a possibility.

Now the north pole lay fifty or sixty kilometers off the North Pole, and the rotation period was between eighteen and nineteen hours, precessing through at least thirty degrees. Of course, these figures were ballpark. They would never be exact, no matter how many decimal places you traced down. The moon oscillated unpredictably; any numbers were no more than those around which the instantaneous actual values would cluster—until the next major shift occurred, at an incalculable moment, to an unforeknowable other set—

"Loren, are you still awake? You must be exhausted." Startled, he twisted his spacesuit about till he spied Bronya dark against the sky. Glancing at his watch: "Good Lord, has it been that long?" Abruptly he felt how weariness had gnawed at him, hour after hour, unnoticed while he was lost from himself. "Well, um, okay, you take over. If we keep moving, we'll reach Madrid that much the sooner."

"Why didn't you call me before? Men!"

Body-needs taken care of, he nevertheless lay gazing aloft for a few minutes. Then the sky began to spin, stars plunged in and out of the Milky Way, he and reality whirled down the maelstrom and through the soft thunders a voice from school days droned:

"The scientific study of chaos originated in pure mathematics. It was found that certain quite simple functions, when iterated and reiterated within certain ranges of values for their constants and variables, yield results that can in principle only be discovered empirically, by doing the calculations. However, regularities do appear, recurring on every level down to the infinitesimal. From this derives fractal geometry.

"Applying such methods to physical systems, it was found that many exist whose behavior is equally impossible to predict. This is not a question of quantum uncertainties; these systems can be perfectly deterministic, governed entirely by differential equations. What makes them unpredictable is their susceptibility to arbitrarily small forces whose effects quickly multiply. A simple example would be a pencil balanced on its point. In which direction will it topple? The least, immeasurably slight impulse decides.

"Realistic, everyday examples include meteorology. We cannot reliably calculate what the weather will be more than a few days in advance. For all our centuries of effort, our data collectors and computers, we cannot. A butterfly fluttering in California may determine what track a hurricane takes three months later in the Gulf of Mexico—except that countless other factors are working too, most of them no heavier than the wing of the butterfly.

"Human affairs are a still more thorough case of the chaotic. What petty accident may change the course of history? Celestial mechanics itself, Laplace's supreme instance of clockwork perfection, exhibits chaos; the paths of the planets cannot be calculated infinitely far ahead in time. As for the shorter term—"

Consider the behavior of Hyperion, masses of varying composition scrambled in any old fashion, shattered by some ancient collision and falling randomly back together, tugged to and fro by the gravitation of hulking Titan, sixteen sister moons in their own ever-varying positions, the multibillionfold moonlets of the rings, Saturn's storm-shifty vastness, companion planets, the variabilities of Sol, stars, galaxy—Magnificently worth an ongoing vigil to see how Hyperion veered among its attractors, as if here nature gave man a chance to peer a little further into the very heart of things—

Loren dropped from the universe.

He came back slowly, gave his timepiece a blurred stare and saw he had been gone for hours. The sun was just up, limning ruggednesses black ahead of a plain across which the buggy toiled. Its harsh brilliance drowned most stars. His body ached, stiff and scooped-out ravenous. After connecting to the sanitor and using it, he went forward and took the seat beside Bronya.

She turned her head to look at him. He saw hers as a chiaroscuro where features were nearly lost, topped by hair that seemed to have whitened. Her voice was the one small familiar thing. "Are you rested, dear?"

"Sort of," he grunted. "Hungry as hell."

"Hell is always hungry—" Her whisper broke off. Louder and fast: "Me, too. I waited for you."

"That was sweet." He owed her an acknowledgment. His head felt too full of gravel to leave room for much warmth.

"We have only one another here—"

"And—" he began. Hoping to cheer them both up a little, he meant to continue, "—once we're in shelter, I sure mean to take advantage of the privacy!" But she went on: "—and God."

"You do," he said, unreasonably annoyed.

"And you," she answered with an earnestness he remembered from their first acquaintance. "Everybody does, unless—" he heard her swallow—"they refuse."

"Come on, let's eat," he growled.

She nodded, turned the controls over to him, and went to the food locker. She had already put rations forth on top of it and now needed simply heat them in the microwave. Meanwhile he decided that this was terrain where the vehicle could drive itself, and set the autopilot. Bronya gave him his lap tray and sat down again with hers. He started to bring his drinktube up to his helmet.

"Please," she asked. "A minute." She bowed her head, signed herself, and murmured what he recognized as a Polish prayer.

He waited it out, suppressing remarks he knew would be unkind. Still, he ought to say something, oughtn't he? "You never did that before . . . with me," he ventured.

Her reply came quiet. "You never heard me praying for you when I was alone."

"You did?" he exclaimed, startled. "What I meant was—after we'd agreed to disagree, you didn't act this pious." Immediately he knew how tactless that had been, and that it made no sense when his anger about it flashed out at her.

"We may be near death, *ukochany*."

"And you're afraid? Don't be."

"Afraid?" He heard the hurt. "I thought you knew me better than that."

"I didn't mean cowardly afraid," he said in haste. "Of course not."

She touched his arm, briefly, glove against metal. "Surely you too feel, well, solemn."

"I don't want to die," he admitted. "I don't want you to." A shudder passed through him. He had seen a space-dead body once.

His hand shook a bit as he plugged in the nipple. Hot tea helped mightily, and he could try to explain his intent. Or make it; he had not been clear in his own mind, had mostly been trying to fill in the silence that surrounded them. "No point in brooding on the, uh, the worst case. A bad idea, in fact. The thing to think about is the practicalities of how to survive—how to better our chances of surviving." In his ears it sounded pompous and empty.

"Do you then believe I am wasting my time?" she asked low.

"Praying? No, no. Nothing else to do right now, and if it soothes you, that's all to the good."

"You do not understand, do you?" she said sadly. "Or is it that you will not understand?"

He raised his hands aloft. "Oh, Lord, how often have we been over this ground? Spare me, I beg you."

Again she reached for him, and this time clung. "Please. I won't try to convert you or anything like that. It is only that even here, you will think of nothing but the practicalities."

"What else?"

She waved at the few visible stars and the pitted, shadow-blotted desolation. "Look around you."

They might as well have this out and be done, he thought. "Am I supposed to feel humble? Sorry. Insignificant, yes. An accidental and temporary collection of molecules in a universe that neither gives a damn nor knows it doesn't give a damn." If he could just see her face. The glare and the darknesses masked it from him. Through hunger and inward chill, he sought back to their years together, drew a long breath, and said, "I love you. That's what counts."

He hoped she would make a similar response and they could let the matter fall. Instead, he was aware of how she regarded him, and he heard: "I love you. Can you really believe that is merely instinct in us, and—and social conditioning and—No, Loren. Your reason should tell you otherwise."

Somehow he could not let that pass unchallenged. Because he must defend the importance of his opinions and so, after all, of himself? "It hasn't yet."

She sighed. "To you, then, love is tragic."

Taken aback, he sat still for a little before he muttered, "Well . . . yes." Someday one of them would lose the other, and who afterward could know that once she brightened the world? "Not to you?"

He saw her head shake. "To a Christian, the only tragedy is damnation."

He knew she didn't expect he'd burn in hell, though he die in his denial. But suddenly he recognized her fear, that apartness might be eternal.

"I'll think about it," he promised clumsily, not very sincerely. "I do respect your faith."

"And I respect your honesty," she answered.

They leaned closer. Faceplates thudded together. A laugh of sorts rattled from both gullets. "Quick," he said, "let's eat before this gourmet meal gets cold."

For the rest of their trek, words came few and far between, soon trailing off. "Remember when" and "What if" and "After we're home" called up no rejoinders that meant anything. It was easier to plead tiredness and lie down, and for the partner to stand watch meanwhile. Besides, they kept declaring, to get well rested was advisable.

Time reached without end.

They arrived at Madrid, and the time in their memories was almost nothing.

Saturn and the sun had risen again, nooned, and gone halfway down the sky. Their carrier mounted the ringwall of a three-kilometer-wide crater, and from the top they beheld the base near the central peak, twin round brightnesses toward which shadows crept across pocked blue-gray regolith.

Loren's heart beat thickly. "Here goes," he said, and started the buggy downward. Glancing aside, he saw Bronya's face white in the mingled light, against a blackness that he now perceived as absolute.

They reached the bottom and started across. Movement ahead. "Yes, robots, all right, coming out of the work unit." It was hard to speak when his throat felt so constricted. "That's what they use for their quarters."

"They are supposed to," she answered as needlessly. "The habitation unit is for humans. Us."

The machines numbered three. Presumably the rest were scattered around the moon, making the observations that were their programmed reason for existence. One of these must newly have reported in with its load of data, for it was the field type, like an unearthly sort of beetle two meters long, tool arms and sensors bristling from the silvery carapace. Another was a mechanician, its multiple specialized limbs making it resemble a bush that walked. The third was a constructor and emergency rescuer, an armored vehicle with a bulldozer blade, a crane, and eight powerful hands.

They halted in the buggy's path. Loren braked to a stop four meters short of their line. He and Bronya had discussed what to say, but suddenly he was dumbstruck.

She took over: "G-greeting. We are . . . from Luna." As she talked, her voice firmed. "Our vessel made a crash landing. Chicago base was deserted and closed to entry, which it should not have been. So we have come here. First we require access to life support."

The reply, directly synthesized, flowed musical, not quite a monotone. "Chicago is barred against the messengers of the dark. It is one-one-one. You saw the one-one-two by the one-one-three, did you not? You will understand."

Insanity indeed! tore through Loren. But how could it happen? Even on this delirious world, the brains should be safe, should stay healthy and aware.

Brains, health, awareness. Dismay had kicked him into anthropomorphism. No, maybe not entirely. Machines that performed complex tasks in an alien and mutable environment, evaluated the results, laid plans, made decisions, constructed explanations, did science—must necessarily be the intellectual equals or actual superiors of humans. If they thought with electrons and molecular configurations rather than with neurons, nevertheless they thought.

Of course, they didn't think as he did. Their programs constrained them. Their work was their whole purpose, their sole desire was to further it. Anything else—and exploratory robots often found ingenious new ways of doing things—was incidental, auxiliary. Nor did Bronya confront a true individual. These three meshed their intelligences, together with the central computer in the base. All their kind did the same at need, when in communication range of each other. She had remarked once that whether or not the Jungian racial soul had ever existed on Earth, it did on every planet where robots were.

He jerked his attention back. She had risen, to stand in clear view. "We are humans," she said. "Obey us."

Did the artificial speech waver the least bit? "We see your form. You may be messengers of the light. If you are, you know that we must verify you are not messengers of the dark. If you are not one-zero, you are zero-one, and know that we must not and will not give you access to the instruments of the light."

"Listen! You can see our air, our supplies are limited. If we don't get into the proper quarters, we will die. Would you kill—would you cause the termination of humans?"

"Show us that you are messengers of the light, and you shall have our total service. You understand that the messengers of the dark seek always to mislead us. If they gain more powers, they may become able to destroy the cosmos. Whichever you are, you know this."

Breath went raggedly in and out of her. "What must we do . . . to prove ourselves?"

"If you do not know, then you belong to the dark, since you cannot deal with one-one-one." Silence, until: "It seems improbable that messengers of the light would appear to us as you have done after arriving as you state you did. We will not attempt your termination, for we are uncertain, and in any event the consequences would be incalculable." More silence. "The light will know—" a plea?—"that we only do what we must, as best we are able to understand it."

Bronya's fingers strained together. "What is it . . . that you must do?"

"Serve the one-one-one. Maintain the seven-five. If you come closer without better evidence, we shall be forced to resist; and then we will be certain that you are of the dark."

Loren gazed at the beetle, the bush, and the huge engine. He found his own voice. "No, we won't. We'll withdraw for a while so you, uh, you can think about this, and realize how, uh, mistaken you are."

"Yes," said Bronya faintly, and sat down. He backed their vehicle, turned, drove off. Sounds in earphones pursued them, *"One-one-one, forever one-one-one. One-one-two opposes zero-zero-zero—"*

A tongue of rock curved from the inner ringwall. When they went behind it, the chant was screened off, together with sight of the three machines standing under Saturn. The planet cast light and shadow into the corner where Loren stopped. Strength drained out of him and he slumped in his seat.

Bronya laid an arm around his waist. They sat mute.

"Crazy, yes," he mumbled at last. "We didn't believe it could be done, but Hyperion drove our finest manufactured brains mad."

She shook her head within the caging helmet. "No, I cannot agree. I am . . . familiar with the systems, the protections and fail-safes. Something has happened with consequences we do not grasp. If we can make sense of it—"

"We can't. We've just a few days left. Unless we can flange up some kind of, of weapon or something we can use to fight our way through."

"Impossible, I fear. Especially since I expect robots will swarm here when the news reaches them. This is, well, clearly it is a tremendous event to them. An apocalypse."

"Yeah. Doomsday, that's right. Ours." He snapped after air and stiffened his back. "No, I'm sorry, that was pure self-pity."

She smiled. He heard how she tried to bring both their minds away from desperation, toward a steadiness that would allow them to think. "You are wrong, my dear infidel. It is a common error. 'Apocalypse' does not mean 'Judgment Day.' It means 'revelation.' Our advent—"

She broke off. The stillness hit him like a hammer. He stared at her. She sat looking upward, lips parted, eyes full of the light from Saturn and its rainbow rings.

"What is it?" he choked.

She waved him to silence. He caught a murmur, and later "*Tak, tak,*" which he knew was "yes, yes" in Polish. She crossed herself, and he identified the Hail Mary.

His pulse quivered. He waited.

She turned about. Both hands seized his arm. "Loren, I think I know."

He could only gape.

"What the robots are doing," she hastened onward. "What is in that great, lonely mind. Magic. Yes, and worship. We have met a faith."

Has the weirdness reached in and grabbed her, too? On his left the ringwall top broke into serrations, a row of fangs that tore at sinking Saturn. "The scarecrow," she said. "We should have known, then and there."

What could the scarecrow scare, with never a wind to move it?

Bronya caught her breath. When she spoke again it was rapidly but evenly.

"You said everybody knew those images do nothing to stop the birds, yet for centuries they put them out in the fields anyway. Why? Traditions like that had meaning once. Ages ago, people danced around the Maypole because this was a fertility rite and it was phallic. They became Christian and forgot, but the custom lived on. A scarecrow was—it must have been— Osiris, Adonis, Kupala, Frey, the god of the land and its increase, holding off the evil spirits that bring drought, hail, blight, famine. . . . The robots set theirs up against chaos."

"But they know better!" he insisted.

"Do they?" she answered fiercely. *"Can* they? Oh, yes, they know physics and chemistry, science, by rote. They work with it, at it. Ancient humans weren't groveling savages either. They had their practical knowledge, they were good craftsmen and engineers, they made inventions. But they knew that in the end they were helpless before the unseen Powers, unless they could bring those Powers to aid them. Well, a robot thinks for itself, too. It must, if it is to serve its purpose. That purpose is written into it, as strong as sex is in us and as mysterious as sex, with all that it means, was to our ancestors. The robot feels!

"Imagine it, Loren. Year after year after year on Hyperion, beneath yonder planet, the moons, the stars, when everything can change at any time, the seasons, the cycles of heaven, meteor strikes like lightning bolts out of nowhere. Yes, they know the astronomy, they know something about chaos mathematics, but does that take away the awe? This is what they live in, live by and for. How can they not come at last to the fear of God?"

Chill went up and down the man's spine. "The war," he said "Fragments of terrible news, and then the hiatus. To them, senseless catastrophe. As it was to us. If the war had gone on as long as one day—"

She nodded. "I suppose that tipped the scale. Robots elsewhere must be troubled too, but they don't have surroundings this fitful and frightening. On Hyperion they . . . they coped with nature, but they must also cope with their emotions, and they did that by finding religion."

She sat quiet beneath the sky for another minute before she whispered, "They are not just mechanisms carrying out an algorithm. They have souls."

At that, reason and common sense struck home into Loren. *Or I snatch after them,* went a fugitive thought at the back of his mind. "Hey, wait!" he protested, "this is getting ridiculous!"

"How?" she demanded.

"Why, well, they *are* machines. Their functioning is purely algorithmic. Emotions? Not anything we'd understand by that. We should know. We, we humans designed and built them." He paused. "Oh, yes, the computations often get too complex for us to predict. And given bad input, they can go wildly wrong, yes, maybe into something like magical thinking. But you're being as, uh, as irrational as any of those primitives you mentioned." It broke loose from him: "We aren't going to save ourselves by superstition."

He saw her fists clench, and did he hear a sob? Yet when she turned her head his way, it was with a glare that made him lower his eyes. "We humans make babies too, and, and we know their biochemistry, but if you call them meat machines, you're the one who is superstitious." Breath hissed inward. "We have the key now. We can talk to the robots. Quickly, before they go away, or before their ideas harden against us."

"Huh?"

"Back to them."

"No, wait, hold on, this is crazy, let's at least think further—"

She reached for the controls. He leaned forward and laid an arm across the panel to block her. "Don't you see," he pleaded, "if we say the wrong thing, it could trigger them to kill us?"

Tears gleamed behind her faceplate. "They are not automatons, they are not insane, they are seeking for the t-truth," she stammered. Then abruptly her voice rang. "If we die giving them the word of God, that's a better death than you want for us."

He sagged back as if hit in the belly. She jumped from her seat and off the car, feather-softly down to the stones. In long leaps, she departed from him.

"Bronya!" he shouted. "Bronya, don't!" She disappeared around the barrier rock. The universe seethed in his earphones.

He fumbled after his wits. Might he catch up, seize her, keep her prisoner till he'd talked some sense back into her? No, the robots would see them struggle, and God knew what that would touch off in them. . . . God! . . . She must be closer to outright hysteria than he'd realized.

The question shocked: *How sane am I?*

Think, damn it, think hard and straight. Nothing came to mind except that he couldn't wait here, cut off. He took advantage of it to utter several phrases blasphemous and obscene before he started the buggy. Having rounded the wall, he stopped and peered.

Let her make her forlorn try. Not that he had any choice. But if she was attacked, he'd rush to her aid. And no doubt die, too.

Well, she'd been right, there were worse deaths than defense of his woman.

The three robots still stood where the humans had left them, together below the planet. The cursed chant was still going on, "—one-one-two for the one-one-one—" It ceased as Bronya approached. How tiny her form was in the tumbled landscape, how lost to him in the spacesuit.

She drew close and halted. The constructor hulked above her, the mechanician bristled at her, the explorer crouched as if readying to leap. Somehow, more daunting than the sight was the musical sound: "What is your intent?"

Loren heard her gulp. She had her mortal share of afraidness. When she replied, it was low, but steady and distinct. "I am sorry to interrupt you at your prayers, but I must."

The silence that followed was long enough for him to perceive. Was the conjoint mind reaching out by radio to search through its original database? "The word 'prayers' is not in the vocabulary," it stated.

Loren could imagine pity welling up through all apprehension. "It means that you commune—you try to communicate with God."

"The word 'God' is not in the vocabulary."

You see? he wanted to scream. *Get away while you can!*

Bronya sighed. "You found the idea for yourselves," she said, "and made words out of numbers. 'God' is the name in English for the one Being Who created all things and, and governs them. In my home country we call Him Bog, and elsewhere—The name doesn't matter. He and those things that are used in His service and those people who have come into His light, those we call holy. 'One-one-one,' does that mean 'God' or does it mean 'holy,' or both?"

The signal keened for an instant. *Troubled?* wondered Loren dazedly. Then: "Do you assert that you are holy?"

"No, never, I am sinful and—"

If she'd made the claim, leaped through him, *they might have accepted it and we'd be safe. She's too goddamn honest.*

"But that signpost at Chicago, is that sacred to you?" Bronya asked. *One-one-two,* Loren remembered. "Did you raise that figure and make it as, as humanlike as you were able, to watch over the signpost? Do you go there for your highest rites—for oneness with the one-one-one?"

The machines stood moveless as the stones around them. *But on Hyperion, a stone may at any moment stir.* Their answer tolled: "Humans put us here and gave us our purpose, which is to know our surroundings." *As the Christian's purpose is to know God,* Loren remembered. "It is clear that they, limited and fragile, cannot be much like the one-one-one. At the same time, they must be Its agents, and from them we have received messages related to that task It, through them, charged us with."

Bronya was right, not to claim everything at once, Loren saw. *She's got to feel her way forward.*

"Messengers," he heard her breathe. "In our language, a messenger of God is an angel. That figure above Chicago is an angel's. St. Michael standing guard over a church . . ."

A messenger of light, Loren remembered. *But the robots also spoke of messengers of the dark.* Recollection surged, the Bible big and heavy on the lap of his father, who read aloud majestic passages that a little boy scarcely understood. Demons. *They'd plausibly wear human shape, too. Fallen angels, serving the Devil, serving the chaos that's seized on the robots' world. How else to explain the war?*

"So you have come that far," Bronya said slowly. "You know you must obey and aid the messengers of the light, you must resist and deny the messengers of the dark."

The voice went hideously flat. "We do not know which you are."

"Let us reason," Bronya said. Her own voice was not quite steady, for with a single blow the constructor could smash her helmet and skull. "If I show you that I know why you have done what you have done, will you listen to what else I have to tell you?"

"Display your logic."

"Why have you sent false reports to Earth? Wouldn't that be a work of darkness? No, not to you. It must be . . . what I'd call word magic. You state the opposite of something strange that's happened here, but make it greater as well, because—it might help. Words and numbers are weak things to set against the Enemy, but they're the best you can think of. You hope this will keep the chaos from overwhelming everything. Am I right? Then I'll also say your real observations are in the proper database, waiting for humans to come claim them."

Again, for a space, Loren sensed his heartbeats and the susurration of the stars. *This is not something the algorithm was ever meant for,* he knew, *but nevertheless the mind that the algorithm generates has gone down the road our forebears did, stumbling in search of a meaning for existence. I was too sure of my philosophy.*

"You employ certain terms that are not in the vocabulary, but basically you state what is correct," he heard at last. "That does not constitute proof of identity. The darkness can make use of the truth."

The Devil can quote Scripture. Loren bit back a lunatic laugh.

A calm that would have been beyond him had come upon Bronya. "Yes," she murmured, "you have a Manichaean kind of religion. Ormuzd and Ahriman, Law and Chaos, Light and Dark, forever at war. A very natural faith, here. . . . But that's all incomprehensible to you, isn't it? Never mind." Her voice lifted. "Hear me. Your conclusions are false because your data have been incomplete. Let me give you the right information."

Loren leaped to his feet. The impetus bore him off the deck. He fell back shouting, "Oh, no! Bronya, you can't—" The machine response overrode him: "Proceed."

"Why has the world gone wrong?" she challenged.

"The power of the darkness," said the other mind.

Loren imagined her shaking her head. She spoke firmly. "No, not as you suppose. Consider your hypothesis. Does it really make sense that

Chaos is as strong as Law? How then could the world have come into being? How could the stars, the rings, the other moons stay in their courses, age after age, as you know they have done? The Creator has to be all-powerful. Nothing else will account for the facts."

Again a sibilant stillness—a hesitation? When the robots replied, was it with more amplitude, louder, than need be? "An omnipotent one-one-one would not allow the world to go wrong. We observe that it has." Fear snapped shut on Loren as the voice finished, "A messenger of darkness would maintain otherwise."

"No," said Bronya instantly. "Sin, suffering, evil, death—things gone wrong—those are facts, too. Agreed. How is this possible when God is all-powerful? Because He's also all-good. He did not make His creatures puppets operated by blind natural forces. He made them free, able to choose, to find their own ways to Him." It was as if Loren had tuned to her inner self: *Yes, even unto these poor man-built machines was given free will, a soul.* But she was continuing: "Freedom must include the freedom to choose wrongly, make mistakes, or actually rebel against God. The Evil One, whatever you call him, he did rebel, and he led humans to sin, and so death and pain came into the world."

"The zero-zero-zero—" The machine words chopped off.

"But God has not forsaken us," Bronya went on. "It is not logical that He would, is it? In His person of Jesus Christ He offers us salvation—peace, rightness, nearness to Him—if we will take it.

"That is my message. I, human, imperfect, am just the same a messenger of light, the eternal light."

She means it, Loren knew. *But she reckons, too, that it'll convince them to accept us, and save our lives.* His throat grew tight as though he were being hanged.

Through the racketing blood he heard: "You continue to use words that are not in the vocabulary."

"I will be happy, honored, to explain them," Bronya said.

"That will not be necessary."

After another half second the voice, gone toneless, smote like the constructor's fist. "What you have presented is not a result of assertions about the nature of things. Have you empirical evidence?"

Bronya stood before the machines, alone, and replied softly, "Doesn't it seem reasonable to you?"

It does to her. It does not to me. And we're a long way from Bethlehem.

"It is a conceivable hypothesis. Many others are conceivable, and have been rejected as inadequate. If you are one-zero, yours is correct. If you are zero-one, it is false and intended to mislead us. We may not judge without evidence. In the absence of that, the optimum is to stay with the accepted hypothesis. Under it, the world has at least remained in being. Action on the basis of ideas contrary to fact could bring total destruction.

"Have you proof that you and your companion are messengers of light?"

Across the stony distance, Loren saw Bronya brace herself. "No," she said, "not your kind of proof," and waited for the steel fist.

"It is logically possible that you are," decreed the machine mind. "In the absence of certainty, you may not be demolished. Go."

The last word spat. Bronya made the sign of the cross, turned, and trudged back to her man.

Loren lifted his face aloft, as if toward the God he did not acknowledge. The waxing crescent of Saturn filled his vision, pale amber dimly banded, the rings where chaos played with wondrous braids and spokes. *Let me take strength,* he implored the vacuum—strength from the knowledge that chaos, the chaos of mathematics and nature, is not evil, that it is rather the wellspring of newness and marvel and freedom, that there is in it an ultimate ordering as there is in music.

Insight did not burst upon him. It flowered.

Bronya reached the car. He beckoned her to spring aboard and drove back behind the screening rock. After he had stopped, he said, "I know what to tell them. You prepared the way."

She gasped, once, and then listened.

Quickly, together, they considered and readied themselves. When the humans brought their vehicle again in sight, the robots were again at prayer. They went silent. To Loren, fantastically, they seemed expectant. Hopeful?

He came to a halt, stood up beside his wife, and summoned all the courage he possessed, for his idea might prove lethally wide of the mark. "We will show you what no messenger of the dark ever could," he declared, "because this is of the pure light. It is what lies behind and beyond the appearance of lawlessness—reason, harmony, meaning."

And he recited one of the simple quadratic equations whose iterations become chaotic. The robots came to him, gathered around, heard him name the numbers he would use, saw him call up their representations on the computer screen. Before them unrolled images of fractals, the infinitely complex Julia sets that spring forth outside the immeasurably long yet finite boundary of the Mandelbrot set, endlessly varied and endlessly repeated in beauty born of the unforeseeable, like surf and shorelines, leaves and love.

"You are indeed messengers of light," said the robots to the humans, and brought them into sanctuary.

Wang's Carpets

Greg Egan

GREG EGAN LIVES IN PERTH, AUS-
TRALIA, AND HAS PUBLISHED A NUMBER OF INTRIGUING SHORT STORIES AND
THREE NOVELS: *AN UNUSUAL ANGLE, QUARANTINE* AND *PERMUTATION CITY.*

READING "WANG'S CARPETS" ANCHORED FOR ME THE THEME OF THIS AN-
THOLOGY—DIALOG BETWEEN CREATORS. SCIENCE FICTION AT ITS BEST IS A KIND
OF TURING MACHINE THAT AUTOMATICALLY CALCULATES THE FUTURE—AND
HELPS TO MAKE IT. I SEE IN THIS STORY ELEMENTS AND IDEAS SCIENCE FICTION
WRITERS HAVE EXPLORED OVER THE PAST TWENTY YEARS—AND A NUMBER OF
IDEAS I TAKE A PROPRIETARY INTEREST IN, HAVING PUSHED THEM A FEW TIMES
MYSELF. BUT THE RULES OF THE SCIENCE FICTION GAME SAY THAT ALL IDEAS ARE
OPEN, SO LONG AS THE CREATOR TAKES THEM AT LEAST ONE STEP FURTHER.
EGAN HAS DONE MUCH MORE THAN THAT. HE PLAYS THE GAME VERY WELL.

THIS STORY MAY BE DIFFICULT FOR THOSE NEW TO SCIENCE FICTION. IT IS
CONCEPTUALLY HIGH-LEVEL, CRAMMED WITH IDEAS AND INSIGHTS, BUT THAT
DOESN'T PRECLUDE IT FROM BEING ELEGANT AND WITTY, FULL OF BELIEVABLE (IF
INCREDIBLY ADVANCED) HUMAN CHARACTERS. IT MERITS REPEAT READINGS.

WAITING TO BE cloned one thousand times and scattered across ten million
cubic light years, Paolo Venetti relaxed in his favorite ceremonial bathtub:
a tiered hexagonal pool set in a courtyard of black marble flecked with gold.
Paolo wore full traditional anatomy, uncomfortable garb at first, but the
warm currents flowing across his back and shoulders slowly eased him into
a pleasant torpor. He could have reached the same state in an instant, by
decree—but the occasion seemed to demand the complete ritual of
verisimilitude, the ornate curlicued longhand of imitation physical cause
and effect.

As the moment of diaspora approached, a small gray lizard darted across
the courtyard, claws scrabbling. It halted by the far edge of the pool, and
Paolo marveled at the delicate pulse of its breathing, and watched the lizard

watching him, until it moved again, disappearing into the surrounding vineyards. The environment was full of birds and insects, rodents and small reptiles—decorative in appearance, but also satisfying a more abstract aesthetic: softening the harsh radial symmetry of the lone observer; anchoring the simulation by perceiving it from a multitude of viewpoints. Ontological guy lines. No one had asked the lizards if they wanted to be cloned, though. They were coming along for the ride, like it or not.

The sky above the courtyard was warm and blue, cloudless and sunless, isotropic. Paolo waited calmly, prepared for every one of half a dozen possible fates.

An invisible bell chimed softly, three times. Paolo laughed, delighted.

One chime would have meant that he was still on Earth: an anti-climax, certainly—but there would have been advantages to compensate for that. Everyone who really mattered to him lived in the Carter-Zimmerman polis, but not all of them had chosen to take part in the diaspora to the same degree; his Earth-self would have lost no one. Helping to ensure that the thousand ships were safely dispatched would have been satisfying, too. And remaining a member of the wider Earth-based community, plugged into the entire global culture in real-time, would have been an attraction in itself.

Two chimes would have meant that this clone of Carter-Zimmerman had reached a planetary system devoid of life. Paolo had run a sophisticated—but non-sapient—self-predictive model before deciding to wake under those conditions. Exploring a handful of alien worlds, however barren, had seemed likely to be an enriching experience for him—with the distinct advantage that the whole endeavor would be untrammeled by the kind of elaborate precautions necessary in the presence of alien life. C-Z's population would have fallen by more than half—and many of his closest friends would have been absent—but he would have forged new friendships, he was sure.

Four chimes would have signaled the discovery of intelligent aliens. Five, a technological civilization. Six, spacefarers.

Three chimes, though, meant that the scout probes had detected unambiguous signs of life—and that was reason enough for jubilation. Up until the moment of the pre-launch cloning—a subjective instant before the chimes had sounded—no reports of alien life had ever reached Earth. There'd been no guarantee that any part of the diaspora would find it.

Paolo willed the polis library to brief him; it promptly rewired the declarative memory of his simulated traditional brain with all the information he was likely to need to satisfy his immediate curiosity. This clone of C-Z had arrived at Vega, the second closest of the thousand target stars, twenty-seven light-years from Earth. Paolo closed his eyes and visualized a star map with a thousand lines radiating out from the sun, then zoomed in on the trajectory which described his own journey. It had taken three centuries to reach Vega—but the vast majority of the polis's twenty thousand inhabitants had programmed their exoselves to suspend them prior to the cloning, and to wake them only if and when they arrived at a suitable destination. Ninety-two citizens had chosen the alternative: experiencing every voyage of the diaspora from start to finish, risking disappointment, and even death. Paolo now knew that the ship aimed at Fomalhaut, the target nearest Earth, had been struck by debris and annihilated *en route.* He mourned the ninety-two, briefly. He hadn't been close to any of them, prior to the cloning, and the particular versions who'd willfully perished two centuries ago in interstellar space seemed as remote as the victims of some ancient calamity from the era of flesh.

Paolo examined his new home star through the cameras of one of the scout probes—and the strange filters of the ancestral visual system. In traditional colors, Vega was a fierce blue-white disk, laced with prominences. Three times the mass of the sun, twice the size and twice as hot, sixty times as luminous. Burning hydrogen fast—and already halfway through its allotted five hundred million years on the main sequence.

Vega's sole planet, Orpheus, had been a featureless blip to the best lunar interferometers; now Paolo gazed down on its blue-green crescent, ten thousand kilometers below Carter-Zimmerman itself. Orpheus was terrestrial, a nickel-iron-silicate world; slightly larger than Earth, slightly warmer—a billion kilometers took the edge off Vega's heat—and almost drowning in liquid water. Impatient to see the whole surface firsthand, Paolo slowed his clock rate a thousandfold, allowing C-Z to circumnavigate the planet in twenty subjective seconds, daylight unshrouding a broad new swath with each pass. Two slender ocher-colored continents with mountainous spines bracketed hemispheric oceans, and dazzling expanses of pack ice covered both poles—far more so in the north, where jagged white peninsulas radiated out from the midwinter arctic darkness.

The Orphean atmosphere was mostly nitrogen—six times as much as on Earth; probably split by UV from primordial ammonia—with traces of water vapor and carbon dioxide, but not enough of either for a runaway greenhouse effect. The high atmospheric pressure meant reduced evaporation—Paolo saw not a wisp of cloud—and the large, warm oceans in turn helped feed carbon dioxide back into the crust, locking it up in limestone sediments destined for subduction.

The whole system was young, by Earth standards, but Vega's greater mass, and a denser protostellar cloud, would have meant swifter passage through most of the traumas of birth: nuclear ignition and early luminosity fluctuations; planetary coalescence and the age of bombardments. The library estimated that Orpheus had enjoyed a relatively stable climate, and freedom from major impacts, for at least the past hundred million years.

Long enough for primitive life to appear—

A hand seized Paolo firmly by the ankle and tugged him beneath the water. He offered no resistance, and let the vision of the planet slip away. Only two other people in C-Z had free access to this environment—and his father didn't play games with his now-twelve-hundred-year-old son.

Elena dragged him all the way to the bottom of the pool, before releasing his foot and hovering above him, a triumphant silhouette against the bright surface. She was ancestor-shaped, but obviously cheating; she spoke with perfect clarity, and no air bubbles at all.

"Late sleeper! I've been waiting seven weeks for this!"

Paolo feigned indifference, but he was fast running out of breath. He had his exoself convert him into an amphibious human variant—biologically and historically authentic, if no longer the definitive ancestral phenotype. Water flooded into his modified lungs, and his modified brain welcomed it.

He said, "Why would I want to waste consciousness, sitting around waiting for the scout probes to refine their observations? I woke as soon as the data was unambiguous."

She pummeled his chest; he reached up and pulled her down, instinctively reducing his buoyancy to compensate, and they rolled across the bottom of the pool, kissing.

Elena said, "You know we're the first C-Z to arrive, anywhere? The Fomalhaut ship was destroyed. So there's only one other pair of us. Back on Earth."

"So?" Then he remembered. Elena had chosen not to wake if any other version of her had already encountered life. Whatever fate befell each of the remaining ships, every other version of him would have to live without her.

He nodded soberly, and kissed her again. "What am I meant to say? You're a thousand times more precious to me, now?"

"Yes."

"Ah, but what about the you-and-I on Earth? Five hundred times would be closer to the truth."

"There's no poetry in five hundred."

"Don't be so defeatist. Rewire your language centers."

She ran her hands along the sides of his ribcage, down to his hips. They made love with their almost-traditional bodies—and brains; Paolo was amused to the point of distraction when his limbic system went into overdrive, but he remembered enough from the last occasion to bury his self-consciousness and surrender to the strange hijacker. It wasn't like making love in any civilized fashion—the rate of information exchange between them was minuscule, for a start—but it had the raw insistent quality of most ancestral pleasures.

Then they drifted up to the surface of the pool and lay beneath the radiant sunless sky.

Paolo thought: *I've crossed twenty-seven light-years in an instant. I'm orbiting the first planet ever found to hold alien life. And I've sacrificed nothing—left nothing I truly value behind. This is too good, too good.* He felt a pang of regret for his other selves—it was hard to imagine them faring as well, without Elena, without Orpheus—but there was nothing he could do about that, now. Although there'd be time to confer with Earth before any more ships reached their destinations, he'd decided—prior to the cloning—not to allow the unfolding of his manifold future to be swayed by any change of heart. Whether or not his Earth-self agreed, the two of them were powerless to alter the criteria for waking. The self with the right to choose for the thousand had passed away.

No matter, Paolo decided. The others would find—or construct—their own reasons for happiness. And there was still the chance that one of them would wake to the sound of *four chimes.*

Elena said, "If you'd slept much longer, you would have missed the vote."

The vote? The scouts in low orbit had gathered what data they could about Orphean biology. To proceed any further, it would be necessary to send microprobes into the ocean itself—an escalation of contact which required the approval of two-thirds of the polis. There was no compelling reason to believe that the presence of a few million tiny robots could do any harm; all they'd leave behind in the water was a few kilojoules of waste heat. Nevertheless, a faction had arisen which advocated caution. The citizens of Carter-Zimmerman, they argued, could continue to observe from a distance for another decade, or another millennium, refining their observations and hypotheses before intruding . . . and those who disagreed could always sleep away the time, or find other interests to pursue.

Paolo delved into his library-fresh knowledge of the "carpets"—the single Orphean lifeform detected so far. They were free-floating creatures living in the equatorial ocean depths—apparently destroyed by UV if they drifted too close to the surface. They grew to a size of hundreds of meters, then fissioned into dozens of fragments, each of which continued to grow. It was tempting to assume that they were colonies of single-celled organisms, something like giant kelp—but there was no real evidence yet to back that up. It was difficult enough for the scout probes to discern the carpets' gross appearance and behavior through a kilometer of water, even with Vega's copious neutrinos lighting the way; remote observations on a microscopic scale, let alone biochemical analyses, were out of the question. Spectroscopy revealed that the surface water was full of intriguing molecular debris—but guessing the relationship of any of it to the living carpets was like trying to reconstruct human biochemistry by studying human ashes.

Paolo turned to Elena. "What do you think?"

She moaned theatrically; the topic must have been argued to death while he slept. "The microprobes are harmless. They could tell us exactly what the carpets are made of, without removing a single molecule. What's the risk? *Culture shock?*"

Paolo flicked water onto her face, affectionately; the impulse seemed to come with the amphibian body. "You can't be sure that they're not intelligent."

"Do you know what was living on Earth, two hundred million years after it was formed?"

"Maybe cyanobacteria. Maybe nothing. This isn't Earth, though."

"True. But even in the unlikely event that the carpets are intelligent, do you think they'd notice the presence of robots a millionth their size? If they're unified organisms, they don't appear to react to anything in their environment—they have no predators, they don't pursue food, they just drift with the currents—so there's no reason for them to possess elaborate sense organs at all, let alone anything working on a sub-millimeter scale. And if they're colonies of single-celled creatures, one of which happens to collide with a microprobe and register its presence with surface receptors . . . what conceivable harm could that do?"

"I have no idea. But my ignorance is no guarantee of safety."

Elena splashed him back. "The only way to deal with your *ignorance* is to vote to send down the microprobes. We have to be cautious, I agree— but there's no point *being here* if we don't find out what's happening in the oceans, right now. I don't want to wait for this planet to evolve something smart enough to broadcast biochemistry lessons into space. If we're not willing to take a few infinitesimal risks, Vega will turn red giant before we learn anything."

It was a throwaway line—but Paolo tried to imagine witnessing the event. In a quarter of a billion years, would the citizens of Carter-Zimmerman be debating the ethics of intervening to rescue the Orpheans—or would they all have lost interest, and departed for other stars, or modified themselves into beings entirely devoid of nostalgic compassion for organic life?

Grandiose visions for a twelve-hundred-year-old. The Fomalhaut clone had been obliterated by one tiny piece of rock. There was far more junk in the Vegan system than in interstellar space; even ringed by defenses, its data backed up to all the far-flung scout probes, this C-Z was not invulnerable just because it had arrived intact. Elena was right; they had to seize the moment—or they might as well retreat into their own hermetic worlds and forget that they'd ever made the journey.

Paolo recalled the honest puzzlement of a friend from Ashton-Laval: *Why go looking for aliens? Our polis has a thousand ecologies, a trillion species of evolved life. What do you hope to find, out there, that you couldn't have grown at home?*

What had he hoped to find? Just the answers to a few simple questions. Did human consciousness bootstrap all of space-time into existence, in order to explain itself? Or had a neutral, pre-existing universe given birth to a billion varieties of conscious life, all capable of harboring the same delusions of grandeur—until they collided with each other? Anthrocosmology was used to justify the inward-looking stance of most polises: if the physical universe was created by human thought, it had no special status which placed it above virtual reality. It might have come first—and every virtual reality might need to run on a physical computing device, subject to physical laws—but it occupied no privileged position in terms of "truth" versus "illusion". If the ACs were right, then it was no more *honest* to value the physical universe over more recent artificial realities than it was honest to remain flesh instead of software, or ape instead of human, or bacterium instead of ape.

Elena said, "We can't lie here forever; the gang's all waiting to see you."

"Where?" Paolo felt his first pang of homesickness; on Earth, his circle of friends had always met in a real-time image of the Mount Pinatubo crater, plucked straight from the observation satellites. A recording wouldn't be the same.

"I'll show you."

Paolo reached over and took her hand. The pool, the sky, the courtyard vanished—and he found himself gazing down on Orpheus again . . . nightside, but far from dark, with his full mental palette now encoding everything from the pale wash of ground-current long-wave radio, to the multi-colored shimmer of isotopic gamma rays and back-scattered cosmicray bremsstrahlung. Half the abstract knowledge the library had fed him about the planet was obvious at a glance, now. The ocean's smoothly tapered thermal glow spelt *three-hundred Kelvin* instantly—as well as backlighting the atmosphere's tell-tale infrared silhouette.

He was standing on a long, metallic-looking girder, one edge of a vast geodesic sphere, open to the blazing cathedral of space. He glanced up and saw the star-rich dust-clogged band of the Milky Way, encircling him from zenith to nadir; aware of the glow of every gas cloud, discerning each absorption and emission line, Paolo could almost feel the plane of the galactic disk transect him. Some constellations were distorted, but the view was more familiar than strange—and he recognized most of the old signposts by color. He had his bearings, now. Twenty degrees away from Sirius—south, by parochial Earth reckoning—faint but unmistakable: the sun.

Elena was beside him—superficially unchanged, although they'd both shrugged off the constraints of biology. The conventions of this environment mimicked the physics of real macroscopic objects in free-fall and vacuum, but it wasn't set up to model any kind of chemistry, let alone that of flesh and blood. Their new bodies were human-shaped, but devoid of elaborate microstructure—and their minds weren't embedded in the physics at all, but were running directly on the processor web.

Paolo was relieved to be back to normal; ceremonial regression to the ancestral form was a venerable C-Z tradition—and being human was largely self-affirming, while it lasted—but every time he emerged from the experience, he felt as if he'd broken free of billion-year-old shackles. There were polises on Earth where the citizens would have found his present structure almost as archaic: a consciousness dominated by sensory perception, an illusion of possessing solid form, a single time coordinate. The last flesh human had died long before Paolo was constructed, and apart from the communities of Gleisner robots, Carter-Zimmerman was about as conservative as a transhuman society could be. The balance seemed right to Paolo, though—acknowledging the flexibility of software, without abandoning interest in the physical world—and although the stubbornly corporeal Gleisners had been first to the stars, the C-Z diaspora would soon overtake them.

Their friends gathered round, showing off their effortless free-fall acrobatics, greeting Paolo and chiding him for not arranging to wake sooner; he was the last of the gang to emerge from hibernation.

"Do you like our humble new meeting place?" Hermann floated by Paolo's shoulder, a chimeric cluster of limbs and sense-organs, speaking through the vacuum in modulated infrared. "We call it Satellite Pinatubo. It's desolate up here, I know—but we were afraid it might violate the spirit of caution if we dared pretend to walk the Orphean surface."

Paolo glanced mentally at a scout probe's close-up of a typical stretch of dry land, an expanse of fissured red rock. "More desolate down there, I think." He was tempted to touch the ground—to let the private vision become tactile—but he resisted. Being elsewhere in the middle of a conversation was bad etiquette.

"Ignore Hermann," Liesl advised. "He wants to flood Orpheus with our alien machinery before we have any idea what the effects might be." Liesl was a green-and-turquoise butterfly, with a stylized human face stippled in gold on each wing.

Paolo was surprised; from the way Elena had spoken, he'd assumed that his friends must have come to a consensus in favor of the microprobes—and only a late sleeper, new to the issues, would bother to argue the point. "What effects? The carpets—"

"Forget the carpets! Even if the carpets are as simple as they look, we don't know what else is down there." As Liesl's wings fluttered, her mirror-image faces seemed to glance at each other for support. "With neutrino imaging, we barely achieve spatial resolution in meters, time resolution in seconds. We don't know anything about smaller lifeforms."

"And we never will, if you have your way." Karpal—an ex-Gleisner, human-shaped as ever—had been Liesl's lover, last time Paolo was awake.

"We've only been here for a fraction of an Orphean year! There's still a wealth of data we could gather non-intrusively, with a little patience. There might be rare beachings of ocean life—"

Elena said dryly, "Rare indeed. Orpheus has negligible tides, shallow waves, very few storms. And anything beached would be fried by UV before we glimpsed anything more instructive than we're already seeing in the surface water."

"Not necessarily. The carpets seem to be vulnerable—but other species might be better protected, if they live nearer to the surface. And Orpheus is seismically active; we should at least wait for a tsunami to dump a few cubic kilometers of ocean onto a shoreline, and see what it reveals."

Paolo smiled; he hadn't thought of that. A tsunami might be worth waiting for.

Liesl continued, "What is there to lose, by waiting a few hundred Orphean years? At the very least, we could gather baseline data on seasonal climate patterns—and we could watch for anomalies, storms and quakes, hoping for some revelatory glimpses."

A few hundred Orphean years? *A few terrestrial millennia?* Paolo's ambivalence waned. If he'd wanted to inhabit geological time, he would have migrated to the Lokhande polis, where the Order of Contemplative Observers watched Earth's mountains erode in subjective seconds. Orpheus hung in the sky beneath them, a beautiful puzzle waiting to be decoded, demanding to be understood.

He said, "But what if there *are* no 'revelatory glimpses?' How long do we wait? We don't know how rare life is—in time, or in space. If this planet is precious, *so is the epoch it's passing through.* We don't know how rapidly Orphean biology is evolving; species might appear and vanish while we agonize over the risks of gathering better data. The carpets—and whatever else—could die out before we'd learnt the first thing about them. What a waste that would be!"

Liesl stood her ground.

"And if we damage the Orphean ecology—or culture—by rushing in? That wouldn't be a waste. It would be a tragedy."

* * *

Paolo assimilated all the stored transmissions from his Earth-self—almost three hundred years' worth—before composing a reply. The early communications included detailed mind grafts—and it was good to share the excitement of the diaspora's launch; to watch—very nearly firsthand—the thousand ships, nanomachine-carved from asteroids, depart in a blaze of fusion fire from beyond the orbit of Mars. Then things settled down to the usual prosaic matters: Elena, the gang, shameless gossip, Carter-Zimmerman's ongoing research projects, the buzz of inter-polis cultural tensions, the not-quite-cyclic convulsions of the arts (the perceptual aesthetic overthrows the emotional, again . . . although Valladas in Konishi polis claims to have constructed a new synthesis of the two).

After the first fifty years, his Earth-self had begun to hold things back; by the time news reached Earth of the Fomalhaut clone's demise, the messages had become pure audiovisual linear monologues. Paolo understood. It was only right; they'd diverged, and you didn't send mind grafts to strangers.

Most of the transmissions had been broadcast to all of the ships, indiscriminately. Forty-three years ago, though, his Earth-self had sent a special message to the Vega-bound clone.

"The new lunar spectroscope we finished last year has just picked up clear signs of water on Orpheus. There should be large temperate oceans waiting for you, if the models are right. So . . . good luck." Vision showed the instrument's domes growing out of the rock of the lunar farside; plots of the Orphean spectral data; an ensemble of planetary models. "Maybe it seems strange to you—all the trouble we're taking to catch a glimpse of what you're going to see in close-up, so soon. It's hard to explain: I don't think it's jealousy, or even impatience. Just a need for independence.

"There's been a revival of the old debate: should we consider redesigning our minds to encompass interstellar distances? One self spanning thousands of stars, not via cloning, but through acceptance of the natural time scale of the light-speed lag. Millennia passing between mental events. Local contingencies dealt with by non-conscious systems." Essays, pro and con, were appended; Paolo ingested summaries. "I don't think the idea will gain much support, though—and the new astronomical projects are something of an antidote. We have to make peace with the fact that we've stayed behind . . . so we cling to the Earth—looking outwards, but remaining firmly anchored.

"I keep asking myself, though: where do we go from here? History can't guide us. Evolution can't guide us. The C-Z charter says *understand and respect the universe* . . . but in what form? On what scale? With what kind of senses, what kind of minds? We can become anything at all—and that space of possible futures dwarfs the galaxy. Can we explore it without losing our way? Flesh humans used to spin fantasies about aliens arriving to 'conquer' Earth, to steal their 'precious' physical resources, to wipe them out for fear of 'competition' . . . as if a species capable of making the journey wouldn't have had the power, or the wit, or the imagination, to rid itself of obsolete biological imperatives. *Conquering the galaxy* is what bacteria with spaceships would do—knowing no better, having no choice.

"Our condition is the opposite of that: we have no end of choices. That's why we need to find alien life—not just to break the spell of the anthrocosmologists. We need to find aliens who've faced the same decisions—and discovered how to live, what to become. We need to understand what it means to inhabit the universe."

Paolo watched the crude neutrino images of the carpets moving in staccato jerks around his dodecahedral room. Twenty-four ragged oblongs drifted above him, daughters of a larger ragged oblong which had just fissioned. Models suggested that shear forces from ocean currents could explain the whole process, triggered by nothing more than the parent reaching a critical size. The purely mechanical break-up of a colony—if that was what it was—might have little to do with the life cycle of the constituent organisms. It was frustrating. Paolo was accustomed to a torrent of data on anything which caught his interest; for the diaspora's great discovery to remain nothing more than a sequence of coarse monochrome snapshots was intolerable.

He glanced at a schematic of the scout probes' neutrino detectors, but there was no obvious scope for improvement. Nuclei in the detectors were excited into unstable high-energy states, then kept there by fine-tuned gamma-ray lasers picking off lower-energy eigenstates faster than they could creep into existence and attract a transition. Changes in neutrino flux of one part in ten-to-the-fifteenth could shift the energy levels far enough to disrupt the balancing act. The carpets cast a shadow so faint, though, that even this near-perfect vision could barely resolve it.

Orlando Venetti said, "You're awake."

Paolo turned. His father stood an arm's length away, presenting as an ornately clad human of indeterminate age. Definitely older than Paolo, though; Orlando never ceased to play up his seniority—even if the age difference was only twenty-five percent now, and falling.

Paolo banished the carpets from the room to the space behind one pentagonal window, and took his father's hand. The portions of Orlando's mind which meshed with his own expressed pleasure at Paolo's emergence from hibernation, fondly dwelt on past shared experiences, and entertained hopes of continued harmony between father and son. Paolo's greeting was similar, a carefully contrived "revelation" of his own emotional state. It was more of a ritual than an act of communication—but then, even with Elena, he set up barriers. No one was totally honest with another person—unless the two of them intended to permanently fuse.

Orlando nodded at the carpets. "I hope you appreciate how important they are."

"You know I do." He hadn't included that in his greeting, though. "First alien life." *C-Z humiliates the Gleisner robots, at last*—that was probably how his father saw it. The robots had been first to Alpha Centauri, and first to an extrasolar planet—but first life was Apollo to their Sputniks, for anyone who chose to think in those terms.

Orlando said, "This is the hook we need, to catch the citizens of the marginal polises. The ones who haven't quite imploded into solipsism. This will shake them up—don't you think?"

Paolo shrugged. Earth's transhumans were free to implode into anything they liked; it didn't stop Carter-Zimmerman from exploring the physical universe. But thrashing the Gleisners wouldn't be enough for Orlando; he lived for the day when C-Z would become the cultural mainstream. Any polis could multiply its population a billionfold in a microsecond, if it wanted the vacuous honor of outnumbering the rest. Luring other citizens to migrate was harder—and persuading them to rewrite their own local charters was harder still. Orlando had a missionary streak: he wanted every other polis to see the error of its ways, and follow C-Z to the stars.

Paolo said, "Ashton-Laval has intelligent aliens. I wouldn't be so sure that news of giant seaweed is going to take Earth by storm."

Orlando was venomous. "Ashton-Laval intervened in its so-called 'evolutionary' simulations so many times that they might as well have built the end products in an act of creation lasting six days. They wanted talking reptiles, and—*mirabile dictu!*—they got talking reptiles. There are self-modified transhumans in *this polis* more alien than the aliens in Ashton-Laval."

Paolo smiled. "All right. Forget Ashton-Laval. But forget the marginal polises, too. We choose to value the physical world. That's what defines us—but it's as arbitrary as any other choice of values. Why can't you accept that? It's not the One True Path which the infidels have to be bludgeoned into following." He knew he was arguing half for the sake of it—he desperately wanted to refute the anthrocosmologists, himself—but Orlando always drove him into taking the opposite position. Out of fear of being nothing but his father's clone? Despite the total absence of inherited episodic memories, the stochastic input into his ontogenesis, the chaotically divergent nature of the iterative mind-building algorithms.

Orlando made a beckoning gesture, dragging the image of the carpets halfway back into the room. "You'll vote for the microprobes?"

"Of course."

"Everything depends on that, now. It's good to start with a tantalizing glimpse—but if we don't follow up with details soon, they'll lose interest back on Earth very rapidly."

"Lose interest? It'll be fifty-four years before we know if anyone paid the slightest attention in the first place."

Orlando eyed him with disappointment, and resignation. "If you don't care about the other polises, think about C-Z. This helps us, it strengthens us. We have to make the most of that."

Paolo was bemused. "The charter is the charter. What needs to be strengthened? You make it sound like there's something at risk."

"What do you think a thousand lifeless worlds would have done to us? Do you think the charter would have remained intact?"

Paolo had never considered the scenario. "Maybe not. But in every C-Z where the charter was rewritten, there would have been citizens who'd have gone off and founded new polises on the old lines. You and I, for a start. We could have called it Venetti-Venetti."

"While half your friends turned their backs on the physical world? While Carter-Zimmerman, after two thousand years, went solipsist? You'd be happy with that?"

Paolo laughed. "No—but it's not going to happen, is it? *We've found life.* All right, I agree with you: this strengthens C-Z. The diaspora might have 'failed' . . . but it didn't. We've been lucky. I'm glad, I'm grateful. Is that what you wanted to hear?"

Orlando said sourly, "You take too much for granted."

"And you care too much what I think! I'm not your . . . heir." Orlando was first-generation, scanned from flesh—and there were times when he seemed unable to accept that the whole concept of generation had lost its archaic significance. "You don't need me to safeguard the future of Carter-Zimmerman on your behalf. Or the future of transhumanity. You can do it in person."

Orlando looked wounded—a conscious choice, but it still encoded something. Paolo felt a pang of regret—but he'd said nothing he could honestly retract.

His father gathered up the sleeves of his gold and crimson robes—the only citizen of C-Z who could make Paolo uncomfortable to be naked—and repeated as he vanished from the room: "You take too much for granted."

The gang watched the launch of the microprobes together—even Liesl, though she came in mourning, as a giant dark bird. Karpal stroked her

feathers nervously. Hermann appeared as a creature out of Escher, a seg-
mented worm with six human-shaped feet—on legs with elbows—given to
curling up into a disk and rolling along the girders of Satellite Pinatubo.
Paolo and Elena kept saying the same thing simultaneously; they'd just
made love.

Hermann had moved the satellite to a notional orbit just below one of
the scout probes—and changed the environment's scale, so that the probe's
lower surface, an intricate landscape of detector modules and attitude-
control jets, blotted out half the sky. The atmospheric-entry capsules—
ceramic teardrops three centimeters wide—burst from their launch tube
and hurtled past like boulders, vanishing from sight before they'd fallen so
much as ten meters closer to Orpheus. It was all scrupulously accurate, although it was part real-time imagery, part extrapolation, part *faux*. Paolo
thought: *We might as well have run a pure simulation . . . and pretended to follow
the capsules down.* Elena gave him a guilty/admonishing look. *Yeah—and
then why bother actually launching them at all? Why not just simulate a plausible
Orphean ocean full of plausible Orphean lifeforms? Why not simulate the whole
diaspora?* There was no crime of heresy in C-Z; no one had ever been exiled
for breaking the charter. At times it still felt like a tightrope walk, though,
trying to classify every act of simulation into those which contributed to an
understanding of the physical universe (good), those which were merely
convenient, recreational, aesthetic (acceptable) . . . and those which con-
stituted a denial of the primacy of real phenomena (time to think about
emigration).

The vote on the microprobes had been close: seventy-two percent in
favor, just over the required two-thirds majority, with five percent abstain-
ing. (Citizens created since the arrival at Vega were excluded . . . not that
anyone in Carter-Zimmerman would have dreamt of stacking the ballot,
perish the thought.) Paolo had been surprised at the narrow margin; he'd
yet to hear a single plausible scenario for the microprobes doing harm. He
wondered if there was another, unspoken reason which had nothing to do
with fears for the Orphean ecology, or hypothetical culture. *A wish to prolong
the pleasure of unraveling the planet's mysteries?* Paolo had some sympathy with
that impulse—but the launch of the microprobes would do nothing to un-
dermine the greater long-term pleasure of watching, and understanding, as
Orphean life evolved.

Liesl said forlornly, "Coastline erosion models show that the north-
western shore of Lambda is inundated by tsunami every ninety Orphean
years, on average." She offered the data to them; Paolo glanced at it, and it
looked convincing—but the point was academic now. "We could have
waited."

Hermann waved his eye-stalks at her. "Beaches covered in fossils, are they?"

"No, but the conditions hardly—"

"No excuses!" He wound his body around a girder, kicking his legs gleefully. Hermann was first-generation, even older than Orlando; he'd been scanned in the twenty-first century, before Carter-Zimmerman existed. Over the centuries, though, he'd wiped most of his episodic memories, and rewritten his personality a dozen times. He'd once told Paolo, "I think of myself as my own great-great-grandson. Death's not so bad, if you do it incrementally. Ditto for immortality."

Elena said, "I keep trying to imagine how it will feel if another C-Z clone stumbles on something infinitely better—like aliens with wormhole drives—while we're back here studying rafts of algae." The body she wore was more stylized than usual—still humanoid, but sexless, hairless and smooth, the face inexpressive and androgynous.

"If they have wormhole drives, they might visit us. Or share the technology, so we can link up the whole diaspora."

"If they have wormhole drives, where have they been for the last two thousand years?"

Paolo laughed. "Exactly. But I know what you mean: *first alien life* . . . and it's likely to be about as sophisticated as seaweed. It breaks the jinx, though. Seaweed every twenty-seven light-years. Nervous systems every fifty? Intelligence every hundred?" He fell silent, abruptly realizing what she was feeling: electing not to wake again after first life was beginning to seem like the wrong choice, a waste of the opportunities the diaspora had created. Paolo offered her a mind graft expressing empathy and support, but she declined.

She said, "I want sharp borders, right now. I want to deal with this myself."

"I understand." He let the partial model of her which he'd acquired as they'd made love fade from his mind. It was non-sapient, and no longer linked to her—but to retain it any longer when she felt this way would have seemed like a transgression. Paolo took the responsibilities of intimacy seriously. His lover before Elena had asked him to erase all his knowledge of her, and he'd more or less complied—the only thing he still knew about her was the fact that she'd made the request.

Hermann announced, "Planetfall!" Paolo glanced at a replay of a scout probe view which showed the first few entry capsules breaking up above the ocean and releasing their microprobes. Nanomachines transformed the ceramic shields (and then themselves) into carbon dioxide and a few simple minerals—nothing the micrometeorites constantly raining down onto Orpheus didn't contain—before the fragments could strike the water. The microprobes would broadcast nothing; when they'd finished gathering data, they'd float to the surface and modulate their UV reflectivity. It would be up to the scout probes to locate these specks, and read their messages, before they self-destructed as thoroughly as the entry capsules.

Hermann said, "This calls for a celebration. I'm heading for the Heart. Who'll join me?"

Paolo glanced at Elena. She shook her head. "You go."

"Are you sure?"

"Yes! Go on." Her skin had taken on a mirrored sheen; her expressionless face reflected the planet below. "I'm all right. I just want some time to think things through, on my own."

Hermann coiled around the satellite's frame, stretching his pale body as he went, gaining segments, gaining legs. "Come on, come on! Karpal? Liesl? Come and celebrate!"

Elena was gone. Liesl made a derisive sound and flapped off into the distance, mocking the environment's airlessness. Paolo and Karpal watched as Hermann grew longer and faster—and then in a blur of speed and change stretched out to wrap the entire geodesic frame. Paolo demagnetized his feet and moved away, laughing; Karpal did the same.

Then Hermann constricted like a boa, and snapped the whole satellite apart.

They floated for a while, two human-shaped machines and a giant worm in a cloud of spinning metal fragments, an absurd collection of imaginary debris, glinting by the light of the true stars.

The Heart was always crowded, but it was larger than Paolo had seen it—even though Hermann had shrunk back to his original size, so as not to make a scene. The huge muscular chamber arched above them, pulsating wetly in time to the music, as they searched for the perfect location to soak up the atmosphere. Paolo had visited public environments in other polises, back on Earth; many were designed to be nothing more than a perceptual framework for group emotion-sharing. He'd never understood the attraction of becoming intimate with large numbers of strangers. Ancestral social hierarchies might have had their faults—and it was absurd to try to make a virtue of the limitations imposed by minds confined to wetware—but the whole idea of mass telepathy as an end in itself seemed bizarre to Paolo . . . and even old-fashioned, in a way. Humans, clearly, would have benefited from a good strong dose of each other's inner life, to keep them from slaughtering each other—but any civilized transhuman could respect and value other citizens without the need to have *been them,* firsthand.

They found a good spot and made some furniture, a table and two chairs—Hermann preferred to stand—and the floor expanded to make room. Paolo looked around, shouting greetings at the people he recognized by sight, but not bothering to check for identity broadcasts from the rest. Chances were he'd met everyone here, but he didn't want to spend the next hour exchanging pleasantries with casual acquaintances.

Hermann said, "I've been monitoring our modest stellar observatory's data stream—my antidote to Vegan parochialism. Odd things are going on around Sirius. We're seeing electron-positron annihilation gamma rays, gravity waves . . . and some unexplained hot spots on Sirius B." He turned to Karpal and asked innocently, "What do you think those robots are up to? There's a rumor that they're planning to drag the white dwarf out of orbit, and use it as part of a giant spaceship."

"I never listen to rumors." Karpal always presented as a faithful reproduction of his old human-shaped Gleisner body—and his mind, Paolo gathered, always took the form of a physiological model, even though he was five generations removed from flesh. Leaving his people and coming into C-Z must have taken considerable courage; they'd never welcome him back.

Paolo said, "Does it matter what they do? Where they go, how they get there? There's more than enough room for both of us. Even if they shadowed the diaspora—even if they came to Vega—we could study the Orpheans together, couldn't we?"

Hermann's cartoon insect face showed mock alarm, eyes growing wider, and wider apart. "Not if they dragged along a white dwarf! Next thing they'd want to start building a Dyson sphere." He turned back to Karpal. "You don't still suffer the urge, do you, for . . . *astrophysical* engineering?"

"Nothing C-Z's exploitation of a few megatons of Vegan asteroid material hasn't satisfied."

Paolo tried to change the subject. "Has anyone heard from Earth, lately? I'm beginning to feel unplugged." His own most recent message was a decade older than the time lag.

Karpal said, "You're not missing much; all they're talking about is Orpheus . . . ever since the new lunar observations, the signs of water. They seem more excited by the mere possibility of life than we are by the certainty. And they have very high hopes."

Paolo laughed. "They do. My Earth-self seems to be counting on the diaspora to find an advanced civilization with the answers to all of transhumanity's existential problems. I don't think he'll get much cosmic guidance from kelp."

"You know there was a big rise in emigration from C-Z after the launch? Emigration, and suicides." Hermann had stopped wriggling and gyrating, becoming almost still, a sign of rare seriousness. "I suspect that's what triggered the astronomy program in the first place. And it seems to have stanched the flow, at least in the short term. Earth C-Z detected water before any clone in the diaspora—and when they hear that we've found life, they'll feel more like collaborators in the discovery because of it."

Paolo felt a stirring of unease. *Emigration and suicides? Was that why Orlando had been so gloomy?* After three hundred years of waiting, how high had expectations become?

A buzz of excitement crossed the floor, a sudden shift in the tone of the conversation. Hermann whispered reverently, "First microprobe has surfaced. And the data is coming in now."

The non-sapient Heart was intelligent enough to guess its patrons' wishes. Although everyone could tap the library for results, privately, the music cut out and a giant public image of the summary data appeared, high in the chamber. Paolo had to crane his neck to view it, a novel experience.

The microprobe had mapped one of the carpets in high resolution. The image showed the expected rough oblong, some hundred meters wide—but the two-or-three-meter-thick slab of the neutrino tomographs was revealed now as a delicate, convoluted surface—fine as a single layer of skin, but folded into an elaborate space-filling curve. Paolo checked the full data: the topology was strictly planar, despite the pathological appearance. No holes, no joins—just a surface which meandered wildly enough to look ten thousand times thicker from a distance than it really was.

An inset showed the microstructure, at a point which started at the rim of the carpet and then—slowly—moved toward the center. Paolo stared at the flowing molecular diagram for several seconds before he grasped what it meant.

The carpet was not a colony of single-celled creatures. Nor was it a multi-cellular organism. It was a *single molecule,* a two-dimensional polymer weighing twenty-five million kilograms. A giant sheet of folded polysaccharide, a complex mesh of interlinked pentose and hexose sugars hung with alkyl and amide side chains. A bit like a plant cell wall—except that this polymer was far stronger than cellulose, and the surface area was twenty orders of magnitude greater.

Karpal said, "I hope those entry capsules were perfectly sterile. Earth bacteria would gorge themselves on this. One big floating carbohydrate dinner, with no defenses."

Hermann thought it over. "Maybe. If they had enzymes capable of breaking off a piece—which I doubt. No chance we'll find out, though: even if there'd been bacterial spores lingering in the asteroid belt from early human expeditions, every ship in the diaspora was double-checked for contamination *en route.* We haven't brought smallpox to the Americas."

Paolo was still dazed. "But how does it assemble? How does it . . .

grow?'' Hermann consulted the library and replied, before Paolo could do the same.

"The edge of the carpet catalyses its own growth. The polymer is irregular, aperiodic—there's no single component which simply repeats. But there seem to be about twenty thousand basic structural units—twenty thousand different polysaccharide building blocks." Paolo saw them: long bundles of cross-linked chains running the whole two-hundred-micron thickness of the carpet, each with a roughly square cross-section, bonded at several thousand points to the four neighboring units. "Even at this depth, the ocean's full of UV-generated radicals which filter down from the surface. Any structural unit exposed to the water converts those radicals into more polysaccharide—and builds another structural unit."

Paolo glanced at the library again, for a simulation of the process. Catalytic sites strewn along the sides of each unit trapped the radicals in place, long enough for new bonds to form between them. Some simple sugars were incorporated straight into the polymer as they were created; others were set free to drift in solution for a microsecond or two, until they were needed. At that level, there were only a few basic chemical tricks being used . . . but molecular evolution must have worked its way up from a few small autocatalytic fragments, first formed by chance, to this elaborate system of twenty thousand mutually self-replicating structures. If the "structural units" had floated free in the ocean as independent molecules, the "lifeform" they comprised would have been virtually invisible. By bonding together, though, they became twenty thousand colors in a giant mosaic.

It was astonishing. Paolo hoped Elena was tapping the library, wherever she was. A colony of algae would have been more "advanced"—but this incredible primordial creature revealed infinitely more about the possibilities for the genesis of life. Carbohydrate, here, played every biochemical role: information carrier, enzyme, energy source, structural material. Nothing like it could have survived on Earth, once there were organisms capable of feeding on it—and if there were ever intelligent Orpheans, they'd be unlikely to find any trace of this bizarre ancestor.

Karpal wore a secretive smile.

Paolo said, "What?"

"Wang tiles. The carpets are made out of Wang tiles."

Hermann beat him to the library, again.

"*Wang* as in twentieth-century flesh mathematician, Hao Wang. *Tiles* as in any set of shapes which can cover the plane. Wang tiles are squares with various shaped edges, which have to fit complementary shapes on adjacent squares. You can cover the plane with a set of Wang tiles, as long as you choose the right one every step of the way. Or in the case of the carpets, grow the right one."

Karpal said, "We should call them Wang's Carpets, in honor of Hao Wang. After twenty-three hundred years, his mathematics has come to life."

Paolo liked the idea, but he was doubtful. "We may have trouble getting a two-thirds majority on that. It's a bit obscure . . ."

Hermann laughed. "Who needs a two-thirds majority? If we want to call them Wang's Carpets, we can call them Wang's Carpets. There are ninety-seven languages in current use in C-Z—half of them invented since the polis was founded. I don't think we'll be exiled for coining one private name."

Paolo concurred, slightly embarrassed. The truth was, he'd completely forgotten that Hermann and Karpal weren't actually speaking Modern Roman.

The three of them instructed their exoselves to consider the name adopted: henceforth, they'd hear "carpet" as "Wang's Carpet"—but if they used the term with anyone else, the reverse translation would apply.

Paolo sat and drank in the image of the giant alien: the first lifeform encountered by human or transhuman which was not a biological cousin. The death, at last, of the possibility that Earth might be unique.

They hadn't refuted the anthrocosmologists yet, though. Not quite. If, as the ACs claimed, human consciousness was the seed around which all of space-time had crystallized—if the universe was nothing but the simplest orderly explanation for human thought—then there was, strictly speaking, no need for a single alien to exist, anywhere. But the physics which justified human existence couldn't help generating a billion other worlds where life could arise. The ACs would be unmoved by Wang's Carpets; they'd insist that these creatures were physical, if not biological, cousins—merely an unavoidable by-product of anthropogenic, life-enabling physical laws.

The real test wouldn't come until the diaspora—or the Gleisner robots—finally encountered conscious aliens: minds entirely unrelated to humanity, observing and explaining the universe which human thought had supposedly built. Most ACs had come right out and declared such a find impossible; it was the sole falsifiable prediction of their hypothesis. Alien consciousness, as opposed to mere alien life, would always build itself a separate universe—because the chance of two unrelated forms of self-awareness concocting exactly the same physics and the same cosmology was infinitesimal—and any alien biosphere which seemed capable of evolving consciousness would simply never do so.

Paolo glanced at the map of the diaspora, and took heart. *Alien life already*—and the search had barely started; there were nine hundred and ninety-eight target systems yet to be explored. And even if every one of them proved no more conclusive than Orpheus . . . he was prepared to send clones out farther—and prepared to wait. Consciousness had taken far longer to appear on Earth than the quarter-of-a-billion years remaining before Vega left the main sequence—but the whole point of being here, after all, was that Orpheus wasn't Earth.

Orlando's celebration of the microprobe discoveries was a very first-generation affair. The environment was an endless sunlit garden strewn with tables covered in *food,* and the invitation had politely suggested attendance in fully human form. Paolo politely faked it—simulating most of the physiology, but running the body as a puppet, leaving his mind unshackled.

Orlando introduced his new lover, Catherine, who presented as a tall, dark-skinned woman. Paolo didn't recognize her on sight, but checked the identity code she broadcast. It was a small polis, he'd met her once before—as a man called Samuel, one of the physicists who'd worked on the main interstellar fusion drive employed by all the ships of the diaspora. Paolo was amused to think that many of the people here would be seeing his father as a woman. The majority of the citizens of C-Z still practiced the conventions of relative gender which had come into fashion in the twenty-third century—and Orlando had wired them into his own son too deeply for Paolo to wish to abandon them—but whenever the paradoxes were revealed so starkly, he wondered how much longer the conventions would endure. Paolo was same-sex to Orlando, and hence saw his father's lover as a woman, the two close relationships taking precedence over his casual knowledge of Catherine as Samuel. Orlando perceived himself as being male and heterosexual, as his flesh original had been . . . while Samuel saw himself the same way . . . and each perceived the other to be a heterosexual woman. If certain third parties ended up with mixed signals, so be it. It was a typical C-Z compromise: nobody could bear to overturn the old order and do away with gender entirely (as most other polises had done) . . . but nobody could resist the flexibility which being software, not flesh, provided.

Paolo drifted from table to table, sampling the food to keep up appearances, wishing Elena had come. There was little conversation about the biology of Wang's Carpets; most of the people here were simply celebrating their win against the opponents of the microprobes—and the humiliation that faction would suffer, now that it was clearer than ever that the "invasive" observations could have done no harm. Liesl's fears had proved unfounded; there was no other life in the ocean, just Wang's Carpets of various sizes. Paolo, feeling perversely even-handed after the fact, kept wanting to remind these smug movers and shakers: *There might have been anything down there. Strange creatures, delicate and vulnerable in ways we could never have anticipated. We were lucky, that's all.*

He ended up alone with Orlando almost by chance; they were both fleeing different groups of appalling guests when their paths crossed on the lawn.

Paolo asked, "How do you think they'll take this, back home?"

"It's first life, isn't it? Primitive or not. It should at least maintain interest in the diaspora, until the next alien biosphere is discovered." Orlando seemed subdued; perhaps he was finally coming to terms with the gulf between their modest discovery, and Earth's longing for world-shaking results. "And at least the chemistry is novel. If it had turned out to be based on DNA and protein, I think half of Earth C-Z would have died of boredom on the spot. Let's face it, the possibilities of DNA have been simulated to death."

Paolo smiled at the heresy. "You think if nature hadn't managed a little originality, it would have dented people's faith in the charter? If the solipsist polises had begun to look more inventive than the universe itself . . ."

"Exactly."

They walked on in silence, then Orlando halted, and turned to face him.

He said, "There's something I've been wanting to tell you. My Earth-self is dead."

"*What?*"

"Please, don't make a fuss."

"But . . . why? Why would he—?" *Dead* meant suicide; there was no other cause—unless the sun had turned red giant and swallowed everything out to the orbit of Mars.

"I don't know why. Whether it was a vote of confidence in the diaspora"—Orlando had chosen to wake only in the presence of alien life—"or whether he despaired of us sending back good news, and couldn't face the waiting, and the risk of disappointment. He didn't give a reason. He just had his exoself send a message, stating what he'd done."

Paolo was shaken. If a clone of *Orlando* had succumbed to pessimism, he couldn't begin to imagine the state of mind of the rest of Earth C-Z.

"When did this happen?"

"About fifty years after the launch."

"My Earth-self said nothing."

"It was up to me to tell you, not him."

"I wouldn't have seen it that way."

"Apparently, you would have."

Paolo fell silent, confused. How was he supposed to mourn a distant version of Orlando, in the presence of the one he thought of as real? Death of one clone was a strange half-death, a hard thing to come to terms with.

His Earth-self had lost a father; his father had lost an Earth-self. What exactly did that mean to *him?*

What Orlando cared most about was Earth C-Z. Paolo said carefully, "Hermann told me there'd been a rise in emigration and suicide—until the spectroscope picked up the Orphean water. Morale has improved a lot since then—and when they hear that it's more than just water . . ."

Orlando cut him off sharply. "You don't have to talk things up for me. I'm in no danger of repeating the act."

They stood on the lawn, facing each other. Paolo composed a dozen different combinations of mood to communicate, but none of them felt right. He could have granted his father perfect knowledge of everything he was feeling—but what exactly would that knowledge have conveyed? In the end, there was fusion, or separateness. There was nothing in between.

Orlando said, "Kill myself—and leave the fate of transhumanity in your hands? You must be out of your fucking mind."

They walked on together, laughing.

Karpal seemed barely able to gather his thoughts enough to speak. Paolo would have offered him a mind graft promoting tranquillity and concentration—distilled from his own most focused moments—but he was sure that Karpal would never have accepted it. He said, "Why don't you just start wherever you want to? I'll stop you if you're not making sense."

Karpal looked around the white dodecahedron with an expression of disbelief. "You live here?"

"Some of the time."

"But this is your base environment? No trees? No sky? No *furniture?*"

Paolo refrained from repeating any of Hermann's naive-robot jokes. "I add them when I want them. You know, like . . . music. Look, don't let my taste in decor distract you."

Karpal made a chair and sat down heavily.

He said, "Hao Wang proved a powerful theorem, twenty-three hundred years ago. Think of a row of Wang Tiles as being like the data tape of a Turing Machine." Paolo had the library grant him knowledge of the term; it was the original conceptual form of a generalized computing device, an imaginary machine which moved back and forth along a limitless one-dimensional data tape, reading and writing symbols according to a given set of rules.

"With the right set of tiles, to force the right pattern, the next row of the tiling will look like the data tape after the Turing Machine has performed one step of its computation. And the row after that will be the data tape after two steps, and so on. For any given Turing Machine, there's a set of Wang Tiles which can imitate it."

Paolo nodded amiably. He hadn't heard of this particular quaint result, but it was hardly surprising. "The carpets must be carrying out billions of acts of computation every second . . . but then, so are the water molecules around them. There are no physical processes which don't perform arithmetic of some kind."

"True. But with the carpets, it's not quite the same as random molecular motion."

"Maybe not."

Karpal smiled, but said nothing.

"What? You've found a pattern? Don't tell me: our set of twenty thousand polysaccharide Wang Tiles just happens to form the Turing Machine for calculating pi."

"No. What they form is a universal Turing Machine. They can calculate anything at all—depending on the data they start with. Every daughter fragment is like a program being fed to a chemical computer. Growth executes the program."

"Ah." Paolo's curiosity was roused—but he was having some trouble picturing where the hypothetical Turing Machine put its read/write head. "Are you telling me only one tile changes between any two rows, where the 'machine' leaves its mark on the 'data tape' . . . ?" The mosaics he'd seen were a riot of complexity, with no two rows remotely the same.

Karpal said, "No, no. Wang's original example worked exactly like a standard Turing Machine, to simplify the argument . . . but the carpets are more like an arbitrary number of different computers with overlapping data, all working in parallel. This is biology, not a designed machine—it's as messy and wild as, say . . . a mammalian genome. In fact, there are mathematical similarities with gene regulation: I've identified Kauffman networks at every level, from the tiling rules up; the whole system's poised on the hyperadaptive edge between frozen and chaotic behavior."

Paolo absorbed that, with the library's help. Like Earth life, the carpets seemed to have evolved a combination of robustness and flexibility which would have maximized their power to take advantage of natural selection. Thousands of different autocatalytic chemical networks must have arisen soon after the formation of Orpheus—but as the ocean chemistry and the climate changed in the Vegan system's early traumatic millennia, the ability to respond to selection pressure had itself been selected for, and the carpets were the result. Their complexity seemed redundant, now, after a hundred million years of relative stability—and no predators or competition in sight—but the legacy remained.

"So if the carpets have ended up as universal computers . . . with no real need anymore to respond to their surroundings . . . what are they *doing* with all that computing power?"

Karpal said solemnly, "I'll show you."

Paolo followed him into an environment where they drifted above a schematic of a carpet, an abstract landscape stretching far into the distance, elaborately wrinkled like the real thing, but otherwise heavily stylized, with each of the polysaccharide building blocks portrayed as a square tile with four different colored edges. The adjoining edges of neighboring tiles bore complementary colors—to represent the complementary, interlocking shapes of the borders of the building blocks.

"One group of microprobes finally managed to sequence an entire daughter fragment," Karpal explained, "although the exact edges it started life with are largely guesswork, since the thing was growing while they were trying to map it." He gestured impatiently, and all the wrinkles and folds were smoothed away, an irrelevant distraction. They moved to one border of the ragged-edged carpet, and Karpal started the simulation running.

Paolo watched the mosaic extending itself, following the tiling rules perfectly—an orderly mathematical process, here: no chance collisions of radicals with catalytic sites, no mismatched borders between two new-grown neighboring "tiles" triggering the disintegration of both. Just the distillation of the higher-level consequences of all that random motion.

Karpal led Paolo up to a height where he could see subtle patterns being woven, overlapping multiplexed periodicities drifting across the growing edge, meeting and sometimes interacting, sometimes passing right through each other. Mobile pseudo-attractors, quasi-stable waveforms in a one-dimensional universe. The carpet's second dimension was more like time than space, a permanent record of the history of the edge.

Karpal seemed to read his mind. "One dimensional. Worse than flatland. No connectivity, no complexity. What can possibly happen in a system like that? Nothing of interest, right?"

He clapped his hands and the environment exploded around Paolo. Trails of color streaked across his sensorium, entwining, then disintegrating into luminous smoke.

"Wrong. Everything goes on in a multidimensional frequency space. I've Fourier-transformed the edge into over a thousand components, and there's independent information in all of them. We're only in a narrow cross-section here, a sixteen-dimensional slice—but it's oriented to show the principal components, the maximum detail."

Paolo spun in a blur of meaningless color, utterly lost, his surroundings beyond comprehension. "You're a *Gleisner robot,* Karpal! *Only* sixteen dimensions! How can you have done this?"

Karpal sounded hurt, wherever he was. "Why do you think I came to C-Z? I thought you people were flexible!"

"What you're doing is . . ." *What?* Heresy? There was no such thing. Officially. "Have you shown this to anyone else?"

"Of course not. Who did you have in mind? Liesl? *Hermann?*"

"Good. I know how to keep my mouth shut." Paolo invoked his exoself and moved back into the dodecahedron. He addressed the empty room. "How can I put this? The physical universe has three spatial dimensions, plus time. Citizens of Carter-Zimmerman inhabit the physical universe. Higher dimensional mind games are for the solipsists." Even as he said it, he realized how pompous he sounded. It was an arbitrary doctrine, not some great moral principle.

But it was the doctrine he'd lived with for twelve hundred years.

Karpal replied, more bemused than offended, "It's the only way to see what's going on. The only sensible way to apprehend it. Don't you want to know what the carpets are *actually like?*"

Paolo felt himself being tempted. Inhabit a *sixteen-dimensional slice of a thousand-dimensional frequency space?* But it was in the service of understanding a real physical system—not a novel experience for its own sake.

And nobody had to find out.

He ran a quick—non-sapient—self-predictive model. There was a ninety-three percent chance that he'd give in, after fifteen subjective minutes of agonizing over the decision. It hardly seemed fair to keep Karpal waiting that long.

He said, "You'll have to loan me your mind-shaping algorithm. My exoself wouldn't know where to begin."

When it was done, he steeled himself, and moved back into Karpal's environment. For a moment, there was nothing but the same meaningless blur as before.

Then everything suddenly crystallized.

Creatures swam around them, elaborately branched tubes like mobile coral, vividly colored in all the hues of Paolo's mental palette—Karpal's attempt to cram in some of the information that a mere sixteen dimensions couldn't show? Paolo glanced down at his own body—nothing was missing, but he could see *around* it in all the thirteen dimensions in which it was nothing but a pin-prick; he quickly looked away. The "coral" seemed far more natural to his altered sensory map, occupying sixteen-space in all directions, and shaded with hints that it occupied much more. And Paolo had no doubt that it was "alive"—it looked more organic than the carpets themselves, by far.

Karpal said, "Every point in this space encodes some kind of quasi-periodic pattern in the tiles. Each dimension represents a different characteristic size—like a wavelength, although the analogy's not precise. The position in each dimension represents other attributes of the pattern, relating to the particular tiles it employs. So the localized systems you see around you are clusters of a few billion patterns, all with broadly similar attributes at similar wavelengths."

They moved away from the swimming coral, into a swarm of something like jellyfish: floppy hyperspheres waving wispy tendrils (each one of them more substantial than Paolo). Tiny jewel-like creatures darted among them. Paolo was just beginning to notice that nothing moved here like a solid object drifting through normal space; motion seemed to entail a shimmering deformation at the leading hypersurface, a visible process of disassembly and reconstruction.

Karpal led him on through the secret ocean. There were helical worms, coiled together in groups of indeterminate number—each single creature breaking up into a dozen or more wriggling slivers, and then recombining . . . although not always from the same parts. There were dazzling multicolored stemless flowers, intricate hypercones of "gossamer-thin" fifteen-dimensional petals—each one a hypnotic fractal labyrinth of crevices and capillaries. There were clawed monstrosities, writhing knots of sharp insectile parts like an orgy of decapitated scorpions.

Paolo said, uncertainly, "You could give people a glimpse of this in just three dimensions. Enough to make it clear that there's . . . *life* in here. This is going to shake them up badly, though." Life—embedded in the accidental computations of Wang's Carpets, with no possibility of ever relating to the world outside. This was an affront to Carter-Zimmerman's whole philosophy: if nature had evolved "organisms" as divorced from reality as the inhabitants of the most inward-looking polis, where was the privileged status of the physical universe, the clear distinction between truth and illusion?

And after three hundred years of waiting for good news from the diaspora, how would they respond to this back on Earth?

Karpal said, "There's one more thing I have to show you."

He'd named the creatures squids, for obvious reasons. *Distant cousins of the jellyfish, perhaps?* They were prodding each other with their tentacles in a way which looked thoroughly carnal—but Karpal explained, "There's no analog of light here. We're viewing all this according to ad hoc rules which have nothing to do with the native physics. All the creatures here gather information about each other by contact alone—which is actually quite a rich means of exchanging data, with so many dimensions. What you're seeing is communication by touch."

"Communication about what?"

"Just gossip, I expect. Social relationships."

Paolo stared at the writing mass of tentacles.

"You think they're *conscious?*"

Karpal, point-like, grinned broadly. "They have a central control structure with more connectivity than the human brain—and which correlates data gathered from the skin. I've mapped that organ, and I've started to analyze its function."

He led Paolo into another environment, a representation of the data structures in the "brain" of one of the squids. It was—mercifully—three-dimensional, and highly stylized, built of translucent colored blocks marked with icons, representing mental symbols, linked by broad lines indicating the major connections between them. Paolo had seen similar diagrams of transhuman minds; this was far less elaborate, but eerily familiar nonetheless.

Karpal said, "Here's the sensory map of its surroundings. Full of other squids' bodies, and vague data on the last known positions of a few smaller creatures. But you'll see that the symbols activated by the physical presence of the other squids are linked to these"—he traced the connection with one finger—"representations. Which are crude miniatures of *this whole structure* here."

"This whole structure" was an assembly labeled with icons for memory retrieval, simple tropisms, short-term goals. The general business of being and doing.

"The squid has maps, not just of other squids' bodies, but their minds as well. Right or wrong, it certainly tries to know what the others are thinking about. And"—he pointed out another set of links, leading to another, less crude, miniature squid mind—"it thinks about its own thoughts as well. I'd call that *consciousness,* wouldn't you?"

Paolo said weakly, "You've kept all this to yourself? You came this far, without saying a word—?"

Karpal was chastened. "I know it was selfish—but once I'd decoded the interactions of the tile patterns, I couldn't tear myself away long enough to start explaining it to anyone else. And I came to you first because I wanted your advice on the best way to break the news."

Paolo laughed bitterly. "The best way to break the news that *first alien consciousness* is hidden deep inside a biological computer? That everything the diaspora was trying to prove has been turned on its head? The best way to explain to the citizens of Carter-Zimmerman that after a three-hundred-year journey, they might as well have stayed on Earth running simulations with as little resemblance to the physical universe as possible?"

Karpal took the outburst in good humor. "I was thinking more along the lines of the *best way to point out* that if we hadn't traveled to Orpheus and studied Wang's Carpets, we'd never have had the chance to tell the solipsists of Ashton-Laval that all their elaborate invented lifeforms and exotic imaginary universes pale into insignificance compared to what's really out here—and which only the Carter-Zimmerman diaspora could have found."

Paolo and Elena stood together on the edge of Satellite Pinatubo, watching one of the scout probes aim its maser at a distant point in space. Paolo thought he saw a faint scatter of microwaves from the beam as it collided with iron-rich meteor dust. *Elena's mind being diffracted all over the cosmos?* Best not think about that.

He said, "When you meet the other versions of me who haven't experienced Orpheus, I hope you'll offer them mind grafts so they won't be jealous."

She frowned. "Ah. Will I or won't I? I can't be bothered modeling it. I expect I will. You should have asked me before I cloned myself. No need for jealousy, though. There'll be worlds far stranger than Orpheus."

"I doubt it. You really think so?"

"I wouldn't be doing this if I didn't believe that." Elena had no power to change the fate of the frozen clones of her previous self—but everyone had the right to emigrate.

Paolo took her hand. The beam had been aimed almost at Regulus, UV-hot and bright, but as he looked away, the cool yellow light of the sun caught his eye.

Vega C-Z was taking the news of the squids surprisingly well, so far. Karpal's way of putting it had cushioned the blow: it was only by traveling all this distance across the real, physical universe that they could have made such a discovery—and it was amazing how pragmatic even the most doctrinaire citizens had turned out to be. Before the launch, "alien solipsists" would have been the most unpalatable idea imaginable, the most abhorrent thing the diaspora could have stumbled upon—but now that they were here, and stuck with the fact of it, people were finding ways to view it in a better light. Orlando had even proclaimed, *"This* will be the perfect hook for the marginal polises. 'Travel through real space to witness a truly alien virtual reality.' We can sell it as a synthesis of the two world views."

Paolo still feared for Earth, though—where his Earth-self and others were waiting in hope of alien guidance. Would they take the message of Wang's Carpets to heart, and retreat into their own hermetic worlds, oblivious to physical reality?

And he wondered if the anthrocosmologists had finally been refuted . . . or not. Karpal had discovered alien consciousness—but it was sealed inside a cosmos of its own, its perceptions of itself and its surroundings neither reinforcing nor conflicting with human and transhuman explanations of reality. It would be millennia before C-Z could untangle the ethical problems of daring to try to make contact . . . assuming that both Wang's Carpets, and the inherited data patterns of the squids, survived that long.

Paolo looked around at the wild splendor of the star-choked galaxy, felt the disk reach in and cut right through him. *Could all this strange haphazard beauty be nothing but an excuse for those who beheld it to exist? Nothing but the sum of all the answers to all the questions humans and transhumans had ever asked the universe—answers created in the asking?*

He couldn't believe that—but the question remained unanswered. So far.

Afterword

They meet now and forever on the shores of Lake Geneva—Dante, Milton, Aphra Behn, Mary Wollstonecraft Shelley and Percy Bysshe Shelley, Byron, Dickens, Twain, Verne, George Bernard Shaw, H. G. Wells, Olaf Stapledon, Aldous Huxley. Joining them after a time, Jorge Luis Borges, Anthony Burgess, C. L. Moore, and James Tiptree, Jr., Theodore Sturgeon, and Fritz Leiber, Isaac Asimov, and Robert Heinlein. The list grows. They greet each other warily, testily, pick quite a few bones together, but soon they settle in and relax. They have all the time in the world.

There are books spread around the great villa. Soon, as they tire of their pens and typewriters, tire of swimming or eating, of arguing old points that never seem done, they turn to these books and begin to catch up, reading our stories of the future, our philosophical excursions and querulous speculations, and scowling, or smiling, or laughing out loud.

We give them ever so much more to argue about.

The long day wanes. They linger over their cups of tea or glasses of wine or whiskey, talking, talking . . .

Long into the night and past the dawn.

—Greg Bear